LISTED DEAD

Jan Edwards is a UK author with several novels and many short stories in various mainstream, crime, fantasy and horror fiction publications, including *The Mammoth Book of Folk Horror* and several volumes of the *MX Books of New Sherlock Holmes Stories*. Jan is also an editor with the award-winning Alchemy Press.

She is a recipient of the Karl Edward Wagner Award and has won the Arnold Bennett Book Prize for *Winter Downs* – the first in her World War Two crime series *The Bunch Courtney Investigations*. The second volume, *In Her Defence*, is also available from Penkhull Press.

The Bunch Courtney Investigations

Winter Downs
In Her Defence
Listed Dead

Other Titles by Jan Edwards

Sussex Tales
Fables and Fabrications
Leinster Gardens and Other Subtleties
A Small Thing for Yolanda

https://janedwardsblog.wordpress.com/

LISTED DEAD

A Bunch Courtney Investigation

Jan Edwards

The Penkhull Press

First Edition

ISBN 978-1-9164373-7-1

Published by The Penkhull Press
www.penkhullpress.co.uk

❧ Acknowledgements ❧

Countless books and web sites were consulted to confirm facts. I bent the ears of Sue Burns and Bev Adams for horsey things, and Mike Herwin on discussions for 'the right breed of dog'. As ever, the Renegade Writers Group sat through many readings of gnarly sections that were in desperate need of a rewrite. Thanks go to Kerry Parsons, Steph Lawrence and Jill Doyle for their endless support on their blog pages, and also to the book readers who make my writing efforts worthwhile.

As always, however, my biggest thanks go to the Penkhull Press crew: a special call to Misha Herwin for her endless patience in our brain-storming sessions and her ruthless red penning in the writing stages; to Jem Shaw and Mike Chinn for their techie info on cars, planes and firearms; and most of all to Peter Coleborn for culling typos and glitches for the final edit, laying out the manuscript, and for his superb design skills.

I hope you get as much fun in reading *Listed Dead* as much as I did in writing it. This is the third *Bunch Courtney Investigation* and with luck and a fair wind there will be many more to come.

✆ One ✇

Two Land Girls were clattering across the yard as Bunch Courtney emerged from the dairy, their voices gin clear on the frosted air.

'According to that Roly Jenner it's been out there half the night,' Gwenny said, eager at the chance to pass on the news. 'He says the driver's copped it. Dead as this bucket, he told me.' Her tone dipped to a breathless stage whisper. 'Just think. Some chap layin' out there on his own, in the cold and the dark, and just dyin' like that.'

'There's bad,' Vera agreed. 'Black ice I s'pect. That hill'd be dangerous this weather.'

Bunch eyed them curiously. They were freshly arrived from the Welsh valleys and she had yet to speak with them at length, but Kate, the farm's senior Land Girl, had given a verdict of 'odd', which seemed to be ringing true. *Because people,* she thought, *don't generally relish talking about death quite that much.* 'Morning girls,' she called. 'Something going on?'

'Mornin', Boss,' they answered in unison.

'There's a car crashed about halfway down Lych Hill,' Gwenny added. 'Police've been there for hours.'

'What happened?'

'Went into the ditch,' said Gwenny. 'Bang. Driver's dead, accordin' to Mr Jenner.'

'How awful. Was it anyone from around here?'

'Not a clue, Boss. The car was a red one, though.'

'Red. Was it indeed.' Bunch looked out across the Downs and rubbed at her lower lip. The road they spoke of bordered the far southwest edge of the estate. Not far across country, but she had a mountain of estate paperwork awaiting her attention. On the other hand, Perringham estate's retired steward lived close by. *And he drives a red Austin Ruby.* She realised the chances of Mr Parsons being out in the blackout were slim to zero given his poor state of

7

health. *I could never forgive myself if something happened to him and I did nothing. Besides – Perry does need a longer ride out than Dower House to farm and back again. It'll save getting someone to exercise him later.*

'If you're going in for breakfast tell Kate I rode over with those Ministry milk forms she needed and I've left them in the dairy,' she said aloud. 'I'm just going to pop over to Lych Hill now and see about this red car of yours, so if she needs to go over the figures I'll be an hour or so.'

'Righto, Boss.'

Bunch crossed the yard to where her black Fell Pony waited patiently, mounted up, and headed across the Downs. The skies were just losing the pinks of dawn in favour of a wintery blue, and a crisp November frost had turned the ground to iron beneath Perry's hooves. It meant she was obliged to keep to a slow trot, but the air was sweet and the hillsides quiet. Not a whisper of the fighter craft from Tangmere and Parham that had been fending off the Luftwaffe on a seemingly daily basis. She revelled in the peace of that scant twenty-minutes ride before she was reining Perry in near the coppice overlooking Lych Hill.

She slapped the pony's neck and crooning softly for him to 'steady up, Perry, steady,' stood in the stirrups to view the crash site from a discreet distance.

An ambulance shared a stretch of icy verge with a police Wolseley. Doctor Lewis's old Type E Vauxhall was pulled into the entrance to Chells Farm where the road dived between the trees toward Inchett village, and between them, just where the bend was sharpest, the rear end of a wrecked sports car protruded from the ditch at a giddy angle – its spare wheel pointing eye-like at the sky while its red bonnet was buried deep in glutinous Sussex mud. Bunch knew a Jaguar Roadster when she saw one. *That,* she told herself, *is about as far from being an Austin Ruby as it's possible to get. And it's not Parsons, thank God.*

It was a little before eight o'clock but a small handful of locals had already gathered on the opposite side of the lane. Bunch always marvelled at how newsworthy events never failed to draw an audience at any given time or place. *In a place like Wyncombe,* she thought, *just about everything is grist for the gossips' mill. Strange that Tilly Parrish isn't out here to see what was going on in her driveway. Doubtless she'd view gawking as common and vulgar.*

8

She gave Perry another pat and settled back in the saddle. 'The Honourable Rose "Bunch" Courtney, on the other hand,' she told her pony, 'has no such qualms. If there's something going on this close to Perringham I want to know about it.'

As Wyncombe residents, PC Botting and the ageing Doctor Lewis were not unexpected. The ambulance crew were quite naturally strangers to her. Detective Chief Inspector William Wright, however, was a curiosity. *What on earth are you doing here?* she thought. *You're rather too senior to be investigating an auto crash. Something's brewing.*

Wright stood hunched against the chill, making him seem even leaner than she remembered. The brim of his trademark fedora was pulled down against the cold air, and his town shoes were wholly inadequate against the crackles of icy tyre tracks around his feet.

She urged Perry out onto the road, his hooves ringing loud on the metalled surface, and halted just a few yards from them. Wright glanced briefly in her direction and then looked back to his bag man, DS Ernie Carter, without so much as a nod of recognition.

'Damn you,' Bunch muttered. 'Are we really going to go through all this territorial nonsense again?' She slid from the saddle and hitched Perry to the field gate. 'Good morning, Chief Inspector Wright. What brings you here?' She jerked her head toward the corpse, draped with a meagre grey blanket. She'd already noted how its wet feet, clad in bespoke brogues, were exposed to the cold. She wanted to tug the cloth over them because somehow it seemed to matter that the mud on those Argyll socks had already begun to freeze.

'Miss Courtney.' Wright raised his hat briefly. 'I might say the same of you.'

'I was told there'd been an accident on the edge of the estate so I came across to make sure it was not any of our people.'

'How very conscientious,' he said.

'Oh, you know. Noblesse oblige, and all that.'

'I'm sure. I assume you know Doctor Lewis?'

'I do indeed. Good morning, Lewis.'

'Miss Courtney.' The GP doffed his hat, adding a slight bow. 'Tragic event. Awful way for a young chap to go.'

'Do we know who it is?' Bunch asked, craning her neck for a closer look.

Lewis attempted to sidle between Bunch and the dead man. 'I'm afraid not. The Chief Inspector is looking into that now.'

'Bit beneath you isn't it, William?' She smiled sweetly at Wright. 'Isn't a motor shunt more PC Botting's bailiwick?'

'No police work is beneath me,' he replied. 'I am a serving officer.'

Bunch grinned. She had hit a raw spot and nothing was going to deflect her now. 'Of course you are. I'm just surprised you'd traipse up from your little cubby hole in Brighton simply because some bear-cub has come a purler. Come on. Out with it. What's special about this chap?'

'Not sure as yet, Miss,' Carter muttered. 'PC Botting put a call out for re-enforcements, and here we are.'

'Enough, Carter,' Wright growled. 'I didn't want to drive out here this morning either, but here we are. Make yourself useful and take statements from those chaps over there. They won't have seen anything but it'll move them on.'

'Yes, sir.'

Wright watched his sergeant stalk across the lane and sighed. 'You'll have to excuse him. We had a busy night. Barely two hours sleep and we're called out to this. Carter's not getting any younger.'

'Can I help with anything?' Bunch asked.

'Since you're here, perhaps you might be able to identify our victim.'

'See here, Chief Inspector.' Lewis laid a protective hand on the stretcher. 'Expecting a young lady to identify corpses by the roadside is simply not done.'

'Oh, come now, Lewis. I'm not some shrinking violet, you should know that.' Bunch treated him to a saccharin smile.

'This is not a fit place for a young lady. Let the police do their work.'

'Oh I shall. Once I've assisted the Inspector, since he asked so politely.'

Wright grasped the edge of the blanket and stared at her, his face serious. 'Given your passion for horsey pursuits,' he said, 'I thought you might recognise the man's hunting tie pin.'

'Tie pin?' Bunch had her suspicion Wright was trying to put

her off but this felt like an olive branch, and mention of a hunt was only ever going to pique her interest. 'If this poor chap rode out with a local pack I'm sure I'd know him,' she said. 'At least in passing.'

'Thank you.' Wright began to raise the edge of the blanket. 'A corpse is never a pleasant sight. Are you ready?'

Bunch straightened her shoulders and nodded. She didn't relish the idea of dead bodies before breakfast, despite seeing her share of them in her time with the FANY and ATS. Wright issued a challenge and she was determined not to be made a fool of.

As the woollen blanket was drawn back her insides lurched, in the way that they do when a train comes to a sudden stop. The pale cheeks were close shaven and, she noted in somewhat macabre fashion, almost a match for his blue-grey eyes that stared off somewhere to his left. *You'd think someone would have closed them by now.* She shook the thought away and examined the body in what she hoped was a more professional manner.

She noted how his brown hair had been cut by an expert hand; how his white shirt was of good quality linen; how his suit had been cut from indestructible Harris tweed, which only the county set could afford. She also noted that two buttons of the jacket had been ripped from their moorings. The tie's knot was a hand's span from his chin and pulled impossibly tight. *Probably not by his own hand.* She bent to peer at pin in question, which dangled pitifully to one side. It was a fox's head on a plain gold bar.

'Nothing out of the ordinary,' she told them. 'Club emblems usually include a crest or some initials. I doubt this has anything to link it with any hunt. Local or otherwise.' Bunch resisted the impulse to lean down and straighten the pin. From what she recalled of this chap, she was certain he would have been mortified to be seen in such disarray.

'Anything else you can say about him?' Wright asked her.

She tightened her fingers into fists and took a closer look at the dead man. The blue-tinged pallor was to be expected so she concentrated instead on the possible causes of death. In addition to a head wound there were small marks to his neck, highlighted by a crusting of dried blood. Very obvious signs of violence, though whether from the crash or an attack she had no way of knowing. *Is that why Wright's here? Not just for a road crash. Even a fatal one*. She shuddered as the image of Johnny Frampton's mutilated and, as it had turned out, murdered body crowded her memory. Almost a year ago now but still so fresh in her heart.

Bunch took a slow breath through her mouth, trying to ignore the odours of a voided bladder and gut, and leaned in once again. She pressed a tentative finger against his flesh and felt a resistance that was not down to muscle. *Rigor. But coming in or going out?* 'When did this happen?' she asked.

'We can't give an exact time. Probably after midnight.' Wright shot a quick glance at the Doctor who nodded. 'PC Botting was summoned by a dairyman on his way to Chells Farm at around four a.m.'

'I see.' Bunch waited for more but neither man offered to state even the obvious point that this body could not have lain undiscovered for longer than a few hours.

'So. Is he known to you?' Wright asked. His voice was low and gentle but, she realised, slightly insistent, as though he had asked the question several times. 'Rose. You do know him?'

'Pardon?' Bunch looked away from the dead man's face. She felt as if she were staring, being rude. *Though he's beyond all that now.* 'Yes, I know him. It's Claude Naysmith. He's more Dodo's set than mine, though a tad older than some of the others.'

Wright peered down at the newly identified corpse, his face revealing little of his thoughts.

'What else do you want to know?' she said.

'You should leave that to the police, Miss Courtney.' Lewis's voice cut across the moment and his tone held more than a hint of disapproval. 'I am sure your father wouldn't wish you to be embroiled in any unpleasantness.'

She turned her head slowly to glare at him. 'The police need my help.'

'You just happened by,' said Wright. 'And I agree with Doctor Lewis. Your family won't thank me for even that much.'

'There is no call to be so po-faced about it.'

Lewis tutted loudly. 'We have your best interests in mind, my dear. Now the Chief Inspector has finished here, I suggest you run along home.'

He turned away from her, plainly feeling that was the end of the matter, and Bunch was having none of it. She was no longer his child patient who could be dismissed. 'You may go now, Lewis.' She drawled. 'Be good enough to call at the Dower House later today. My grandmother wishes to see you.'

Doctor Lewis glowered, moustache bristling, and for a moment Bunch thought he might have a coronary on the spot. The moment passed as he bowed his head stiffly and tipped his hat. 'Yes, of course, Miss Courtney. Now I really must go, Chief Inspector. I have other calls to make and I am already late. I shall look forward to seeing what the autopsy has to say, though one imagines that the results will be self-explanatory. Good day, Miss Courtney.' Lewis signalled to the ambulance crew to load Naysmith's body into the ambulance and marched back to his own vehicle.

Wright, Bunch realised, was staring at her. 'So rude,' she said. 'Now, we were talking about Claude?'

'Good to have a name for the face.' Wright flipped through the pages of his notebook. 'He wasn't carrying any papers and it seems the car was not his. It is registered in the name of Penelope James, a resident of Newhaven. Carter contacted the Newhaven police station and the only address available was bombed out a few weeks ago.'

'Penelope James? I do recall hearing she and Claude were as thick as thieves. In which case his driving Penny's motor wouldn't come as any surprise. I believe her family live over Chichester way, if that helps?'

'That is a huge help. Thank you. Identifying our victim was the main priority. You are sure about the name?'

'Absolutely. This is, or rather this was, Claude Naysmith. Can't tell you if he had a middle name.'

'Was he trekking do you think? People are still flooding out of the cities every night despite this weather, and we can't blame them for that. Not with the lack of bomb shelters in half the lodgings along the coast,' Wright said.

'So I'm told.' She pursed her lips, allowing herself a glance at Naysmith's bloodless face. 'I'd be very surprised. More likely he was stationed somewhere around here, don't you think? These days people are forever signing up and getting sent hither and yon. We have two new Land Girls from the Rhondda Valley, would you believe.' She looked at the ambulance that was backing onto the road, and touched her fingers to her lips. A vague remembrance of deeper links were tickling at her brain, but whatever it was refused to surface and she was not about to make rash statements that might have her look an idiot before this man. 'His family have an estate in Oxfordshire. Can't recall where because I really don't have Granny's gift for those details. I swear she has the whole of *Debrett's* committed to memory.'

'But you're certain this is Claude Naysmith?'

'Absolutely positive.'

'Then we have two names to be going on with,' Wright said. 'If he and this Miss James were close, we should be able to trace her through Naysmith's circle.'

'Indeed you will,' Bunch replied. 'They ran with the same crowd. I say, isn't it possible that Penny is waiting for Claude, for her car? Completely unaware that he's had an accident?'

'This was not an accident.'

So he was murdered, she thought. *Or William thinks he was. That explains a great deal.* 'How awful,' she said aloud. 'You think she handed over her car because he was in trouble? I know they were pals but it still seems odd she would do that.'

'Not knowing Miss James I could not possibly say. Legally, the use of petrol rations belonging to someone else may be dubious, even when the car belongs to a close friend.'

'You really do like to complicate things, don't you?' she said. 'It hardly matters now whose ration he was using. I can pop over to see Dodo later and ask her. We'll get to the bottom of it quick enough.'

'We?' Wright looked at her from the corner of his eye.

Bunch made sure he could read nothing from her expression. Pique at his lack of communication over recent months had made walking away her first thought, but she had recently set plans in place and this was her chance to unveil them. 'Of course "we". You casually asked me to look at a body and then you think I shall trot off and leave you to it? Come now, William. I think you know me a little better than that.'

'Well, I...'

'I shall have a chat with Dodo and also with Granny, and you shall let me know if you have any news at your end.'

Wright shook his head. 'You've been helpful but we shan't need your further assistance.'

'Oh for God's sake,' Bunch snapped. 'You keep telling me you're so terribly short staffed. Can Sussex Constabulary truly afford not to accept my offer of help? Just say "thank you" nicely.'

'Help how? Enrolling as a Special Constable?'

Bunch laughed loudly, drawing odd glances from those around them. 'Good heavens, no. I have an estate to run, as my family are always eager to remind me at every turn.'

'Your father would hardly allow it. The Honourable WPC Courtney? I can't see it.'

She sighed. Like most of the family she seldom used her title. Her father rarely displayed his peerage outside of the FO, and only inside it when absolutely essential. 'Does it matter what my father thinks?' she said. 'Or who we are?'

'Your uncle told me to look it up.' Wright shrugged. 'He seemed to think it was relevant. Blood lines do matter to some people.'

'Not to me. Unless it has four legs and a nosebag. You keep harping on about being so short on officers – how can it matter if I'm a Right Hon or God forbid, a Lady. I'd much rather be your consulting detective.' She stepped close, brushing a fleck from his lapel. 'I shall be taking a consultation fee – if it makes you feel better.'

'So no WPC Lady Rose?' He grinned at her, tilting his head a little.

Bunch took half a step back. She hadn't intended to give him the impression she was flirting, and knew his use of her given name, rather than the diminutive that he knew she preferred, was a sly put down. 'WPC Rose? If you ever, ever, dare call me that I shall slap you. Hard.'

'I've no doubt you will. I'm grateful for your helping us out.'

'Consulting,' she said. 'Remember that. A consulting detective.'

'Ahh. Consulting detective.' He laughed with little humour. 'Somehow I can't picture you as Sherlock Holmes.'

'Try harder, because I have no intention of being your Watson, I can assure you.'

'Hmm. Your help was most welcome today.' He hesitated, looking down at his mud-splattered brogues. 'As for the future? There's just the small matter of the Commissioner. I cannot believe he is going to agree to this. The whole idea is contrary to a few dozen regulations.'

'Uncle Walter? Oh pish. You leave him to me.'

❧ Two ❧

Bunch's promised ride to Banyards was a short one and, in view of the freezing rain that had been falling over the previous few hours, surprisingly dry. *Possibly might have been worth a little petrol,* she thought. *On the other hand, it's the Marsham's shooting party later this month.* The need to conserve fuel supplies was logical and she fully accepted the need, but calculating every thimbleful irked her.

Bunch had been expecting a quiet tête-à-tête with Dodo so finding the lean figure of Emma Tinsley, Dodo's sister-in-law, lounging in an armchair near the fireplace was a surprise. 'Emma. How lovely to see you. I thought you were up staying up in Town somewhere.'

'I am but I was delivering some items to the Admiralty types at Haslemere, and it seemed like a good opportunity to visit the family.' Emma grinned at Dodo.

'Where is the little tyke by the way?'

'Sleeping, thank heavens. I told Nanny Tanner to bring her down for a visit after lunch to see both of her aunties.' Dodo turned to Bunch and winked. 'Everything going well with you, Aunt Rose?'

Bunch elected to ignore her sister's goading on the subject of children. 'Things are getting rather interesting, actually. I met up with William Wright yesterday.'

'Really? Your policeman? Business or pleasure?'

'Business of course. He was investigating that motor accident outside of The Chells.'

'The one that killed poor Claude?'

'You've heard about that already? Yes of course you have. No secrets in Wyncombe. You knew Claude rather well, didn't you?'

'He was on the circuit the year I came out so we went to all the same dos. He came to Perringham House a few times but I've not seen him for quite a long while.'

17

'I never really had what you could call a conversation with him. Just polite chit chat. Without wishing to speak ill of the dead, I found him a little tedious. I was hoping you could tell me something more.'

Dodo held her sister's gaze thoughtfully. 'Are you getting involved with police business again?'

'In a manner of speaking. There were some odd things about the accident and I told William I'd see what I could find out.'

'Daddy will go mad if he finds you are dabbling in crime yet again.' Dodo held her hands up to fend off her sister's glare. 'I know. None of my business. What can I tell you?'

'I seem to remember George knew Naysmith quite well.' Bunch held her breath, as she always did when Dodo's deceased husband came up in conversation.

'Probably no more than I did.' Dodo's gaze flickered toward George's photograph on the side table. 'I think the only one of that crowd George kept up with was Larry Parrish.'

'Really? Wright may be interested in that, given that this happened on Larry's doorstep.'

'What accident was this?' said Emma.

'Lynch Hill, just up from Chells Farm.'

'And you think it odd that it happened just there? So close to Lawrence Parrish's house?'

'Why would you think that?'

'Because I know you rather too well,' Emma replied. 'If you ask about anything that doesn't have four legs there's a jolly good reason for it.'

'I got pulled into it by accident,' Bunch admitted. 'Wright asked me if I knew who the victim was.' She grinned. 'I think he was calling my bluff but I rather called his instead.'

Over lunch Bunch gave an expurgated version of her meeting with Wright. With the maid dodging in and out at odd moments and able to listen in, Bunch did not wish to set any more rumours flying than necessary. She reached for the butter dish as her narrative ended and topped a small bridge roll with the smallest of butter curls. 'Look at this. How can anyone possibly make two ounces last a week?' She regarded the mangled roll dolefully. 'Cook makes her own butter but I've heard a whisper that she won't even be allowed to do that much soon.'

'You think it will come to that?' said Dodo. 'Surely the government can't stop us making our own. Butter and such, I mean.'

'Father has all but said so. At least you do have this.' Bunch waved the butter knife at the room in general. 'Barty may be all kinds of nincompoop but he's in far better condition than one might have expected.' She paused, realising how that must have sounded when Dodo's father-in-law had come so close to languishing at His Majesty's pleasure the previous winter. She ploughed on, considering it best not to dwell on the situation. 'I was asking what you knew about Claude and his family. I'd heard they sold their Town house back in 1933?' Bunch carried on mangling the roll and waited for a reply.

'They have property between Oxford and Banbury. I only know that because Bunny Ince told me she went to a party there last month.' Dodo shrugged. 'I haven't seen much of that set for a while.'

'Including Claude?' Emma glanced at Bunch and shrugged. 'I gather from Father that he was some exceptionally distant cousin on his mother's side. Umpteen times removed, so no call for mourning.'

'Did you know him at all, Emm?'

'Not in the slightest. I think George and he were at the same school but in different years.'

'So if their school was anything like ours, even a year below one put people beneath one's notice. What about the rest of that little coterie?'

Dodo shook her head firmly. 'Other than Larry, George had no time for those chaps. Not for a long while. There was some huge falling out, by all accounts. I never did discover what it was all about. They were all part of some rather exclusive little supper club, but not one I'd ever want to join. I still see one or two of the girls now and then.' She tailed off, staring down at her plate. 'I heard nothing from Claude when George passed away, which did surprise me.'

'I heard they joined up at the same time. Perhaps he was away and never heard?'

'Perhaps.' Dodo smiled at her sister-in-law. 'It's so hard keeping track of people these days.'

19

'How very true,' Bunch observed. 'My old ATS unit has been scattered all around the country. Half of them are driving generals around the country like glorified bloody chauffeurs and the rest are changing spark plugs in various motor pools. It's even harder keeping track of the chaps, and I've been to two military funerals since the new year.' Bunch crumbled a little of the roll into her soup and spooned up a mouthful, pretending not to watch her sister's reactions.

'I never realised we'd lost a cousin at Dunkirk until Granny mentioned it a few weeks ago. I felt so guilty because I know I've let things slide this past year.'

'You have nothing to blame yourself for. You've had a terrible year and nobody expects it. I can name half-a-dozen people gone missing from the ranks.'

'Like George?' Dodo snapped.

'Well, yes. Like George. And Johnny. And I very nearly ended up the same way. There's war and it's awful, but you cannot allow yourself to feel guilty.'

'I still can't help feeling sorry for Claude, even if we weren't best chums.' Dodo straightened up and busied herself with pouring tea before leaning in to whisper. 'I say, girls, did you hear about Isla McVie? Carrying on with some Canadian chappy while her husband's out in Singapore?'

'Really—' said Emma.

'We were discussing Claude,' said Bunch.

Dodo avoided looking Bunch in the eye. 'It just came to me,' she said, her voice remained light but her shoulders slumped once more.

Bunch's mind tipped back to Claude Naysmith's body lying on that ambulance stretcher. He had reminded her of a discarded mannequin she had seen in a London street after a raid a few weeks before. Broken and soiled and devoid of humanity. And on her doorstep. Dodo preferred to gossip in muted tones about some illicit affair involving people that Bunch only knew in passing and it was very apparent that the younger woman simply did not want to acknowledge yet another violent death within her circle. In many ways that was understandable but Bunch was concerned all the same. Dodo seldom brought up George's name of her own volition, despite naming her child in honour of him.

She wondered how much little Georgi would ever know about her namesake. It would be tragic for her to grow up in the shadow of a man she would only know through whispered hints. Dodo was doing as she always did – changing the subject, or changing its direction at very least.

'What was Claude doing, do you think?' Bunch said. 'Wright suggested he was sleeping under the stars but that doesn't sound likely. I know his family lost a lot of money but they're not quite destitute. Emm, do you know any of them?'

'I can hardly be expected to know everyone in the city of Oxford. It all depends on whether one is Gown or Town. They hardly ever move in the same circles,' Emma replied. 'Lot of academics barely acknowledge the world beyond the quad. Probably a little different now that we're all scattered to the winds. Bit of a rude awakening for some, I imagine.'

'Wasn't your faculty house requisitioned by the Ministry of War?' Bunch said.

'Admiralty,' Emma replied. 'Mostly Wrens, thank God. We none of us wanted a few hundred bloody matelots rampaging about the place.'

'I doubt they'd station matelots in Oxford. Officers maybe. Boffins more likely.' Bunch sloshed more water into her glass, slopping a small tidal wave over the sides. 'Not that you can trust what the Ministry tell you.' She paused to suck the water from her hand. 'Perringham House was meant to be full of Canadian pilot officers and instead we've Colonel bloody Ralph and his stream of oddities.'

'Still no idea what they are up to in there?'

Bunch laughed sharply. 'I've a bloody good idea.'

'Bunch. Language.' Dodo glanced toward the door, a light frown on her face.

'I think little Georgi is a tad young to worry about a few expletives, darling.'

'I know. But the staff…'

'Don't give a damn.' Mopping the last of the spill with her napkin Bunch reached for her cigarette case. 'Daddy said you were meeting him up in Oxford next week, Emm.'

Emma shot her a cautious glance. 'He told you?'

'Only that you and he had a lunch appointment.'

21

Emma nodded. 'He wants to consult me on a new project.'

'Are you going to make the trip?'

'Yes, but not just for that meeting. I also have a College formal to attend. Why do you ask?'

'I would never ask about the Whitehall stuff. I know better. Would you mind awfully if I tagged along for the ride?'

Emma leaned back in her seat and looked her up and down. 'What are you up to, Rose?'

'I don't know as yet. Curiosity, I suppose. Naysmith's family live around there, and since I've had myself taken on as a police consultant I need to earn my crust.'

'Police consultant? Oh dear God, does Daddy know?' Dodo asked. 'He's not going to be very happy about that. Granny will turn blue and explode.'

'Uncle Walter is my godfather and he can never turn me away. I asked him back in the summer, after my last case. Rather nifty, don't you think?'

'Case? Listen to you, a regular Dick Barton. A good way of keeping your detective chappy in your sights, however.'

'Oh do behave Dodo. Even if I saw him in that way, which I don't, he's married to his job.'

'He did retire once so he can't be that attached.'

'He was invalided out. Rather a different matter.' Bunch scowled at the knowing grins passing between the other two women. 'And it really is none of your business. Either of you.'

'And yet...'

'Daphne Elizabeth Tinsley, I am warning you!'

Dodo adopted the wide-eyed ingénue look, tucking in her chin to stare with her forefinger pressed to her lips and Bunch swotted at her with a napkin. 'Are you home for long, Emma?' she said.

'Lord no. I did have a request from the vicar to tutor the local brats. I gather their teacher has joined up and he wants me to fill in. Just until the end of this term.'

'God help them. You'd have them translating Homer and playing match chess.'

Emma sniffed loudly. 'Never going to happen. I have a post lined up elsewhere so I've persuaded him to crowbar Miss Tuff out of retirement. She taught at that school for so many years she could do it standing on her head.' She chuckled quietly. 'I think the reverend was hoping to avoid that. He's a little frightened of her.'

'Most people are.'

'Indeed. Fortunately almost all of the evacuees have been moved further north or west, and so many Wyncombe folk have sent their children to stay with relatives the old girl won't have more than ten or twelve, so she should cope, even at her age.'

'Half the county seems to be on the move,' Dodo said. 'Can't blame them. There have been raids along the coast since September '39. One of Granny's cronies told me there wasn't a cottage to rent – or a bed – in any guest house to be had in the Lakes and Dales at any price. People are getting as far away from Jerry as they can – if they can.'

'You've not thought about taking Georgi away?' Bunch leaned toward her sister. 'With Barty here, it isn't as if there's nobody to keep an eye this place. We have a cousin in Berkshire, and another in Devon, I believe. It may be safer.'

'I've thought about it. Given the speed Hitler's troops moved across Holland and Belgium and into France… If we *are* invaded, I doubt moving a couple of counties away would make a great deal of difference. Meanwhile, the air raids are not that much of a worry. Banyards Manor has good solid cellars.' Dodo shook her head. 'I know you are worried about this business with Claude but really, Bunch, these things can happen anywhere.'

When did you suddenly grow up to be the philosopher? Bunch thought. 'If you're sure.'

'I am.'

'Excellent. Now I really must dash. The estate doesn't run itself, as Daddy is so fond of reminding me.'

'Good to see you, Bunch,' said Dodo. 'As always.'

'Seconded,' Emma added. 'I shall let you know about the jaunt up to the spires.'

'Absolutely my pleasure, old thing. Dodo, I shall report back to Granny that you're resting as requested and positively brimming with health. Oh, by the way, I am meeting Mummy tomorrow.'

'Is she still refusing to move down to the Dower?'

'Yes, and now she has asked me to help her out with some mystery meeting up in Town. God knows what she is up to now. Wish me luck.' She dropped a light kiss on her sister's head and bounded out to the yard where Perry, rugged up against the chill, snatched wisps of hay from a fine net.

ॐॐॐ

The stretch of hillside being cleared by the Land Girls for ploughing was on the southwest side of Perringham, and as she had promised to drop in and view their progress it was easier for her to go directly there. She left the road and followed the headlands past Genet coppice and down to the stream. It ended up on the same road, eventually, but cut across a large corner of the estate.

The far side of the coppice sloped gradually down to the small stream that wound back and fore across the estate, one of the many tributaries of the River Chilt. She urged the Fell Pony down to the ford that was deeper and murkier than its summer levels.

Perry paused, almost knee deep in fast-flowing shallows, and lowered his head to drink. The further bank was set at the base of a cut, rising almost high enough to obscure her view, even from horseback. 'Come on, you.' She tugged gently on the rein and pushed Perry on with voice and heels. 'Get on, boy.'

The pony clambered up along the track worn by generations of cattle descending for water, and emerged in the skeletal remnants of grass and nettles that lined the bank. At the top Bunch dismounted, hitched the reins to a fallen trunk, and walked across the open space

The meadow there formed a small flood plain between the stream and what was left of a stretch of a long-abandoned canal. In past years it had been used for summer grazing the beef steers, but with the Ministry of Agriculture demanding every inch of ground be put to work, even land prone to flood was expected to pay its way. Silage and hay as winter feed for the dairy herd was essential. Just over half of the meadow was already mown with wiggling lines of raked cuttings slicing across an open space of green stubble. On the far side, three figures surrounded a patch of briars.

One of them noticed her approach and paused to wave. 'Hey, Boss!'

'Good afternoon Kate. Girls.'

'Boss.' 'Miss Courtney.' The Land Army women sounded off cheerfully and used her arrival to take a break. They scrabbled for flasks of tea and perched on whatever came to hand to rest their backs and legs.

'How is it going?'

'Slowly. It's bloody hard work,' a short brunette complained.

'Language Brenda.'

'Sorry, Boss, but it is. I've got blisters like ruddy golf balls.'

'Eggs and vinegar,' Ruth said. 'Best thing for blisters.'

'My old grandad were a brickie,' said Brenda. 'He reckoned you should piss on 'em.'

'Oh Bren! Really? That's revolting.'

Bunch was not about to be drawn in to what was plainly an on-going debate. She looked across the meadow and nodded satisfaction. 'You've got this stretch three-quarters finished,' she observed. 'I'm very impressed. Do think you'll get it finished this week?'

'Maybe. We still have to get rid of the cuttings and we were just thinking it would be easier to burn it here.'

'I can't see a problem in the early mornings but not a good idea this late in the day. The Luftwaffe don't need you lighting them beacons.'

'Hadn't thought of that. We'll start on it tomorrow. Don't want to attract attention, as you say.'

Bunch shaded her eyes and looked toward two cars parked off in the distance. 'I say, any idea who that would be over by Penning Lane?'

Kate stretched up to look over the hedge and snorted. 'Trekkers. We've had them stopping up by the old viaduct most nights this past two weeks.'

'Trekkers? This far out from the coast?'

'We've seen them a few times this,' Kate replied.

'They were definitely there last night?'

'Yes. They arrived earlier than usual, which is why I noticed them.'

Bunch looked toward the triangle of land between canal, road and stream, and noted a flurry of pigeons starting up from it. Penning Lane led down toward the Y-junction that fed into the road to Inchett. *They would have packed up and gone by the time Wright went through ... but I wonder...* 'Have they been any trouble?' she asked.

'One of them didn't latch the gate a couple of days ago. We

didn't have the sheep in that section fortunately. Mr Parsons had a few words with them and he thought they were harmless enough.'

'Let's hope so, Kate. I shall have PC Botting take a regular ride past. I think I shall trot on over and have a brief word, myself.' She glanced at her watch. 'Give this until three and then pack up for the day. It's going to be getting dark by then and the cow sheds will need a good sweep out after milking.'

'Yes, Boss.'

'See you all tomorrow.'

৯৵৯৵

Bunch cinched Perry's girths whilst examining headland. It was barely wider than the average hay wagon with tufts of grass pushing up through the central band where wheels seldom made contact. That lack of use made it an ideal spot for wanderers to spend an undisturbed night.

She rode up to the gate at the corner of the meadow that stood open ready for the silage cart's final load of the day. Perry clattered out onto the crumbled and pitted tarmac surface toward the junction where road, stream and canal converged. The road bridge spanned the fast-flowing water where it bubbled around the stone wreckage of the viaduct that had once carried a small spur of canal. There had been loading sheds at a quay close to the top of small flight of locks, but all that remained were cobbles interspersed with scrubby undergrowth as nature had set about reclaiming its own.

The abandoned canal quay had apparently found a new lease of life. Parked amongst the hawthorn and brambles and sapling birch were a Bedford van and a rather old Austin.

Two women were bent over a pair of paraffin stoves, one supported a large brown enamel kettle and the other a vast and battered saucepan. Steam rose from both wafting the unmistakable scents of stewed rabbit and steeping tea, and Bunch hoped in passing they were not in the same vessels. Two boys played tag amongst the undergrowth, watched by a lanky man from his perch on one of several logs dragged into a rough horseshoe around the stoves.

'Hello.' Bunch remained in the saddle waiting to see what reception she was about to receive.

26

'Hello.' The man got to his feet and took a few steps toward her.

From the sides of her vision Bunch noted the children run for maternal cover, as wary as any spooked deer. 'My Land Girls have been clearing the fields across the way,' she said, 'and they tell me you have been staying here for the last few nights.'

He shrugged wearily. 'Just stopping overnight,' he mumbled. 'We'll move if it's a problem. We mean no harm. I'm Arthur Vale.' He held out an ID card for her to see. 'We're not here every night, and not this early usually, but the eldest lad's been fretting so we took an afternoon off.'

Bunch slid from the saddle and glanced around her before she pulled out her cigarette case, offering it round with a smile. The three adults relaxed visibly as each accepted a smoke. 'No, it's fine. Make sure you keep the gates closed,' Bunch replied. 'And put your fires out when you finish. Bombings been bad where you are?'

'Have been,' Arthur admitted. 'Shoreham harbour's been getting it on and off since the start.'

'You work there?'

He nodded. 'Customs and Excise. Me and my pal, Les.'

'Reserved occupations. What brings you this far out?'

'The quiet. We only come up now and then cos we've fire warden rosters most nights. And Beth and Grace both do part-time hours at the exchange.' He lit his cigarette and shielded the match for Bunch. 'Shelter in our street took a hit and young Ben's been having nightmares ever since. Les knew about this place cos his father used to bring him – tench fishing in the pools.' He glanced toward the children. 'Can't keep this up, though. It's too far out and the lad's still not getting any sleep.'

'Would it be hard to move away?' She took a deep lungful of smoke and watched the children playing, and realised how that had become rarer now so many had been shunted off to the west and north. 'Could you not find houses further inland?'

'Not so far. I'm Beth. Beth Jenkins.' One of the women rubbed her palm on her coat before offering to shake hands. 'I'm trying to get our Aunt Freda to have the children for a bit. This is no life for them.' She gazed anxiously at her sons and then at Bunch. 'Do you have children Mrs—'

'It's Miss. Miss Courtney, so no children.' They watched a car swish past and vanish into the gathering dusk. 'Someone's in a hurry,' Bunch observed.

'Trying to get somewhere before blackout,' Beth replied.

'You can't blame anybody for that.' Bunch watched the vehicle vanish out of sight and then asked, 'I can see why you picked the spot. It's always quiet. Did you see any cars last night? Or early this morning?'

'Not saw.' Grace spoke up for the first time, softly spoken and calm. 'Heard them. We weren't asleep because it was such a proper cold one. So yes, we heard them all right. It was just like Monte Carlo races.'

'Close to each other?'

'Yes. Zoom. One went by and then maybe five or six seconds after it, zoom again.' She shook her head. 'My sister heard it as well. Didn't you Beth?'

'I did.'

'You saw nothing? Or hear a bang? There was an accident just a mile or so along this road. Was one of them a red car?'

'I saw them but it was too dark to see clearly,' said Vale. 'The first one was a sporty type, if that helps. If there was a bang, I doubt we'd have put it down to a crashed car.'

'How early was that, do you think?'

'Early hours. I would guess one o'clock, or a little after.'

'That early?' Bunch said. 'Are you sure?'

'Yes. I remember it was not long after the last of the bombers went over. Was it serious, this accident?'

'A man died.'

Grace grimaced at her sister. 'That's it. Bombs or no bombs I'm not coming out twenty-five miles again. It's not worth it.'

'But the boys…' Beth Jenkins shook her head. 'Ben has got so nervous. Slightest bang has him shaking like a rabbit. We only come this far so he can't hear when the bombers come over. Except that they do. Even here.' She looked toward her sister, her lip beginning to quake.

'Take them to Auntie Freda's,' Grace snapped, and then more kindly, 'she won't say no once she sees 'em.'

'I can't do that. I can't just leave them there.'

Bunch realised she was not going to find out any more now the conversation was dissolving into domestic squabbles, which she didn't even do with her own family. She lobbed her cigarette into the stream and mounted up whilst Grace and Beth continued to bicker, as only siblings can. 'You are quite welcome to stay here, Mr Vale,' she said as she gathered up the reins.

'We'll stay tonight but we won't be back again,' Vale replied.

'Understood. Thank you for your time.'

He nodded suddenly, as if making a decision. 'Glad to help.' His lips lifted in a lop-sided smile. 'I'm a customs officer. I do know an interrogation when I see one. You're not police, I can tell that much, but you're asking official questions. If you need any more answers you can contact me at the harbour.'

'Thank you. I must go or it will be dark before I get home. Good evening.'

'Good evening, Miss.'

ᔥᔢᔥᔢ

Determined to prove her worth, Bunch was more than happy to have something to tell Wright when he called her that evening.

'Arthur Vale, you say?' he said.

'Shoreham Customs house.'

'Hearing two cars in the dark is not a lot to go on, and the timing is all wrong. But we'll follow it up and I shall get Botting to make a few house calls. It's possible that someone else saw something.'

'If it was our man it does sound very much like Naysmith was being pursued. You have to admit that.'

'He may as easily have been the pursuer.'

'Do we know how he died?'

'Severed spinal cord.'

'Snapped neck?'

'Not in the way you think. Letham, our pathologist's opinion is a short blade inserted into the victim's neck at the base of the skull. Death would have been very quick.'

'So was going into the ditch deliberate?'

'It looks to have been staged, yes. Shove him in the driving seat, put the Jag in gear and away he'd go. Or he could have been shunted into the ditch and then finished off by an unknown assailant.'

'Someone with medical knowledge?'

'Possibly. Or just sheer luck with a stabbing from behind. No sign of a weapon, of course. Letham guesses a short flattish blade of some kind. Nothing unusual.'

'So tracing that second car is vital.'

Wright hesitated and in the background Bunch heard a deep voice calling *Hello? Wright? Are you still there?* 'Yes, I am,' said Wright. 'Will you hang on for just one moment.' The phone was muffled, by a hand over the mouthpiece, Bunch assumed, so that she could not hear what was being said, and then, 'I have to go. Bit of a flap on. I need to go up to the Yard.'

'Excellent I shall be in Town tomorrow as it happens. Mummy has an appointment and wants me to go with her. Perhaps we can meet up?'

'I'd like that but I have no idea when I'll be able to get away. '

'Call and leave a message. You have our number at the house in Thurloe Square?'

'Yes I do. I shall look forward to it. Now I really do have to go.'

'Roger that. Until tomorrow then. Toodle pip.'

✎ Three ✎

The coffee cup at Bunch's right hand was Cooper & Woods, stylish angular deco of the finest quality, but not the Spode or Royal Doulton she might have expected. Yet it remained in keeping with the curiously antiseptic space despite its deep leather armchairs and dark oak occasional tables.

The Times was laid out on the coffee table, carefully pressed and pristine, and Bunch felt a simultaneous wave of sadness and anger at the headlines. The details of the raids on Coventry were sparse, as these things often were. Propaganda dictated losses be downplayed, but reading between the lines she guessed it had been quite devastating. It was easy to forget that though London had suffered so much over the past weeks, as had the south coast, the rest of the country had also taken its share of punishment. The reported devastation sent shivers to her core – and placed her reasons for being there in the Ephrin's' Harley Street clinic into perspective.

A different matter of life or death, she thought. She glanced at her watch for the umpteenth time. 'Five and twenty past twelve. Mother has been in there rather a long time.'

She abandoned her seat and prowled the room for another five minutes before the door opened and a young receptionist, trim in her fashionable dark-wool suit, asked her to step into the consultation room.

Bunch followed her in and crossed to sit next to Theadora without waiting to be asked. 'Everything all right, Mummy?' She looked from her mother to the woman seated across the desk from them, wondering why she had been called in and yet afraid to ask.

'Perfectly fine, Rose.' Theadora patted her hair, a rigid smile on her face.

'Miss Courtney? I'm Doctor Felicity Ephrin.' The doctor stood

31

and extended her hand across the desk to Bunch.'

'Oh. I was expecting Doctor…'

'The other Doctor Ephrin?' Ephrin smiled a little tightly. 'People often say that. My *father* has been called back to the Regiment. His expertise is rather in demand down at Queen Mary's in Roehampton. Do sit down, Miss Courtney. I asked you in because your skills may be useful over the next few months.' She glanced at Theadora, who stared toward the window in silence. 'Miss Courtney, I seem to recall my father telling me that you were a nurse at some point?'

'Almost. I did some training with FANY but never actually qualified.'

'This is less a medical and more a caring role that I have in mind. I've supplied your mother with the necessary diet sheets and medication and I would like you to help her with those. I shall be in contact when I've spoken to Sir Oswald Blakely about the possibility of surgery. It may take a few weeks until we have all of the test results confirmed.'

'Surgery? What surgery?' Bunch looked again from Ephrin to her mother.

'Your mother's X-rays show some shadowing on the liver.'

'Oh.' Bunch glanced at her mother who was uncharacteristically silent. A chill ran through her at the implication. 'Is it cancer?' she whispered.

'That is one possibility.' Ephrin conceded. 'I shall be seeking the opinion of Sir Oswald. He is an expert in the field and a renowned surgeon.' She smiled, a professional tweak of muscles that barely touched the rest of her face.

Not committing herself, Bunch thought. *Not going to say too much – because she doesn't know? God help us. Cancer.*

'Please don't think the worst just yet. Your mother's problems may still lie with cirrhosis,' Ephrin was saying. 'Which is a serious condition in itself, but one that we can treat far more readily. In either eventuality, abstinence is paramount.'

She turned back to Theadora. 'Lady Chiltcombe, I must insist on complete rest and a total abstinence from alcohol in any form. Plenty of fresh air and fresh food. Not easy these days, but I understand that you have an estate in Sussex so it should make obtaining good food a little easier. With the correct regime we shall have you feeling better very soon. I shall want to see you again in a month's time with the results of our tests.'

'You can contact me here. I shall be staying at the Town house...'

The doctor shook her head. 'Rest and abstinence.'

Theodora glanced at Bunch, rolling her eyes. 'I've just spent the summer up in the glens. How much more rest can one possibly take? Up there one can't be rude enough to refuse a wee dram when you are host or guest. It's unforgivable.'

'Rest.' Ephrin repeated. 'And no "wee drams" – under any circumstances.'

'Now see here, Doctor—'

'Lady Chiltcombe, regardless of what our tests may confirm, you must call an immediate halt to your alcohol consumption or the consequences will be very serious indeed. I cannot stress strongly enough how vital it is. If you continue to drink your life expectancy will be greatly reduced.'

'I'm hardly a stripling. I don't see how losing a year or two will make any difference,' Theodora replied. 'In the current circumstances how long can any of us expect.'

Ephrin took a noisy breath. 'You are not old by any means, and we are not speaking in terms of years.' She gazed at the Courtney women, appraising them for possible reaction and then sat back in her chair. 'If you continue as you have been, I would say you may only have a single year left to you. Quite possibly less.' She waited as the Courtneys registered the news.

There was little Bunch could say at that bombshell and her mother's silence was unnerving. 'Of course, I shall do what I can to help,' she said.

'If you can get your mother to rest as much as possible that will be a great help. I can recommend several good clinics.'

'No.' Theodora turned away, her face set. "I've taken cures in the past. They're a waste of my time.'

'I can see that from your records. I can assure you we've progressed beyond calf's foot jelly and leeches in the past thirty years.'

'No rest homes,' Theodora snapped. 'If I'm put out to grass, I swear I'll expire through sheer boredom.'

Ephrin frowned and looked away.

'Mother.' Bunch swivelled to glare at Theodora. 'For God's sake, listen for once in your life. Think of Daddy. And little Georgi.'

None spoke for several seconds. The noise of rubble being cleared from fire-damaged buildings came clearly to them from the street outside.

'Very well.' Theodora began to pull on her gloves. 'I shall go down to the country for a week or two, if you insist, but no clinics.'

'Then I shall make sure your local doctor comes to see you in a week's time. Lady Chiltcombe, Miss Courtney.' Doctor Ephrin smiled brightly and went to open the consultation room door.

∽◈∽◈

'There,' Bunch said. 'I fully applaud the order to rest. It isn't your normal style but if it's what's required then rest you shall.'

'Oh, what do doctors know?' Theodora snapped. 'She's just spinning out her fee. Lady this and Lady that.' Theodora laughed and waved a hand in dismissal. 'I thought we would go for a nice spot of tea, and shopping. And perhaps dine out later?'

Her smile was sudden, turning on like a lamp, and Bunch spied the diplomat's wife's guise. Her mother was obviously feeling on the defensive and Bunch recognised her own obstinacy in that face. *There are times when one wonders who is the child and who the adult.* 'I'm not sure.' Bunch looked at the sheaf of paper that she had been handed. 'It doesn't sound much like resting. Besides, I was supposed to be meeting Wright later this evening.'

'Tonight? Oh really, Rose. I hardly see you for months and now you're racing off with your little policeman pal.' Theodora pursed her lips. 'Do you really need to go tonight? What are you meeting this chap for, anyway?'

'We agreed to meet this evening. Official business, I'm afraid, and quite urgent.'

'Not more scandal? I don't often agree with your grandmother but on this occasion I do. Your father's career does not need that sort of notoriety. It's too bad of you.'

'Do you think your drinking hasn't been noticed?'

The two women glared at each other, each convinced the other was at fault and determined not to give ground. Bunch rarely argued with her mother, considering it a waste of breath, yet Ephrin's ultimatum rendered her usual indifference moot. It was

Theadora who blinked first. 'Rose, my darling, your little policeman chum can surely wait? I need to have some fun for one last night if I'm going to be stuck out in the country for who knows how long. I can rest tomorrow.'

'The Dower House is not that bad.'

'All my friends are in Town.' Theadora paused at a mirror to adjust her hat and her reflection glared back at Bunch. 'Don't look at me in that way.' She jabbed a silver pin topped by a black pearl through the side of her hat. 'Bad enough your father is on the telephone to me morning, noon and night.'

'He cares. We all do. You shouldn't blame us too much for that. I am surprised that he isn't here with you today.'

'Edward had some fresh War Office meeting. They have a new crisis every half hour and the place has been in chaos since dear Neville passed away. Not that it wasn't expected, of course, because he was terribly ill when he resigned his premiership. I wasn't going to bother with all of this resting nonsense but Daphne insisted, or she would speak with your father, and Edward has enough to deal with already.' Her garbled nonsense saw them out onto the pavement and once away from the doors she grabbed her daughter's arm and pulled her to a halt. 'Say nothing to Edward about this visit. You understand?'

'You can't possibly think you can hide this from Daddy?'

'I—'

'Mother, he knows you're unwell. We all do. That it is affecting your liver is obvious to anybody with the slightest medical training.'

'Nonsense.'

'How could you think we don't know? One only has to look at the colour of your skin. You might be expected to have had a tan when you came back from Singapore, no matter how much you hid from the sun, but there's no hiding your yellow skin now, and your eyes are positively canary. You must tell Daddy. And if you don't, I shall.'

'This is exactly why I don't want to stay at the Dower House. Nobody can ever mind their own business.'

'You're his wife. My mother – Georgi's grandmother! For Pete's sake Mother, this is madness.'

'I just so hate people fussing over me. Such nonsense saying I

35

can't stay here in Town. I am quite capable of looking after myself.'

Bunch sighed. Theadora had always been a slave to drama and used to having her own way, but whilst such tricks might work on Bunch's father, who, even after forty years, was still devoted to his beautiful wife, as a long-suffering daughter Bunch saw through her. 'Then go back up to Scotland,' she drawled. 'It would be so much safer than staying in Town and you can do what you like without family fussing over you.'

Theadora's eyes glittered with impatience. 'You will be pleased to hear that it is simply not on the cards.'

'I won't pretend I'd rather you weren't up there alone. So all right, tell me one good reason why not.'

They stared at each other for a long moment, bristling like two cats on a fence. Theadora glanced away. 'Ask your darling father. It seems half of Scotland has been requisitioned, practically overnight. Or the western side has, at least. So we've been evicted twice over. No doubt the only reason we still have Thurloe Square is because they all think it could be bombed at any moment.' The sentence was delivered with a superficial smile and a vicious undertone. Theadora pulled up her gloves and looped her handbag over her left forearm before turning to meet Bunch's curious gaze with another smile, more brittle this time. Thin-lipped and bland. 'Shall we go?'

Bunch opened her mouth and closed it again. It had never occurred to her that her parent's marriage had more than hairline cracks. She always realised it was not a perfect bond. It was a marriage like any other, with its flaws and failings, but in essence a partnership that was forged by mutual respect and duty. She even supposed Theadora must love as equally as she was loved, given how much time her parents spent together. *Shock*, she decided. *It's not every day you're told you are likely to die.* 'Oh come on, Mummy.' She linked arms and leaned her head against Theadora's. 'Neither of us are angels. Let's forget all that for the afternoon. There are shops to peruse.'

ॐॐॐ

Shopping took longer than anticipated, picking their way past stores hit during raids over the previous two months. Bourne & Hollingsworth, John Lewis, and Selfridges remained valiantly in business despite bomb damage. Throughout the spree, Theadora rebuffed all attempts to discuss either her illness or how much she would allow Edward to know. She kept up a constant flow of chatter about clothes and upcoming balls and about little Georgi, and it was almost five o'clock when they piled a small mountain of packages in a cab to be delivered to Thurloe Square.

'I am not used to driving my own car,' Theadora observed. 'We need to get a proper chauffeur again. Edward still has Sutton, of course, but he's Edward's valet so he's not always available when I need him, and it's so damnably hard to find cabs at times.'

Bunch nodded but said nothing. It was pointless trying to point out that there were no longer any young men available to drive her mother around, and Theadora refused to acknowledge anything that did not meet her expectations. Bunch checked the time and wondered if she should call the house yet again to see if Wright had left a message. She had made three calls during lulls in her mother's frenetic shopping and had been increasingly frustrated at hearing nothing. *Now it's getting dark and I'm too busy shoring up Mummy's ego to worry about that man.*

They found a small restaurant but she barely had time to use their telephone and then join Theadora at a snowy-clothed table before the sirens wailed out across the West End.

'The Luftwaffe are late today,' her mother observed. 'We've usually had sirens by this time. The weather was bad earlier so perhaps they were not coming tonight.' She stared out of the window at darkened streets. 'Probably some incompetent has let a blimp off its moorings. Happens a couple of times a week.'

Since mid-September, the capital had been subjected to raids and appalling devastation every single day and Bunch was not sure if her mother was being hopeful or satirical. *Possibly the latter given the news she had earlier.* She signalled to the waitress. 'Could you call us a cab?'

'Miss?' The girl looked toward the doors. 'I can try but they get snapped up quick once the sirens go.'

'Then do you have a shelter here?'

'No, Miss. You could try Dickins & Jones. They've got a cafe in their basement shelter but it gets crowded early on. Or you can try the tube? That's safe as a rule except…' She hesitated. 'It gets 'orrible crowded. My mum doesn't like me going down there, these days, in case I gets pushed off the platform.'

'Crowded so early in the day?' said Bunch.

'Yes, Madam. I've heard some people that are bombed out are just about livin' down there. Specially now there's bin bunks and things put in. And people are still bagging platform spaces well before four o'clock.' Her lips set into a pursed line and she handed the two women their coats and hats with practised speed. 'If you'll excuse me, we have to be shutting up now or we'll have the wardens down on us.'

'What does she mean by "bagging"?' Bunch asked as they hurried along the street.

'That the platforms will be full of people. You must have seen them when you came up? It becomes unbearable when the raid starts. I have been in the Tube in a raid and have no intention of repeating the experience,' said Theadora. 'We need to get a taxi to Thurloe Square, but they rather do go to ground when the sirens are sounding.'

Bunch stared at her mother wondering how much of that was bravado and how much sheer lack of common sense. 'I dare say it's sensible of them. I suspect the wise head underground faster than a rat in a hayrick.'

'I'd prefer not to be part of such a comparison,' Theadora snapped.

Bunch tugged her hat tight down over her ears. 'Not such a bad one in many respects. Rats know how to survive. I would call that admirable, under the circumstances. Ready?'

'Yes.' Theadora drew her fur tippet closer under her chin and nodded to the doorman to pull back the blackout around the door, and they stepped out into the street, pausing for a moment to gain their night vision.

Sirens still wailed overhead and spotter lights already criss-crossed the sky, flickering across occasional blimps and vanishing into the inky darkness beyond. The full moon had yet to rise over the buildings that surrounded them but its glow gave off enough light for the two women to join the general march along the dark street toward the Underground station.

The siren stopped abruptly and like many of those around her Bunch could not resist the impulse to look upwards. She listened for the drone of engines but the noise of people hurrying to reach their destination before the bombers came within range drowned any distant approach. She grasped Theadora by the arm and nodded toward the taxi rank close by the tube entrance just as a black cab coasted up to the line.

They made it across the road and piled in.

'Ritz,' Theadora snapped.

'Yes, Madam,' the cabbie called back to them as the cab pulled away into the dark.

Theadora sat back and smiled to herself and looked at the empty rank before she turned to Bunch. 'The Ritz sounds rather jolly, don't you think? Café de Paris is fun but perhaps a little later in the evening. We really aren't dressed for it.'

'We're not dressed for the Ritz, either,'

'Oh, at this time of day we shall be fine.' Theadora smoothed her fox fur tippet and flicked a mote from her sleeve. 'When there's a raid on we Londoners make the best of the situation. There's such a perfectly darling grille there, and I am famished after all that shopping. They make fabulous desserts. You'd barely imagine we had rationing. All perfectly safe in the basement and a lot closer than home.'

'Daddy said he was expecting us to be at The Square for supper, and you know I have a meeting with Wright later this evening.'

'Are you still mithering over him, Rose.'

'He was adamant that he'd be at Scotland Yard today. I told him I have some interesting evidence to share.'

'Theadora tilted her head and gave her daughter a long appraising look. 'Darling,' she said at last, 'you are turning out to be a pleasantly dark horse.'

'It's not like that.'

'It never is. Now, what about supper?'

'We need to get back to Thurloe Square. There may be a message.'

'Nonsense, dear. The raid won't last long, I'm certain. We shall be home in plenty of time. I shall call the house and leave a message for Edward if you are worried. And for your policeman friend. They will both be caught up in the raid the same as we are, you know. Not that Edward is ever at home these days. He works all sorts if odd hours. I am quite used to it and at least now he's out of the Foreign Office he doesn't need me most of the time.

Now, shall we go and get a decent dinner?'

For the wife of a diplomat, Bunch thought, *there are times when Mother could be incredibly insensitive.* In the distance the first crump, crump of exploding ordnance somewhere south of the river cut her objections short.

There seemed little choice but share a cab with Theadora or seek out a public shelter, and Bunch would far rather not go anywhere that would provoke her mother when she was in such a mood. *Mother's had a shock from the doctor. Maybe best she's kept busy.*

The drive from Oxford Street to the Ritz on Piccadilly was not far, as the Tower ravens can flap, but in the total blackness of an unlit London it was taken at a crawl, hugging the white-painted kerbs and avoiding pedestrians who appeared to have little regard for survival.

Theadora and Bunch chattered on with the usual polite banter, discussing the trials of shortages and restrictions as if nothing was amiss, but all the while Bunch watched the flares in the distance, with familiar landmarks highlighted now and then by search beams and ack-ack flare. She noted how her mother's hands clasped and unclasped, the only part of her to move as she also stared into the staccato night sky. Despite her outward calm, the unflappable Theadora was as close to panic as Bunch had ever seen her.

Bunch leaned her head against the window and watched the world passing her by, feeling oddly detached from it by that fragile sheet of cool glass, as if she were watching some Pathé newsreel that was nothing to do with her. Search lights that had been criss-crossing the skies in anticipation of enemy planes began to pick out the pale cross shapes of the bombers more than the bloated shapes of barrage balloons tethered above the city, and then the boom and crack of anti-aircraft fire in Hyde Park.

Even inside the cab the bombs could be heard falling somewhere along the river. Bunch watched the glow of fire springing up beyond the immediate line of buildings, with a growing unease, glancing at her mother who now appeared undisturbed, merely watchful, as they risked casual glances toward the distant halo of light above the building tops. 'Should we get to a shelter, Mummy?' she said at last.

'We'll be all right, Miss. Woolwich getting' it worst. Just a few

40

strays up this way,' the cabbie said. 'They've been getting' a pasting down the docks all week.'

'Aren't we going toward the river?' she asked.

'Yeah, but we're dead close now.' He pulled up and turned to grin at her. ''Ere we are, Miss, The Ritz. Better get in quick.'

'Thank you.' She reached in her bag for her purse and paid with a generous tip.

'Thank you, Miss. Evenin'.'

The cab pulled smartly away and once again Bunch could not stop herself from looking up, despite all of the Public Information films that assured her it was the wrong thing to do. It was an instinctive act that few around her seemed able to resist. Search light beams were more obvious now out of the confines of the cab, and she glimpsed the pale crosses of two bombers caught in their beams. She had seen enough raids across the coast to find the sight entirely alien, yet somehow seeing those shapes over London took her breath. More planes droned high above them. Lights wafted to and fro, seeking the source of their whining hum. Somewhere, fire engines were ringing a frantic approach. Another crump, louder than before, and the unmistakable shiver of breaking glass followed by another a little further away, and Bunch could not prevent herself from flinching.

There had been so many air raids over the Downs. She had watched bombs falling over Worthing and Newhaven but that had been across open country. Here in the city it was more visceral, more immediate. Fire flared along the top of a four-storey block down the road, and the taint of smoke and burning that she had noted pervading the city all day increased by tenfold.

'Miss?' Bunch looked toward the hotel where Theadora and the concierge waited on the steps. The elderly doorman stood like a rock, deflecting the tide of people still hurrying into shelter around him on both sides. 'I think perhaps you should take cover,' he called. 'They're dropping incendiaries.'

'Yes, of course.' Bunch scurried inside, taking a final glance at the sky before slipping through the curtains into a dimly lit foyer.

Inside the building the pounding of guns and occasional boom of falling bombs, though marginally quieter, were still un-mistakable. Bunch linked arms with her mother and they followed the bellboy past the scaffold poles bracing the walls and on down

41

to the shelter. The doors opened onto a long low room partly lined with sandbags. Tables were laid out for dinner and at one end of the room a band was tuning up to play.

Theadora beamed at her daughter. 'If you must be shut in a cellar for the night it may at least be somewhere that has oysters and champagne.' A waiter showed them to a table. Theadora motioned for Bunch to a small table as she gazed around her. 'They must have a telephone here. I shall call the Square and inform Gilsworth we shall be home once the all-clear has sounded. She and Kimber will be glad of the night off, in any case. They can inform Edward and your constable they will have to wait.' Theadora offered a mocking curtsy. 'Whilst I'm gone be a darling and order me a Martini – and then we shall look at the menu.'

'Martini? Mother, really you are the giddy limit. What did Doctor Ephrin tell you just today? You must not drink.'

The two women stared at each other. 'We can't come here and not have a drink, darling.' Theadora paused, listening to the noises filtering through to them even past the sound of the crowd and the band. 'One cocktail, Rose-bunch. I've had rather a shock, don't you know. It's not every day you're told you're dying.' She raised her eyes toward the chandeliers that were shimmering gently. 'And as things stand, does anyone know how long they have?' She laughed, throwing her head back in a full-throated whoop. 'One Martini, darling. Plenty of olives if they have them.' Theadora kissed the air above Bunch's head. 'Back in a trice.'

Perplexed, Bunch watched her mother's slender form weave its way back through the crush. The waiter helped her to her seat and handed her a menu. She scanned the crowd recognising a few faces but none she cared to attract as she had no real wish to be sociable. Neither she nor her mother were dressed for the Ritz, and though there were many others in day clothes, sheltering from fiery rain, there were as many in evening dress and fur wraps.

Breaching the dress code was far from being the greatest fear that loomed over the evening. Theadora had been avoiding the subject of the diagnosis ever since they'd left Harley Street, but the knowledge that drink had rendered her liver a turgid mass hung over them, unmentioned but as menacing as the barrage balloons that festooned the London skyline. Bunch was the first to acknowledge that she and her mother had never been close but faced with this diagnosis she realised familial bonds ran far deeper than she had anticipated. Yes, she could understand Theodora's refusal to buckle under, but what was her alternative? Theodora would need help and it was unfair to place that burden on her maid Kimber, or Thurloe Square's housekeeper, the ever-stoic Mrs Gilsworth.

'Drinks, Ma'am?' She started, realising the waiter was still hovering and she sighed. *No point fighting it. No tonight at least.* 'Two Martinis. One with extra olives. And leave the menu.'

'Two Martinis. Of course, Madam.' He placed the leather-bound menu folder on the crisp linen tablecloth, inclined his head respectfully, and was gone.

Bunch opened the folder, glanced down the list and then closed it again. The band was striking up 'A Nightingale Sang' and couples began to fill the dance floor. *Soothing tones to calm the masses,* she thought. The waiter brought drinks, glancing at the menu, and she shook her head. 'Five minutes,' she said.

He bowed and turned to a group still waiting for a table: three women and two men, one of whom was in uniform. Loud, excitable.

'Bit lively out there,' one of the women said.

'More than it is in here.' The youngest looking of the group waved toward the band. 'Wasn't like this in Munich. I was so cross when Daddy dragged us home last year. A few more months wouldn't have hurt.'

'Perhaps,' one of the men said. 'It can't be helped, Fee. It's a bloody war.'

Bunch could see him from the corner of her eye, the only face she could see without being obvious. His face was a familiar one. *Gordon?* She thought. *Gordon something. Tilman?*

'All such a bloody waste,' the younger said. 'Daddy mentioned it need never have happened if Halifax had—'

'Fee!' The unseen male was sharp. 'It's my last night. Don't start.'

'Oh poo. You're such an old stick, Harry. If I want...'

'We have a table free now. This way please.' The waiter intoned and the group moved away. Bunch risked a look at them, a glance as they vanished into the masses, but that did not help a great deal in identifying them when she could not see their faces. She picked up the glass with the single olive and took a tentative sip. It was heavy on the gin and, she suspected, watered down with soda. *Shortages of vermouth are even hitting this place.* She looked in the glass, shrugged and drained it.

The exchange she had overheard rattled her. She'd heard talk of that kind elsewhere but sitting in a London basement in the midst of an air raid seemed the most bizarre. *And incredibly dim.*

'Waiter.' She signalled for another drink and peered in the direction Theadora had taken.

The band had changed tempo and Bunch watched the dancers spiralling anti-clockwise in a synchronised swarm, hardly noticing their faces. Her mother appeared, taking her seat in silence. 'You were a long time,' said Bunch.

'Yes. It took a while to get through. Then it was your father who answered. He was home just for once.'

'Daddy was home before midnight? That must be a first. Any messages for me?'

'If you mean from your policeman, then no.'

'Nothing at all?' Wright's silence felt like a betrayal. She understood that he might be busy. *But what does it take to make a call? Two minutes at the most. Utter pish.*

'This is a bad raid. You saw how hard it was for us to reach here.'

'Scotland Yard isn't that far away.'

'If your chap's still *there.* He might be anywhere in the city.' Theadora laid her fingers lightly on her daughter's arm. 'This isn't Wyncombe, my dear. Remember that the telephones will be down all over the place. Roads will be blocked by fires, and as if that isn't hard enough we still have the blackout. Don't fret, darling. He will be in touch.'

Something in her mother's tone made Bunch turn to examine her. Empathy was not Theadora's strong suit. 'You said it's a bad raid. What makes it worse than others?'

Theadora breathed in noisily, and out again, and then picked up her glass, taking out the olive-laden stick and drinking the alcohol in one long gulp.

'Mother?'

'It took a while to get an answer. There were incendiaries

dropped at the end of Thurloe Square.'

'Is everyone safe?'

'All accounted for. The staff either were in the cellars or out helping the fire wardens. But I gather Sloane Street Station has taken a direct hit.'

'Oh good heavens. That's just two streets from the Square.'

'It is.'

'Rather close. It will be chaos over there, I'm sure. Perhaps we should go down to Perringham as soon as the raid is over.'

'Don't be ridiculous, child. Driving all that way in blackout? More dangerous than the raids. We'll go in the morning.' Theadora signalled to the waiter for more drinks.

'One,' Bunch muttered. 'You promised. One drink.'

'One?' Theadora looked sideways at her daughter. 'I'm far from being a saint, Rose. You of all people have always known that so you'll excuse me if I exercise my weakness in the face of adversity in the way I know best.'

'Mother, I didn't mean…' Bunch laid a hand on her mother's, feeling guilty. Her mother had suffered so much loss. Her sons to the Spanish flu, her marriage to the Foreign Office, and her homes to the military of one persuasion or another. Bunch sat back and toyed with the stem of her cocktail saucer. 'I am sorry, Mother.'

'I know you are, dear heart.' The solid whine of the all-clear filtered down to them, bringing the band to a halt. Theadora looked at her watch. 'Edward said the raid would not go on for long. Drink up and we shall get home.'

'How does he know it's almost over?'

'How does your father know anything? Come along now.' She gestured at the Martini. 'Spit spot. There's bound to be a rush for cabs.'

ꙮ Four ꙮ

Bunch took the booklet that Wright held out and fanned the pages under her nose, breathing in over the bundle like a Bisto Kid. 'Extra motor spirit coupons. I'm honoured.' She read the top ticket a third time and grinned. 'Undated. Is this a peace offering?'

'I'm not sure I need one.' Wright's neck flushed red and he looked away.

Bunch wondered if that was out of embarrassment or annoyance and she found that irksome. It was hard not to take either as a slight. *He could at least have the good grace to lie.* 'I might be tempted to think you have something to hide. I was disappointed not to get our supper in Town.'

'It was unavoidable. I can't say any more at this juncture, so please, just accept my apology. Those coupons are orders from on high. Allowing you to traipse around the county in your own vehicle uses less fuel than sending a car to fetch you. As they're for your use alone, perhaps they are a little bit of a bribe?'

'Accepted, then.' She slipped the booklet into her pocket and patted it gently. 'Do not begin to imagine this makes up for ducking out of dinner.'

'I can't keep apologising, Rose. I was detained.'

'That is all the explanation I am going to get?'

'For the moment. It has nothing to do with this case, I assure you.'

She had no way of knowing whether he was being entirely open or not. His expression was apologetic and there was a hint of regret, almost sadness, in his eyes that swayed her into giving him some slack. There were so many who were bound to secrecy on so many fronts. Yet she could not help feeling that there were times when a little chat here and there would be beneficial. 'All right, Detective. What did you call me down here for?'

'Another ID, I'm afraid. The body of a young woman was

discovered up on the Downs.'

'Why would you assume I'd know who it is?'

'You'll see. He gestured along the mortuary's main corridor. 'Shall we get on?'

She followed him through the swing doors. 'Where was she found?' she asked.

'On the edge of the escarpment, south of Storrington. An out-of-the-way spot full of brambles and gorse. Only found because the farmer's dog sniffed it out. The farmer had seen lights and thought it might be trekkers using an old shepherds' hut up there. The papers are being told to keep it quiet but people are leaving towns after work in droves.'

'I know. People are frightened already. They don't need to be hounded by clod-hopping coppers.'

'We have every sympathy but several farm buildings have been burned to the ground recently. People have died and there are enough civilian casualties from the raids without folk adding to the toll themselves.'

'I shall get my staff to keep a watch.'

Wright paused as the doors swung closed behind them. 'Ready?' he asked.

'As I shall ever be. What can I expect?'

'We think she may have been dumped at the scene. Seemingly a well-heeled young lady, which is why we wondered if it was linked with the other victim. From the condition of the body there's a good possibility she was killed on the same day as our other corpse. That would be a big coincidence.'

'Claude Naysmith,' Bunch snapped. 'The *other corpse*, as you put it, had a name.'

'It sometimes helps not to think about that.' Wright nodded to the porter on duty and pushed through to the cold room.

Bunch resisted the impulse to cover her nose. She had come across enough death to be prepared for the smell, but in the confined space, and despite being cloaked by the dank blanketing odours of formaldehyde and Lysol, it was stronger than she had anticipated. There were several trolleys covered in white sheets but Wright went unerringly to one on the furthest side where the pathologist was waiting for them.

'You know our pathologist, Doctor Letham?' said Wright.

'I do. Good morning Doctor Letham.'

'Good morning, Miss Courtney. Are you prepared?' Letham asked.

Bunch nodded abruptly for him to tweak back the sheet covering the trolley and stepped forward to view the body, acutely aware of Wright watching her every twitch. She had been called upon in a formal capacity, and knowing this was quite probably a test made her nervous.

What I see and think matters, she thought. *So what can I see?* She edged forward until she was standing over the body.

'Take your time,' Wright said, quietly. 'Tell me everything you see.'

'Average height,' she said. 'Pretty, but she always lacked the bones to be a real beauty. Was there a struggle?' She glanced at Letham, who nodded.

'Go on,' Wright said.

She pulled the sheet back further, schooling her face to ignore the smell emanating from the corpse, and hide the fact that once again this was a person she knew, however slightly. *Oh dear God, why do they always seem to be people I know?* she thought. *What an end to meet.* This was a darker part of police work that she had never considered. *The need for impartiality, that no murder is more serious or no less, that a crime is a crime, no matter who she is … or was.* Bunch's gazed lingered on the woman's face for just a heartbeat longer. 'She's quite clean so she hasn't been buried,' she murmured. 'And she hasn't been submerged in water for any length of time. Was she dumped?'

'We're working on that assumption.' Wright's eyes glittered without humour but a suppressed excitement.

He's enjoying this, she thought. *We shall see.* She bent lower, peering at the girl's head and neck and saw nothing. She pushed the sheet further down and inhaled sharply at the small neat hole directly above the heart. 'Small calibre pistol shot,' she said. 'No sign of bruising or damage to her hands. Almost seems as if she faced her attacker head on.'

'Full marks,' said Letham.

Bunch looked toward the pile of clothes folded on a small trolley beside the body. 'Are these hers?'

'Yes,' Letham replied. 'Your opinion?'

Bunch looked through them, holding items up against the light and respectfully folding them once more. 'Good quality for the most part, except for the home-knitted cardigan. Rather badly made, it must be said.' She inspected the name tag sewn into the back of the neck and glanced at Wright, who waved her to carry on. 'I assume she wasn't wearing this?'

'No,' Letham replied.

Bunch nodded. 'It's not hers. Nothing is soiled or especially wet but then she wasn't left out in the rain, was she? And no shoes? So one has to assume she was carried to this hut place.'

The smell at close quarters proved to be a little much even for her cast-iron constitution. Bunch pulled the sheet up over the corpse again leaving just the head exposed, and stood abruptly. 'Shall we talk outside?' She stepped out into the corridor, opened her cigarette case and offered it to Wright.

'No thank you,' Wright said. 'The big question is do you know her name?'

Bunch knew he was impatient but she needed a smoke. She was not a stranger to death but not under such scrutiny. She lit her tailor-made and took in a lungful of smoke before delivering her verdict on the out breath. 'I knew her. Your victim is the elusive Penelope James.'

'That explains why the poor women we brought in to identify her was so upset.'

'Oh?'

'You noticed the name tag on the cardigan? It appears that the Jane Forest who owns that garment is a clippie on the South Downs buses and still very much alive. She claims not to have any idea why her cardigan was found with the body, but it's a popular spot for courting couples, so I think we can guess.'

'Could Penelope have worked with this girl perhaps?'

Apparently not. And as the deceased was not wearing the garment there's no reason to suspect any connection. Now we have a name for our body. All we need to do is track down her home address and place of work, if she has one. You girls of private means don't always need to earn your crust.'

'That is why you thought I might be able to identify her? Other than her being well dressed, and us posh girls not doing our bit by working? That's bloody unfair. Practically every one of my pals that isn't married has joined up, you know.'

'That wasn't what I meant at all.' He grinned sheepishly. 'May I extend an all-encompassing apology?'

She looked him straight in the eyes and her tension collapsed. She had been angry with him, she still was, but his face held nothing but honest regret. 'Truce,' she said. 'So why else did you ask me here?' Bunch didn't want to consider the alternative, that he was attempting to prove her superfluous. It was no secret that Wright was needled by her wheedling her way into her uncle's favour. 'Stop being such a prize idiot, William. I know that I'm completely and utterly brilliant in every way, but even I can't identify every blue blood in the kingdom. So what did you find that made you think I would know her? Spit it out, man.'

'I was hoping you might be able to shed some light on this.' Wright reached inside his coat and fished a crumpled sheet of paper sandwiched between pages of his notebook. 'It was clutched in her hand.'

Bunch took it gingerly, clasping the edges between her fingertips. The paper was stained in various shades of brown and she was fairly sure that she didn't want to know what had caused them. Peering at it, she could make out a list of names, some of which were crossed through, including Claude Naysmith. 'Interesting,' she said. 'Any idea what might connect them?'

'We have a few ideas. None we can confirm, which is the main reason why you're here.'

'I recognise them all in passing. I know a few of them rather better. Pilkington and Barrington-Soames are both on the hunting circuit, but then they all are, one way or another. Clarice Bell is more into shooting than riding.'

'Anything else? Personal details?'

'Pilkington is a bit of a snake, if we are being perfectly honest. I gave him the brush off a few years back.' She shrugged. 'He had dynastic dreams that I had no intention of sharing.'

'With you?'

'Yes, me. Don't look so surprised. I may have had my coming out season a while ago now but I still get at least two proposals a year. Nothing like a decent inheritance to make a romantic out of these chaps.' She pulled a face. 'I wasn't Pilkington's first choice. He likes his lady friends to be a little more – shall we say, biddable?'

'He didn't think you fitted the bill? For shame.'

Bunch shot him a dark glance. 'The point is, he's a serial proposer in desperate need of wife. Only heiresses need apply. Yes, he's a pill but no, I don't think he has it in him to kill in cold blood. Larry Parrish is probably the best known to me. You know he lives at The Chells, about six hundred yards from where Naysmith died?'

'We had noted that.'

Bunch went back to the list. 'I see Larry is one of the names crossed out. He's not a bad sort. He was a great pal of Johnny Frampton, and George Tinsley, of course. Poor chaps. Not their passing away is relevant here of course.'

'Johnny Frampton was the man who was murdered by Mrs Tinsley's mother-in-law?'

'Yes. My sister married into a delightful family on the distaff side, as it turned out.'

'On which side of the law does Parrish live?'

'He's a good sort, as I said. Barrington-Soames is the one to watch. That crowd liked to run with the bright young things, and the main reason Pilkington lives well beyond his means is because he's trying to keep up with Soames.'

'What about the rest of the list?'

Bunch took another long look. 'Harriett Beamish, and I can't quite read the next two – they are are scored through quite hard. Penelope James and Jemima Harper? The last one is Clarice Bell.' She shrugged. 'I know Clarice Bell to nod to. She lives over Lewis way so we've crossed paths at house parties and things of that sort. I've met Jemima Harper and Penelope James. They were friends of my sister's. Or they were before she married George.' Bunch handed the paper back. 'I don't imagine they'll be too hard to trace. I'm surprised you called on me.' She gazed at him a shrewd smile in her eyes. 'What I find odd is that if Penelope wrote this list why has she included her own name, and crossed it out? Is it her handwriting? What aren't you telling me? Or perhaps I should say, what don't you want to tell me?'

Wright shrugged. 'We had wondered why she included herself. It may be an innocent note with no bearing at all. Odd you should mention Soames … because he came up on another list. I gather he has some dubious links behind enemy lines.'

'You think he's a spy?'

'Not that we can ascertain. More familial links that need to be questioned. He was in Germany quite bit between '34 and '35, and then again in '38 to '39. Came back just ahead of the Panzers.'

'That's because he has German rellies. Haven't we all. Granny tells me I have a cousin in the Luftwaffe. Bit rum watching chaps having dog fights over the Downs not knowing if the chap with the cross on his wings is cousin Friedrich.' She laughed at Wright's face. 'Don't get too concerned. He's at least four times removed, or is it five? I don't think we've ever met. I believe my maternal side also had German antecedents before they were American. I would not set too much store by it.'

'Perhaps.' He took the paper back and slipped it in his pocket. 'We're still looking into the other names and their connections. Have you heard anything on your grapevine?'

'Not that I can think of. I shall give it some thought.'

He nodded, staring off into the middle distance. A muscle ticked along his jaw line

As the seconds lengthened Bunch felt a slight change of tack was called for. 'Anything more on Claude?' she asked.

'There is some progress there. Did you ask your sister what she knew?'

'She had nothing to tell me beyond Claude's family having land in Oxfordshire. I suspect Dodo drifted slowly away from that old set when she married. That happens to a lot of people. You see, old thing, the London season is a little like school. You're dragged back from finishing, herded together like cattle, with no idea who anybody is, and you live in their pockets for a year, until—' Bunch snapped her fingers. 'You have a mad rash of weddings where you only ever see half of them across a crowded space and they drift off into their own family lives, never to meet again.' She laughed suddenly. 'Perhaps I exaggerate a little but it is a beastly process. Until you manage to give the old chaperones the slip. These days that's when the real matchmaking is done, whatever the mothers and grannies think.'

'Except you've never ran the gauntlet. Never walked down the aisle, I mean.'

'True.' Bunch held her hands up. 'Guilty as charged. I am a woman of means without a husband. Scandalous! Fortunately for me, if not for them, there was a whole generation of women before me in that situation, so nobody sees it as too odd anymore.' She rubbed at her arms. 'I say, Will. I am absolutely frozen. This is not the best of places to hang around making idle chit-chat.'

'I agree.' He smiled at her. 'We've nailed down Claude Naysmith's digs. Would you be free to take a look at? Maybe we could have a spot of lunch after?'

'That sounds rather jolly. Is it near here?'

'Newhaven. Do you know it?'

'Not really. I am not that familiar with East Sussex. I know Brighton, of course, and Plumpton. And I've been dragged along with Daddy to Glyndebourne a few times.'

'You don't like opera?'

Bunch shrugged. 'Yes, I do.' She pulled a face. 'I have to admit I am not terribly musical. Had all the lessons, of course. Piano and such, but playing scales was too tiresome. Dodo's far more gifted that way than I am.' She shivered. 'Oh come on, Will. If you want me to view this room of his, let's do it before I freeze solid. Let's take my car.'

సౌ౼ఌౡఌ

Mrs Margaret Tristram was not pleased to find Inspector Wright on her doorstep, and Bunch was not certain what annoyed the woman more, the fact that the police were at her door once again, or that she had not being allowed to re-let the room within days of the previous tenant's demise. *If I had to take a guess it would be the money, every time*, she thought.

'It's very inconvenient.' Tristram stood back to let them into the hallway. 'I run and reputable establishment, you know, and it doesn't take much for the gossips to ruin that.'

Bunch and Wright glanced at each other but said nothing. Both wiped their feet with marked vigour and followed the landlady through the long narrow entrance hall.

Plainly we don't warrant the front parlour. Bunch took careful note of the house as she passed through. An Edwardian villa that had not been built as a small hotel. It would once have been a comfortable family home before it had taken on the mantle of genteel Guest House. The décor was slightly dated in style, and perfectly in keeping with its origin, but immaculate. It felt light and airy and welcoming despite its owner. Mrs Tristram herself

53

was in her sixies. Slender and upright with iron-grey hair cut in an Eton crop. She wore a cowl-necked woollen frock that would have been fashionable five years previously, and a well-polished but somewhat creased pair of chestnut-brown brogue shoes. *What Granny would call a sensible woman,* Bunch thought.

They entered the viciously bleached kitchen where Tristram gestured at the table and chairs. 'Do be seated.'

'Thank you.' Wright looked down the long table and its ten seats. 'How many tenants do you have?' Wright asked her.

'Eight. As you well know, Chief Inspector.'

'And none of them knew Mr. Naysmith?'

'He hadn't been with us here for long, so no. I don't think he said much beyond the polite chit-chat over supper, and he was seldom here for that. He worked strange hours. Then of course with all the air raids we get, I could say that of several of my guests.'

'None of them worked with him?'

'No. *Harbour Side* is more used to retired residents. Not holiday guests. They suit me well, you see. No trouble with "callers". No rowdiness. No drinking. I don't usually take in young gentlemen but when so many of the old brigade have moved away one has to take what there is.'

'You are licensed, I understand?'

'Yes.' She lifted her chin defiantly. 'My husband was the chief steward of a gentleman's club before the Great War. This was to be our retirement fund.'

'And your husband?'

'Mr Tristram died at Ypres,' she replied. 'I fail to see how that is important.'

'Just trying to get a broader picture,' he said. 'Was Mr Naysmith a good resident? Other than keeping late hours?'

'He was polite. Well spoken.' She glanced at Bunch once more, a shrewd assessing, though Bunch had barely spoken. 'He came from a respectable family, you see.' She looked Bunch up and down and sniffed. 'I would not have had him here, otherwise. Times are different now, aren't they? I got on the bus just last week and there was a whole gaggle of flighty young creature in men's overalls and headscarves. All red lipstick and cigarettes.' She pursed her lips. 'I've always worked for my living, Inspector. But a woman needs to have her pride.'

'Indeed they do, Mrs Tristram. Do you know where Mr Naysmith worked?'

'I thought when he first came, he was a gentleman of independent means, but he turned out to be a Naval man, if that helps. I don't normally take younger military types but he was a well-spoken young man with impeccable manners. As was his young lady friend.'

'Did you know her name?'

'I don't pry. She only came here twice, to collect Mr Naysmith in that flashy red car of hers. Never stayed. I don't allow those carry-ons here. I've barely seen either of them this past month or so and I wondered if I should ask if he was moving out, but he paid his rent on the dot so I didn't make an issue of it.'

'Thank you. That is very helpful. Perhaps if we could take a look at the room?' He smiled at her. 'I hope we shall be able to release the room very soon. Mr Naysmith's family will be collecting his belongings once we've ascertained the room has nothing more to tell us.'

She led the way to Naysmith's room and waited, hovering at the door as if unwilling to leave Wright alone. 'What are you looking for?' She said at last. 'What had he done?'

'Apart from dying? Nothing that we know of.' He smiled at her. 'I shall call you when we've finished.'

Mrs Tristram hesitated, her hand on the doorknob, her lips tightening against words unsaid, and then she stepped back onto the landing, 'Of course, Chief Inspector,' she muttered.

Bunch watched her retreat with curiosity and a not a little surprise. She had seen the deferential facets of Wright's character, and seen the superior officer who issued orders to his underlings. The autocratic Wright was new. She recognised the assumption of obedience. She saw it in her parents and grandmother and expected that she did it herself without thinking. It pulled her up a little short to see the unguarded flash of mutiny in the woman's face. Did people do that to her? Grimace when they assumed her attention had moved on? 'She'll turn the milk...'

'Shh...' Wright held up his forefinger, his head tilting as he listened. For few seconds there was silence and then the unmistakable sounds of footsteps descending the stairs. 'Coast is clear,' he said.

'Was that nosiness or something more?'

Wright shrugged. 'Too early to tell.' He looked around the room. 'Let's see what we have here.'

He began to prowl the room, opening drawers and poking through their contents.

After a moment or two watching him, Bunch moved to the dark oak single wardrobe and pulled the door open. Inside she found the clothes expected of any well-raised man, though rather fewer than she might have imagined. *But then he's not here to socialise.* She slid the hangers along the rail one at a time. A light coat, one day suit, evening suit. Two shirts. *It's the kind of tally one expects to take on a short country house weekend.* She fingered the clothes. Suits from a London tailor but shirts off the peg. She turned up the label. *Bourne and Hollingsworth. The kind one might find in the closet of a man servant or bookkeeper. Was he just trying to fit in with a different set?*

'Anything interesting?' Wright appeared at her side and peered at the garment in her hand.

'Not entirely the wardrobe I'd expect, and not nearly enough of it. It's as if he didn't actually live here.'

Wright rubbed his hand over the top his head as he turned to look around. 'Not so much as a ration card.'

'Mrs Tristram would have those. Or the navy.'

'There's nothing. I'd expect a few receipts or letters here, but there's not even a bus ticket.'

'Perhaps Mrs Tristram cleared them away.'

'She said not. Unless he's exceptionally neat, which I doubt, this place is too clean. There is nothing of the man here.'

'I agree. There's neat and there's inhuman, even for a naval officer.' Bunch looked around them and shook her head. 'Where's his uniform? He wasn't wearing it when he died.'

'That is rather odd.'

There was a tap at the door and Mrs Tristram walked straight in. 'There's a telephone call for you Chief Inspector.' Her voice dripped disapproval and Bunch wondered whether she objected to passing messages for anybody or just the police in particular.

Wright smiled and nodded. 'Downstairs?' he said.

'In the public lounge,' she replied. Wright stepped past her, nodding politely, but Tristram did not follow. She waited with folded arms watching Bunch's every move as she continued her search.

A few minutes later Wright returned. 'Emergency call, I'm afraid. Thank you for your help Mrs Tristram. If you think of anything please do call me. You have my number.'

They were hustled out of the door and stood on the driveway alongside the Crossley just as a patrol car pulled up and Glossop jumped out to open the door. He turned back and shook Bunch's hand. 'I have to leave you to get home alone, I'm afraid. Seems we have another body turned up. Nothing like chalking up a list.'

'Anything to do with our case?'

'I doubt it. A body on a bomb site with a bullet through his head. A known villain, so plenty of suspects there.' He slid onto the seat and shook his head. 'No, don't look at me like that. You can't come with me. I'd get that tank of yours home before it gets dark, and find something a bit less thirsty. Those coupons are not going to last long if you are trundling around in that.'

'And the pony-cart's too slow.' She grinned and slapped the Wolsey's roof. 'Off you pop, old chap. Go and examine your latest corpse. I shall carry on and do some checks on your list.'

�����

'You must know them as well as I do, Rose dear.'

'I know the names, Granny. I was wondering if you'd knew something about their backgrounds.'

Beatrice angled Bunch's notebook toward the lamp and stared at it as if the answers could be gleaned from the ink itself. 'Nothing exceptional. All from good families, though this one—' she pointed at the list that Bunch had jotted down '—Harriett Beamish... She's an odd one out.'

'Because she's a bad egg?'

'Not that I've heard. She just doesn't fit well. Quinton Beamish, her father, went into the Church. Youngest son so never inherited as much, but he's risen quite high so he's not destitute. They are distantly related to the Woods, you know.'

'Lord Halifax?' Bunch whistled quietly. 'I bet he'll want the Very Reverend Beamish kept out of any gossip. Where does Beamish ply his sermons?'

'He was a college dean and then he moved on. Or rather he was moved up. He's down in Chichester as I understand it. An *arch*deacon, would you believe, and set to become bishop if rumours are correct. I recall an acquaintance of mine, Alexia Pitman, being quite put out over whatever or wherever it was because her nephew had set his sights on the same post. Quinton was rather overdue his advancement. He ruffled the wrong feathers back at the end of the Great War and was held back.'

'And now?'

'Seems he's rattling ecclesiastical cages once again. Beamish is a rabid pacifist, if that isn't a contradiction.'

'He's a clergyman. One would rather think being a man of peace went with the territory.'

'One would think so. Except like his illustrious cousin he was a vocal supporter of Chamberlain's policy of appeasement – and continues to be so. He's not alone, of course. I understand from your Uncle Hillary that the Church Synod is still debating the matter and the Bishop of Chichester is a kindred spirit, if rumour is to be believed.'

'Not a Sussex family then?'

'No, my dear. Other side of London, I believe.'

'Wouldn't happen to be Oxford?'

Beatrice took a sip of her sherry and held her glass thoughtfully toward the firelight. 'I believe you may be right,' she said.

'Do any of these others have connections there?'

'Not that I am aware of. You know the three chaps, of course. Did you expected there to be?'

'Not as such. It's just a theory. The Beamish girl breeds dogs. I remember that much, though I imagine there's not many people wanting them right now. I can't recall what breed.' She looked at the list and sighed. 'What about Larry Parrish? Any idea what he's up to?'

'I had heard that the Parrish coffers are also a little sparse.'

'What makes you think that?'

'They parcelled off two cottages and forty acres at Chells Farm just after Easter. I hear the boy is selling off his car.'

'Is he, by Jove?' Bunch sat a little straighter. 'Any idea which? The car I mean.'

'Not a clue. Though didn't he buy the Frampton boy's noisy little bone shaker at the auction?'

'I believe he did. I shall give him a call tomorrow. May be just the right sort of coincidence.' Bunch sipped on her own sherry and sat back. 'I thought Mummy was coming to stay this weekend.'

'She should have been here already but she keeps finding reasons why not. I can't say I am sorry that she's not.'

'She needs our help.'

'I am happy to offer it. Please don't think we dislike each other. It is merely that she hates the country.'

'She likes Scotland well enough.'

'Because it's not here,' Beatrice replied. 'Your mother has a positively morbid dislike of Perringham.'

'It makes her sad.'

'I know but she has a duty. She can't do as she pleases. None of us can.'

Bunch knew her grandmother was right. The family had seldom placed limitations on Bunch's life since school ended. Not that she was encouraged in hedonistic activity but she knew she had far greater freedom than many. She had dabbled in flying lessons for a short while, and had been driving cars from the moment she was old enough. Once she had suffered the rigours of the social season she had been allowed to travel extensively. As the declaration of war passed its first anniversary, it was the curtailing of what she had deemed the most basic duties that depressed her.

Yet, despite all of her moaning, she had never seen Perringham House as a burden, and when it had been requisitioned by the Ministry of War, it was a hammer blow. The fact that she could see it from the gallery of the Dower House, rising above the trees beyond the main estate complex, rubbed in salt by the handful. Though the Dower belonged to the estate, her entire life had revolved around Perringham House. She had been born there, as had Dodo, and also the brothers who had never reached adulthood, victims of the Spanish flu at the end of the Great War.

For Theodora, however, Perringham was the place where her sons had died and been laid to rest in the family chapel. They were never spoken of yet were always a part of any conversation. Bunch understood all of that. It was easy to see why her mother had for many years preferred their Town house in Thurloe Square. Except that London was receiving nightly poundings from the

Luftwaffe and the devastation was terrifying, by any measure. Bunch was not sure why anybody would stay there when they did not need to. Sussex had its own share of Dorniers and Heinkels dropping unspent payloads over towns and villages on their way back to the Channel, but all of those things had been sounds off in the distance and not the blast-blackened gaps in the London that Theadora knew so well.

'I am reliably informed, however, that she and your father will be here in time for dinner.'

Bunch dragged her attention back to the present and glanced at the clock. 'If they don't hurry they shall be too late to dress.'

❧ Five ❧

Edward argued long and loud against Bunch buying Lawrence Parrish's car but she had made up her mind. 'I know the car,' she told him. 'Larry bought it at the auction at Hascombe back in February but he's been away most of the time since then. He's been trying to sell it since Easter. He will be practically giving it away.'

'I can't see why you would buy a used car at all.'

'Don't be such a crushing snob, Daddy. There's no shame in a second-hand car these days. Plus the Crossley is a shocking hay burner. I'd use up all of those spirit coupons in one trip. What's required is a smaller vehicle and right now. There's a simply horrendous waiting list for new models now that car production has been moved to war work, so used is my only option.' She didn't add that owning Johnny's MG was also a crucial added attraction. She missed Johnny still even though they were not ever really a couple. He had been her first and had also been her best friend. *And one never forgets that kind of thing.* That the car belonged to one of the men on Penny James's list was a huge bonus, too, which she could not resist or possibly even afford to ignore.

'In any case, I'd never be able to snatch the Crossley out of Granny's clutches.' She grinned at her father in triumph. 'I also happen to know by an incredible stroke of good luck that Lawrence Parrish knew Penny James.'

'I'm assuming this has something to do with your policeman friend's investigations. You do know that I don't approve? Mother certainly does not.'

'Yours or mine?' said Bunch. 'Mothers, I mean.'

'Either.'

'Wright is a colleague,' Bunch said defiantly. She knew what was coming and braced herself for the *Lecture*. Wright's absence on the previous Friday, and subsequent refusal to explain beyond 'police business' still rankled, but she was determined to follow up on both deaths, whatever her father said – if only to pip Wright at the post. 'Granny disapproves whatever I do, and Mummy doesn't care. I need a car. Much as I adore the gee-gees, they will only take me so far. And there's an end to it.'

'Your grandmother will be spitting feathers and you know it, young lady.'

Bunch rolled her eyes, looking like the teenager that she felt herself to be under parental disapproval. 'Granny thinks it's not ladylike. That's rich coming from one of Mrs Pankhurst's trusted lieutenants.'

'Don't be obtuse. We all feel it's too damned dangerous.'

'I ride horses practically every day. How is driving a car going to be worse?'

A pained expression crossed Edward's eyes. 'There are cars and there are cars. And you don't ride Perry out in the blackout. That tiny roller skate of Larry Parrish's won't offer you much protection if a damned great lorry doesn't spot you in the dark. But—' he raised both hands in resignation '—you will do whatever you want whatever I say. You invariably do. Just please be careful. We were all sick with worry when the ATS shipped you out to France with the British Expeditionary Force. With good cause because you came back in a mess.' He glanced at her leg that had been shattered on active service the previous year.

The injury was a sore point in every sense because, though it only gave her pain occasionally, it prevented her from re-joining her ATS section and stuck her at Perringham, minding the family estate instead of being out there in the fray. 'Hardly my fault,' she muttered.

'War is something none of us can avoid right now, though God knows Neville tried hard enough. But this penchant for embroiling yourself in murder worries your grandmother terribly.'

'I know.' She pressed her hand to his arm. 'Thing is, I need something that's for me. Need I remind you I am almost thirty-one years old? I'm quite capable of knowing my own mind. I love you to pieces, Daddy, and I do know about duty and all that goes with it. At the same time I need something that hasn't been mapped out by the family.'

Edward eyed her sadly. 'I do understand. All too well, in fact. I simply wish…'

'Oh, Daddy, you wouldn't let me buy a plane after I had all of those flying lessons. Heavens above, a car is not anything like as… I am so sorry. George died in a plane crash. That was meant to be a joke and it backfired a little. But I need this. For me. Can you understand that?'

'I do. I'd be disappointed if you didn't kick at the traces. All right, Rose-bunch, just take care where you go and what you do. Please?'

'Of course I shall.' She grinned at him and leaned in to kiss him on the cheek. 'If I'm a good girl maybe I'll get that plane for Christmas? It's what all the girls are having this year … and I already have a pony.'

౪౼౪౼

The small Jacobean manor house known as The Chells was one of the oldest in the area, a solid two storey building of gables and mullioned windows and tall chimneys, all built of mellow Sussex sandstone, which seemed to glow, even on such a grey misty afternoon. On the left were double gates, which stood open, and in the cobbled yard between the main building and the coach house was the MG-PA, a compact coupe in Petrol Blue with a black fabric roof – a car that Bunch had ridden in several times when it had belonged to Jonathan Frampton. She could visualise him grinning at her from the driver's seat, and felt a sudden welling in her chest. *God help me. I'm not sure this is a good idea.*

'Here you are, Miss Courtney.' Tilly Parrish leaned forward to open the car door, and the image ended abruptly. 'We've bought Lawrence a hardtop model. So much more sensible now he is toing and froing to the docks.' She watched with thinly disguised distaste as Bunch unhitched the bonnet of the MG to peer beneath it. 'I don't really know why he bought this at all. He barely drove it.' She folded her arms and peered over Bunch's shoulder. 'Do you know what you are looking at under there?'

'ATS training.' Bunch tipped the bonnet back into place and stood back to view the vehicle at a distance. 'Comes in jolly useful.' She looked around her. 'He's not here? Larry, I mean. I was rather hoping for a chat. Just to catch up. Not seen him for months.'

'He's at sea. Can't say where, naturally, but we've barely seen him ourselves.' Tilly laughed, a forced laugh without the smallest trace of humour. 'He and that Naysmith boy joined up early. They seemed to think that way they'd be able to pick which service they went into. You know what Lawrence is like. Always so sure he'll get what he wants.'

'He wanted the navy?'

'No. He wanted the RAF. All these young chaps do. But he was assigned to the RN and I was happy at first because it seemed far less dangerous, but with all of these U-boat—' She wrapped her arms closer around herself and stared at her feet.

'Has Larry told you what he wants for it?' Bunch suppressed a smile at the confusion in Tilly's face. The older woman was of the kind who found the discussing of money an embarrassment. 'I seem to remember he got it for a song at the auction.'

'Larry always talked about how Johnny loved it. He can be such a romantic at times. I worry about him, you know. Before this war started he never seemed to be able to make his mind up about what he wanted. Head in the clouds with his poetry and drawing. It's why he got on so well with the Frampton boy, I think.' She stared at the car, eyes glazing slightly in remembrance.

Perhaps he and Johnny had something a little more than poetry in common? Bunch thought. She slapped the bonnet jolting Tilly back to the here and now. 'He's only a young chap. Give him time. Now … this is a 1936 model?'

'I believe so. Larry hardly used it, if truth be told. He never had enough fuel. I know some of these chaps don't turn a hair at the black market, but Larry would never dream of it. Always the gentleman.' She smiled weakly. 'We were so terribly grateful to Sir Edward for standing references. We had hoped he might get a commission in the Guards if an RAF post didn't happen, but somehow he ended up on a ship. It makes no sense, does it?'

Bunch shook her head. She had been cornered by Tilly Parrish often enough at soirées to know that replies were seldom required, or even noticed. 'There is no rhyme nor reason when it comes to conscription boards.'

'I don't know what he does precisely, but then I suppose he's not allowed to say,' Mrs Parrish went on. 'I do so worry.'

'Naturally.' Bunch walked around the car once more with a little more of the prodding and poking that she thought might be expected, though she had already made up her mind before she'd even arrived. 'I shall take it. Shall we go inside and talk details?'

Mrs Parrish hesitated for a moment and Bunch wondered why the woman was so reluctant to show her into the drawing room.

෴෴

The older woman went to tweak back the blackout curtains and Bunch noticed a small shower of dust dancing in the sudden light. Mrs Parrish noticed it also and smiled weakly. 'We only have a cook and one maid now so we don't use half the rooms. So hard to find staff, don't you find? Do sit down. Tea?'

'A small one. I have to get off soon.'

'At least come and warm up after standing out there for so long.' Tilly went to the fireplace and pulled the bell cord.

Bunch sank into a chair and looked around her. It was some time since she had been here and the room was unchanged, and comfortable. Bunch took out her cigarette case and offered it to her hostess. 'Did all of the other chaps sign up with him?'

'Other chaps?'

'Soames and Pilkington. All that crowd?'

'All but that Soames boy.' Tilly looked away, her brows drawing in. 'I admit I was quite taken in by him at first.'

'In what way?'

'We did share an admiration for Mr Chamberlain and his party. I thought he was a good man who had our best interests at heart,' she replied. 'Mr Chamberlain was a man of the Great War generation and we all thought he was leading us along the right path, making a pact that would avoid another war. We wanted peace and it was hard to imagine how anybody would want anything else. Mr Chamberlain was lied to by that dreadful creature in Munich, and now he's gone, poor soul.'

Bunch nodded and made the expected noises of agreement. The sentiments were ones she had heard often in the year or so leading up to the declaration or war and it was hard not to have had some empathy. The Parrish family had lost five close male relatives, to her knowledge, which made Tilly's hopes and fears all too real. 'Indeed,' she murmured. 'It's very sad.'

'Mr Chamberlain had a private funeral, I understand. I have heard that a state funeral was vetoed because so many people have died in the Blitz.' Tilly cocked her head slightly. 'I suppose you would know all about it, with Sir Edward being in the War Office?'

'Daddy would hardly tell me. Fathers seldom consult their daughters, and in any case he practically lives up in Whitehall these days so we don't have much opportunity to chat.'

'Of course. Silly me. Not that your home is what it was of course. So sad what the military are doing to Perringham. I was driving past there just last week and—'

'I try not to look,' Bunch snapped. The faint hint of satisfaction in Tilly Parrish's voice may not have been intentional but it was no less irritating for all that. *Schadenfreude may not be the right word under the circs*, she thought, *but it fits.*

'No, indeed.' Tilly flushed pink around her collar. 'Larry has an utter disdain for Herr Hitler,' she went on, gushing now, Bunch felt, to cover her embarrassment. 'There were several huge rows with Soames over it right here in this house. It was quite unpleasant and I asked Larry to stop him and Pilkington from visiting.'

'I never took Larry for a political creature.'

'He isn't. He much preferred Rome or Paris to Munich. He went to the Olympics in '36 with Soames and his crowd, you know. He admits to being impressed by what he saw, which is odd because they cut the trip short. Came home a full two days before the closing ceremony. When Larry went to Garmisch for the skiing in '38 he was very sad at how things had changed.'

'In what way?'

'I don't know exactly. Not for the better, I think, because he saw even less of that crowd after that.' Tilly paused, seemingly confused.

Bunch sipped at her tea and waited. Tilly's ramblings were not easy to follow but unguarded snippets might prove useful.

'Poor Larry fell out quite spectacularly with Etta Beamish last winter,' Tilly continued. 'I'd wondered if there was something going on in that quarter for a while. Now she *is* quite an opinionated political young woman. It was her going to some rally or other that upset Larry in the end. He said it was a wonder she hadn't been arrested. Comes of mixing with your sister-in-law's group I suspect.'

'Emma?'

'There are some rather radical thinkers amongst those

university women. So unladylike. I know I might be seen as a rather old fashioned these days, but that's the way I was brought up. Veronica wanted to follow Emma to Oxford but we soon put a stop to that. Larry's education was expensive enough. Letting Veronica sit for a degree seemed such a waste when she'd be off starting families.' A nervous smile crossed her lips. 'She's getting married in the spring, you see.'

'Dodo did tell me.' Bunch had never much cared for the slightly vacuous Veronica Parrish and doubted the girl would ever have passed an entry exam, but she smiled politely. 'You must be delighted.'

'We are. And at least we were right on that score. I believe several of her chums went up to Oxford. None of them have married, of course. Your mother must have been so pleased when your sister took her marriage vows. Such a blessing. I should have hated our little Veronica to become an old maid.'

Tilly's expression was bordering on smug. 'It's not so uncommon,' Bunch replied. 'We had a generation after the Great War that never married. Were you thinking of anyone in particular?'

'Gosh, let me think.' Tilly flushed as she realised her faux pas. 'Well, there was that French girl you had staying here back in the spring. I do recall Larry hinting that the James girl was about to announce an engagement.'

Bunch nodded. There were coincidences and there were coincidences. The same names cropping up over and over again was not one of them in her estimation. She had envied those girls who had been permitted to gain knowledge as well as taking part in the season. *At least I was educated, if only because it was simpler to board whilst the old parents were away. Poor Dodo never even had that much.* 'You believe women don't require an education?' she said aloud.

'I've never been against it in theory, but gels still need to know how to manage a house, don't you think?'

'Or an estate.' Bunch smiled brightly. 'It's not a choice is it? I rather enjoyed school. If I'd had the chance to try for university I'd most certainly have gone. I might even have paid my own way when I finally laid hands on my trust fund. That's never going to happen now.'

Mrs Parrish flushed around her neck, the skin turning deep

pink against her strand of pearls. 'I'm sorry, I rather keep putting my foot in it, don't I? Your sister-in-law is quite the academic.'

'Emma has an exceptional mind and I applaud it. I do wish I had followed her but I was a bit of a dunce when it came to sums and Latin at school. Far more interested in lacrosse and such, so my own fault. Emma doesn't go gadding about the clubs, from what I've heard. I was up there last week with Mother, and the raids were terrifying. It doesn't seem to put off some of that set though, does it?' Bunch buried her nose in her cup for another well-timed sip, peaking at Tilly over the rim. 'In fact I've heard some of Soames's crowd go quite often. Wasn't Claude Naysmith one of that group?'

'I do believe he was. Why would you ask?'

'You haven't heard? The poor man was killed right by your gates. That was Claude.'

'Oh – goodness.' Mrs Parrish looked down at the rug, her hand pressed against her lips. 'Was that – oh my, I hadn't heard.'

For Tilly not to know seemed unlikely, but Bunch pretended not to notice. 'I don't believe the police have released details of names and such,' she said. 'Doubtless it will be in the papers once it's gone through the Coroner's Courts. And then there's poor Penelope James.'

'What about her?'

'Found dead up on the Downs over at the far side of Storrington. It's such a shame. Both inquests have been adjourned, of course.' Bunch watched for a reaction from the sides of her vision and gauged the woman's shock as genuine.

'Penny James?' Mrs Parrish wrapped her arms around herself, her eyes bewildered. 'Oh my goodness. One almost expects it with the chaps who join up. Almost. I mean it's always a terrible shock when somebody one knows is killed in war, but it seems somehow more shocking when it's a woman. Are you sure it was Penelope James?'

'I do wish I could say no, but I'm sure. Had you seen her recently?'

'Not since Larry joined up. He mentioned that he had visited her and Claude a few times. Both were stationed further down on the coast, I believe. That's as much as he told me.'

'Down the coast? Both of them?'

'They aren't allowed to say very much, are they? Probably just as well. I am simply dreadful at secrets. I just wish I knew more about Larry's posting, just to know that he's safe.' Tilly fidgeted her handkerchief from her sleeve and dabbed at her nose as she gazed out of the window. The clock on the mantle struck the quarter hour and she jerked back to the present. 'I suppose we should discuss the car.' She turned back to Bunch, her face bland. 'Will you want to take it for a spin before you decide?'

'Oh no, I've ridden in it so many times when it belonged to Johnny. I shall manage it, I'm sure. If you are agreeable, I shall be back shortly to pick it up. Shall we say thirty guineas to start with? Larry and I can beat the kinks out of that bargain when we meet up next.'

ๆๆๆ

An hour later Bunch was driving the MG back to Perringham Dower at a sedate 30 mph. After the wallowing grandeur of the estate car and the sweeping rumble of the Crossley, she admitted if only to herself that it was a little lacking in all but basic luxury. Cold and drafty and cramped *but*, she decided, *such fun.* The niggling idea that she might have paid Larry Parrish far too much was pushed to the back of her mind. *Better he thinks I'm not quite sharp enough.*

When she had her new acquisition safely stowed in the garage she went in to telephone Wright once more.

'He went back up to Scotland Yard, Miss. Meeting up with his old oppo, Superintendent Murray,' said Carter. 'Following up on his visit last week. That is all he would say.'

Not telling his sergeant, either? Bunch felt a little less slighted at that, but only by a small margin. 'All right then, Carter, tell him to call me when he gets back. I may be out tomorrow. I'm taking a trip up to Oxford. Several of the names on that list were at Thirkiss College and I've been given a chance to attend a social there. It may come to nothing but it's too good an opportunity to miss. I shall be staying there overnight.'

'Oh well, you take care, Miss.'

Bunch's ears pricked at the change in his tone. 'Something I should know?' There were a few seconds of quiet, broken by steady breathing. *I'll swear I can his brain ticking*, she thought.

'That place came up in our background details. Can the boss

69

reach you there?'

'I don't have a number as yet but I daresay it will be easy to obtain. Goodbye Sergeant.'

❧ Six ❧

Though the canvas roof was up, Bunch had forgotten, in her rosy memories of trips with Johnny Frampton, just how desperately cold outings in the little MG could be. She glanced at Emma, clutching her fur wrap to her neck and pulling her hat down to her eyes, and grinned. 'We're almost there and it's not even dark yet.'

'I'm frozen stiff. I know you wanted to give your new motor a spin, but great heavens above, Bunch, if I had known this heap of scrap metal needed a heater I'd have caught the train.'

'Sorry, old thing. There is a heater but it's on the fritz. I asked the chappy in the garage to get it repaired but the spare parts are hard to come by. I did think of trains but it was this or fight our way through three changes of line, and quite frankly I didn't fancy our chances of getting here before midnight.'

'At least then we wouldn't have frostbite.' Emma thrust her hands under her armpits and sank a little lower beneath the heavy car rug. 'We're here. You'll want to take the next left turn after the telephone box.'

'Right ho.' Bunch leaned forward and wiped the back of her gloved hand across the windscreen, and manoeuvred the turn briskly with only a small skitter of the rear end of the car. 'Must say, she handles like a dream.'

'Yes. A nightmare,' Emma snapped. 'Slow down for pity's sake. We don't want to have an accident this close to the college.'

'Just enjoying the drive. Haven't had this much fun since I chauffeured General Gaunt around Paris.'

'So far as I am aware, we don't have an army to evade. Left at the gates just around this corner.

They pulled into the driveway where it split in two, the wider road leading straight across some hundred or more yards of shaggy lawns to a three-storey house built of soft yellow sandstone. The architecture was eclectic, mixing Georgian simplicity with a more organic arts and crafts style, with gables and eaves added on to the front and sides. Its appearance was made all the stranger by the barbed wire barricade straddling across the grounds, with the security point sited where it bisected the driveway.

'Hideous and yet beautiful,' Emma observed. 'Thirkiss is a relatively new college, and quite small. The house itself was a bequest from a rather eccentric lady of means and named after her only son, Andrew Thirkiss, who was killed in a hunting accident in the Punjab in 1865.'

'I know. I've read the prospectus. You said it had been taken over by the War Office. I'm still amazed you can use even some of it.'

'The college building has been completely usurped, as have the faculty residences. You will know how that feels, I'm sure. We negotiated the use of the student house in order to continue our research. We still hold Formal Halls once a month. The Dean insisted on it.' Emma indicated a building through the trees to the left. 'Not everyone attends, which is how I got you a seat at table. Your father's name carries a lot of clout in some circles.'

Bunch nodded slowly. She empathised with Emma, who had essentially been made homeless by this requisitioning. 'Who will be there tonight?' she said.

'A lot of people you will not know,' Emma replied.

'I meant, would there be people from the main house.'

'God no. That would be the absolute end. They're mostly navy. A distinct lack of academics.'

'Interesting. Can we go into the house?'

'I doubt it. It won't help you a great deal. There's nobody left there who would have had anything to do with the college. The people you want to speak to will be at the formal.' Emma glanced at her watch. 'Speaking of which, we'll just about have time to dress. Dinner is earlier now there are no students. Take the road to the left and park near the trees.'

The student accommodation attached to the college was a functional three-story red brick of little architectural merit, so far as Bunch could tell. She followed Emma up to a bedroom with two beds and two wardrobes and a large desk.

'Shared room.' Emma flung her overnight case on the bed

furthest from the door. 'Student rooms are never terribly glamorous, and given that we're all squashed into one building we have to double up on these weekends.'

'Is this your room?'

Emma frowned, jerking her head in one small nod. 'It's where I sleep when I'm here.' She stepped out into the corridor to gesture toward the far end. 'The bathroom is the last door on the right. Lavvies are on the left. Best to be up early in the morning because the hot water never lasts. These top two floors are dorms. Half of downstairs now houses our library. The refectory is there also. Kitchens and laundry are in the cellar, of course. You'll find your way around quick enough.' She flopped upon her bed and shuffled back against the headboard to watch Bunch unpack her dinner frock and hang it for the creases to drop. 'I still can't imagine why you wanted to come here. I've told you pretty much all there is to know.'

'You gave me the facts, yes,' Bunch said, 'but I want the juicy details.'

'Never seen the need for gossip. Lot of pointless cackle'

'No doubt.' *Emma*, she thought, *you are a consummate banger of gums.* Bunch turned her back rapidly to hide a grin and grabbed her sponge bag. 'I'd better go and find this bathroom if we're expected to eat early.'

☙❧☙❧

The refectory was a rather stylish but austere affair. Light oak panelling and dark marble floors. Concealed lighting reflected off a cream-coloured ceiling, though Bunch was not sure if that was its original colour or a side effect of the cigarette smoke that wafted around the tables between courses. Bunch found herself opposite Emma, sandwiched between two elderly classicists who talked to their neighbours in preference to her once they had discovered she wasn't able to converse in Latin. *At least I know they won't be interested in anything that happened in the last few centuries.*

She sat through six interminable courses.

'Less than usual,' Emma told her. 'Due to rationing, which also accounts for the parsimony of each dish.' She pulled a face. 'We've also lost most of our catering staff.'

I really hope so because I'd hate to think the college serves this stuff intentionally. Bunch pushed the pitiful excuse for boeuf bour-

73

guignon around her plate and managed a few mouthfuls. *School dinners prepared me for such things, but it doesn't mean I have to like it.*

She was grateful when the assembly retired to the adjoining common room furnished comfortably, and perhaps just a little shabbily Bunch felt, in the French style that had swept the world in the early half of the1920s. Emma came to sit with her on one of the many slightly saggy leather sofas.

'Not very plush,' Bunch said.

'But practical. This was student halls. Velvet sofas would not last very long.' Emma looked around the room. 'I have no idea who you want to talk to.'

'People who might have heard things. I don't even know if being here will help at all, but several names involved with the case have connections with the college, so it seemed a logical place to start.' Bunch sipped at her coffee, peering around the room over the rim of her cup. 'Who here would recall Penny James?' she muttered.

'Of the faculty? Well, you sat next to one of them at dinner. Professor Lindstrom was to your left. 'She was quite new to the academic staff back then. Don't be fooled by the frizzy white hair and the stick. She's old but not nearly as batty as she makes out.'

'How did she know Penny?'

'She takes Latin and Civilisation, which is compulsory for all of the freshers. I was quite glad to specialise in literature and didn't see her much after that because she has only got madder since then.'

'Are there others here?'

'Ariadne Brown. She's Professor in English Language and Linguistics and has been since Boadicea marched on the south.'

'That old dear knocking back the scotch?'

'It is. I suspect it's what keeps her so well preserved. Believe it or not, she has a quarter of a century's lecturing over Lindstrom.'

'Anything else I should know about them? Where are they from? Do they still live here?'

'My goodness you are getting ensconced in this police thing, aren't you? Courtney of the Yard.' Emma frowned and looked around the room, and then shook her head. 'So many people have decamped if they have families to fall back on, so it's just Lindstrom over there, who hails from Norway. I suspect she's not been back for a long while and not likely to for some time to come. The learned Ariadne is a proud Scot. Not a bad old stick on the whole. Bit of a tyrant but the students like her, and trust her, and they have unerring instincts in that regard.'

'They're not so keen on Lindstrom?'

'I would not go so far as to say that. Brown is eccentric but Lindstrom is odd in a very different fashion. Honest, I think, and harmless. She spends too much time in the city's libraries to talk to anybody.'

'And that's it? Nobody else left from then?'

'There may be a few still on the roll from those times but none of them are here tonight.'

'Any others that live locally?'

'Rather difficult to say. The Dean had a residence on the outskirts of the city but most, like me, lived in residence, and have had to rely on the kindness of friends and relations for succour.'

Bunch was beginning to suspect that to be the truth. The room was full of the older lecturing staff. 'When did Brown come here?'

'She's been here longer than I have.' Emm shook her head. 'I told you it was a waste of time coming here. Watch out, she's heading our way.'

Bunch watched Professor Brown advance on them and realised she was faintly disappointed. She had half-expected a gaggle of rabid eccentrics but what she saw was a gathering of earnest women in sensible frocks. Ariadne Brown, in particular, was one of those capable women who would not be out of place at a gymkhana in tweeds and brogues, issuing orders at riders and mounts alike. Tonight she was clad in a shapeless rusty-brown velvet gown that Bunch judged had been first sewn in 1925 and cleaned on a semesterly basis ever since.

Emma's voice rising in conversation with Ariadne Brown brought her attention back. 'I can't agree, Professor. How can you possibly take that stance?'

'Theoretical, my dear. Purely overlaying our current situation with history.'

'In what possible way?'

'Remember that it was the Romans who subsumed most of the European land mass.'

'You think that Generalissimo Mussolini is a greater danger

75

than Hitler?' Bunch asked her.

'Heavens no. He would like to think he is but the German war machine is far more like the Roman model than his own.'

Emma and Bunch exchanged glances. 'You admire them?' Emma asked.

'Only in as far as they *are* efficient.' Brown sighed, tapping the rings on the fingers of her right hand against her saucer. 'I mourn the exchange of ideas with our German colleagues but I am not an admirer of their current strategies, Miss Courtney. Unlike some.'

'I know several who would prefer we had taken Chamberlain's lead,' Bunch replied. 'The Naysmiths for example. My grandmother knows them slightly.' She lowered her voice and leaned forward, not quite looking the professor in the eye. 'I gather they were very much in favour of Halifax becoming Prime Minister. Wasn't the eldest son a supporter of Moseley at one time?'

'Claude? I doubt it. Or if he was it wasn't for long.' Brown snorted. 'Since Moseley's internment the scales have fallen from many eyes, thank God.'

'You were never fooled?'

'Not at all. Oh, it was nice to imagine Mr Chamberlain's attempts to avoid war would have succeeded. After the last conflict any sane person would find peace preferable. But against Herr Hitler? It was only ever going to be a pipe dream. I only hope we don't lose another entire generation as we did before. She glanced across the room and snorted again, reminding Bunch even more strongly of an elderly horse. 'Lindstrom held out for some sort of accord for the longest time. I suppose her roots accounts for that. What family she has is now under Nazi rule.'

Bunch slotted a cigarette into a small ebony holder and then offered her case to the others. 'Of course.' She accepted a light from Emma and sat back once more. 'So she is not a supporter of Herr Hitler, one assumes.'

'Not at all,' Brown replied. 'I believe she went to one of Moseley's little gatherings because she considered it her duty to see for herself. Any support of Moseley's policies, now he's under arrest, would hardly be acceptable in polite circles. Did you imagine there was support for Moseley at this college?'

'No. My questions sprang from idle curiosity.'

'I understand from Professor Tinsley, here, that you have been something of an amateur sleuth in recent months.'

'Only by accident.'

'You'd have made a fine academic,' Brown replied. 'You have a nose for intrigue, which is essential in this world. It's also a valuable asset in wartime, or an unfortunate affliction, depending on how you use it.' Brown tapped ash into crystal dish and pursed her lips. 'Most people assume I notice nothing outside of my research. They're wrong. I merely choose not to comment.' She exposed a row of small even teeth in a broad smile. 'As I said, most academics share a great many traits of the detective. The pursuit of fact at all costs.' She smiled again, closed lipped and knowing. 'I can assure you there are no budding Nazis in this building. Or at least not any longer.' She took a mouthful of her drink and stared up at the ceiling. 'I think, like old Lindstrom over there, some of our students were dazzled by the Reich for a while. It seemed so very organised and I suppose it appeared rather British, in an odd sort of way. Naturally there were as many inclined to follow Joseph Stalin, which made for some interesting debates. Of course, in the academic world we were aware of colleagues vanishing from the various German chairs. A few have resurfaced here. Most were interned, poor creatures. Is that what you are here to ask?'

Bunch regarded her through the tobacco haze. This woman reminded her of her grandmother with her disconcerting directness. *I could like her.* 'Not entirely,' she replied. 'You may have heard that Penelope James is dead?'

'I hadn't. Dear me, what a terrible shame. The girl had a good head on her shoulders. Shame she wasn't able to finish her studies because she would have made a formidable research lecturer. Forgive me for appearing ghoulish, but what happened to her?'

'She was murdered.'

'Was she, by God.'

'Penny James seemed to have secrets, and her murder may be linked to another suspicious death. A chap from an Oxfordshire family. Claude Naysmith'

'Of course. Anything that involves a family like the Naysmiths will percolate from Town to Gown. Miss James came to see me a few weeks ago, you know. She told me she was staying with the Naysmiths for the weekend.'

'With Claude?'

'They appeared to be close. Miss James came for tea and was asking about that Beamish family. Not people I cared for, personally. Well aware of the name, of course.'

'I understand her father oversaw spiritual care within the college.'

'Yes. He's gone now, thank heavens. I'm as much a church goer as the next person, but Quinton Beamish?' She waved both hands. 'A pompous ass. His daughter was as bad, perhaps worse in many ways because she lacked discretion. Opinionated, both of them. Which is why Quinton never got any higher here at Oxford.'

'What kind of opinions?'

'Most recently? He was very vocal in support of appeasement. Nothing wrong with that, of course. None of us wanted another war but he trod on too many toes in the process.'

'So he was moved on.'

'Yes. To Chichester Diocese. Or was it Guildford?' Brown raised a hand for the steward. 'I will admit I did not take a lot of interest once he'd left. Whisky?'

'That would be lovely. Thank you.'

'Good. We can relax now because I have told you all I can.' She jerked her head at Lindstrom. 'Don't waste your time with her. Poor excuse for a lecturer and absolute menace in a research library.'

'But she may know something.'

'Unlikely. Ah, thank you.' She waited for the steward to step away before raising her glass. 'Chin-chin, my dear.'

'Good evening, Miss Courtney,' murmured the slight middle-aged woman that appeared at Bunch's side. 'There is a telephone call for you.'

'Me?' Bunch glanced at Emma who shrugged. 'Well, let the dog see the rabbit.' She followed the porter out to the foyer and the American-style public telephone fixed to the wall. 'Hello? Rose Courtney here.'

'Good evening, Rose.'

'Oh, William.' She smiled despite herself, inexplicably pleased that Wright had called her by her first name. 'Carter passed the message on then?'

'Such as it was. Sorry it's taken me a while to call you. I was delayed.'

'Nothing serious?'

'Not now.'

Bunch detected a dry humour in his reply. 'Anything you can discuss?'

'I had an interesting exchange with our old friend Percy Guest.'

'Emma's uncle? He's still alive?'

'Yes.' Wright paused and Bunch heard him lighting a cigarette and exhaling softly. 'We both had an unscheduled swim in the Thames.'

'Oh my God. Are you all right?'

'I shall live. I don't think I swallowed too much of what passes for water down at the docks.'

'And Guest?'

'It has nothing to do with this case. I shall tell you all about it some other time. I hear you have some leads?'

'More guesses than anything.' Bunch twisted around to lean against the wall and watch the doorway into the common room. 'I have made a few enquiries about that list and Oxford came up several times. As Emma was coming up for a dinner I rather invited myself along. I gave her a lift in my new jalopy. I took your advice and got something smaller. Rather fun.'

'Have you come across anything worth a trip up to Oxford?'

'Nothing earth shattering.' She brought him up to date on the small details she had gleaned and ended with, 'I can't think there is much else to learn up here.'

'Are you staying overnight?'

'Yes. Emma is staying here in Halls for a while. I have to get back to Perringham tomorrow. Why, would you want to come up here?'

'I have a few breadcrumbs leading that way.'

'Something you found out in London?'

'Sadly not, that was a different case. It was Carter who turned up some more information at Penelope James's digs. She had notes on some of the people on that list of hers. Seems she may have been tracking their movements – but we have no idea why as yet. There were a few notes on this Beamish girl, but from what you say the birds have flown that Oxford coop.'

'They have.' Bunch paused to draw on her cigarette. She was somewhat irritated to realise that her trip here had been largely a waste of time. 'So we need to find her.'

'We do. I shall head straight back to Brighton and call tomorrow to see what you have gleaned, and we should have a meeting soon.'

'I shall look forward to it. Goodnight William.'

'Goodnight, Rose.'

❧ Seven ❧

The drive back to Wyncombe was far longer and more tiring than Bunch had anticipated. Delaying her trip until mid-morning in the vain hope that the weather would improve had been a mistake. The heavy rain slowed her to a crawl. Only sheer bloody mindedness kept her on the move, determined to get home because she knew she had spent far too much time away from estate business, and she could not miss yet another day. That would draw criticism from family and silent recriminations from estate staff.

She peered through the small windscreen, alternately wiping condensation from the inside with her gloved hands, cursing the elements, and mulling over the small snippets she had picked up. She was beginning to wonder if the trip had been worth the amount of effort and precious fuel that it had cost. *Though the spotlight on Etta Beamish is an interesting one. She was such a quiet creature from what I recall. Not that I recall a great deal.*

When she finally pulled into the rear courtyard of the Dower House, shared by stables and garage, it was past four o'clock. She sat for a moment contemplating a considerable pool of rain that had gathered in the passenger footwell. Pulling off her driving gloves, she rubbed at her face with icy fingers, massaging the fatigue from between her eyes. She knew sporty roadsters had their downsides and water infiltrating around the edges of the canvas roof was one of them. The need to wear galoshes inside the car was not something she had anticipated. *This weather is beyond foul. If Noah were here he'd be knocking up a quick ark. I suppose only getting my feet wet is something to be thankful for.* She looked at the petrol gauge still registering almost a quarter of a tank and chuckled as she switched off the engine. *And it uses a lot less juice.*

As she made to decamp, a vaguely familiar figure swathed in an army cape appeared at the driver's door, holding aloft a large black umbrella. 'Welcome home, Miss Rose.'

81

'Why, Lizzie Hurst, I didn't know you were starting here so soon.' Bunch gazed at the young woman, noting how she was far thinner than when her husband had been killed six months ago.

But she was smiling. ''Tis a good job you've offered, Miss, an' there were a cottage empty so Lady Beatrice said me and the liddle maid could move straight in.'

'Your daughter—'

'Tilly,' Lizzie replied. 'Ten month old now, an' the spit of 'er ole' dad.' She grinned. 'Not sure that's a good thing fer a little maid, but there. She's good tempered with it.'

'I hope you both like it here at the Dower. But you're getting soaked standing there. Let's get into the dry, shall we?' Bunch climbed out of the MG and ran with Lizzie in through the rear of the house. She kicked off her wet shoes and draped her mackintosh along the top row of coat hooks to dry. 'Get Cook to dig out something for me, will you? Oh, and tell Burse to see to my bags and bail out the bottom of the jalopy when this wretched rain stops.' She took the towel that Lizzie offered to dry her face and hands, revelling in the warm cloth that had been hanging over the kitchen range. 'Is Knapp here?' she asked.

'Serving tea in the drawing room to both Lady Chiltcombes, Miss.'

'My mother is here? Oh hell, I suppose I'd better show my face.' Bunch had hoped to sidle up to her room for a hot bath, but Theadora's presence, after all her cajoling, was something she could not afford to ignore. She slipped her icy feet into warm slippers and hurried along to the drawing room.

Beatrice poured tea the moment she entered and set it near the chair closest to the fire. 'How was your trip? We were a little concerned with this weather. I'm told the Arun has burst its banks at Pulborough.'

'Hello Granny. Hello Mummy.' Bunch bent to kiss both in turn and stood in front of the blazing logs to warm her hands. 'I am absolutely frozen. Had to turn around twice and find a different route,' she said. 'The River Arun floods when someone flushes the lavatory.'

'Don't be coarse, dear.' Beatrice sighed.

'Sorry. I'm a bit tired.' Bunch flopped into the chair and took a gulp from the bone china cup her grandmother poured for her.

'Anything happened around here whilst I was gone? Apart from taking on Lizzie Hurst.'

Beatrice grinned. 'Our last maid Sheila was so keen to join up and what could I say?'

'She's not a patch on Iris,' Theodora drawled.

'Iris was a treasure but getting any staff at all is next to impossible.' Beatrice set down her tea with a firm clunk. 'Lizzie will do us very well so please don't find fault.'

'I shall say nothing at all. This is exactly why I hate the country. So very dull. At least in Scotland one has decent shooting and fishing. And in Town there are people to see.'

'Yes, Mummy, but staying in Town is not on at the moment.'

'Their Highnesses are still in residence. I don't see why I can't follow suit.'

'Hardly the point, Theadora. You are here for a rest. Cake?' Beatrice laid her well manicured fingers on the silver-handled slice.

'Heavens, no.' Theadora's gaze twitched fleetingly toward the tantalus on the side table.

Bunch pulled a face at Beatrice, who arched a judgemental brow in reply. 'I may have to take a trip down to Brighton tomorrow, Mummy,' Bunch said. 'I need to drive down to see Wright, but I understand there is an afternoon recital at the Pavilion, if you'd like to go? Debussy.'

'Off gallivanting again, Rose?' Beatrice muttered. 'This estate does not run itself, you know. Especially now Parsons has sunk into retirement.'

'I know, Granny, but Kate and Pat are very capable. And they have a full compliment of Land Girls to call on.'

'Nevertheless, you are the estate manager. You cannot just go swanning off whenever you feel like it and leaving the office awash with paperwork. At very least you need another secretary, darling. You cannot do everything.' She glared at Theadora, who busied herself with selecting a cigarette. 'I can do more. You only need ask.'

'You have been run off your feet with the WVS clothing drive, Granny. Doctor Lewis has told you to rest. I feel awful now. I would hate you to have another turn like the one you had in the summer.'

'Think about a secretary, my dear.' Beatrice patted her hand.

'We could share, if only to keep an eye on the calendar. Speaking of which, you do remember we have an invitation to the Marsham's shooting weekend? Rationing should make dinner an interesting prospect, but we have promised to be there.'

'I thought we weren't going.' Bunch took another sip of her beverage and hoped her exasperation was not too plain. Since Perringham House, along with half of the large residences in the county, had being requisitioned by the MOD, the endless round of dinners and weekend parties had slowed to a trickle, and she wasn't so very sorry. It was not that she was lacking in social graces – she preferred to choose her own company and the Marshams were not high on the list, if for no other reason than her grandmother was convinced that Henry Marsham was prospective husband material for her eldest granddaughter.

'I shan't go, but you simply cannot duck their invitation a third time,' Beatrice said. 'One has to maintain the semblances of social nicety, even out here. One might even meet interesting people.'

'Who's going to be there?'

'Oh, usual crowd expect. I heard Ginny Marsham was angling to invite your Colonel Ralph.'

Bunch suppressed a ripe expletive. Her grandmother had not attempted to hide her amusement and she was not going to rise to it. Both of the woman facing her had attempted to throw her in the path of the officer now in charge of Perringham House. Bunch had found him a cold fish and could not forgive him for sucking her friend, Cecile Benoir, into his covert operations. *And even if I could trust him any further than I could throw a horse, I refuse to be manipulated. On the other hand, he may know something useful about Newhaven.* 'Is Dodo going?' she asked.

'She said not. Worried about leaving Georgi, I suspect.'

'Then I suppose I must go. I shall pop over and see Dodo and see if she's changed her mind.'

'She would appreciate that. Poor darling seems quite at sea.' Theadora slipped a cigarette between her lips and lit it. Pondering the lit end for a long moment.

You've barely seen her, Bunch thought, and instantly regretted it, knowing her mother had other worries. 'She doesn't seem to get out as much as she might.' She watched her mother's fingers trembling very slightly making the end cigarette flicker like a scarlet glow worm. 'Good to see you here, Mummy. How are you holding up?'

'Bored out of my wits already, darling.'

'That wasn't what I meant.'

'I know.' Theodora stabbed the smoke out and stood abruptly. 'Not one snip better for you and everyone else badgering me night and day.' She swept out on a cloud of Gemey, leaving the rest to exchange resigned glances.

Beatrice poured a little more Earl Grey into her cup. 'She's being an absolute nightmare,' she drawled. 'All the time she was at Perringham House one could avoid her tantrums, but the Dower only has so much room.'

'Is she in pain, do you think?'

'I doubt she would admit it if she were. I'd call Granville Lewis and see what he can suggest but quite frankly I'm not sure he will have anything of genuine use.'

'Lewis is a doctor. He must have a few suggestions.'

'Granville Lewis is a country quack. He can prescribe a linctus or a sleeping powder, but your mother's ailments are well beyond him. His son has a little more intelligence, I'll own you, but as young Hubert is away with the RAMC we shall have to make do.'

'Aren't you being a little unfair?'

'Am I? Lewis will not be firm enough with her. You know she was something of a liability in Singapore? The Ambassador felt obliged to have a private word.'

'Good heavens, I hadn't realised it had gone that far. It explains why Daddy moved over to the War Office.'

'Not entirely. He and Winnie do go back a long way. I suspect it's why he declined a posting in New York. The Americans are less formal but far less forgiving of that kind of excess.'

'Then Mother knows what she has to do.'

'She has known what she should be doing for the past thirty years, but she's an alcoholic. Those ghastly Parma Violet cachous that she insists in crunching all day will only cover up so much.'

'She is never going to admit she needs our help.'

Beatrice looked out of the window at the rain scudding across the lawns. 'I don't mean to sound quite so heartless,' she murmured, 'but she has burned so many bridges over the years that a lot of people would not believe her if she did ask. I wish she made an effort to meet us halfway. We must at least try to accommodate her, though we have barely enough room for us let alone her staff. She has her maid, Kimber, and your father has his man, Sutton. Edward has got Knapp clearing the attics for the extra staff, though I believe he has her eye on the old groom's quarters for Sutton.'

'Daddy won't like that. He prefers having Sutton close to hand. I have to say, living over the stables away from the hordes has its appeal.'

'As if you don't have enough time with those nags you want to live with them?'

'I've not ridden out for three days, and Daddy hasn't been here to exercise poor old Robbo all winter. He will be fat as butter, lazing about in his stall. There's a meet this weekend. I shall have to get Daddy to come out for a jaunt. Is he not here this weekend?'

'He hoped to get down tomorrow but I doubt he has time. Need I remind you once again that we have a prior engagement?'

'Yes, Granny, I have remembered. It is why I faced hell and, quite literally, very high waters to get back today.' She rubbed her arms and leaned toward the fire. 'I suppose it could have been snowing. I doubt I would've been a great deal colder.'

'Hmm.' Beatrice's features swooped into a thoughtful frown. She stretched for the decanter near to the percolator and sloshed a snifter into both her own and her granddaughter's cups. 'So you left Emma Tinsley in Oxford.'

The sudden change is subject made Bunch stare at her grandmother, and at a loss for easy reply. 'Well ... yes. She had some sort of meeting going on. Why do you ask?'

'I ran in to Tilly Parrish at the WVS. She seemed quite upset with you for asking questions. She seemed to think you were laying blame on Larry for something or other and virtually accused Emma of leading you all astray.'

'Good God, what did she say?'

'She made some rather pointed remarks to the effect that Emma had been a part of the Oxford circle, and that Daphne shared many of the same friends as Larry, but nobody dared point fingers at either of them.'

'Did she indeed?' Bunch was not altogether surprised that Tilly would react that way. Her protectiveness toward her only son was legendary, but she was mildly taken aback that the woman would dare tackle Beatrice about it. *I suppose even the shyest mares defend their young. Damn Tilly Parrish for upsetting Granny. Change the subject.* She crumbled the edges of the rock-hard oat macaroon on her plate. 'I see Cook has been experimenting again,' she said.

'Yes.' Beatrice eyed her own cake and sighed. 'I gather this has come from our WI *Eating for Victory* pamphlets. One has to set an example, I suppose.'

'Don't we all. Speaking of which – Etta Beamish.' She popped the piece of biscuit in her mouth and gazed at Beatrice expectantly.

'You mentioned her before. Moved to Chichester. What else did you need to know?'

'There's a rumour in Oxford that her father had become some kind of radical cleric.'

Beatrice chuckled loudly. 'He's a pacifist, darling. A stance not entirely beyond the scope of church doctrine. Strident might be more apposite. Our Bishop was telling me quite recently that he's been a bit of a nuisance with the synod, but Archdeacon Beamish is far from alone in wanting to promote those theories. The Bishop of Chichester is of the same mind, I gather.'

'What's the buzz about his daughter?'

'Not a great deal. Her health suffered a couple of years ago – 1936, or it may have been seven. Asthma, we were all told. Had a bad turn when she was studying and took herself to the Swiss Alps for the mountain air, and then they went down to Italy for almost half a year.'

'I don't recall her ever being sickly.'

'No, dear.' Beatrice eyed Bunch with a half-smile. 'I don't believe she ever was.'

'Then why – oh, I see.' The penny dropped and Bunch felt herself flushing a little pink at being quite so dense. Pregnancies happened; she was not so naïve that she did not know that, but it still came as something of a shock when cossetted and chaperoned blue-blooded girls succumbed. *And the daughter of a dean, no less.* 'It explains why she left so abruptly.'

'That's why her father took up a ministry well away from Oxford, one would imagine.'

'Did your spy service have wind of who the father was?'

Beatrice's lips tweaked upwards by a fraction. 'Most are hinting at Soames though I had it on good authority he was walking out with Penelope James around that time.'

'Goodness. I know Claude Naysmith was mixed up with the James girl, but you are saying Penny was also linked to Soames? Was that before or after poor Etta's fall from grace?'

Beatrice paused as she fought to retrieve the information, and then frowned. 'I can't recall but about then, I should think. You were away at the time. I heard Soames's name linked to a dozen young girls during that season. There was even a brief engagement, if I recall correctly, but it didn't last. He's a catch, with his family's money, and when he draws eligible debs like bees to honey he's not above spreading himself around.'

'Oh, terribly droll.' Bunch grinned and sat back in her chair, rolling her shoulders to ease the aches of the long drive. 'Soames has been getting around? I always heard Pilkington was a bit of a rotter, but I've never had a lot to do with Barrington-Soames's family.'

'His father had his share of scandals. What is that saying about always being judged by the company you keep?'

'Indeed.' Bunch frowned. 'So Etta Beamish came home alone. No age-old long honeymoon trip after a whirlwind courtship? That must have given her father palpitations. Or should that be *pulpit*-ations?' She stifled a laugh as Beatrice offered an exasperated glance.

'Yes, dear. Now who is being droll. But have some pity. The poor child must have been frantic. Something like that would be impossible to live down if it were to be made public knowledge.'

'As the Soames boy was walking out with another woman it would explain a great deal. It just gets more and more complicated.'

'That little coterie of debutantes and beaus do seem to be quite a nest of vipers. I don't think Larry Parrish is a bad boy. He can't help his mother being such a muddleheaded ninny. And the James girl was well spoken of. The rest of them all seem to have some secret in the wind.'

'Oh? Do tell.'

'It mostly pertains to Soames and Pilkington. They rather got mixed up with some dubious politics. Both spent an inordinate amount of time in Munich before '39. The Beamish girl you know about. Plainly her goings on at Oxford were the reason the Reverend Beamish moved out of the city.'

'Yet I heard nothing of that when I was there.'

'Now you do surprise me. Something like that would be pure nectar for the gossips. Perhaps Constance Frain was wrong.' Her lips twitched. 'It will not be the first time. I swear the WI rumour mill would grind to a halt without that woman, though when she passed that titbit onto me, she did assure me it came from a very reliable source.'

'Speaking of passing things on, has Chief Inspector Wright called at all today?'

'He called last night but I told him where you would be.'

'But not today?'

'Should he have?'

Bunch looked toward the hearth, hiding her expression from her grandmother. This short chat with Beatrice had given her a swathe of information and no way of relaying it to Wright since he insisted on being so evasive. She could not decide if Wright was less reliable than she recalled, was busier than she might imagine, or was trying to distance her from the investigation itself. He had made no secret of the fact that her going over his head had annoyed him, but she had honestly thought he was over that. Yet twice now he had failed to live up to his promises. *One minute he's dragging me down to Brighton to identify bodies and the next he's cutting me out of the herd altogether. It really is too bad.* She tossed her cigarette end into the fire, watching it vanish into ash within seconds. *Rather like Wright and his promises.* 'Not really,' she said, and yawned loudly. 'I think turn in if that is all right, Granny? That drive home was bloody.'

❧ Eight ❧

'Lot of chaps are away, of course.' Henry Marsham led Bunch along the shooting butts toward her allotted peg. 'So it's a quieter turn out than usual,' he murmured, 'but we've had this on the estate's calendar since last autumn, and you know how keepers get about these things.'

'We put on the same kind of do at Perringham before it was overrun. A last hoorah, as it were.' Bunch eased the 12-bore that she carried *broken* over her arm and wondered how much further she had to go. The ground was wet and uneven and pocked with tussocks of dark-green waxy reeds that seemed intent on tripping her up every fourth step. She wished she had been less determined to send the right message of independence by not allowing Marsham to carry both of her shotguns. She stumbled and he paused with a hand held out to steady her, his eyes full of concern – and just a hint of puppy-dog. She sighed and hitched the gun a little higher. 'Any idea who or what the Ministry requisitioned your family pile for?'

'Some sort of government department they want to get away from the bombings in London,' he replied. 'Civilians, thank God. We prayed not to have the military in. Anyway, they must be desperate to come this close to the south coast. The parents are moving into a house on the other side of the farm, so we won't have as much disruption as his lot have caused for you.'

Bunch followed the jerk of Marsham's head and spotted Colonel Ralph, commander of the unit stationed in Perringham House. He was leaning against the edge of his peg chatting with his loader. When he spotted her Ralph raised his hat. She had no choice but to nod in return.

Marsham noted her stiffening posture and waved to Ralph with a cheery 'hello' but at the same time hurried her past. 'Mother invited him. She knows his family. He's rather an odd cove.'

'One way of putting it, Henry.'

'I've found him to be mostly harmless.' Marsham ushered her to the last peg along the line. 'Here we go. I shall have to leave you in Avery's tender care – I have a few other things to see to. He'll load for you, and he has a good dog.'

Bunch handed the guns she had brought with her to the short wiry keeper waiting at the shooting peg.

'Avery, I'm sure you remember Miss Courtney. I want you to look after her especially well.'

'Sir.' Avery tipped his battered tweed fishing-hat with one hand, while tugging a liver-spotted young springer spaniel to heel with the other.

'The next drive will be up shortly, but I'd like to have a quick chat later.'

'Thank you, Henry. Now off you trot.' She watched him walk briskly out of sight, wondering what point he was making. As she scanned the line of pegs for familiar faces, the slight figure of Clarice Bell a half-dozen stakes down the row caught her attention. 'Bingo,' she muttered.

'Miss?'

'Oh nothing.' She smiled and leaned the loaded gun he'd handed her in the holder before looking back along the line. It had not occurred to her that Clarice Bell, a keen huntswoman, might have been here. *Makes this trip worthwhile.*

While she waited for Avery to check and load her second firearm Bunch studied Clarice Bell. Bell held a gun similar to her own, and against her slight frame it seemed almost at long as she was tall. But Bunch knew from previous shoots that Bell was well able to use the 12-bore she held, and dealt with the kickback as well as any of the men.

Bunch was still watching when a lone man, muffled deep into his coat and hat against the cold and damp, crossed the plot. He was drawing notice from several pegs as, judging from his dress, he was plainly not here to take part in any shoot. He stomped heavy-footed along the back of the line with head down to avoid eye contact. *Terrible bad form when a drive is imminent,* Bunch thought. She stood a little straighter to watch as the interloper came to stand near Clarice Bell. He stood side-on with his collar up so that Bunch could not see his face, but she knew him. 'Basil Barrington-

Soames, as I live and breath.' She watched what appeared to be an animated talk judged by the gesticulating, and saw the curious glances from those at the stations either side of the peg. Then Bell raised the barrel up and Soames took a step backwards. Both were stock still, glaring at each other, each seeming to be waiting for an interminable few seconds for the other to continue before Soames broke away and strode back across the rough terrain without a backward glance.

Bell watched him go with her gun held defensively across her body. Only when Soames had vanished from view did she turn to face the sounds of beaters shouting and banging sticks on branches and trunks some way up the scrubby hillside, as if nothing had happened.

He comes from old stock. Soames of all people would know wandering along the line is terribly bad form, Bunch thought. *As is verbal fisticuffs in public.* The unmistakable screech and flurry of birds taking flight drew her back to the day's task but the matter was filed away for later thought.

A couple of hours later, as the light was starting to fade, Bunch moved restlessly, impatient for the final drive. She could see why her peg had been left for the latecomer. It was water-logged and even several layers of strategically placed duckboards were not sufficient to stop icy mud welling up through the slats to wash around her boots. Her feet were numb despite two pairs of woollen socks. Punishment for her tardiness, she supposed.

She slapped her arms around herself a half-dozen times, thinking how her ancient Labrador would have loved this kind of day – but Roger had died a few months previously. On days such as this she missed him badly. She glanced at Avery's springer, quivering eagerly at the sounds of the day's final drive. The dog had fidgeted between Bunch and Avery all afternoon, displaying bags of energy, and was a sweet enough companion in Bunch's opinion, but it was not nearly the same as having Roger's solid warmth leaning against her leg.

The game birds broke cover in a burst of noise, taking a low ragged flight toward the lines, chucking noisily, with wings whirring. Bunch took the gun offered her and released both barrels in rapid succession as two birds headed straight across her sights. The slower of them halted mid-air, as if it had hit a glass divide, and spiralled rapidly downwards. The other glided on, chucking frantically as it sought cover in the fields across the river. Bunch swore. She just *knew* she would not have missed that first shot had she been paying proper attention.

The springer scurried across the field and dived into the cover of a bramble heap, emerging a full three minutes later with a somewhat bedraggled hen pheasant hanging limp in her jaws. Avery had the grace to look chagrined at the dog's slow retrieve. Bunch felt a pang of pity for bird, dog and man. It reminded her quite bizarrely of Penelope James. A sad carcass being brought to her for attention by unknowing witnesses. Another victim of violence to be consigned to memory. She broke both guns and handed them to Avery to carry before heading back to the house and the promise of a large whisky.

Copping House was long and squat and tile-hung in the typical Sussex manner. All tiles and eaves, as Edward Courtney often said. Close to the stable's entrance the day's bag was laid out for the shooters to admire. The lack of newly raised pheasants made the bag something of a mixed lot; for every pheasant flushed out and shot there were pigeons and a few wild partridges, and Bunch was amused to note several rabbits and even a hare amongst them. She had bagged a brace at very least but her interest was fixed solely on getting warm and dry. She hurried past in search of her allocated room where she drew the deepest hottest bath she could.

It was not until after dinner that Bunch had time to assess the inside of the house. It was much as she remembered since the last time she had visited. *Probably the way it's been for forty years or more. Though the valuables have been weeded out a little.* She recognised the signs of reduced circumstances and felt sad for them. *Yet they're hosting a shoot. How odd.*

She prowled the drawing room, chatting with various people that she knew, catching up on news, all the while watching the door for her target. Clarice Bell appeared a little after the rest. *No grand entrance. Just quietly, no fuss. The same way she handles a gun,* Bunch thought. *If there's a woman in this room capable of murder, is it really her?* Bunch smiled into her hand. Wright's voice was clear in her head, honing innate suspicion to a needle-sharp cynicism. *There's no reason to suspect Clarice above the rest. Or at all. Other than she's part of that little knot.*

Bunch grabbed two Martinis from one of the serving staff and wandered across to where Bell stood by the closely curtained window. 'Quiet day's shooting,' she said. 'You look as if you need this, Clarice. Is everything all right?'

The woman looked up, startled to be handed a glass by a fellow guest. 'Oh, thank you.'

'Shall we?' Bunch gestured at an empty sofa. 'I saw you on the pegs earlier. Nice shooting.'

'My father encouraged us all to handle our weaponry.'

'Same here. To fathers.' Bunch waved her glass in salute. 'Shame you were put off your stride by people wandering about behind the butts.'

Bell blinked rapidly and took a large swill of her drink. 'You noticed that?'

'I did. He had a bit of a nerve pestering you on the pegs.'

'Oh no – I mean, yes.' Bell half-smiled, downed her drink, and swept another from a passing server. 'For someone with such impeccable manners he never cares much what people think of him. Such a surprise seeing him here.'

Bunch made a show of looking around the room. 'He didn't stay for dinner. What was so urgent that he dragged himself out into the sticks?'

'The *divine* Mr Barrington-Soames…' Bell grinned widely, the emphasis on divine delivered in throaty pastiche '…came to ask me a favour. Well, demand, I suppose. Not that he's really in any position.' Her eyes glittered suspiciously bright, with pupils dilated wide so that her dusty-blue irises were little more than new-moon parings.

'Favour?' Bunch waited for Bell to continue but the woman's head wobbled as if she had been pushed by an invisible hand; she blinked rapidly in nervous silence. She snapped her fingers quietly before those wavering eyes and Bell dragged herself together with a visible effort.

'I say, how is Dodo these days?' Bell murmured, slurring now. 'Not seen her in an age.'

Bunch now realised where Bell had vanished off to when some of the women had withdrawn after dinner. *Cocaine. I hate people taking that stuff, but she's still au fait enough to try putting me off track. Scared of Soames, is she? Or what he came to say?* 'Dodo's doing very well, Clarice,' she said. 'I think having the baby has helped. Given her something to go on for. You should visit her if you have the opportunity.'

'Babies have a knack of changing people's entire worlds. Even from the side-lines.' Bell took a gulp from her glass, her mouth thinning into an ugly line. 'Ye gods and little fishes.' She fished the cocktail stick from her glass, picking the green fruit from it with small even teeth. 'Thank God for olives. I know vermouth is getting hard to find but there's an awful lot of gin in here.'

She really doesn't want to discuss Soames, Bunch thought, and aloud, 'Just what the doctor ordered. I'm still thawing out.'

'It was cold out there, and so many people missing.' Bell replied. 'People signing up right and left – and then they're gone. Poof!' Another change of tack as her attention span wound down.

Maybe I need to hurry her along. Bunch reached out to touch Bell on the wrist. 'I know how you feel. It's so much worse when you lose someone in an accident.' Bunch examined her glass with a sudden fascination. 'I mean, all kinds of people have accidents.'

Clarice Bell looked up, confused. 'They do don't they. Look what happened to Claude. You heard about that?'

'Yes, indeed. That was less than a mile from Perringham. I wonder, what was he doing over my way?'

'Crashing a car.' Bell gulped half her drink without seeming to notice the gin. 'It wasn't his, you know. It belonged to Penny James.'

Bunch watched her carefully, wondering whether the woman knew about the second death and how she could broach the subject. 'I'd heard she and Claude were involved, so his driving her car would make sense. Hard to keep track of society these days. Dodo probably told me about them. Was there an engagement?'

Bell shrugged. 'Not a clue dear-heart. Etta knows more of the juicy goss than I do.'

'I'd heard that Etta Beamish was living down this way now.'

'Probably why Penny moved along the coast. To get away from her.'

'I thought all you chaps were all such pals. Dodo mentioned a supper club.'

Bell opened her mouth several times and closed it again. Those unfocussed eyes were bewildered and also, Bunch

95

thought, a little afraid.

'We were all in that. Even your brother-in-law at one time,' Bell said. 'The supper club has been going for years.' She slugged the very last hint of drink and scowled into the empty cocktail saucer. 'It's all rather jolly. Café de Paris, you know. The music is divine.' Her voice had fallen away to a whisper that was almost lost as the door opened and the men drifted in on a wave of cigar smoke. 'Excuse me, will you? I need to powder my nose.'

'Of course.' Bunch watched Clarice Bell scuttle through the gathering and out of the door, still clutching her glass. She knew she'd waded in far too soon and had blown it. *The chances are she's not coming back. Poor girl is a mess. Interesting that she didn't mention Penny's demise. Not so close as she pretends – or avoiding the subject?*

'You know she's barking mad?' Henry Marsham slid into the seat that Bell had just vacated and handed Bunch a large single malt. 'Thought you might like a decent drop instead of that lighter fuel you've been drinking.'

'Thank you. The martinis are a little - startling?' She smiled at him.

'Clarice? Or the cocktails?'

'Both. I imagine.'

'Those martinis, as you charitably name them, are my sister's doing, and perfectly vile. And Clarice Bell? I repeat, mad as a hatter.'

'I am surprised you let her indulge … on the premises.' Bunch tapped her nose and sniffed, and took the moment to examine him. He wore evening dress well, being tall and wide shouldered. She acknowledged that he was handsome, in the classic fashion, with those vivid blue eyes and that thick dark hair combed back from his forehead and glistening with pomade. He was not a bad sort, just not her sort. Too affable, too eager to please. She took a cigarette from the box on the side table and waited for him to proffer a light. 'I'm surprised you invited her,' she said, 'if she's such a loon. Though in her defence, I think perhaps Basil Soames rather upset her.'

Marsham inclined his head. 'Oh you spotted him, did you? No sooner was he here than he took off again.'

'Having had it out with Clarice?'

'It would seem so. Though I doubt she needs Soames to set

her off.'

'Makes her a liability around guns, don't you think?'

'I agree completely but Mater has other ideas. He took a puff from his cigar and blew the aromatic fume toward the ceiling. 'The Bells are making rather a killing in munitions, you know, and this old place could do with a little moolah.' He grinned suddenly, displaying even white teeth. 'Your grandmother isn't the only matchmaker.' He rolled his eyes on the direction of the fireside where Beatrice was watching them – and pretending not to. 'Please don't take this the wrong way, old duck. You're a perfectly splendid girl, but—'

'Not *the* girl? Well, that's a blessing because you're not *the* boy.' She laughed and shook her head. 'We're agreed on that, at least. Let's join forces against the common enemy.'

'A toast. To confounding the matriarchy.'

'And foiling their dastardly plans at every turn.'

Glasses chinked and both savoured the peaty liquid. 'I heard you lost your dog.' Marsham said at last.

'Yes. Poor old Roger never recovered from that gunshot injury last winter.'

'He wasn't a youngster. Even a pup would struggle to come back from that.'

'True. I miss him though. Brave as any dog I've known, silly old bugger that he was.'

'Are you in the market for another?'

'I might have said no a few months back, but the ATS have turned down my application to return to service yet again. Third time in a row.'

'The leg?'

'Such nonsense because it really doesn't hurt that much now.'

Marsham nodded, rolling his cigar between his fingers. 'Did you notice my springer on your peg.'

'She's yours?'

'Yes. Would you be willing to take her on? I'm away so much and can't take her with me, so she sits in the kennels getting fat and idle. She doesn't like Pater very much, you see. He shouts rather. And now the house is being taken over and the family is being moved out, there won't be room for her. I think she'd respond well to a woman. Under two years old, so a nice young bitch for training up.' He gazed at her, blue eyes intent upon hers. 'You'd be doing me and her a huge favour.'

Bunch was not sure what to make of the offer. The dog was eager, but very twitchy, and she could see how the gruffness of Marsham's father would rattle such a nervous animal. But she didn't want to be in Marsham's debt, or allow him to gain the wrong impression. 'Can I think about it?' she said finally.

'Of course. She's not going anywhere for a bit.' He took a few puffs on his cigar, bringing the end to a glowing ruby red.

'So, going back to Clarice Bell,' Bunch said. 'Did she come on her own?'

'Probably. Her brother's in the Fusiliers and her sister Mina was scooped up by ATS last month. I gather she and her mother are vacating to Wales quite soon.'

'Along with a lot of others. If it wasn't for the military I think Sussex and Kent would be totally deserted.' She regarded him curiously. 'Taken the shilling yourself, yet?'

'Pater got me a commission in the Horse Guards way back in '39. It keeps me away from this place rather a lot.' He smiled slyly. 'Wangled a weekend pass when I heard you were coming down.'

'Less of the soft soap,' Bunch growled. 'If you're not home a great deal you will not have heard the local chit chat?'

'About what?' His face took on a darker expression, and the amiable Henry Marsham melted away.

'About Claude Naysmith and Penny James?'

'Of course.' Marsham allowed a trickle of smoke to slowly escape his lips. 'I hear it's got you mixed up with that policeman chappy again. Mater is scandalised, of course. You are fast gaining a reputation for trouble. Getting involved in the sad demise of Penelope James, however heroic, will not help.'

'Why would you say that?'

'I'm with ... special duties. I gather facts. One of which dates right back to 1936.' Marsham exhaled the last of the smoke and sipped at his whisky.

''36? Where?'

'Munich.'

'Oh, I see.' Bunch took a mouthful of her own drink to cover the fact that she didn't see in the slightest. 'What has Penny's death, or Claude's, to do with that?'

'I hear there's a list?'

He really is a most infuriating man. Answering questions with questions. 'Really,' she said. 'Go on?'

'Most of the people on that list were never in the spotlight.'

'Whose spotlight? Which names should we be looking at?'

'I really couldn't say.'

'Can't? Or won't?'

'About what?'

'Don't be obtuse, Henry. What do you know about that damned list?'

'What list?' He chuckled, and tapped the grey residue from his cigar into the crystal ashtray. 'I don't have all the answers ... just little snippets here and there, but I will give you one item, gratis.'

'How generous of you.'

'A favour, because I like you. My superiors would have my rear end in a sling for telling you this much. They don't trust each other never mind a provincial police force.' He shrugged. 'Don't give me the evil eye. Your father would say just as much. Tell me, Rose, have you ever belonged to a supper club?'

'What?' His constant change of subject was making her senses reel. *Unless it's this fall-down juice,* she thought. *Note to self. Less drinking on the job.* 'No, I've never joined a supper club. Nor have I been up the Eiffel Tower but I can't see that it's connected to the case in hand. How is any of this relevant?'

Marsham smiled at her. 'Glad the rain held off this afternoon. Aren't you?'

Bunch recognised a diplomat's code. He would tell her no more. They sat in silence for a while, oddly companionable since the spectre of courtship had been laid. She finally drained the last of her drink and stubbed her cigarette in the dish. 'I think I shall turn in. Farming involves early starts so I'm rather out of the habit of late-night socials.'

'Goodnight then, Rose. Hope your investigations go well.'

'So do I.' She leaned across to land a kiss on his cheek. 'That should give the old cats something to think about,' she whispered in his ear. 'Goodnight, Henry.'

Once safe in her bed she made the decision not to stay for the second day's shooting. She needed to meet up with Wright as soon as possible.

❧ Nine ❧

'I'll be right our here if you need anything, Miss.' DS Carter had shown Bunch into Wright's office, somewhat reluctantly, she thought, and half-closed the door.

'Thank you, Carter,' Bunch called after him. She had yet to get his measure. Dragged out of retirement, he was an old-fashioned copper who made it clear that giving credence to young ladies, however well connected they might be, was against his better judgement.

Bunch prowled Wright's office as she waited for him to arrive. It was a big room, yet a cramped space. The vast desk was surrounded by filing cabinets and bookcases that lined most of the walls. The meagre light coming through criss-crossed yards of blast tape made it seem gloomier than it should. She wondered how many of the mountains of paper adorning every flat surface belonged in those cabinets, but she could hardly criticise when her own estate office was a similar disaster area. However, as she looked a little more closely, the chaos had a surprising level of order given the sheer volume of work that he was juggling. *All the more reason for me to help him out.* She barely had time to take in the map dotted with coloured pins that covered the wall behind the desk before Wright burst in.

'Rose. Good morning. I thought you were out slaughtering pheasants with the aristos this weekend. What arcane power has brought you here to my door?'

'Only so many pheasants a girl can eat.' She pulled a second chair from the side of the desk and sat down. 'I was on my way home and thought I'd bring you up to date.'

'I've also dug up a few interesting things as well. Carter,' he yelled. 'Get Wills to rustle up some tea, could you?'

He looks please with himself. 'First of all, it would appear that this list of Penny's has come up with some very interesting relationships.' She filled him in on the details she had gleaned from both her grandmother and the hints dropped by Henry Marsham, and ending with an assessment of Clarice Bell's state. 'Don't be so po-faced,' she said at his disapproving frown. 'The season can be like that for the bright young things. All calmness and propriety on the surface and a veritable Sodom and Gomorrah in the shadows. Most of it ends at the altar, and no harm done.'

'People who've been used to champagne on tap,' he replied, 'what will they do now the Germans have all the vineyards under occupation?'

Bunch looked away from a moment concealing a wry smile. 'The Moet still flows, my dear. There are enough bottles laid down in cellars across the land to last them a while yet. It's not only the bubbly that fuels it all, especially in Clarice Bell's case.'

'Hash?'

'Oh really, William, how desperately proper you can be. It's more than a little giggle weed. She is on the toot.'

'Cocaine?'

'By the snoot-full, my dear boy. Clarice Bell was totally panned. God knows how she drove home through black out in that state, but she left soon after dinner. She was frightened and Basil Soames had something to do with it.'

'Do you think Soames may have had some part in encouraging her in that?'

Bunch thought for a moment. 'Not in the way you think. The drugs act only came in, what, twenty years ago. Most of that set indulge now and then because they can, but I'd never seen many of them as a habitual drug takers. Seeing Clarice in such a state was a bit if a shock, to be honest. I had the impression she was not used to being quite so out of control.'

'Interesting. The autopsies on Penelope James and Claude Naysmith didn't show any recent drug use. I'll get Letham to check specifically for those kinds of thing, but I don't think we should get dragged down that rabbit hole. I'll stake my pension on this not being about cocaine.' He stared at the pen he had been absently juggling in his fingers and laid it down with a snap. 'It appears that Claude Naysmith and Penelope James were intending to marry.'

She whistled quietly. 'So Naysmith and James were doing the

deed and said nothing to anyone. How peculiar. It's not as if their families were likely to object. Quite a good match, socially. Was she up the duff?'

Wright blinked at her and flushed a little pink around the collar at her candid query. 'Err ... no. The post-mortem doesn't report a pregnancy. Why would you jump to that conclusion?'

'I keep telling you, don't be such a prude. It's as logical a reason for jumping into the wedlock stakes at short notice as any. Perhaps she wanted to avoid some family hoo-hah? On paper Claude was a very good match but some mothers have very set ideas on who their offspring breed with, and it would be a way of knocking any previous assumptions on the head. Waltz into the family pile seven months preggers, waving the paperwork at the old rents, and voila. The deed is done. They are both over twenty-one, after all. No legal need for consent.'

'That is true.'

'We are checking registry offices in the area but the Admiralty is not very forthcoming on details.'

'I wish Henry hadn't been so vague. Not sure Munich was a great lead. It's hardly as if we can pop over there for a nose around. However, he wasn't the first to mention a supper club.'

'I imagine he's told you what he could.'

'That most of the people on that list were not under their spotlight.'

'But one of them is. Perhaps more than one.' Wright got up to peer out of the window between the slanting stripes of breakage tape. He stood for several moments, hands in pockets, easing up onto his toes and back again.

Like some refugee from The Pirates of Penzance. Bunch squashed the urge to laugh – and waited.

The door opened and Carter backed into the room, a cup of tea in each hand and a slim manila file tucked under one arm. 'I sent Wills over to get that report on the motor incident you asked for.' He set the two thick white cups on the desk and handed Wright the file. 'Interesting reading, Guv.'

Wright lowered himself into his seat, his attention fixed on leafing through the papers. 'Interesting.' He glanced up at Bunch. 'It seems there are several large dents to the rear of the vehicle, some of which bore traces of paint. A mixture of white guard-paint and also the black paint that was underneath. Seems the car Naysmith was driving had been rammed. So we can safely assume that he was forced off the road. Didn't your trekker witness say there were two cars that night?'

'Yes they did.'

'Any hope of them identifying the makes?'

'Not in the dark. And the hedges are awfully high. They would only have caught glimpses at the most.'

'Track down the file, will you Carter? See if we can get any more information.'

'Sir.' Carter left closing the door carefully behind him, but Bunch could tell he was not happy at being dismissed once more, like a green constable.

'So what do you think Naysmith was involved with that got them both killed?' she asked Wright.

'It may be something we'll never find out, if it's down to the Admiralty.'

'On the other hand – what if Naysmith was killed by accident and Penny James was the target?'

'The report is quite precise. Naysmith was murdered.'

'Yes, but in Penny's car. What if she *was* the one they're after?'

'That's a big conclusion to jump to,' said Wright. He reached for his tea and gave it a brief stir in memory of absent sugar. 'It's a theory that's worth looking into, though I doubt it. If he wasn't the target why kill him? My question would be, what coincidence brought him into your neck of the woods?'

'Given where he crashed, I think it likely he was trying to reach Larry Parrish.'

'Parrish is also on that list.'

'Indeed he is.'

'Do you think he's involved?'

'Until we know what it was that was going on, there is no saying. Parrish was away at sea when that car was run off the road. According to his mother he'd rather fallen out with the pack.'

'Which helps us not at all.'

'Not in the slightest. What do you suggest we do now?'

'I suggest we go out in search of a decent cup. Our canteen lady swears this is tea and it may have been, once upon a time – about eight brew-ups ago.'

'And then?'

'We can take a run out to Newhaven. See if we can ruffle a few seagoing feathers.'

'Admiralty won't like that.'

'All we have been getting from them up until now is an arctic silence, so anything will be an improvement.'

'Fine. Have you found Penny's digs? If they were stationed at the same place she has to be living around there somewhere.'

'Not so far. WRNS are usually billeted together so we started trawling the sort of small boarding houses that the navy have been using.'

'I sense a *but* in the offing.'

'We've drawn a complete blank.'

'Surely they're assigned a barracks, even if it's a guest house?'

'We thought so but not being permitted access to personnel records has rather shackled our enquiries.'

'I can't see why they are being so touchy now she's dead?'

'I got the impression it was precisely because she's dead.'

'Ahh.' The vagaries of officialdom were never a surprise to Bunch. 'Maybe being married, she wasn't assigned to the usual mess? The navy would have to have given permission for the wedding, one assumes. Parents might not have had a say but our armed forces tend to be rather picky about these things, which brings us to the other elephant in the room. If they were married why was he still in bachelor digs?'

'Seems neither didn't tell their COs, either.'

'Brave chaps. If the high-ups decided to cut up rough...'

'I doubt they worried too much. There seemed to be no reason why barriers should be put in their way. I have found there's only one way to answer these kinds of conundrums: kick over a few cans and see what scurries out. Come on, we have a commodore or two to question.'

'Sadly you are going to have to do that alone. I dropped by to pass on my information but I have a prior engagement that can't be put off.'

'A date?'

'Would that it were. I'd like to be home before the blackout. One of my Land Girls has absconded and all hell's let loose. But keep me posted?'

Standing in the kitchen of one of the two farm cottages that formed the Land Girl's bothy, Bunch was wishing she had taken Wright up on his offer of dinner because she could see where this conversation was heading. *Not that I want to avoid it, I just feel so sorry for her, and helpless.* 'So none of you have any idea where Brenda has gone?' she said aloud.

'She's been a bit quiet, like,' said Vera, 'ever since her young man and she parted ways. Funny though, she took all of her kit.'

'So she's left rather than gone missing.'

Kate glanced at Pat and said, 'We thought so. I thought I should make sure she was all right so I left a message for her mother. They don't have a telephone so the number is the corner shop. It seems Brenda hasn't turned up there. Her mother called the police in a panic, and it rather snowballed from there. I'm sorry, Boss.'

'Oh, it's not your fault, Kate. These things happen. You say she fell out with her chap?'

'I don't think it was a choice. I rather think she was the deserted party,' Kate replied. 'Courtesy of His Majesty's Armed Forces.'

Bunch rubbed both hands across her face. 'Is she PWOP?' The telling looks passing between the girls told her all she needed to know. Pregnancy seemed to be a common theme for the weekend, and more common than ever it was in peace time. Finding comfort in the arms of a man was understandable with the fear of bombings and the constant battering of losses on personal and national levels. There wasn't a single person she knew who had not lost a family member or friend. 'Brenda didn't confide in anyone about her condition? Any idea where this chap of hers has been sent?'

'They're never told, are they,' said Kate. 'I heard a rumour his unit was shipped out to North Africa.'

'So she's not going to catch up with him in a hurry. There isn't a lot we can do, here and now. She's a grown woman and her family seem to have it all in hand. I'm sure she'll turn up either back here or else in Town by tomorrow. Once she does, we'll give her all the help we can.'

'Yes, Boss.'

'Is everything else running smoothly?'

'Yes … Boss.'

The hesitation before Kate's chirpy assurance was minute but it was there. 'Good to hear. There's a few things I want to go over before the morning. Walk up to the stables with me?'

'Yes, Boss.'

They walked quickly, muffled against the chill of the evening that was promising an early frost. The beam from Bunch's small torch lit the ground just in front of their feet. With the moon past the third quarter, all was dark beyond the torch's feeble glow and they concentrated on the terrain, stumbling now and then and not speaking for most of the way from the terrace of farm cottages to the Dower House. The smooth stone sets of the stable yard were a relief.

'Clear night.' Kate gazed up at the Milky Way sweeping overhead. 'Weather forecast is for a dry day tomorrow.'

'Good. It will be a fair chance to get the team clearing the last of the slopes below Genet Copse and start on the ploughing.'

'Now that's what I wanted to talk about. Slight problem.' Kate opened the door leading into the stalls and stood back for Bunch to walk in.

The inside of the stables was several degrees warmer than out, warmed by the body heat of the estate's three horses. Bunch lit one of the storm lanterns and hung it on a hook. All three horses came to hang their heads over their doors. Robbo, Edward Courtney's hunter, was closest to the entrance and he snickered quietly as Bunch reached him. She gave him a rub, feeling his rumbled greeting ripple through that muscular neck, and fed him one of the tid-bits she had brought with her. Next to him, Magpie, known as Maggie, the piebald she had bought a few months before to pull a pony cart, kicked peevishly at her door and squealed indignantly. 'Oh, be quiet, you greedy monster,' Bunch called, but moved on to proffer a chunk of carrot on her palm. Maggie took it and retreated a pace to crunch the treat just beyond reach of any patting. 'Bad tempered little baggage.' Bunch felt in her pocket for the third vegetable as she reached Perry. He took her offering more gently, nodding his head as he mumbled the root veg before biting noisily. She rubbed his greying forehead and buried her face into his mane for a moment, and made a mental note to get the vet out to file his teeth. He was getting old and she didn't want to risk poor molars endangering his health. Perry was her best pal and been the receiver of all her innermost secrets for so many years.

Kate cleared her throat. 'Boss?'

'Oh, sorry Kate. I'm apologising to the old chap. I've neglected him horribly this past week.'

'I don't suppose he minds not riding out when it's this cold.'

'Probably not. Now then, what was it you wanted to tell me?'

'It's a bit tricky, as it happens.'

'Is that slope harder to clear than we thought?'

'No. I mean that is hard but not impossible. No, it's something rather different.' She looked down for a moment. 'Lady Chiltcombe has ordered us onto another duty.'

'Oh?' Bunch heaved a loud sigh. 'What is it this time?'

'She wants us to prune the nut walk and clip all of the yew hedges.'

'Does she now.'

'When I tried to explain that we had other duties she gave me notice.'

'She what?'

'I was given a week's notice.'

It was the kind of nightmare that Bunch had been foreseeing ever since her father had bestowed the basic running of Perringham estate on her. She and her grandmother had reached a working arrangement, made easier by the fact that Beatrice had relinquished her throne to Theadora when Bunch's grandfather had died. With Edward still very much alive there had been no such handing on for Theadora. Edward was happy to leave Bunch in charge, with judicious suggestions and guiding nudges about the day-to-day running, but there was no history of shared stewardship between mother and daughter. 'Was my father not around?' she asked.

'He's been in Town. Only came in an hour before you.' Kate shuffled awkwardly. 'He seemed – pre-occupied.'

'He has a lot on his plate.' Bunch stared at her feet and pressed her fingers to her lower lip. 'My mother can't sack you, Kate. You do know that.'

'Yes, I know, but she is used to having her orders carried out.'

'And you thought she would pull strings?'

Kate said nothing.

'Was my mother quite herself when this is happened?'

'Boss?'

There was no mistaking the panic in the Land Girl's expression and Bunch felt a pang of pity for her. 'Let's not be coy about this.' She put her hand on Kate's shoulder. 'Was my mother—' She laughed, aware of the irony in her reluctance to put her fears into words. Admitting that her mother was liable to be off her head to someone outside of the family was not easy. 'My mother is unwell, Kate. She has been for a while. It makes her cranky and frankly, against all medical advice, she's rather inclined to take a little more medication than she should this early in the day.'

'We realise that.' Kate ran her hand through her hair. 'I had thought that perhaps—'

'I shall put it right. The chances are she won't even remember. It may be an idea to keep out of her way for a few days.' She dropped her hand and unhooked the hay net hanging beside Perry's door. 'It's not six o'clock yet but may as well feed up now.'

'Yes, Boss.'

They spent a few minutes fetching feed and water and stuffing hay nets. 'Anything else going on?' Bunch asked into the unnatural quiet.

'Not really.' Kate paused with her hand on Robbo's light rug. 'Think he needs a rug indoors?'

'Yes. He was only clipped a month ago and it's going to be a cold night.'

'What about the other two?'

'No. Perry's got a decent coat. Fells are tough old things. As for this one—' Bunch slapped Maggie affectionately on the neck '—I swear she's part goat. I doubt there's a rug yet made you could put on her that wouldn't be in tatters by midnight.' Bunch slipped out of the stall and bolted it firmly. 'Heard any more about the accident?' she asked.

'No. I heard the police have been asking for witnesses but I think they'll be lucky. Not many people about at that time of the morning.'

'Except the trekkers.'

'Who haven't been back since then.' Kate finished fastening Robbo's rug and bolted the stall behind her. 'Boss ... the girls are nervous about Brenda. Some of them still haven't got over Mary's murder. I know it's almost a year ago, now, but it's not something you forget.'

Bunch did not need reminding of the Land Girl who had died on the Bothy's doorstep in the January snow. It was something they all avoided talking about. Mary had been an innocent victim. *Like Naysmith*, she thought. She had no idea why she was so sure of that but it seemed to fit, only because there seemed no reason to suspect him guilty of anything other than a clandestine marriage. 'I am not at all surprised.' She adjusted the net by Maggie's stall and went to pick the storm lantern from its hook. 'I'll deal with my mother, Kate. Don't worry on that score. And I am sure Brenda is fine. Or as fine as she can be if she really is in the family way.' She snuffed the lamp and both women stepped out into the yard. It was completely dark now and even the additional light from the small torch Kate produced from her pocket was barely adequate. 'Any other problems? I know I've been gadding around rather a lot and left you to it. Parson's retired, but you can always call on him for advice if I'm not around.'

'Yes, Boss. We've been getting a lot more done since Gwenny and Vera arrived, but Brenda going missing…'

'I shall see if I can pry a couple more recruits from headquarters,' said Bunch. 'Have a quiet night and see you tomorrow.'

૭૦ન૭ન

Bunch waited until dinner was over before raising the subject of estate management. She watched her mother pouring herself yet another scotch and marvelled that Theadora showed no signs of inebriation. The fervent promise of abstinence after the visit to Harley Street had not lasted.

She glanced at her father to see if he would say anything. He was engrossed in reading a sheaf of documents that only dinner had interrupted. She wondered if that was a genuine lack of awareness or wilful myopia. It would be unlike him not to be aware and she could not believe it was indifference. The only other conclusion was an unwillingness to cause a scene, and given his willingness to lecture her at every turn she found it exasperating that he gave Theadora quite so much leeway. *Perhaps that is just the way of marriage? Perhaps it's the way of love?*

'Are you sure you wouldn't prefer coffee, Mother?' Bunch said at last.

'Don't be a nag, Rose.' Theodora sank into the sofa and took a large swallow. 'You are becoming shrill, darling. Shrill and bitter.'

The inference was like spring water, as clear as it was cold, and it hit Bunch with the same effect. 'As opposed to just plain bitter?'

'Rose!' Edward snapped his despatch box shut. 'Show a little respect, please.'

'But Mother—'

'Is your mother.'

His warning glance dampened her anger. 'I'm sorry you feel that way, Mother,' she said. 'I am concerned for you, that's all.'

'It's none of your damned business.' Theodora drained her glass and slammed it on the coffee table at her elbow.

'Then in future I shall respect your right to keep it. Provided you offer me the same courtesy.'

'Meaning?'

'I know you've not been here for a while, and yes the garden is a little unkempt, but you can't commandeer my Land Girls as your private gardeners – and you certainly can't give them notice.'

'Oh that.' Theodora slotted a cigarette into a short holder and lit it, taking her time, studied in her indifference. 'I can't see what the problem would be. Strapping girl like her will find work anywhere.'

'Who would?' Edward asked.

'Kate Wooldridge. Mother gave her notice simply because she would not prune the nut walk.'

'Is that true, Theodora?'

'The girl was being insolent,' Theodora snapped. 'It is not for her to dictate how I direct staff.'

'Except that they're not estate staff. They are Land Army troops employed by the government.'

'Stuff and nonsense. Tom Varsing had his Land Girls rebuilding his orangery. I don't see why this is any different.'

'What Tom Varsing does is not my concern. I left Kate clear instructions that she was not to take the girls off farm duties without my direct orders,' Bunch said. 'She needs to know that what I say goes. If you start countermanding me the girls won't know where they are.'

'You really are making a fuss over nothing, and it's hardly my fault that we don't have enough outdoor staff.'

'It is a cause for some regret,' said Beatrice. 'The gardens were always so lovely, but I already have plans to hire some village boys to turn the far side of the nut walk into a vegetable patch.'

'Vegetables?' Theadora's voice rose a pitch. 'You've spent years getting it fit for croquet and now you're going to plant cabbages?'

'*Dig for Victory*,' Beatrice replied. 'There's never anybody around to play croquet, darling. Some of the WVS ladies have sons and grandsons, strapping boys too young to join up as yet, who will do the job for a small fee. Certainly no need to take people from the farm.'

'I know all of that.' Theadora stroked a crease out of her gown, trying hard to appear nonchalant. 'I think everyone is blowing this out of proportion. I merely asked for some simple tasks to be carried out.'

'Nothing is simple anymore, Mother. I can't run this place if you keep interfering.'

'Quite right, Rose-bunch.' Edward held up both hands to ward off another outburst. 'It would help if we all remained calm.'

'Calm? Daddy, you told me I was in charge of the estate. Gave me a load of absolute guff about duty, yet the moment you and Mummy are back it's all change.'

'Do be reasonable, Rose darling,' Theadora said. 'You're in charge of running the farm, of course, but I thought I still have some authority.'

Bunch looked from one face to another and felt helpless in the face of family pressure. She knew that one day she would have to take up the reins of estate management fully, but not quite so soon. Yet she had stepped up to the task. If she was not allowed to do that job then what choice did she have? 'Authority?' she said. 'That's rather the point isn't it? Who has it and who doesn't.'

'I have run entire embassies,' Theadora snapped. 'I think a small country house is well within my scope.'

'Yes, of course, you are so right, Mother. There can only be one person issuing orders and you are the current Lady Chiltcombe. So take charge. I can throw my lot in with Emma Tinsley. She tells me her people in Whitehall are looking for French speakers. I'll be out of your hair in no time.'

'Enough.'

Both women spun round toward Edward. 'I know it is not easy for any of you having to rub along together in this house. That is what we must do, however, so I would appreciate it if you both stopped this war of attrition. Rose is correct, Theadora. You should not be drinking. You know that.'

'Can you blame me for partaking a few remaining pleasures? I may not be around that long.'

'Don't talk that way. You know what the doctors have said. If you keep to the diet you have years yet – provided you look after yourself. Which is why you would benefit from a change of scenery my dear. I've found a nice little place in Bath.'

'Bath?'

'Yes, my dear. Delightful place.'

'So I am being packed off to a rest home?'

'A spa. To take the waters and to rest. Just for a few weeks and be back in time for Christmas.'

'Damn you, Edward. Damn you to hell.' She swept out of the room, slamming the door behind her with enough force to set the chandelier chiming.

Beatrice made a show of brushing imaginary dust from her shoulders. 'I shall retire,' she said. 'We could all do with an early night.'

'I shall look in on Theadora on my way to bed.' He waited until the door closed behind his mother. 'Now, Rose, my dear child. Please don't do anything hasty. Your mother was wrong to interfere but we can put it right. When we left for Singapore she was lady of the manor. She still is, of course, but she came back to a far different world than the one she left.'

'We've all had to make changes.'

'I know, and you've felt it more than the rest of us, watching it all take place. Theadora has never adjusted well to changes. We appear to zip around here and there like migrating birds, except that life in one consulate is pretty much like any other. Here, she's a fish out of the water. Mother runs the house and you run the estate. I'm hardly ever out of the War Room, and on top of all that, she has this sword of Damocles hanging over her.'

'The cancer.'

'We still don't have a firm diagnosis. It may still not be cancer.

112

It could be cirrhosis. It's why Ephrin has suggested she takes a few weeks at a spa.'

'To dry her out yet again? How terribly optimistic.'

'Try not to judge. She never got over the loss of the boys. When we got word you'd been injured in France ... well I thought I was going to lose her.'

'She was so very heartbroken she spent the next God knows how long skulking in the Highlands, as far from me as she could get.'

'You were hardly home and we had all the kerfuffle over the requisition. She can cope with kings and potentates because they are her business, but when it's people she cares for her nerves go to pieces. I should be here for her but as things stand.' Edward looked defeated, exhausted, as Bunch had never seen him before and she felt guilty.

Her mother's fragility was no secret and she knew she should not expect a great deal. Kicking off only added to the burden that her father bore. 'Sorry, Daddy, I've been a bit of a brat, haven't I? I was so angry at Mother giving Kate notice I wasn't thinking.'

'Then you're not running away to the circus?' He smiled and shook his head. 'Rather apt. That's Jebb's name for the Admiralty department Emma Tinsley works for.' He raised a warning finger. 'Word of advice, if I may. Do not go anywhere near them. They're a bunch of hotheads. Patriotic, of course, but reckless to the point of lunacy. I have no doubt they are what we need right now but I'd rather my daughter and heir wasn't sucked into their shenanigans.'

'I thought the navy was all boats and submarines?'

'So it is. Most of it. The army doesn't have the monopoly on madness, you know. British Naval Intelligence stretches back beyond Henry VIII and has more than its fair share of Everett Ralphs.' He patted her arm. 'Playing detective with your policeman friend must seem like fun, and we shan't go into your manipulating your Uncle Walter, but with Parsons retired I do need you here. Rose-bunch, you are Perringham's estate manager and the running of the estate must trump everything for you right now.'

'And Mummy going for her spa?'

Edward pulled a face. 'When we've talked her into it.' He leaned forward and kissed Bunch on the forehead. 'I am relying on you Rose.'

'I know. I shall go up now, I think. Storrington Market tomorrow so it's an early start for me. Goodnight, Daddy.'

❧ Ten ❧

Bunch left the Storrington auction barn early. Orders by the Ministry Inspectors to cull surplus stock left farms with fewer beasts than ever to go under the auctioneer's gavel. She wandered through the market square and noticed how subdued it all seemed. Meat and butter rations had made gaps in the lines of covered stalls and there seemed little of the seasonal cheer Bunch had expected, with Christmas just a few weeks away.

The biggest advantage of this early finish was the lunch she had arranged with Wright. If nothing else it delayed her return to the Perringham Dower House and yet another icy mealtime with Theadora, and it was a perfect opportunity to see what the Chief Inspector had uncovered over the week.

At a little after ten she set off for Newhaven, against a tide of military vehicles and roadblocks, in numbers she had seldom encountered before, and arrived at the Continental Hotel just after noon. The hotel dining room was of the slightly shabby Edwardian kind, with white moulded-plaster ceilings and the palest gold walls punctuated by more plaster panels surrounding Victorian rococo mirrors. The curtains, Bunch noted, would doubtless have been red velvet to match the faded red carpets but had been given over to heavy blackouts, urgent verticals that gave it a vaguely cell-like feel.

'So sorry I'm late,' she said as she handed the waiter her coat and hat and flung herself into a chair. 'The roads are absolutely bloody. Is there something going on?'

'Newhaven is a prime port.' Wright glanced at the lurking waiter. 'And we couldn't discuss it if we did know anything. I am sorry, also.'

'What for?'

He waved both hands at the room. 'This. Not what you are used to I imagine, but it was hard to find anywhere to eat. The

Admiralty has commandeered just about every building for billets or offices.' He glanced at the clock on the far wall. 'I was told to be here by eleven but no sign of our contact as yet.'

'Surely they'd let you know if they were going to cancel?'

'You would think.' Wright laughed sharply. 'They may have avoided a meeting on Naval territory but this is still their waiting room – in all but name.'

'And we are being kept waiting.'

'Exactly.'

'It will be fine,' she said, and took the menu from the elderly waiter. 'Is the fish good?'

He nodded. 'No boats out from here, not since June, but we do have some flatfish fresh from the harbour this morning, and some excellent crab.'

'Then the fish it shall be. And if you have a decent Sauvignon to go with that, please.'

'I shall have the same,' Wright added.

'Yes, Sir.'

Bunch watched the server go out of earshot before turning to Wright. 'Why here, old chap? What's the buzz in Newhaven?'

'We traced young Naysmith's base,' Wright murmured. 'Not that we need a grid reference, just someone who can tell us if his work might have got him killed.'

'So we're going to chat with his CO?'

'That is what I was told. Commander Hopkirk. Odd business, altogether, when they spent days insisting our Captain Naysmith's last posting did not exist.'

'He made captain?' Bunch whistled quietly. 'Why has nobody offered up that snippet before now?'

'I suspect most people are not aware. He's still down on the official roll as Sub Lieutenant: Signals. It must have been a very recent promotion. People rise through the ranks quite quickly these days. It took Carter a week of being passed from one department to another before we had confirmation that Naysmith was Royal Naval personnel. As if being billeted in the town wasn't a bit of a clue.'

'Signals, hey? You'd think he'd be over in Portsmouth.'

'Units are being shifted out of the dockyards because of all the raids.'

'And Penny James?' Bunch asked.

'Now … she has been even harder to track down. Oxford graduate, which we knew, and a Wren officer. Beyond that the Admiralty has been especially closed mouthed.'

'Extra hush-hush?'

'So it would seem. They are making a good fist of burying us in tape and tradition. The navy, in my experience, are not called the Senior Service for nothing. They'll be sending someone who will deny everything, probably claim it's above his rank. I've been passed three times around Whitehall, right up to and including the office of the Lords of the Admiralty, and back down again. They can hide facts indefinitely. Certainly for months. Years, even.' He pulled a face. 'I don't suppose you have some sea-faring relative who can oil the wheels?'

'Sorry.' Bunch shook her head. 'All army. And one in the police.' She gave him a bared-teeth smile. 'I do know how you feel. You forget you are talking to the daughter of a diplomat. It's all so much very gracious eyewash. My surprise was that you got a chap as high as Commander right out of the gate. Unless I am very much mistaken, here he comes.'

A stocky naval officer of middle to late years was wending his way through the chairs toward them. He came to stand near them, hand outstretched. 'Inspector Wright? Commander Evelyn Hopkirk at your service.'

Wright stood to shake the proffered hand. 'Detective Chief Inspector William Wright.'

'Jolly good.' Hopkirk smiled at Bunch expectantly.

'And this is the Honourable Miss Rose Courtney.'

'Honourable, hey?' He bowed and offered his hand and an arch smile. 'Pleasure to meet you, *Miss* Courtney.' His emphasis on the Miss was aimed at Wright.

'Miss Courtney is assisting Sussex Constabulary as a consultant. Her insights on the deceased are invaluable.' Wright avoided Bunch's eye as he introduced her, but she could see why he had pulled her rank. The Commander's back straightened perceptibly at her title.

'Do sit down, Commander. My card.' She handed over a paste oblong, smiling an apology to Wright that she had not yet had time to show him her latest weapon.

'Hon. Miss Rose Courtney – Consulting Detective.' Hopkirk bowed his head once more, a little more mocking this time. *Calculating,* Bunch thought. *You can practically see him flicking through Debretts to place me. Or my father, at the very least.* 'Consultant detective?' He returned the card and took his seat. 'Should I call you Inspector Watson?' he said to Wright. 'No ... it was Lestrade, wasn't it?'

Wright smiled a little grimly and moved on. 'Miss Courtney is familiar with the case so you can be quite open.'

'Jolly good,' Hopkirk replied. 'Capital.'

'Would you like to see a menu, Sir?' The waiter asked.

Hopkirk gestured toward Bunch.

'I'm afraid we've already ordered lunch, thank you,' said Bunch. 'We didn't know how much longer you would be.' *Or,* she thought, *if you were going to turn up at all.*

Hopkirk stared at her for a moment. 'Oh, don't worry about me, Miss Courtney.' His smile widened. 'I ate at the mess. Bit of a flap on you see. Can't stop long.'

How convenient, Bunch thought and glanced at Wright. 'Surely you can you have a glass of wine?'

'Sorry, no. It wouldn't do if I went back on watch three sheets to the wind. But coffee, perhaps.' Hopkirk watched the waiter retreat to the kitchen. 'Well now.' He removed his cap and settled back in his seat. 'How can I help the Sussex Constabulary?' The officer's hazel eyes beamed bon homie from a complexion that Bunch thought rather defied Hopkirk's claim to abstinence.

'I was rather hoping we could help each other,' Wright replied. 'Concerning the late Captain Naysmith.'

'Yes. That was unfortunate. Poor chap pranged his jalopy I understand? Lot of that in the blackout.'

'Yes, but we have reason to believe it was not entirely accidental.'

'Really?' Hopkirk's brow tightened with concern. *He doesn't look that surprised,* Bunch thought. *Probably knows more than we do.* 'What made you draw that conclusion?' he went on.

'The pathologist seems to think he was killed elsewhere and the crash was staged afterwards.'

'Was it really? Gosh. That's rather unfortunate for the poor chap.'

Now he looks worried. Bunch sipped at her glass of water. *And a touch shaken, perhaps?* 'Is there anything he was involved with that might have made him a target?' she asked.

'Was he tortured?'

'An odd jump to make,' said Wright.

'Naysmith was a good officer,' Hopkirk replied. 'If he was waylaid because of his duties then violence would be the only way information would have been extracted from him.' He sat back as the waiter approached with a tray of coffee and the wine, his fingers steepled together against his bottom lip as they waited in silence for the server to retreat. 'You must realise I can't reveal the nature of his duties. Do you have reason to believe information retrieval was the reason for his demise?'

'We've no obvious reason to think that was the case,' Wright replied. 'He seemed to have been killed outright and the murder disguised as an accident. But then Sussex Constabulary had no reason to believe Naysmith had any information worth the taking, other than the usual "careless talk costs lives" variety. The Admiralty has been completely close lipped so we had no way of judging that. Have you any idea why he would be on that road at that time?'

'We assumed he was on his way to see his wife,' said Hopkins. 'She'd been transferred at short notice and they both had two day's shore leave.'

'Why was she transferred?' Bunch said.

'The marriage was terribly recent,' Hopkirk replied, 'and totally against regs, but in these times?' He shrugged the idea away. 'Young things need to be able to live whilst they can. Seemed like a good idea, I don't doubt, but she was transferred immediately, you understand? Can't have married personnel serving together. Not good for discipline.'

Bunch wasn't entirely sure why that should be. She nodded, however, as if it were quite natural to her. 'Do you know how we can get in contact with her unit?'

'Well, there's a thing. I don't know where she was transferred to. Somewhere rather more on the quiet side, I'm told.'

'You knew her then?'

'Penelope? Rather. We were sad to see her go.'

'Penelope was a sweet girl,' Bunch said.

'Was?' Hopkirk said

'Yes. I assumed that you knew. She's dead.'

Hopkirk glanced out of the window briefly. 'No, I hadn't heard. Poor girl. What a terrible coincidence.'

'She was murdered,' Wright replied. 'A fact we've been trying to get through to your superiors for a while now. We've been blocked at every turn.'

Hopkins took a gulp of coffee, staring at Wright over the rim and then set the cup down with exaggerated precision. 'Do you think these two deaths have something to do with Naval affairs?'

'Without knowing what those affairs could be we have no idea what to think.'

'Now that could be a problem. Lieutenant James's new posting was classified. You'll understand if I don't elaborate. I am grateful for your bringing it to my attention. I shall have our Master-at-Arms keep a close eye on anything they were working on. If we can help you with any other aspect of their lives then of course we shall do what we can.'

'National security is your concern. Murder is mine, Commander. Is there anybody who was especially close to them?'

'I couldn't say. They were both junior officers. I saw them in the mess, naturally, but we didn't mix outside of it. I think Naysmith saw himself as a cut above many of our chaps, and as most of those were Naval Ratings, I suppose he was. Of course, Naysmith wasn't going to be chums with an old fossil like me – I saw service in the last lot. Career navy.' He grinned at Wright. 'I expect you saw your share.'

'I did. Royal Engineers.'

'Army?' Hopkirk chuckled. 'I can't hold that against a chap.' Ignoring the large hotel clock, he made a show of shooting back his sleeve to consult his watch. 'Unfortunately I am going to have to desert you. I'm on three bells watch.' He stood more agilely than his figure hinted at and settled his cap into place with a sharp tug. 'If you need anything just run a message up the old flagpole.'

Wright rose with him. 'Thank you, Commander. One more thing, though. Do you happen to know where they married?'

'It was a civil do, so Brighton I should think.'

'Witnesses?'

'Can't help you there, I'm afraid. Now I really do have to go.

Goodbye Chief Inspector. Miss Courtney.' He shook Wright's hand and tipped forefingers to his cap at Bunch before wheeling around and striding rapidly toward the exit.

'Well?' Bunch murmured. 'Did you buy any of that?'

'He confirmed that they knew of the marriage and that James and Naysmith had served together. Beyond that? Load of old hooey. I very much doubt he was even Naysmith's direct CO.'

'What makes you think that?'

'Because if he were, we'd have been his mess guest, where he'd be on familiar ground. Commander Hopkirk suggested very neutral territory. There are a dozen Naval establishments in this area he could have used if he were a bona fide commander of a local station. I would hazard a guess that he's a little bit more than a mere commander.'

'Admiralty Intelligence?'

'That would be my guess. Out to stamp on any curiosity we might have about their work. There is no way that Naysmith could have been killed and his CO not try to contact his wife of less than two months. Using that same logic there is not a chance he wouldn't also be aware that she was also dead by now.'

'So why come at all?'

'To see how much we know and to stop us badgering them for any further interviews. They will leave it to us to investigate while they continue to deny knowing anything at all. All covered by the Official Secrets Act.'

'We're being fobbed off?' Bunch demanded. 'If it was something to do with official secrets acts, we're never going to find out any more from them.'

'Absolutely.'

'Ye gods. You'd never know we are supposed to be on the same side.'

'Ah, but he didn't deny anything,' Wright replied. 'If he had we'd be warned off a little more forcibly. They are happy enough to allow us to carry on for now, if only to see what we uncover.'

'Meaning it genuinely has nothing to do with them.'

'Most likely.'

'So what now?'

'So we eat our fish and hope it really is brain food.'

'This thing is a death trap.' Wright pulled his collar up and huddled down in the passenger seat as Bunch raced her MG along the coast road toward Brighton. She risked a glance at him. Little of his profile could be seen between his overcoat and hat but the dark shadows beneath his eyes were unmistakable.

'You could have ridden with your own driver in your nice cosy Wolseley,' she said. 'We're going to the same place. Besides, you could've had a little snooze. When was the last time you had a decent night's sleep?'

'I can't remember. Between warning sirens and a crime wave of epic proportions I'm lucky to get four or five hours at a stretch.' He yawned as if to prove his point, lips pulled back from white teeth. For a tiny moment he reminded her of the wolf she had once seen on a hunting expedition in the Tuscan mountain ranges – grey and lean and watchful. 'Oh don't be such a ninny. We are on a perfectly straight road which absolutely nothing else is using, and in broad daylight.' She zipped around a half-dozen drab-green Bedford lorries and slewed to a halt for another roadblock, slamming the MG in gear the moment Wright flashed his ID.

'How many more of these?' she grumbled.

'That was it this side of town. It's why we avoid the coast road,' said Wright. 'It's far longer to go round the north side but quicker in the long run.'

'And you didn't think to warn me?'

'You get so used to them you tend to forget.' He yawned. 'No more army, at least. Navy are all along this stretch now.' He waved a hand toward a turning to their right. 'Roedean School.'

'I know. I went there for a short while.'

'You did?' He threw his head back and laughed. 'Now why doesn't that surprise me? I'm only puzzled that it was only for a short time. I wouldn't have thought it was about the fees. So what?'

'We didn't suit each other,' she growled. 'I hear they were all packed off up north somewhere.'

'They were. It's now the abode of Naval cadets.'

'Bet the girls' were disappointed they were all moved out.'

'Steady on.'

His shock was quite real, which amused her, and Bunch wondered how much he knew about well-brought-up young women of a certain age when they escaped the confines of home.

'Hope they treat it better than the army is treating Perringham,' she said. 'I haven't been in the house for a few months but when I was last there it was a wreck. I am only glad Granny has not been up there to see it. It would break her heart.'

'Hard to imagine your grandmother resisting a little peek.'

Bunch glanced at him and nodded. 'You're probably correct. Probably had Ralph give her a grand tour. I gather she knows his family.'

'Is there a family of note that she doesn't know?'

'I doubt it.'

'And what does she know about the James's?'

'In what department? Pedigree? Wealth? Gossip?'

'I'm not sure. Anything will help. Meanwhile we need to know more about where she was stationed without waiting six weeks to go through channels. I'll get Carter on it. There can't be too many James families in this area.'

'We need to talk with the others on that list. Have we tracked them down yet?'

'We've talked with them all. Each one has an alibi for both deaths, when Naysmith was run off the road and when Penelope James was killed.'

'How reliable are their accounts?'

Wright laughed. 'Now you are thinking like a copper. I don't really know. As they were all out of the county, at least some of the time, we've had to rely on other constabularies.'

'Weren't they all called up?'

'Soames has a medical "E".' Wright grunted and spread his hands. 'A chap who goes hunting, plays golf and was in both a rugby eleven and a rowing eight at his school – he suddenly develops a heart condition.'

'Convenient. And Pilkington?'

'He had a penchant for figures at Oxford so his family have him ensconced in some War Office department.'

'Really? That's worrying. I shall ask Daddy to look into that.'

'Do. We can't find anything out.'

'That leaves Jemima Harper and Harriett Beamish.'

'The Harper girl has gone into the ATS, I gather. Stationed somewhere in the North Surrey region. She has a pretty good alibi – she was on duty.'

'Not if she's a driver. She could be out anywhere.'

'I hadn't considered that. Harriett Beamish doesn't seem to be signed up anywhere as yet. Working for her father, perhaps?'

'It would make sense.' Bunch pulled the car into the yard behind the Brighton Police HQ and switched off the engine. 'I am told she's a dog breeder so maybe I could go and see her on that pretext?'

'I thought you were getting a gun dog from some chap?'

'Not arranged anything about that, as yet. I shall toddle over and see Etta this week, but I shall naturally need some more spirit coupons.'

❧ Eleven ❧

Bunch called Harriett Beamish to arrange a visit on the pretext of viewing her dogs though there had been a distinct reluctance on the woman's part, which struck Bunch as odd. *The dog breeding business can hardly be blossoming just at this moment,* she thought. *Can't imagine my reputation has preceded me that far, so there's no reason why Etta should be so cautious. Unless someone has been warning her off. Clarrie Bell, perhaps? Whatever the reason, it's a risk I shall have to take.*

She was tempted to take the train to Chichester but an overnight raid had caused chaos on the railway lines and she dismissed the idea as impractical. *I would need to change at Brighton and I simply can't face being at it all day. A chat on the off chance with someone like Etta Beamish is simply not worth it.* As it was, the thirty-mile drive took almost two hours in patchy fog and drizzle, and she was frozen by the time she reached the Chichester Deanery in Canon Lane, a three-storey double-fronted building in red brick and sandstone. Not as grand as the Bishop's Palace but suitably imposing. The kind of building she expected to house a senior cleric.

A housekeeper led Bunch through the panelled lobby into a sitting room at the corner of the house, with views of both the driveway and the garden.

'Miss Beamish will be with your shortly.' The door closed behind the woman and Bunch prowled the room for a minute or two. It was elegantly furnished if a little Victorian, a look of fading grandeur that Bunch was accustomed to in half of the county houses that she visited. The portraits on the wall were of past incumbents of the Deanery rather than of the Beamish family. In fact there seemed little that was personal to the Archdeacon or his daughter and Bunch wondered if there was a Mrs Beamish. A divorced man of the cloth would be unheard of, and it struck her as odd that so many people she knew were bereft of one parent or the other.

'Pestilence and war,' she muttered and spun around guiltily as the door opened to admit the slender woman that was Harriett Beamish. Her dark hair was pulled back in a ferociously pinned chignon which made her complexion all the paler; her small neat features were dominated by heavy spectacles. It lent her a scholarly air which was aided and abetted by a sensible wool skirt and beige twin set. Bunch had expected something very different, knowing how Etta Beamish was viewed by people she had spoken with. *None of it fits with her reputation. A bit flighty. One of the fast set. Not this frumpy housekeeper.*

'Harriett.' She held took off her glove and held out her hand. 'Hello. I am so glad you could see me.'

'You're most welcome,' Beamish said, closing the door firmly behind her. 'I only have three pups on the books.' She turned to look at Bunch, all seriousness. 'As I told you on the telephone, they are very young and I haven't done much by way of training as yet. Are you fond of Sussex Spaniels?'

'Not had a lot to do with them, if I'm honest.'

'I should warn you they aren't for everybody.'

'Still worth a look,' Bunch replied. 'There's not that much available since the voluntary cull.'

'Good animals destroyed for no good reason. The Kennel Club is having quite a time keeping blood lines going.' Beamish smiled, a bleak twitch of her lips. 'Shall we take a look?'

She led Bunch back through the lobby, down a dark passage to the rear of the house, and ushered her out into the garden where wooden kennels emitted doleful baying. 'I have just the sire and bitch and the last of this year's litter,' she said. 'I had to cut my breeding stock when we left Oxford. Mother said it was not seemly for an Archdeacon's family to be seen feeding so many pets when people are in such dire straits.'

So there is a mother. 'Your parents are not at home today?'

'Goodness, no. I thought it was hectic at Thirkiss College but this is like a circus. My father has business with the Bishop in the palace all morning, and my mother is chairing yet another committee or other. You know how that can be. Your grandmother has always been a busy woman in that regard.'

'And you? Everyone seems to be doing something these days.'

126

'I help Father with his diary. He has secretaries of course, but there's always so much to do, and even clergy are needed by the military, so we're a little short handed.' Beamish unlatched the side door of the kennel. 'Then there these damned dogs. Excuse the noise,' she said. 'They get bored when they don't get out, so every visit is an excitement.'

'Understood.' Bunch followed her inside and the door was shut forcefully on her heels. The noise that greeted them was an assault on the senses. Five dogs milled around their pens. Three youngsters at that leggy stage of near adulthood milled around in one pen, whilst two adults occupied another. *If Sussex Spaniels could ever be leggy,* she thought. *What can I say about them? Hate to be disloyal to the county but Sussex's are not my favourite breed.* She watched them pushing and shoving for the place nearest to where she stood. Occasionally one would rear up to place paws against the partition. Their long, square backs and short legs seemed mismatched, to her, as were their broad jowly heads. These pups had wonderfully silky brown pelts which she found quite attractive. *But those huge ears?* To Bunch they might have been borrowed from another breed entirely and tacked on as an afterthought. All of the dogs were gazing up at her with lugubrious eyes and wide grins so that those floppy jowls and pink tongues exuded copious strands of drool.

She knew it would be so very easy to adore them.

'I don't heat the outside runs, at least not in daytime,' Beamish was saying, her voice raised over the din. 'Most people want them bred hardy.'

'So you keep the adults outdoors all year?' Bunch yelled back.

'They are always inside at night. My mother was concerned about "damage to the floors and fixtures" so they are here quite a bit when we're at work.' She pulled a face. Then she leaned over one of barriers avoiding eye contact as she patted and scritched indiscriminate heads and backs, and the baying gave way to ecstatic groaning.

'They are all bitches,' Beamish added. 'The male dogs went first.'

Bunch looked at the pups scampering around the pen, moaning eagerly for attention from a potential purveyor of food, and she had some sympathy for the Archdeacon's spouse. *These pooches could do some damage with those enormous feet. Not to mention the smell.* The oily pelts of this breed was efficient but nobody could deny their being aromatic. She put her finger to her upper lip and breathed through her mouth. 'Nice lookers.' She leant over the rail and was mobbed over by a noisy mass of curly ears and wagging bodies. She patted each in turn, smiling despite herself. 'Sussex Spaniels always look as if their ears have just had a quick permanent wave.' Beamish didn't reply so she plunged on. 'None of them are gun trained, I suppose?' She seriously doubted they had any training at all judging by the parent dogs who were no less vocal, throwing their heads back as they saw attention being paid to the pups and letting out a doleful cacophony. *Something,* Bunch thought, *very close to Hound of the Baskervilles, I would imagine, only shorter.* The combined baying reached fever pitch and Bunch put her hands over her ears. She was used to dogs making noise but in the close confines of the kennels it closed in on her as an almost physical pressure. Beamish seemed not to notice and made no attempt to quiet them. *Nice creatures but I am heartily glad acquiring a pup is not on the cards.*

'It's not really part of early training with these dogs,' Beamish was saying.

'Oh, all right. This is not a breed I've had much to do with.' Bunch shouted over the noise. 'We've always been more of a Labrador house. I won't count the Peke Mummy had a while back. Poor creature didn't reach two years old. Something to do with his nose.'

'That can happen with those breeds. Be quiet! Basil, Pasha. Enough now!' Beamish gave the brood bitch a brief pat and in the absence of a tail it curled its body back and forth so that she was wagging her entire body at her mistress's attention. 'They are so very excitable as pups but they do calm down. Very even temperaments.'

'So I've heard. I see you dock their tails.'

'Done young enough they barely whimper, and it saves injury out in the field. In fact I did this litter for myself. Saved a trip from the veterinary.' Beamish picked a penknife from a shelf by the side of the door and unfolded it.

The blade was bright and well cared for, the edge honed to a keen edge. Bunch still shuddered. She had paunched enough game not to be squeamish, and tail docking was commonplace, but usually done by a vet. 'Not something I think I could do for myself,' she said. 'Sheep yes. Tails can be a nuisance with flies and such.'

'A tail is a tail, no difference.' Beamish slipped the knife into the pocket of her cardigan and waved her visitor out of the kennel. 'Shouldn't leave it out here. It will rust,' she said. 'Have you seen enough? Do come in for tea and we can discuss the details in comfort.'

Bunch had a suspicion those last words were said through gritted teeth, more politeness than any desire to be sociable. She was not ready to abandon this woman just yet, however. 'Tea would be super,' she replied and soon found herself back in the sitting room at a sulking fireside.

'Only room with a fire this time of day.' Beamish gave the embers a prod with the poker. 'My father is usually out on diocesan business until dinner, or else in his study.'

'An archdeacon's life must be a busy one,' Bunch said, though she had only a passing knowledge of an archdeacon's duties.

'It is. He is happy with his new duties in spite of that. Oxford had become a very different place now that half of the faculties are closed.'

'True. I was there very recently.'

Etta Beamish grunted quietly. 'I didn't know you'd ever had any links to the halls of academe.'

Bunch bridled at the unmistakable sneer. 'Emma asked me to a formal,' she replied. 'It was all rather dull, to be perfectly honest. I suppose it suits some people.'

'The excellent Professor Tinsley? How is she? Last I heard she was avoiding her family.'

'Things are better there since her mother died, I gather, but the college has been requisitioned. I believe she's working for the Admiralty now.'

'I'd heard about her mother. Families can be such hard work.'

'At least we can choose our friends.'

'Always.'

Beamish plastered on a smile, *Which*, Bunch thought, *never strays north of her nostrils.*

'Now, about the dogs?' the younger woman said.

'Not for me I'm afraid. Smashing hounds but I really need something at least partially trained. With all of the estate work to deal with I don't have the time to start from scratch.'

'You want a working gundog?'

'Yes, I suppose I do. I was at a shoot at the Marsham's just recently and realised how much I missed my old Labrador for the fetch.'

'Then my girls are not for you. Not sure where you'll find anything part-trained at the moment but I shall keep my ears open, if it helps.'

'That would be awfully good of you. Actually I was offered an older dog at that shoot. Then I spoke with Clarice Bell and she said you had some youngsters going.'

'Tinker Bell?' There was no mistaking the shock in Harriett's face, though she covered it well, busying herself with tweaking the teapot into line with the milk jug, and the sugar tongs at right angles to them all. 'You know her well?'

'Only in passing, as one does. I've never heard Clarice called Tinker before.'

'Basil's little joke. We had private nicknames for everyone. Larry Parrish was always *The Vicar*, for obvious reasons, and he always called Penelope James *the Penny Dreadful*.'

'That seems a little unfair.'

'She deserved it. The woman led Basil on something awful.'

'Did she?' Bunch watched the woman carefully. There was no mistaking a tension in her at the mention of Clarice Bell, and the idea of Soames being Penelope James's innocent victim went against everything else Bunch had heard. 'Didn't you all come out in the same season? You're quite the party crowd, by all accounts.'

'Yes, I suppose our little coterie have been known to cut a little above the average.' The reply was sharp and followed by a silence that stretched like a well-used rubber band.

'You heard what happened to Claude Naysmith?' Bunch said at last. 'It was so close to our estate. Dodo has been quite upset over it.'

Beamish eyed her cautiously and with a hint of suspicion. 'Of course I'd heard. The police called and asked all manner of rather personal questions.'

'How perfectly beastly for you.' *And why didn't Wright tell me he'd had her questioned.* Bunch realised it was naïve to think he hadn't. *He could have said something, dammit.*

'Poor Penelope.' Her face set at the mention. 'Terrible news. However we might tease we were all very close at one time.'

That was a very rapid about-face. And how does she know so much so quickly? 'I'd rather gathered Penelope's death wasn't common knowledge.' *Small fib, but I have to play this fish.*

'Secrets seldom stay that way. Her father is a sidesman at a one of the Chichester churches, so Father and Mother know him quite well.'

'Of course. I'd forgotten about that.' Bunch glanced around the room, floundering for way to start a new topic. 'Devastating, isn't it. Losing the people we know. I suppose with all of this we shall lose a few more faces with every wave.'

'It need never have come to this.'

'Ah, yes. Your tribe are related to Lord Halifax so I suppose you heard a lot about that debate.'

'He and Mr Chamberlain fought so hard to avoid it all.'

'The time for talk has long passed. War is always such a waste, I agree. Bad enough without people crashing cars and such. Though—' Bunch leaned toward Beamish and lowered her voice '—dear Claude's death was a tragic accident but I heard tell Penny was actually bumped off. Dodo said she was rather a popular sort so God knows what brought that on her head.'

'Unfortunate,' Beamish agreed. 'Penny was more than popular with some. Especially with the chaps.'

There was an emphasis on the last word that pricked Bunch's attention. 'Clarrie Bell said she was a special pal of Jemima Harper.'

'Did she?' Beamish laughed, louder this time. 'Clarrie Bell barely knows the time of day.'

'Was she wrong?'

'Penelope and Jemima have been daggers drawn for months.'

'I didn't know that. Why were they rowing?'

'Over a man, of course. Why else do girls fall out?'

'I say. Yes, well, nothing like a chap to cause ructions. Do you know who?' She paused. Breamish's expression closed down, becoming a mask of cold detachment. 'It's not important but Dodo is bound to ask. Poor lamb feels a bit cut off, I think, with a new sprog and no petrol to get about visiting.'

'Lack of everything is a blight on us all.' Beamish looked pointedly through the window at the MG sitting in the driveway. 'Dodo rather cut herself off when she married, you know. Forgive me for saying so, but George Tinsley could be in insufferable bore.'

'I never found him that way. He would have disapproved of Clarrie's personal habits, I suspect.' She touched a finger to her nose. 'She was in a bit of a state when I saw her.'

Beamish inclined her head and then appeared to come to a decision. 'It will not hurt to say now that Penelope and Jemima had a falling out over Basil Soames,' she said. 'They both ran after him like puppies, you know. Quite shameless. Drove him quite mad at times.'

'Oh I say. I thought Penny and Claude...'

Beamish sat a little straighter in her seat. 'One hates to speak ill of the dead, but Penelope James ran wild with every man in sight. She also set her cap at Aubrey Pilkington.'

'How gauche.' Bunch smiled brightly while thinking, *So much for Christian kindness.* 'Soames and Pilkington both had reputations as men about town. I imagine you were warned about their dubious charms, your father being a man of the cloth.' She kept smiling but knew from the frozen horror and pain in Etta Beamish's eyes that she had hit a nerve. *Seems Granny's rumours may have been on the money.*

'Father never approved of him it's true, no matter how rich the family is. People don't understand Basil. He gives the impression of being something of a cad but he's jolly good fun.' Beamish smoothed the moment with a forced laugh that made Bunch feel guilty for scratching the girl's wounds.

'I had heard some such.'

'It's all in the past now.'

'Do you really think so? People do change I suppose.'

'Basil is going into politics. He can't afford to have gossip flying around.' She pursed her lips and gave Bunch a knowing stare. 'Now, I do hate to hurry you when you've come all this way but I promised to help Father with committee work, and we have a meeting in an hour's time.' Beamish got to her feet and Bunch had no option but to follow suit.

'I quite understand,' Bunch said as she was escorted to the door. 'I do hope you manage to sell your pups. I should have known they would not be right for me and I feel awful for wasting your time.'

'Not at all.' Beamish held the door open. 'Remember me to your sister.'

಄ೞ಄ೞ

Bunch could not help feeling annoyed with herself for being so clumsy in her questioning. *God, I'm such an absolute dolt. William makes it look so easy.* It was quite obvious to her that Harriett Beamish had been rattled, angered even. Yet, despite using up almost all of her petrol coupons Bunch had gained almost nothing from the meeting. *If I didn't know better, I'd say she was deliberately trying to confuse matters. Was Soames involved with Jemima? And Penny? Seems he went through those girls like a dose of salts. Odious little man, so full of himself.* There was the distinct possibility that he had indeed dallied with each of the women in turn. *If that was the case why did they stick around? Any right-thinking women would have told him to buzz off. Money or no damned money.* She needed to speak with Jemima Harper and then both Soames and Pilkington. *But God knows how, where or when.*

When she arrived home a little after lunch it was to find the Land Girls in turmoil. 'We've heard from Brenda's mum,' said Annie.

'Woah. Let me catch my breath, won't you, girls?' Bunch prised herself out of the MG and stretched her back. 'I shan't need it again today, Burse,' she called to the groom-chauffeur. 'Give her a clean and put her away, thank you. Now, Kate, let's get out of this rain, shall we? First things first, has Perry been exercised today?'

'We thought it was a bit cold and wet for him. Mrs Westgate took the cart down to the village yesterday, so Maggie has had a stretch, but Perry and Robbo haven't ridden out for a couple of days.'

'Well, it's slackening off so I can take Perry out for a bit of a hack, over to see Mrs Tinsley later. Poor old Robbo will have to wait, I'm afraid. Shame the hunt isn't running so often or I'd loan him out. I can saddle Perry up so no need for you to hang around.' She crowded the two young women into the temporary estate office sited in the stable yard and settled herself in the battered

133

captain's chair. 'Now, what's the buzz with young Brenda?'

'Her mother sent us a letter,' said Annie. 'Too much to put in a telegram.'

'Has something happened to her?'

'"Fraid so.' Annie glanced at Kate.

'She in hospital.' Kate looked down at her clasped hands. 'Very ill by all accounts.'

'Goodness. Was she caught in a raid?' Bunch caught another guilty glance pass between the two Land Girls and a certainty came to mind. 'The baby?' she asked.

'Gone.'

'A miscarriage? Or – by other means?'

'She went to some local woman that her aunt knew and well, you can imagine.'

Bunch sat back with hands together, fingertips pressed against her bottom lip. It was impossible not to draw comparisons between the fate of Harriett Beamish and that of Brenda Green, in not dissimilar circumstances. *A discreet Swiss clinic versus some backstreet in Lambeth. It's no kind of choice, at least not for poor Brenda.* 'She's in danger?' she said at last.

'Terribly ill, I gather – from what her mother said.' Kate was looking down at her hands again.

'I sense a *but* in the offing.'

'Police have arrested her 'cos she won't tell 'em who she went to.' Annie leaned forward. 'Handcuffed 'er to the bed, so 'er mum says. I don't hold with what she did but she ain't no criminal, Miss. It ain't right.'

'She does need our help, Miss,' said Kate.

Their abandoning of the affectionate "Boss" in favour of formal deference spoke of desperation. She knew her band of Land Girls had always been tightknit – more like sisters in the way they squabbled amongst themselves, but stood united should one of them be under attack. It was a bond that had grown stronger since Mary Tucker had been shot and killed in January. The two women stared at Bunch with expectation oozing from every pore.

Bunch was not entirely sure what they expected she could do. Such an abortion was illegal. Because their very nature was clandestine, when things went wrong and lives were put in danger the hospital had no choice but to inform the police. She'd heard of charges being dropped provided the unfortunate women had given details of the abortionist, but life was seldom that simple. Many would rather chance prison because the penalty for a 'snitch' amongst her neighbours would be far harder and last longer than a short stretch at His Majesty's pleasure. Or perhaps those potential mothers had been taken to some uninhabited and insanitary building for the procedure and they never knew who their abortionist was. Knowing the area Brenda came from, Bunch felt it unlikely the young woman would reveal anything to the police. 'How can I help?' she said.

'Well … we thought perhaps you could put in a word, somehow.' Kate produced an envelope from her pocket. Besides, Mrs Green says Brenda may not survive. Even if she does, she'll never have children. Isn't that punishment enough?'

'I totally agree but it is the law.' She looked at the faces in front of her, two pairs of puppy-round eyes gazing back, mute, imploring. They reminded her of Roger, and she sighed. Dogs were on her mind today and she missed canine company all the more. It took an effort not to drop her hand to the side of the chair where Roger had often sat. 'I will ask but I promise nothing. Let's hope the Metropolitan Police have more urgent business than prosecuting a gravely ill young woman.'

'Thank you, Boss.' Kate got to her feet. 'We really are most awfully grateful. Shall I write to Mrs Green?'

'Yes, do. I shall write myself when I have something to say, but meanwhile do send her my regards.'

'Yes, Boss. Come on Annie. We've got cows to milk.'

The door swung to behind them and Bunch listened as they clattered out of the stable yard in the direction of the farm. She felt a little guilty that she had earlier put the disappearance of Brenda Green to the back of her mind. Though she was no longer Land Army Co-ordinator for the area the women working for the estate were her responsibility. Brenda Green had not been with them for long but she was a pleasant girl who had pitched into any task handed her.

It was not the day to disturb her uncle and use his position in the police force to pull strings. She reached across and pick up the telephone to put a call through to DCI Wright.

'Can't talk now. I have a crime scene to attend.' Wrights voice was gravelly, his fatigue evident in every syllable. 'Nothing to do with the James case, I hasten to add. Some poor squaddie ended up stabbed in a dark alley.'

'Poor chap.'

'With people moving around the country as much as they are, nobody knows who's alive and who's dead up there right now.'

Bunch heard his breath whisper across the mouthpiece as he sighed, and she could picture him rubbing his hand back and fore over the top of his head, the way he always did when a query bothered him. *Poor old duck is totally fagged,* she thought. 'Was it in Brighton?' she said aloud.

'No, as it happens. It's in Shoreham.'

'Not so far from here then. Come for dinner. We can have a jolly good chinwag, compare notes, and you can have an evening's peace and quiet. I will have Knapp prepare a room to save you driving all that way back in the dark.'

'I…'

'You need the rest,' she said. 'Cook always expects one more at table as a matter of course, and you'll be doing me a favour, anyway. Mother is less likely to kick off when we have a guest.'

'How is she?'

'Bloody hell incarnate. I wish she'd go to that spa Daddy has been on about. She's hates the country at best of times, she feels trapped here now. Keeps referring to the Dower as the "nunnery". I swear Granny was going to clock her one with the dinner gong last night. I can tell you, it takes some effort to ruffle the feathers of Beatrice Courtney, at least on the outside.'

'You make it sound so inviting.'

'Look on it as a blood sport. They may have discovered an ancient arena in Chichester a few years back, but those Romans had nothing on us Courtneys. See you at six?'

'Okay, fine. Now I have to go, Rose. I shall see you later.'

'Don't forget, Granny insists we dress so bring your best bib and tucker.'

'I won't forget.'

She replaced the handset and picked it up again within seconds, jiggling the cradle and asking the exchange to get her the Senior Commandant, Leonora Fairdene at the ATS Barracks at Camberley, Surrey.

'Fairdene.' Just hearing those familiar fruity tones was enough to make her slide her feet from the desk edge and sit to attention.

'Commandant Fairdene. Good afternoon, Ma'am. Rose Courtney here.'

'Deputy Commander Courtney. Good to hear from you. Now before you ask, no, you can't take a third medical, and yes you are invalided out for all of the foreseeable. Now that we've got that over and done with, for what else might I owe you the pleasure?'

I asked for that one, Bunch thought. She could not help grinning at the officer's bluntness. There had been a time, after her return from France, when she had been calling her old CO almost weekly in an effort to claw back her commission. To her credit, Fairdene had always been very polite but totally implacable on the matter. 'No, I've given up on that one. Daddy has me pushing pens here at the old pile.'

'I'd heard he was practically living at the War Office.'

'Needs must.'

'As you say. So what's bothering you enough to call me?'

'I was rather hoping you could help me track down an ATS girl. I was told she was under your command but that's as far as it got. You know how it can be when you hit that wall.'

'Lord yes. British Army runs on red tape and tea. Who did you want to find?'

'A young woman by the name of Jemima Harper?'

'Oh, her.' Fairdene's tone grew cooler. 'What would you want to ask?'

'I just needed a quick chat really.'

'She's in demand. Some damnable civvie plod named Carter has been pestering my clerks about Harper all week. What's doing?'

Bunch pursed her lips, staring straight ahead at the bulldog clip full of receipts dangling down the wall on frayed hemp string. She could dissemble, spin Fairdene a yarn. *Probably not a good idea. Fairdene's not one to forget or forgive.* 'A friend of hers was murdered and she might have some little snippets that could help us.'

'Us?'

Damn it. Bunch grimaced at her slip up. 'I'm a consultant for the Sussex Constabulary,' she replied.

'Then I shall tell you that I have ordered the police to go

through channels. I will not have them disrupt my command. I am rather disappointed in you, Courtney. Thought you were above playing games.'

'I'm not actually a police officer,' she said. 'Merely helping with this case because, well, there have been two murders actually. Both naval types. I can't say too much but you can imagine anything they were involved with could be vital.' She grimaced, eyes closed, as she waited for an interminable pause to pass. 'National security,' she added.

'If that is the case surely the relevant Admiralty departments would be involved.'

'Yes, Ma'am, but they've kicked it into the rough. You know how those chaps at Greenwich can be. Positively obstructive.'

'They can be tiresome I agree.' Fairdene's breath was even but distinctly audible in the long quiet. 'All right, Courtney. I shall have Harper informed that you called.'

'Thank you, Ma'am, I won't forget it.'

'No.' Fairdene's voice was dry. 'You won't.'

'And about my commission...'

'For the fortieth and final time, no.' Her voice lowered slightly. 'Look, I would have you in a flash. Company Commander at very least, but the decision came about way above my grade so please don't ask me again.'

'No, Ma'am. Sorry, Ma'am.'

'Was that all?'

'I suppose so.'

'Then I shall have to go. I have a cart load of brass descending in an hour's time. Good to hear from you, Courtney. I shall pass a message on to Harper. Goodbye for now.'

The connection cut abruptly and Bunch was left staring at that bulldog clip once more, feeling a little bruised by the encounter. She had seen Fairdene as a friend as well as officer so she had not expected to be given the military sidestep. The question of who above Fairdene was doing the dance was not something she felt she wanted to ask.

The answer's bound to be one that I don't want to hear. In which case there is only one course of action open to me. She got abruptly to her feet. *I may just get in a half-hour's ride before Wright arrives.*

'But first, the not so small matter of young Brenda.' She picked up the phone once more and asked for Chief Police Commissioner. 'Hello? Uncle Walter?'

ৡৢৡৢ

Bunch rode, first of all, to the viaduct to check for any sign of the trekkers. It was turning colder and she was concerned at the thought of a young family out in such weather. Dismounting at the spot where she had seen the Vales and Jenkinses, she examined the remnants of their fire, which was little more than a few sticks of blackened wood and ash washed into the grass by the recent downpours. Otherwise there were only a few faint tyre prints. She pushed at their raised edges and noted grimly how they were already icing up. It was going to be a cold night and she was glad that the families were gone, for their own sake; it was not the weather for sleeping in vans however many blankets they might have.

A glance at her watch told her she had an hour's daylight left and she remounted and followed the Inchett road to Lych Hill and stared at the spot where Naysmith had died. 'Or where the car ended up at least,' she muttered. The car had long since been towed away; there was little sign of the crash other than churned earth.

'Walk on.' She urged Perry forward, tracking back up the slope until she came across the marker left by the police where it was thought that the car had started its final run. There had been a thorough search of the area. The girls working on the field had had a bird's eye view and given her a good report. Nothing had been found there to indicate who had set the car containing Naysmith's dead body in motion. Or if he had even been killed here.

She pushed Perry forward at a slow walk, her attention fixed on the ground. She had no idea what she was looking for, and she was well aware that this road had also been searched thoroughly. She arrived at the Y-junction. Left went back toward Inchett; sharp right was a narrow lane, little more than a car's width, with the added impediment of a fording place impassable in bad weather, but which was a short cut that eventually join up with the main road.

'What if he never intended to go to Parrish's?' She turned Perry down the right fork and trotted a short way along it to the first

139

passing point. Dismounting she examined the space that curled into the bank, long enough to accommodate a Sussex cart and horse. *Or two cars.* Why would he have stopped, if at all? Nor could she understand how he had been run off the road when driving such a high-powered car. Yes, the witnesses had said he was pursued by something equally fast. *Or what if he'd stopped to confront his pursuer? Unlikely but possible.*

Bunch looked up and down the road. Not a building in sight, no window or garden overlooking the spot. *Hard to find a better place for an ambush – or maybe an assignation? Did Naysmith arrange to meet this person, who then turned out to be his killer? His car was rammed, according to the report, which makes it unlikely.*

The day was growing darker and colder by the minute and she could feel Perry's cooling muscles trembling with the cold. She pulled her scarf a little tighter round her neck and took a final look at the lane. There seemed no point searching ground that Wright's men had already covered. She headed back to the Dower.

The sun, somewhere behind the cloud cover, was sinking below the horizon when Perry clattered across the cobbled yard. She slid from the saddle and led him into the stables. The interior was gloomy but she was reluctant to light lamps with all the faff of blackout that it involved. She removed saddle and tack by touch and long practice, and rugged him against the cold with a light cover. He uttered low whickering noises at her as she fastened the straps beneath his belly, pushing against her so that she could feel the noise as vibrations that began deep in his broad chest and emerged as a throaty rumble. She pulled a wedge of hay from the bale in the walkway and re-stuffed his net, laughing as Robbo and Maggie snickered more loudly, heads nodding emphatically as they demanded their share.

'All right you greedy creatures.' Bunch lobbed a small wedge of hay over their stall doors with a chuckle. 'That will keep you busy. It's too early for your mash. Burse will mix that later. Goodnight.'

She stood by the main door for a few moments, breathing in the sweetish odour of horse and hay and ancient dust, and listened to the three beasts shuffling and muttering. They were at peace, and being in their company brought her a peace of her own. She slipped out into the yard and latched the double doors behind her. The shadows were deep now and there was a stiffening southerly breeze coming straight from the continent, with a hint of brine plucked from the channel en route. She took a deep breath of its cold sharpness. The forecast had not been for snow but she would not be surprised if there were a flurry or two.

The moaning of a lone plane made her freeze, staring up and listening intently. It was a small craft headed out toward the coast, which seemed odd. It was not a fighter or even a solitary bomber and she relaxed. Raids continued in the capital, across the night skies over the southern counties, and people in the 'bomb alley' of Sussex and Kent had learned to take cover on the return flights as crews who had not managed to reach a suitable target dropped their payload before returning to base. She was no expert but had taken flying lessons a few years previously. *And that,* she thought, *is not the usual military craft.*

She was still standing there when the police Wolseley swung into the yard.

'Tradesman's entrance?' she called as Wright emerged from the driver's seat and stretched.

'I know my place.' Wright hauled himself from the driver's seat and stretched. 'It's been a very long day so I hope you have plenty of scotch put by.'

'No Glossop?' she said.

'She's got a four-day pass. Family emergency.'

There was no answer to give. Family emergency had become a common euphemism for someone missing, or worse. Bunch bobbed her head by way of acknowledgement. 'You're just in good time.' She gestured toward the Dower house. 'Granny will be serving tea shortly and she will have a fit if I waltz in wearing jods.' She grinned. 'She was quite the radical in her day, but she has standards that will not be argued with. Your parking round the back is handy. We can pretend we're not in yet and have tea in the kitchen, if that's all right with you?'

'Whatever you say.'

'Trust me. The atmosphere in the drawing room as far chillier than out in this yard.' She led the way into the kitchen and slid onto the bench seat at the long kitchen table, looking at Cook and Knapp and Lizzie in turn, a finger to her lips.

Knapp, who had been loading a tray, silently removed the two cups and saucers she had just added to it, placing them instead in front of Bunch and Wright. She added plates with several sandwiches and some cake, and withdrew leaving Cook and Lizzie Hurst at the far end of the room busying themselves with preparations for dinner.

Bunch relayed her meeting with Harriett Beamish as she poured tea.

'So you think she was lying?' Wright helped himself to one of the dainty triangles of potted-meat sandwiches, which Bunch thought looked faintly incongruous. *He looks more like a doorstop-and-wedge-of-cheese man.*

'It was hard to be sure either way,' she said. 'She certainly was not telling me everything, not by a long chalk. My fault, I dare say. I wasn't as subtle as I might have been. She did say that the local police had questioned her, and that seemed to rankle. Perhaps she was just being touchy.'

'I've read her statement and she does appear to have been in Chichester at the time of Penny James's death.'

'You don't think that's right?'

'The lads over at that station dealt with it. Her alibi is a special service for the victims and survivors of the Coventry Blitz. Half of the Bishop's staff were there.'

'If they saw her that's it, isn't it?'

Wright chewed for a moment, gazing toward the women intent on their tasks and lowered his voice a fraction. 'Nobody at the service seemed to have spoken with her. Some are positive they saw her but they could easily have simply assumed she was there.'

'That's a little harsh. I mean if they saw her, they did.'

He grunted and took a gulp of tea.

'What about the other names on the list?' she said.

'The Pilkington chap told DS Carter that he was at his club, which seems to be correct from the signing-in book. I had the Metropolitan force check it out. Barrington-Soames claims to have been at his family's estate but we've no way of verifying that. The constable sent up to the house to make enquiries told Carter the butler was not inclined to be very helpful. Kept repeating that, "the young Mr Soames had been at home that weekend, but no, he could not possibly say what the young gentlemen's movements had been".'

'The perfect servant.'

142

'Seems that way. The Harper girl was on duty, but since she's a driver she could have been anywhere.'

'I've been onto that. Waiting for her secondment details.'

'You may get further than us. Her CO was stone walling. All these military types do when it comes to dealing with civilian authorities. They resent us and it makes it damned difficult to get anything without permission in triplicate.'

'Through official channels. Which can take weeks.'

'Exactly so.'

'I have my contacts there so we shall see. What are you doing about chatting with Soames and Pilkington? I assume their statements don't really cut it?'

'Tricky. Pilkington's movements are protected by his job. Can't even get a pass to enter the place.'

'Then we shall have to beard him outside of the den. Leave it with me. Ah, Knapp.' Bunch paused to greet the housekeeper. 'Can you get a room ready for Chief Inspector Wright, please?'

'Yes, Miss Rose. There is the China Room. Lizzie, will you see to that.'

'Thank you, Mrs Knapp,' Wright said.

'Good, then I shall go and bathe before I dress. Lizzie will show you your room, William.'

ঌয়ঌয়

There was a certain amount of guilt in abandoning Wright for the two hours before dinner would be served, but only a very little. Bunch felt the need for a break. Her drive to Chichester followed by riding out had exhausted her, and her old injury was radiating a deep nagging pain. *Like toothache in my bones.*

She wafted the water around her, mixing the cooling liquid closest to the cast iron of the bath with the rest, and breathed in Attar of Roses with a deep sigh, wishing she could just doze there in that warming solitude. But there were only so many times she could top-up with hot water, and her fingertips were beginning to pleat into deep ridges.

She hauled herself out, standing for a moment to easy her aching leg and then went to dry herself. Though she preferred to forgo the lady's maid her mother had, or the assistance Beatrice demanded from Knapp, she was grateful that Lizzie had laid out the blue-grey silk bought in Milan three years previously. She almost put it back as it seemed rather dull at first glance, but as she picked it up it shimmered under the lights. Against her dark complexion it always flattered.

Sitting before her mirror she contemplated her hair, bobbed even shorter now, just grazing her jawline. She reached for a snood to satisfy expectations of evening dress but put it back again. *Why should I pretend I have long hair for form's sake?* Instead she fastened a pair of sapphire drops to her ears and a matching necklace and surveyed the result. *You'll do.*

She descended the stairs just as Knapp sounded the first gong. Wright was talking with, or rather listening to, her father and Barty. She crossed to side table and poured a small sherry. Wright glanced at her as she entered and gave a small tweak of his head in acknowledgement. Whatever Edward had to say appeared to engross him and she had time to think how Wright looked surprisingly at ease in evening jacket before her sister called her over.

'Hello stranger.' Dodo held her hand out for Bunch to grasp and tilted her head to greet her with a kiss to the cheek. 'Where have you been? I haven't seen you for ages.'

'Yes, sorry. Been a bit tied up. Hard to fit everything in.'

'I can understand the distraction.' Dodo gave Wright a significant look. 'He scrubs up rather well, doesn't he?'

'Stop that this instant. Wright is a colleague.' Bunch scowled into her sherry as she took a sip. 'No Emma?'

'She's out. We hardly see her these days.'

'Not surprised. Tell her to give me a call when you see her next.'

'All right. Any reason?'

'No ... just something she might be able to throw light on. Did you know Penny James and Claude Naysmith were married?'

'Gosh, no. That would put Etta's nose out of joint. She had rather a thing for him, you know.'

'I thought she had her sights set on Droopy Soames?'

'She may well have at some point. By all accounts, I heard that crowd were at it like rabbits.'

'Daphne!' Theadora snapped. 'Don't be course. Bad enough your sister has abandoned social graces.' Theadora timed her entrance to coincide with the dinner gong's second roll.

Bunch confined her outward reaction to winking at Dodo and

they drifted toward the dining room. Theadora's bright cheeks, despite the powder, had not escaped Bunch's notice, nor the perfumed sweetness of violet cachous. She had seen almost as little of her mother as her sister in the past week notwithstanding their recent argument. Theadora took breakfast in her room and often failed to appear for dinner. Bunch was not sure if it was down to her health or a wish to avoid Beatrice. *Probably a little of both.* The old adage that two women could not be mistress of the same house was apt, at least with those two, and it was not improving with time.

Beatrice was using that advantage even now, asserting her seniority and commandeering Wright as the unattached male at an uneven table, to lead him into dinner, pushing her son and daughter-in-law into second place. Dodo as always was escorted by Barty, leaving Bunch to bring up a solitary rear.

From the looks her mother was giving her, when it was Wright and not Barty Tinsley that Bunch was seated next to, she realised that she may have maligned Beatrice. *I have no idea why Mummy has the idea there is anything between me and Wright. Even if there were, which there isn't, why is she throwing a fit? He's a good sort. But then Mother is being dizzy headed over just about everything.* Bunch was surprised at her mother's blatant hostility. She had years perfecting her skills as hostess for dinners and balls and house parties, and it was out of character. *Which is deeply worrying. I should really be around more.*

She watched Theadora's waspish mood make for stilted conversation throughout dinner, and realised it was not through any kind of personal enmity. *Mummy is being equally vile to everyone.* She wondered if her mother had received any further news on her health. *Or maybe it's just the booze.* She surveyed the plethora of glasses. It was too much to hope that Theadora would abstain when the table was awash with wines, with a fresh vintage to accompany every course.

'Ladies.' Beatrice got to her feet. 'Shall we? If you would, Rose?' She waited, leaning on her stick with her right hand and left elbow raised for her granddaughter to take.

Bunch had wanted to chance her arm and stay for port and cigars but Beatrice knew her too well, and the three generations of Courtney women withdrew without a murmur. Knapp brought them coffee in the drawing room as Bunch was busying herself, agitating the logs in the grate into fresh life.

'Oh, for God's sake, Rose. I know you don't care about fashion but one doesn't stoke fires wearing a Schiaparelli frock. Knapp? See to it, will you,' Beatrice said.

'Yes, Granny,' Bunch crossed to the table to pour herself a large scotch, carefully avoiding the sight of the housekeeper bending to add logs to the blaze.

'Will that be all, Madam?' Knapp looked pointedly past Theadora to Beatrice.

'Yes, thank you.' Beatrice replied. 'Tell the staff they may retire. Lizzie can clear up in the morning. Good night, Knapp.'

'Thank you, Madam.'

Bunch lit the cigarette in her holder and watched in silence as Theadora refilled her glass, noting the slight tremor in her mother's stick-thin wrist that struggled to lift the crystal decanter. Theadora swilled back half of the large tumbler that she had poured and glared at her daughters and mother-in-law. 'What?' she snapped. 'What? Too late for parsimony. Felicity Ephrin was quite clear about that when she called.'

So she had more news. 'When did she call?'

'Yesterday.'

'And—'

'Nothing we don't already know.' She reached for the tantalus once more.

'Enough.' Beatrice's cane slapped the floor. 'This is not how we do things.'

'You may not. Or her.' Theadora sloshed what remained in her tumbler as she waved at her eldest daughter. 'All for one and one for Perringham. Hoorah for Courtneys.'

Dodo reached forward to catch her hand. 'Mummy, don't. We know you're unwell and we want to help. Truly. I want Georgi to know you. Please…'

'That will be a distinct change to—'

'That is hardly fair,' Bunch said. 'If we share more with Granny, it's only because she's here with us.'

'You think we had a choice? Don't be naïve.'

'When you're home in Sussex you are never… I know there are bad memories here, but Edward and Benedict are gone but we are still here.' Bunch was aware of a collective intake of breaths at the mention of her deceased brothers, names never mentioned in Theadora's presence, and Bunch felt an immediate guilt. Theadora was glowering at her elder daughter, eyes glittering, and Bunch almost took a step back. Stubbornness alone made her tilt her chin and meet the ancient anger head on. 'We were here,' she whispered, 'are here. Dodo won't remember them, naturally, because she was only a baby but I was ten years old, and I remember them quite clearly. Daddy does quite obviously – they were his sons too. And Granny's only grandsons. We do understand, truly we do. No amount of time will erase their memory.' *Twenty years ago. God, how did I miss that?* 'We would miss you every bit as much.'

Theadora stood motionless, her stare still locked with her daughter's. Their relationship may not have been as close as many mothers and daughters, but active dislike had not been a part of it. *The ability to communicate, however, has always been sadly lacking.* Bunch broke eye contact first, glancing at Dodo and Beatrice in turn. There was resignation in both their faces, each expecting an ice war to erupt. At Perringham House it had been easy to avoid seeing people for days at a time so that disagreements were not so much settled as passed by. *Perhaps now is the time, of all times, to break the cycle.* 'I'm not trying to make much of all that. Far from it. I – we are all terribly worried about you. Surely the stiff-upper lip thing can be relaxed a little with us? Tell us what the doctor said, please Mummy.'

'I have a great many duties, Rose. Not one of them will benefit from weakness.'

'Hardly weakness.'

'Isn't it?' Theadora dropped her head forward, chin almost touching the ornate necklace glittering at her throat. 'I think it most probably is. That and resentment. Excuse me, but I have a headache.'

The door closed quietly on Theadora's heels leaving a silence that none of the remaining three felt adequate to puncture for some seconds. Theadora's parting shot hurt and Bunch wondered how much of it was true. Had she resented the grief her mother had shown for the boys? Did Theadora resent the fact that Bunch had survived the flu where her older siblings had not? Beatrice's voice broke into her thoughts. 'Rose, my dear child, you do know it's the drink talking.'

She turned to smile. 'I know, Granny. Have you any idea what Ephrin told her?'

'Rather confirming what was said before, according to Edward.'

'Yet still she drinks. What can we possibly do to help her?'

'I think your father has it in hand. The gentlemen are coming through and I think Edward would much rather not have this discussed in front of your policeman friend.'

♚ Twelve ♛

'Is that you, Courtney? CCO Fairdene here. You asked me to track down Jemima Harper.'

Bunch glanced at her watch and suppressed a yawn. 'I did indeed, Ma'am. Have you found her?'

'We are not in the habit of misplacing personnel. Harper is part of our driver pool in the southern division.'

'Naturally,' Bunch said. 'The high-ups should be able to find better things for intelligent women to do that doesn't involve filing, cooking or driving.'

'It's getting better. We shall be doing a great deal more, quite soon.'

'Only because they are running out of men.'

Fairdene chortled quietly. 'Did you want to hear about Harper or not?'

'Sorry, Ma'am. Go ahead.'

'She's stationed out of here at Camberley but by a stroke of sheer luck she is currently driving for Colonel Langford, Royal Sussex regiment. You may even know him. It was the same outfit you drove for with the BEF, I believe. Currently based not twenty miles from you, just outside of Brighton.'

'That's rather splendid. How may I get hold of her?'

'Langford has stood her down until later tonight. She is driving up to see her parents and tells me she will visit your sister on her way.'

'Dodo? Why not here?'

'I am not your messenger, Courtney. Make the most of it. You know how hard it is to get a grip on drivers when their passengers are pottering about all over the shop.'

'Twenty percent of their duty hours driving their assignment all around the place and the remaining eighty or so kicking their heels outside some officer's club, or worse.'

'In a nutshell.'

'Thank you, Ma'am. I very much appreciate your help.'

'Pleasure. Always glad to hear from you. Provided it's not about another dammed medical. Between you and your father, I was getting quite dizzy. Now, duty calls. Speak to you soon, Courtney. Toodle-pip.'

The connection was cut and Bunch was left fuming after learning that her father was calling her old commander. *He has no right.* She replaced the receiver and wandered back to a somewhat depleted breakfast gathering. She did not expect to see Theadora but Beatrice, despite her frailty and years was usually up bright and early for the ten o'clock service, was also absent.

'Mother is feeling a bit under the weather,' Edward said.

'Granny has been a little fragile since the weather turned colder,' Bunch agreed. 'We need to find her a new maid-companion. She's adamant she doesn't need anyone but Knapp simply doesn't have time to give her all the attention she needs. Granny struggles far more than she will admit.'

'You're right. Meanwhile, she says she won't be up in time for church so that duty will fall on the two of us. All hell will break loose if we don't attend.' He glanced at Wright. 'No pun intended. You do attend services?'

'Not as often as I should,' Wright replied. 'My job makes it impossible to keep regular hours. If I have a rare Sunday morning—'

'Quite.' Edward smiled. 'I hope it's a habit my daughter will regain. Rather a sense of duty involved with such things. The family is expected to be there.'

'Understood. I shall have to forgo the pleasure this morning however.'

'Oh, do hang around,' Bunch said. 'That was my old CO on the blower. She tells me Jemmy Harper will be dropping by today.'

'Here?'

'At Dodo's, I gather.'

'Why not here?'

Bunch raised her shoulders, head tilted. 'I have no idea but we should get over there when we've eaten.' She pulled a face at her father. 'Sorry, Daddy, I shall do my best to make Morning Service. May even arm twist Dodo, but if I can't make it, I shall do

Evensong. I promise.'

'You'd better,' Edward grumbled.

'You're a brick.' Bunch crossed to the serving dishes and lifted a couple of lids and returned to her seat with bacon and scrambled eggs. 'I miss the old days,' she grumbled. 'Not had any kidneys for ages. Nor kedgeree.' She helped herself to toast from the rack and scrapped butter onto its crisp surface and paused to watch Wright trying to spread half a single curl across his slice, and pushed the butter dish a little closer to him. 'Thank heavens Cook made us a little extra butter this week. I do so hate dry toast, don't you?'

'Us town folk don't have a choice.' He grunted but scooped a second curl.

'You don't ride do you?' she said.

'No. I have a perfectly good car, thank you.'

'Spoilsport. All right we shall drive if you insist.'

♥♥♥♥

The drab-green Austin staff car already sitting in the driveway seemed bright against the frost rime that covered the grass, gravel and shrubs that surrounded it.

'December comes in with a crackle.' Wright pulled the black Wolesley up beside it and opened the door allowing in a cold bubble of air to prove his point. 'Clear nights make for cold days.' He looked up at the cloudless sky. 'Bombers love a clear night.'

'The girls will be pleased. They have been hating the field work in the rain,' said Bunch.

'Cold mud isn't any fun,' he replied. 'I saw enough of it to know.'

She didn't reply. Wright seldom referred to his short time in the trenches but as it had ended close to the armistice, she guessed he had seen his share of semi-frozen clay. 'Let's get in and see Jemmy Harper.'

'She beat us here,' said Wright. 'I hope your sister hasn't given too much away.'

'Dodo's a good egg. She knows exactly what to say.'

'We can hope.' He put on his best smile as the door was opened by the elderly butler.

'Morning, Mason. Is my sister up and about?'

'Yes, Miss Rose. Mrs Tinsley is in the breakfast room. She has an early guest.'

151

'So I gather. Pop down and tell Cook to send up extra cups and coffee if you have any?'

'I believe there is coffee already on the trivet, Miss. You were expected.'

'Good show.' Bunch handed him her jacket and headed across the hallway to the manor's small breakfast room. 'Morning Dodo. Up and about early I see. Morning Barty. And good morning Jemima.' She proffered her hand to the slender young woman in army serge seated next to her sister. 'We have met before, though you may not remember me.'

'I do. We were all a little in awe of you. Dodo's big sister.' Harper shook hands and smiled. 'Even the chaps.' She looked beyond Bunch to Wright. 'I understand this is Chief Inspector Wright. How do you do? My CO told me I was wanted by the police. In the nicest possible way. Daphne told me your name.'

She smiled again at Wright, flashing perfect teeth in a full-lipped mouth. She had high cheek bones, wide-set brown eyes and a firm chin, and her light-brown hair was scraped back into a neatly coiled bun. Bunch recalled it being braided and coiled over her head in the past, but she could imagine how unpopular that Germanic style would be right now. 'Did Dodo tell you what we need to ask?' Bunch poured two cups of coffee from the pot sitting on the trivet for herself and Wright and took a seat. 'If you don't mind?'

'Don't mind at all. CO said you wanted to ask about poor Penny. If it helps to find her killer then fire away. All in strict confidence?'

Bunch looked at Barty. His face fell for a brief moment and she felt sorry for him. The exposure of his wife's criminality, in this very house almost a year ago, had lost him his seat as a magistrate and came close to losing him his freedom. Though he had reclaimed a great deal through his Home Guard activity, she knew he keenly felt the loss of trust by the authorities.

Barty managed a laugh as he got to his feet. 'I have to get the horse ready. Taken a leaf out of your book, Rose. Got a cart for Dodo's mare. She's a rather small beast for a hunter but just fits with some adjustments to the shafts.'

'You put Tilly into harness?' Bunch laughed. 'That creature has bees in her bridle!'

'Good as gold provided she's blinkered. She's a better temperament than that the Vanner brute you bought back in the summer. I don't understand how a horsewoman such as you has a penchant for such ugly horses.'

'They generally have more interesting characters,' she replied. 'And I like a challenge.'

'I prefer a horse that isn't going to take chunks out of the hired help.' Barty laughed, a loud braying, pleased at his own joke. 'Now I shall leave you to your discussion. Ladies. Wright.' He smiled all round and left.

'I feel a little mean,' Harper said. 'Driving a man from his breakfast.'

'He'll be fine,' said Dodo.

'Miss Harper, can you tell me where you were on the night of twelfth into thirteenth of November?' said Wright.

'Thought you'd ask that. I looked up my log sheets and I was outside the *In & Out* club most of the night. Or rather the car was. I was sitting in a basement shelter with a bloody air raid raging overhead.' She grinned. 'There are plenty witnesses. Other drivers. Some of the Club members.'

'That settles that, at least.' Bunch beamed at Harper. 'Such a nuisance asking people these questions but it has to be done. Now, tell me about Penny and Claude. How long were they sweet?'

'Can't recall. Quite a while I think.'

'And you were happy for them?'

Harper looked puzzled. 'Yes. Of course.'

'I'd heard you weren't always so keen.'

'What?'

'I'd heard you were angry at Penny for her involvement with Basil Soames.'

'Me?' She ran a hand over her head. 'Yes, I had a few dates with Basil but it was never serious. He's such a hound. Quite charming and tremendous fun but a complete hound. I was quite glad when he moved on to another conquest.'

'Why would that be?'

'Because there wasn't room in that head of his for any girl plus his ego. He's amazingly generous, though. First bottles of Moet at the Café de Paris are always on him. He's not the kind of chap I would attempt to waltz down the aisle, however, whatever my sainted mother would have liked.'

'Your mother?' Wright said. 'What role does she have in all this?'

'The role of any mother. Landing a rich son-in-law is the raison d'etre for all mothers of good breeding,' Bunch replied. 'After a title they hold the greatest respect for the size of a chap's wallet. They can get quite despondent if a girl voices a preference for personality to go with it.' She looked at Jemima Harper. 'So it was your mother who was disappointed? Not yourself?'

'Oh heavens, yes.'

'Because we heard a different story entirely. That you held a torch for Soames and got rather upset when he dropped you for someone else.'

'I may not be a genius but I do know my own mind. Believe me, I never had any intention of marrying Basil Barrington-Soames!'

'Harriett Beamish claims you and Penny James rowed over him. That it was one step short of a cat fight and you'd hated each other ever since.'

'Etta said that?' Harper scratched thoughtfully at her cheek. 'I think most of the girls had a little tilt for him at some point. He was quite the catch in debutante terms. Still is, I suppose. Then I had a few dates with Pilky, and Larry Parrish, and I didn't marry either of them, either. Pilkington also took Etta out a few times. And Clarrie Bell. And so on and so on. You know how the season goes. We try these chaps on for size. Most are a shocking fit and we move on to the next.'

'A lot of frogs to be kissed,' Bunch said with a slow grin, 'and very few princes to show for it.'

The women exchanged nods; mutual understanding had been reached. 'Truth to tell, this war, awful as it is, has been a godsend from that standpoint.' Jemima Harper waved a hand at her uniform. 'Perfect excuse to jump off that merry-go-round, for a while at least. Why this obsession with my love life? It's no better or worse than Penny James's. Better than Etta Beamish's. Don't be fooled by her vicar's daughter charade. She's a piranha.'

'I hear she had a trip to a Swiss clinic?' said Bunch. 'Sorry to be indelicate, but were you aware of that?'

'Of course.' Harper snorted. 'You can't drop off the scene for six months or so and not expect people to add it up. Did you know Clarrie Bell went with her?'

'We didn't.'

'Clarrie Bell is Etta's lapdog. Always has been. But Etta's mystery trip is ancient history. Nineteen thirty-six was it? Or seven? Why would that interest you now?'

'We are simply eliminating the impossible,' Wright replied. 'Can you think of any reason why someone else would want Penny and Naysmith dead?'

Harper shook her head. 'No. They were both rather sweet. Not anywhere near so flaky as the rest of us. We were seeing less and less of them. Something to do with their postings? They were both really secretive about that.' Harper sat back in her chair. 'It raised a few eyebrows, to be frank. Our crowd are not exactly discreet, so those two refusing to cough up the where and the what didn't go down so well. Soames was quite put out. He sees it as his right to know everything about everyone.'

'Isn't Aubrey Pilkington also in some secret department?'

'Yes. Whitehall, he proudly informed me.' She smiled at Wright's expression. 'I told you. Not the most discreet of men.'

'You think him capable of leaking secrets?' Wright asked. 'Beyond your group, that is.'

'Heavens no. He and Basil gossip like a pair of debs but it goes no further.' She looked anxiously at Wright, points of pink flushing her cheeks. 'I don't want to get them into trouble.'

'Had they disagreements with either of the deceased?'

Harper shook her head. 'Not that I ever saw.'

'You heard they were married, I suppose?'

'You know about that?' Harper raised a hand to her mouth. 'Yes, I knew. Such a tragedy. Both of them dying a month after their wedding. Perhaps that was why they married – in case they didn't survive?'

'Why such a secret?'

'That's simple enough. They knew the navy would never let a married couple serve together on the same base.'

'Yet you knew.'

'Naturally. I was a witness. They wanted it kept secret and I can be terribly discreet when called for.'

'One assumes there was a second witness?' said Wright.

'Larry Parrish, of course. He was Claude's best pal so no surprise that he was asked to be best man. All terribly romantic, isn't it.'

'Didn't Claude have a brother? I should have thought he was the obvious choice.'

'If he were in the country. Not sure where Mungo is, right now. Out East, maybe? Not here, anyway.'

'Any idea why they married now if they knew they'd be reassigned?'

'Larry and I assumed she was preggers.'

'Not according to the pathologist's report.'

'Oh.' Harper deflated visibly. 'That's a shame. They were terribly in love, you know. Perhaps that was reason enough. With things looking so grim perhaps they just thought, why the hell not.' She stared at the floor, a watery smile bending her features. 'There are worse reasons I suppose.'

'And this was at Brighton registry office?' asked Wright.

'No, it was Lewes. They thought going there that it would be less likely their COs would find out.' She spread her hands. 'I have no idea where that logic came from.'

'The date this wedding took place?'

'Sixth of October.' Harper's chin trembled. 'So sad looking back. She wore a divine dress in powder-blue silk. It was just the four of us.'

'And none of the rest knew?'

'Rest of what?'

'This Café de Paris supper club?'

'It's barely a club anymore.' Jemima Harper paused, mentally counting. 'It started with about thirty of us and dwindled to half-a-dozen. So many have joined up, you know.'

'What started it? Beyond the girls coming out in the same season.'

A dull flush suffused Harper's neck. 'It was terribly naïve of us, looking back. We'd spent part of August '36 in Munich. Etta and Clarrie got hold of handfuls of front-row seats for the track and field events. Not sure how.' She smiled at Dodo. 'You were there, weren't you? And George?'

'Only at the beginning,' Dodo said. 'George fell out with some of the chaps over something. He never told me what it was.'

'You always were the sensible ones.' Harper rummaged for a cigarette and lit it, and Bunch noted how her hands were slightly unsteady. 'Larry and Claude bitterly regretted arguing with George. By time they realised he was right it was too late to mend the rift. If it's any consolation, we left before the closing ceremonies. I don't know why.' She smiled an apology. 'Claude did write to George so perhaps they were better pals by the time...' She shrugged. 'Most of us had come around by the summer of '39.'

'We think Penny had some concerns about some in that group. Would that have been with anyone in particular?'

Harper blew smoke, deep in thought, and then shook her head. 'She never said. She even asked me to jot down who was still part of the supper club. I have hardly been this past year but I put down the ones I'd seen at the last one.'

'We heard otherwise.'

'In what way?'

'Etta said you were still a regular.'

'What a rat! I have been there perhaps twice in the past six months. The Blitz scares me witless.'

'Yet you joined the ATS.'

'Yes.' She let out another mirthless snort. 'Not much of a person, am I?'

'You're doing your bit,' said Dodo. 'Don't be so hard on yourself, Jemmy. If you could let us know the next time the club meets that would be useful.'

'I shall.' She stubbed out the half-smoked cigarette and looked at Wright. 'Do you mind most awfully if I go now? My parents are expecting me for lunch and then I have to pick up the Colonel at his club in Town before midnight.'

'Of course.' Wright got to his feet and held out his hand. 'I am very grateful that you stopped by to speak with us. Where can we contact you?'

'Brighton Barracks.' She shook his hand and bent to kiss Dodo in the cheek. 'It was good to see you, and you too, Rose.' She tugged on her cap and driver's gloves. 'I shall drop by again when I am passing, Dodo. I'd love to meet young Georgi next time. I shall see myself out. Bye!'

Bunch made a performance of lighting a cigarette to fill the silence after Jemima Harper gone and sat back finally to gaze at Wright. 'What do you make of that?' she said.

'I think she may be telling the truth,' he replied.

'Of course she was. Jemmy's a good sort.' Dodo poured more coffee and slammed the pot down on the trivet. 'And she has an alibi.'

'Which we shall check, of course.' He held up his hands against Dodo's anger. 'All of these people were friends of yours, but do remember that two of them are dead.'

'You think it has something to do with this Café de Paris coterie?' Bunch demanded.

'It's looking increasingly like it, though how many are still involved is open to question. I am fairly sure your Miss Harper had no direct hand in this.'

'But is she wholly innocent?'

His head shook once. 'I rule nothing in nor out at this stage.'

'I am with Dodo on this one,' said Bunch. 'Jemmy was being totally honest with us.'

'And the rest?' Wright laughed sharply. 'We cannot pick and choose. Everyone on that list has to be investigated.'

'So next up are Pilkington and Soames?' Bunch took a deep lungful of smoke and held it until blue-grey mist began to trickle from her nose and lips. Staring into the fire in the hearth, she exhaled like a small explosion. 'Not looking forward to that.'

'You don't like them?'

'Not in the slightest. When do you intend to question them?'

'When I have something to ask them,' he replied. 'Chaps like them tend to summon lawyers the moment you put anything they say into your notebook. I want to make sure we have good evidence to wave at them.'

❧ Thirteen ❧

Had a call from Clarrie Bell. Supper club is meeting tomorrow night around nine or ten p.m. See you there. Jemmy. Bunch studied the telephone message from Jemima Harper carefully. 'When did she call?' she asked Knapp.

'About an hour ago, Miss.'

Bunch flipped the note over and back again. 'Is that it? She didn't leave a number to call her back?'

'Miss Harper informed me that she would be on duty and unavailable, but she would see you tomorrow evening if you are able to be in Town.'

'Understood.' Bunch gazed into the middle distance, tapping the note against the edge of her hand. After a lack of movement on the case for almost a week it was exciting to have some hint of progress. 'I shall need to get up to Town this afternoon, Knapp. Have Burse get the car ready.'

'Shall I tell Lizzie to draw you a bath?'

After a morning with the Land Girls digging drains in the cold and wet she had been looking forward to a long hot soak. *But that's not going to happen.* 'Sadly I shan't have time. If you can get an overnight bag, please. I shall be dining out tomorrow evening.'

Knapp looked her up and down and failed to suppress her sigh. 'Shall I also have her bring those corduroys down to be dried and brushed?'

'Yes, do.' Bunch smiled as she mounted the stairs. There were times when she felt the housekeeper was more disparaging of her habits than the family.

As she washed and changed she mused over what Jemima Harper might have to tell her that was urgent, and why she had not called Wright. *He's on her doorstep, after all. Something so delicate and personal she feels it too private for the police?* That seemed odd to her mind.

When she called Brighton Police Station she found the reason why. 'Chief Inspector Wright', she was told, 'will be in court all day.'

She left a message and went into lunch and was surprised to find it was just herself and Beatrice.

'Where's Mummy?'

'Gone up to Town.'

Bunch could not help noting what looked suspiciously like a smirk flit across her grandmother's face. 'What happened?'

'Edward thought it best to tell her that her booking for the spa had been brought forward.'

'So she's going to Somerset?'

'Lord, no. They had a huge row and she flounced off to Thurloe Square.' Beatrice made no attempt to hide her amusement. 'Edward has gone after her, of course.'

'Is there anything we can do?'

'I'd leave her to Edward.'

'With pleasure.' Bunch ladled soup from the tureen. 'Look, Granny, I have to go up to Town myself. Will you be all right here?'

'I managed perfectly well before you moved in, Rose dear.'

'You had Nanny as a companion then. I worry about you.'

'I may be old but I am not totally incapable. Besides, Knapp here will assist me, won't you, Knapp?' She smiled at the housekeeper ladling soup into her bowl. 'Added to which, we now have the invaluable Lizzie Hurst, who is proving such a treasure. And Daphne is only a mile away.' She shook out her napkin and broke open a bread roll. 'Meanwhile we should eat.'

'Absolutely. This smells delicious, Knapp. What is it?'

'Chestnut. Cook had the foresight to have Burse collect several baskets of sweet chestnuts up at Perrett woods and dry them in the garage loft.'

'I've not had chestnut soup since we were last in Megéve. I don't suppose we'll be back there at any point soon.'

'If at all.'

Bunch looked curiously at her grandmother and wondered how she should take that simple statement. That none of them would see the French Alps in the near future, or that Beatrice was feeling her mortality more keenly than before. On the whole it seemed wisest not to ask anything on that score. The topic was best changed. 'What have you planned for tomorrow?' she asked.

'WVS meeting. There has been a drive to provide homes for bombed-out families. Women and elderly mainly but some children. In theory they were all evacuated but in practice an awful lot managed to stay put.'

'Do we have any spare accommodation on the estate?' Bunch said. 'Not in the Dower I suspect, though I suppose if Mother is being shipped out there might be room.'

'We shall be left alone,' Beatrice replied. 'The places required as yet need to be close to railways so that people can get to work. A four-mile drive in a pony and trap doesn't appeal even to the desperate. Not if they can avoid it. We have any number of unused cottages around Wyncombe that can be commandeered before we start putting bunk beds in our attics.' Beatrice smoothed her napkin on her lap as she added, 'I hear you're gadding about with your policeman chappy yet again.'

'Hardly gadding. Jemima Harper tells me there is some information to be had on Claude Naysmith's death and this is the only chance to get it. Did I tell you I'm meeting Wright in Town?'

'Yes you did. Your Inspector is a nice young chap.'

'Granny!'

Beatrice spooned soup with all the innocence of a dozen cherubs. 'One can't let an opportunity go unexamined,' she murmured. 'Time isn't ever on our side.'

'Excuse me, Miss,' said Knapp. 'Someone else also called for you, too. They seemed quite anxious to speak with you. On the strength of the message from Miss Harper I informed them you'd be going up to Town later and they could probably reach you there.'

'Was it Jemima Harper again?'

'They didn't leave a name. They rang off quite abruptly.'

'Wouldn't be her. She's quite a sweet kid.'

'Is she one of the Berkshire Harpers?' Beatrice asked.

'Possibly. Her parents live in Richmond, but Dodo knows her better than I do. Is there anything I should know about them?'

'Old families always have a few skeletons rattling around, but nothing this side of the old Queen with them, that I am aware of.'

'Glad to hear it.' Bunch picked up her spoon and dipped it into the fragrant contents of her dish. 'If you are sure you will be all right here, I shall catch the three o'clock train.'

��������

Bunch boarded a later train than expected. It was packed tight, even in first class, and she did not shunt into Victoria Station until well after six. When she finally emerged from the station, tired and soot smudged, she found there was not a cab to be had.

It was hardly surprising when by that time of the evening most of the buses had ceased to run. The majority of her fellow passengers were descending into the Victoria Underground station. Comforting herself with the knowledge that South Kensington was only one stop along the District Line she picked her way past the bombed-out families settling on the platform for the night and found herself a space in the designated waiting zone for the next train.

Travelling the London Underground was not something she did often, but she had done it enough to know that it was far busier than usual. She felt ill at ease in the crush. She had heard of how people were crowding on the platforms at night but it was not something she had witnessed first-hand until now. She held her gloved hand to her nose against the stagnant odours of sweat and stale food mingled with decades of oil and brake dust that hung in the closed space, and tried not to breathe in too hard.

Bodies were pressing against her, moving her closer and closer to the platform edge. She was teetered on the very edge and felt herself falling, arms flailing for a handhold that wasn't there. Her body was jerked backwards, hands grasping at her arms and waist, and suddenly she was swinging back into the melee.

A small patter of applause rippled through the people close enough to witness the event and she felt herself reddening, embarrassed at needing to be rescued at all and in such a public place, but eternally grateful nevertheless to the pair of soldiers, one of whom was small and greying at the temples, and the other a young man with the look of a boxer to his broad shoulders and flattened nose. He still had the shoulder of her coat grasped in a massive fist. 'Are you all right, Miss? That was a narrow squeak.' He relinquished his hold and brushed at the creases his vast hand had made.

'Yes, I am … or at least I think so.' She resettled her hat and gazed at the tracks. 'I was almost over them. Can't think how it happened.' She stared around her, remembering the shove that had almost sent her into the oily depths of the train tracks. 'I was pushed.'

'It happens, Miss,' the other said. 'More'n one person's got pushed onto the line in these crowds. It's goin' to happen with this many folk trying to get home and half the platform full of other folk.' He nodded in the general direction of the stairwell. 'It's a jungle down here.'

'I am not surprised. I wouldn't have come down but there were no cabs.' She smiled at them both. 'Sorry, there's no reason I should tell you all that. I really am most awfully grateful. Here, let me—' She reached for her bag but the larger of them tapped her hand with a warning finger.

'Now then, Miss. No call for that. Never show your cash down here. It's not safe.'

'I'm sorry. I wouldn't offend for the world but you did save my life.'

He nudged his pal in the ribs and laughed. 'Not used to the Tube, this one. You were safe enough bar a bruise or two.' He pointed to the lights at the end of the platform changing from green to red. 'Now would be a different matter. You just take care, Miss.'

The train pulled in as he spoke and Bunch was swept into the carriage. The men were out of sight before she could thank them again and she found herself clinging to one of the poles as they rattled westwards, wondering about what had just happened.

She tottered onto the South Kensington platform a few minutes later, picked her way through a slightly denser crowd of platform-sitters, and up the escalator until she was standing on the pavement on Cromwell Place. For the second time that evening there was not a cab to be found.

'Between raids,' a porter informed her. ''Ad a short'un started just after four and all clear a bit before six. I s'pect they'll be back later, If they ain't bein' been nabbed for fire duty, that is. If you ain't going far I should walk. Just watch yerself wiv traffic and that. It's bleedin' mad out there.'

Though she knew the way, and living in the country all of her life was accustomed to night-time darkness, it was an odd feeling for these streets to be so very black. She stood outside the station for a moment wondering if she should call the house and ask for the car to fetch her. *But it's only two streets away. I can walk that distance by the time it got here.*

The Tube travellers were dispersing in all directions until just two or three remained, shadowy figures swathed against the cold, lurking on the pavement edges. *Presumably all dithering, like me, hoping a cab will turn up,* she thought.

A Number Fourteen bus loomed out of the dark, the last run of the day. It crawled past, its unlit interior peppered by the few pallid faces who had not headed for sanctuary. From instinct Bunch sidled to the furthest edge of the pavement, her hand against the nearby wall as the vehicle trundled past. The regular pattern of the bricks and mortar was reassuring as it told her which was the right route. Sadly for her, buses did not travel around the Square; she decided her only option was to walk. She felt in her pocket for her torch and stepped smartly in the direction of Thurloe Square.

White-painted kerb stones lent some assistance, and as she regained her night eyes she was able to make out most of her surroundings. A few jagged gaps where familiar buildings no longer existed confused her a little but she knew where she was. There were other pedestrians, many with dim glimmers of hand torches lighting a scant two feet before them; and some walkers bravely striking out blind. A taxi passed by on the far side of the street, its motor loud to her ears, and she mused on the way they had all got used to a traffic-free existence.

She was opposite the entrance to the Square and peered into the darkness for any slatted car lights. She stepped off the kerb and heard a shouted warning from a few yards away. Heard the noise of an engine as she turned to see where the voice had come from. Sensed rather than saw movement in the darkness. Bunch leaped backwards, slammed hard against the wall before sprawling onto the pavement. She had a vague image of something dark and predatory passing close the kerb edge, travelling fast. The glimmer of masked head lamps and taillights not merely faint but completely absent. The darkness swallowed the unlit vehicle in seconds – and then even the sound of its engine was gone.

Bunch lay there, dazed, staring after it until passers-by ran up to help her.

'Are you all right, Miss?' An elderly gent in a long wool coat was leaning down and offering her his hand. 'Can you walk?'

'Yes. I'm fine. I wasn't hit. I just sort of bumped against the brickwork.' Bunch staggered to her feet. 'Nothing broken,' she said, but put her hand to her head as the words reverberated through her skull. 'I had a hat somewhere. And a bag.'

'Here it is, Miss.' A young woman held out the felt fedora. 'Its rather grubby I'm afraid. It fell into the gutter.'

'It will clean. Thank you.' Bunch pulled the hat on and took the bag, and smiled at them both. 'You must think I'm an absolute goose.'

'Under the circumstances you were very lucky. These things happen more often than you would think,' the man replied. 'Cursed blackout makes it impossible for everyone. Though that vehicle did seem especially reckless.' He gazed in the direction the car had taken. He seemed about to say more but from some unseen height a siren began to wail and they all looked up.

'Here we go again,' the girl muttered. 'Wailing-Winnie clocking on.'

The elderly gent grunted. 'Like clockwork. Luckily, we've not far to go. And you, Miss?' He peered at Bunch, eyes seeming to glitter even without light.

'No,' she said. 'The far end of the Square.'

The man leaned a little closer to peer at her. 'Ah yes. You're Edward's daughter. Rose, isn't it? You probably don't remember me. I've been away a lot but we're neighbours of a kind. Godwin Newcombe.' He shook her hand briskly. 'This is my niece, Betty.' He grasped Bunch's arm, looked both ways along the junction then hurried them both to the other side. 'I think we should get home, don't you?'

They walked as briskly as the dark allowed, without speaking, concentrating on not walking into lampposts or falling off the edge of the kerb, until they reached the steps that marked the Courtney residence.

'Here we are. Will you be all right now?'

'Yes. Yes I shall and thank you.'

'Don't mention it my dear.' He raised his hat and gave a small bow.

In the distance a faint crump-crump of exploding ordnance

made them all pause and look toward it, even though there was nothing to be seen over three-story Regency buildings.

'Nice to meet you, Miss Courtney,' Betty said as she took Newcombe's arm. 'We should go.'

'Of course, my dear. Good evening.' He tipped his hat once more and the two vanished quickly into the night, leaving Bunch to mount the three steps to the door, fumbling for the house key because she realised everyone inside would be down in the cellars.

Bunch closed the door and leaned against it, pulling off hat, scarf and gloves and dropping them on a hall table. She ached and was aware that the shake in her legs were not entirely due to any physical damage as the thoughts she had not dared to give room vied for attention.

Inside, the house was warm and quiet, and a small shaded lamp had been left on for her arrival. Its reach was limited which lent depth to the shadows, both calming and eerie at the same time. She felt for her cigarette case and a small seed of panic took root. It was not in her pocket. She patted her coat, rummaged in every pocket, her movements quickening by the second. Nothing. Both her case and lighter that she knew had been in her right pocket were missing. 'Dammit. They must have fallen out of my pocket.' It had been a gift from her father. It was only a plain case but irreplaceable, for sentimental reasons.

Bunch laid her hand on the door handle, thinking she should go back to the crossroad and search for it and then listened to raid growing louder. 'Maybe not.' She let her hand drop and spun back to contemplate vague outlines of staircase and doorways before making her way into the drawing room across the hall where she knew there would be a cigarette box.

Her hands were still shaking and it took her three fumbles with the lighter to get a flame. Standing in the dark, the only light coming from the hallway, she thought over the incidents.

Two near misses in under an hour? What if someone followed me from the Underground? No it had to be before that, at Victoria. Had they been on the same train? Were they watching the Dower House? How had they known where I was going, and when? She sucked in another lungful of smoke and forced herself to run through the options as a tick list. Bunch prided herself on being unflappable, and knowing she was in shock didn't prevent her annoyance with herself.

Or maybe it was just plain old crime followed by some bad driving. She took another puff and stabbed the butt venomously. The idea that she had thanked the very men who had quite probably picked her pockets shifted her fear into anger.

The muffled chatter of the ack-acks in the park dragged her attention back to the present. The more distant detonating of bombs was more felt than heard but seemed less threatening. 'For heaven's sake, standing here shivering like a cur will solve nothing.' She strode out to the hallway to check that the door was locked and blackout curtains were tightly drawn. The cigarette soothed her rattled nerves but the lure of a stiff drink still called to her, and the best place to seek it out lay down the servant stairs into the bowels of the house, where she would find the household sheltering from the raid.

ᔕᗝᔕᗝ

'Hello Mummy.'

'Rose, darling— Oh my goodness, what happened to you?'

'I very nearly got mown down by a car.'

'Oh my goodness! Kimber, fetch a brandy. Quickly. Are you all right, Rose? Come and sit down. Have you eaten?'

'I had a rather nasty sandwich on the train an absolute age ago. It took hours to get here and then this bloody car came racing around from Exhibition Road and damned near ran me down. I might have been killed but for Mr Newcombe coming to my rescue.'

'Newcombe? Was he out in this? He's a game old chap,' she said. 'Do sit down. Oh, you are bleeding. Edward! Rose has been hurt! Kimber, fetch the first aid box, please.'

Rose put her hand to her head and probed gently at her scalp. 'It could have been a lot worse. Hello Daddy.'

'You know how to make an entrance,' he said. 'My mother taught you well.' He came to stand behind her and parted her hair to examine the injury. 'It's more graze than cut. Gilsworth will be happy to make you tea.'

'I'd rather have hot chocolate.' Rose heard the hint of the nursery in her own voice and sat a little straighter in her seat to counter it.

'Crossing roads can be hellish.' Edward gently smoothed the hair on the undamaged side of her head. 'You should be more

167

careful.'

'I do know how to cross the road, Daddy. This car was going at a hell of a lick. Way more than the regulation twenty miles an hour.' She grabbed the bag of ice that a maid had brought her and slapped it against the erupting lump, wincing at the contact but refusing to make a sound.

'I suppose you didn't recognise it. The car I mean.' Edward went on. Bunch could hear the subtext beneath his simple query. 'Do you recall the make? Colour?'

'Nothing.' The shake of her head made her hiss at the pain. 'I didn't get much of a look at it, to be honest. A large saloon. Possibly black? Dark coloured anyway, not that dark helps much. It was gone almost before I realised it was there. If it hadn't been for Mr Newcombe shouting at me I wouldn't have known to jump clear. I must thank him. He said he knew you. I couldn't place him myself, but it was so very dark.'

'Admiral Newcombe? Yes, I know him and so do you. You've met him many times when you were smaller but he's been abroad until quite recently. Capital chap. He rattles around in that house on his own, but you may know his heir who drops in from time to time. Some young cousin several times removed who goes by the name of Henry something or other? Mother would know.'

'The Admiral had his niece with him. I think her name was Betty. Or Beryl?'

'Is that what he's calling her?' Edward chuckled quietly. 'The young lady in question is no relation of his, I can assure you.'

'Oh.' Bunch smiled as she caught on. 'Well … they were both very sweet.'

'Glad to hear it.' He frowned at her. 'I wonder if we should call the police. Speeding cars on any road in the blackout seems unusual.'

'What can the police do in a raid? The car will be miles away by now, and Wright will be here tomorrow. I have an idea this will mean more to him than the locals.'

Edward sat next to her and put an arm around her shoulders. 'Rose—' he lowered his voice '—is there anything else you should be telling me?'

'My cigarette case…' She halted. Telling them about the incident on the tube suddenly seemed too difficult. *And it will solve nothing*. 'The one you gave me for my twenty-first. I think I dropped it when I fell.' She looked down at her glass of brandy and swilled it gently around the glass.

'Oh, that hardly matters. Easily replaced.' Edward tipped her chin to look her full in the eye. 'And nothing else?'

There had never been a time when she could hide anything from her father but she was aware that the whole room was listening in. 'Don't Daddy. Please. Not now.' She smiled brightly and looked around her. The cellar room had once been a staff dining hall when the house had been used more fully, which meant that it had a hearth to warm them. Nevertheless, the walls had been lined with rugs to keep out the cold and various screens drafted in from bedrooms to divide it into sections. Sofas provided space to sleep or sit, which, she realised for the first time, were occupied by the much-reduced staff. 'This is cosy,' she said. 'We should get something similar sorted out at the Dower.'

'We seem to spend half of every night down here of late. I see no reason to be any more uncomfortable than absolutely necessary,' Theadora replied.

'In that case you'll enjoy the spa,' said Bunch. 'Terribly nice, I am told.' She heard her mother's intake of breath to protest and raised her hand to her head. 'I really do feel rather awful. I think I might lie down for a while.'

'Masterly deflection,' Edward whispered into Bunch's ear. 'Well done.'

❧ Fourteen ❧

Bunch arrived at the Café de Paris a little before eight o'clock. Dressed in her deep-green watered silk gown, silver shoes and arctic fox coat, she blended in with the evening crowd and drew a few casual glances only because she was alone.

She grabbed a table near the edge of the room with a grandstand view of the staircase and dance floor where she could sip at her Martini as she waited for Wright to arrive, and pretended to peruse the menu. A haze of smoke hung across the room despite the air conditioning. It mingled with the odours of food, cologne and body sweat to form that unmistakable 'club' odour that went largely unnoticed in opening hours. *Which,* she thought, *was perfectly hideous the morning after.* Snake-hips Johnson's resident band was warming up for the evening's entertainment with his signature swing sound drowning out the noise of cutlery and diners' chatter.

A few eager dancers took to the floor, obscuring her view of some of the tables. As far as she could see, none of Barrington-Soames's supper club had shown their faces. *Though it's very early,* she reminded herself. She spotted Wright the moment he entered the room and watched him descend the staircase with approval. He lacked Henry Marsham's physique but possessed a presence that suited evening dress equally well. She was amused to find herself thinking she was glad he had made the effort.

Bunch wondered if she should proffer her cheek for a kiss. They were here disguised as a couple, after all. As if reading her mind Wright made the gesture, kissing the air a good hand span from her ear as she turned slightly, and they grinned at each other like a pair of children. He moved his chair round a little so that he had a similar view to herself.

'I hope I haven't kept you waiting?'

'Lord no, I was early. Wanted to give myself a little time to get my bearings. I have a few rather disturbing things to catch you up on.'

'Disturbing?' He turned to the waiter who came to stand close to his right.

'Would sir like to order?'

'Bring us some hors d'oeuvres,' said Bunch, 'and then we shall have steak with a bottle of the Malbec.' She handed the waiter her menu and waved away Wright's glare. 'I said it was my treat. The steak here is sublime, a real treat, and God alone knows I need one.'

'You do?'

'I could put yesterday down to a bad day for accidents.'

'Or?'

'Or someone had a bloody good try at bumping me off.'

'They what?'

'I was very nearly killed.' She gave him a run down of events. 'I may be blowing it all up out of proportion, of course.'

'It doesn't sound like it,' Wright replied. 'Are you hurt?'

'Amazingly, not. Bump on the noggin and a few bruises but nothing drastic. The thing on the platform seemed to be a simple case of theft, but if it hadn't happened I should have been paying more attention because the car was a different matter.'

'I hope you reported that to the local station?'

'Daddy called them a bit later but I think they were inclined to dismiss it as a hazard of blackout conditions.' She shrugged. 'Without anything more than 'a dark-coloured saloon car, make and model unknown, I can't say I blame them. To them it was no more suspicious than the Underground incident.'

'About that. You didn't see anyone else nearby who might have been responsible?'

'Like someone in a black cape and twirling a moustache?'

'This is serious. You know full I meant somebody you recognised.'

'No. Though my entire family could have been there and I'd have been hard pressed to pick them out. It was packed to the gunnels.'

'You never had the feeling you were being followed?'

'No, I hadn't given it the slightest thought until then. Why would I?'

'No reason you should,' he agreed. 'It may well be an amazing run of bad luck but you should have called me, all the same. I would have collected you tonight from Thurloe Square.'

'I did call the station but Carter told me you had left mid-morning. I don't have any number for you here in Town.'

'No. I am sorry about that. I shall notify the Transport Police. There are teams operating this kind of trick all the time and they are sure to have some clues. You may even get your cigarette case back.' He adjusted his tie and looked around the room. 'Just in case there was more to it, I'd be happier if you didn't travel alone until we have this case wrapped up.'

'That may rather cramp my style,' Bunch spread her hands. 'I'm sure I am making more of this than there was. I wasn't paying attention.'

'Or someone really did take a chance to silence you.' Wright replied. 'A lot of people know your family's Town house. Yes?'

'I suppose so.'

'For someone to be on the train to rush ahead of you and happen by some miracle to have a car just handy for that purpose seems highly unlikely.' Wright frowned, passing his hand over the top of his head several times. 'But the car itself feels odder. I will have someone look into it. Who did you tell you were travelling up here?'

'Granny. The house staff. Knapp said there was a phone call and when she told them to call Thurloe Square, they rang off.'

'No name I assume. It does explain a lot'

'Rather chilling thought.' Bunch took a large swill of her drink, emptying the glass, and called the waiter to bring champagne. 'Better not swig cocktails the entire evening,' she said at his raised eyebrow. 'I can drink champers like fizzy pop, and we are meant to be blending in, old chap. A bottle or three of Du Pape would be expected.'

She lit a cigarette and surveyed the room. She noted how many men were in uniform to avoid the stigma of being young fit and civilian. Yet very few the women followed suit though many were undoubtedly in the military. There was a dual standard at work and she was unsure who was at the biggest disadvantage. It made her medical board rejection sting all the more. 'I don't intend to come up to Town again before the New Year,' she said at last. 'Don't worry yourself on that score.'

They ate and chatted and managed to avoid the whole subject of assassins and murder for almost an hour before the noise of the sirens could be heard rising over the music. A few heads went up, like hounds catching a scent. Most ignored the warning wail. This was a shelter in every sense, deep under street level, and nobody had the slightest fear that the raids going on above could touch them.

Snake-hips Johnson and his band were in full swing as sporadic booms of a raid began once again. The ordnance could be heard and felt from the street above, and Bunch noted how the vibrations rippled the surface of her drink, but the people around her did not allow the doings of the upper world to impinge on their night, applauding the band as they finished one song and swung into the next.

'Are they applauding the band or the bombs?' she called to Wright over the orchestra's swing sound.

'Probably a little of both.'

A fresh influx of people flooded down the staircase as people sought refuge and Bunch nudged Wright's arm when a noisy group clattered past to take their places at a reserved table near to the stage. 'Soames's supper club,' she said. 'I vote we let them settle and maybe bump into one or other on the dance floor.'

'Not very subtle.'

'Doesn't need to be. The alternative is to just march over there... I say, that's Larry Parrish.' She watched the naval officer making his way toward the party. 'I thought he was still safely out at sea.'

'There's a few U-boats out there that might make "safe" questionable.'

'Safer than he is with amongst these sharks,' she replied. 'His name was crossed through on that list.'

'Which was not written by Penny James, as it turns out.'

'Oh?'

'We had it analysed. Definitely not her handwriting.'

'Any idea whose?'

'That would be asking too much at this stage.'

'I take it we've no idea whether she found the list or was given it?'

'Not a clue, but it's a fair bet she and Naysmith died as a result.'

'Meanwhile, what should we do about Larry Parrish and Jemmy Harper? Are they in danger?'

'Ask him yourself. He's coming back this way.'

'May I?' Lawrence Parrish pulled up a spare chair up to join them. 'Miss Courtney. I thought it was you. How are you?' He tipped his forefinger to the peak of his Naval cap in salute.

'Very well, thank you, Larry.'

'Good. I heard you wanted to speak with me.'

'Yes, indeed. And what is all this "Miss Courtney" nonsense?' She punched his arm gently. 'We've been neighbours all our lives.'

'I wasn't sure how official you were being. I hear you've been chatting with some of Penny and Claude's friends.'

'We have,' Bunch replied. 'Routine enquiries, as William here would say.'

'I've been hearing about it. Chapter and verse. Jemmy said you might be here, and why. Once Etta and Clarrie compared notes and realised your visits had ulterior motives they were filled with righteous indignation. Or rather Etta was and Clarrie always follows suit.' He glanced at Wright as if noticing him for the first time, and back to Bunch. 'Are you going to introduce me to your friend?'

'Oh, I'm sorry. Where are my manners? This is Chief Inspector William Wright.'

'Ah. Of the Sussex Constabulary.' He grinned. 'Your fame runs before you, Chief Inspector. Pleased to meet you.'

'William is fine for tonight, Mr Parrish. I'm not on duty.'

Parrish held out his hand. 'Then it's Larry. So what was it you chaps wanted to talk to me about? I can't tell you much about these deaths. I've been out at sea most of the past month.'

'We know,' said Wright. 'We understand you were an official witness at the Naysmith wedding, along with Miss Harper?'

'Yes. Rather puts a big hole in our club. I don't think it will survive. Such a shame to lose them both. They were good friends and hardly married five minutes.'

'Awful,' Bunch agreed. 'Thing is, there's this list of names, all of whom are in your supper club. Eight names in total and four of those struck through.'

'Two of those are now dead and we have reason to believe

there have been attempts on others connected with the case,' Wright added.

The sailor's expression was solemn and his lips pursed. 'Do I assume my name is on this list?'

'One of those crossed-out names,' Bunch added. 'We think you may be in very real danger.'

'I appreciate your concern but why just the four of us? Why not all of the eight?'

'Well—' Bunch turned to Wright '—he has a point.'

'Information from on high,' Wright replied. 'And no, I can't say where that information came from.'

'You never thought to tell me?' Bunch glowered and Wright sighed.

'Politics,' he said.

There was a moment of stasis before Parrish threw his head back and let out a guffaw. 'That won't make any difference to me.' He shook his head. 'Not when I'm spending my days and weeks chasing U-Boats.' He touched his clenched fist to his lips. 'You are serious, aren't you,' he said. 'Who was the fourth name crossed through?'

'I'm afraid I can't divulge that,' Wright replied.

'Understood.' Parrish tapped his knuckles several times against his chin. 'If you think we're in danger why haven't any of us been warned?

'It wasn't much more than a theory until last night,' said Wright. 'Besides, you seemed safe while you were out at sea. Now it does appear that things have changed.'

'You really think this is some kind of hit list?'

'We have no real proof of that. I think it may have started out as a list for this evening and ended up being used for other purposes. Either way, we would be happiest if you went back to your ship, for now at least.'

'After the past few months I've had—' Parrish shook his head. 'I have a seven-day pass and I am going to take it. I was intending to be in Town for the first few days, but I'm sure my mother will be happy to have me home. Have you any idea why all this is happening?'

'Our initial investigations pointed toward the work certain individuals are doing,' said Wright. 'It's a little less likely now.

Anything you imagine might help us, however small, would be useful.'

'I know Claude and Penny were working on some special project. I never asked them what it was because one doesn't these days. Why Jemmy and I have been linked with that is bit of a mystery. If it's official secrets this killer is after... What would they gain by killing the people closest to them?'

'That I cannot say,' Wright said, 'but as I said before, you should seriously consider cutting this evening short and getting back on board ship with a few dozen matelots watching your back.'

'Are you serious?' Parrish said.

'Never more so.' Wright nodded toward the rowdy table close to the stage. 'One of the people over there in that supper party is likely to be a cold-blooded killer. We have no idea which one. Or if it's more than one.'

Bunch gazed at him, a little stunned by his hard words delivered as sotto voce as conditions permitted. 'When did we come to that conclusion?'

'Since you told me somebody made at least one attempt on your life.'

'That seems ... logical.' She stared in the direction of the supper club group. 'We seem to be attracting some attention.'

'Larry, you're been neglecting us.' Basil Barrington-Soames drifted up to join them, smiling at each of them in turn. He was not especially tall but undeniably handsome with high cheek bones and wide-set grey eyes over a slightly prominent nose, and fair hair that had been carefully comb and Brilliantined into submission. He had charisma, Bunch had to give him that, *but there's a distinct whiff of weasel about him*. 'I can't recall when we last met, Rose,' he said. 'Before dear Johnny left us, I'm sure.'

'I do believe it would have been before you all toddled off to the Games.'

'You missed that. It was tremendous fun. I heard you were invalided out of the army and you're working with the forces of the law now. Bravo.' Soames smiled at Wright. 'Won't you introduce me?'

'Of course. This is my good friend Chief Inspector William Wright. William, allow me to introduce Mr Basil Barrington-

Soames.'

'Ah. I have heard a lot about you.'

'All bad I hope.' Soames hooted at his own joke. 'Good evening, Mr Wright. Please do join us. We are raising a glass to fallen comrades.'

They skirted around the dancers to the supper club table where Soames held a chair for Bunch to be seated. 'There's usually more of us,' he said. 'Claude and Penelope's deaths have reduced our merry band rather.'

'So Larry was just saying.'

'Was he now? Yes. Such a terrible shock coming after poor George Tinsley, and dear sweet Jonathan Frampton such a short time ago. I swear our little coterie seems cursed. Don't you think Inspector – Wright isn't it?'

'Lot of people are losing friends and relatives,' Wright replied. 'Though murder does feel a little more personal. I hoped to speak to you about that, Mr Soames.'

'My man said you called a few times – but one gets so busy.'

'I wasn't aware you had regular duties,' said Wright. 'Not being in the Services.'

'Sadly, I have a medical condition.' Soames replied. 'There is the estate for me to run, however. My father is here in London such a great deal so someone has to do it. You know how that is, Rose. You are in much the same boat.'

He beamed at her though Bunch felt more provoked than amused. She had never known him well and never liked what she had seen. There was something now, in the way he was looking at her, that made her spine tingle.

'We all do what we can in our own way,' said Soames. 'Alas, my medical condition prevents me doing as much as I might.'

'Then you don't dance?' said Bunch.

'One doesn't let these things get in the way if one can avoid it.' Soames leered at her.

The music changed tempo from Swing to Slow and Soames held his hand out to her. 'Would you do me the honour, Rose? If the good Inspector can spare you?'

Bunch took his hand and allowed herself to be led into the gathering vortex of dancers on the floor. She was as tall as Soames, which she was glad of as it avoided the embarrassment of her leaning her head on his shoulders as many couples were doing. Soames was a good dancer, supporting her with a steady arm, and she began to relax despite her instincts.

'I heard you were injured in action. Quite the little soldier,' he said. 'Clarice tells me she saw you at a Henry Marsham's shoot and you were barely favouring your leg at all.'

'I'm fine.' Bunch flashed him a smile and hoped her surprise was well buttoned in. If he knew what had happened last night then it was a bold opening gambit. 'Hardly bothers me at all. Though a speeding car very nearly did for me. Blackout is such a damned nuisance isn't it.'

'Sorry to hear that. Yes, wandering about in the dark can be rather an interesting pastime. These days.'

He was smiling, a curve of the lips that seemed genuine enough but Bunch couldn't help wondering what it was that he found amusing. 'It is,' she said. 'I was lucky a neighbour was there to help me. It may have been my fault. I was a little distracted, to be perfectly honest. Penny's death has been a shock...'

'Do tell.'

He's a ghoul, she thought but schooled her face into polite condolence. 'You knew her better than I did. I was told you and she were an item at one time.'

'We went to a few balls together. Lovely girl but terribly proper. Much like Jemmy there.' He nodded at Jemima Harper out on the dance floor with Aubrey Pilkington.

'Jemmy seems rather a good sort.'

'She is a *nice* girl. I hear she came to talk with you the other day.'

'You're very well informed.'

'I intend to run for Parliament when this debacle with Germany is over. It pays me to be informed.' He smiled down at her. 'Can't think what she'd have to say that was so urgent she'd hunt you down in the wilds.'

'Actually it was Dodo she went to visit. They were chums, a few years back.' Bunch felt a small chill run down her spine as she wondered if mentioning her sister was a good idea. Time for a change of tack. 'Is it true you were once engaged to Penny James?' she said.

Soames's grip tightened on her arm. 'Old news. Yes, I was with her for a time. I also partnered Etta to a few events, and even

Clarrie Bell once or twice. I like the company of women. Why would any of it be of interest you?'

'Nothing at all. Just gossip. You know how it is,' she said. 'When you're in line to pick up a substantial estate—' she laughed sharply '—I do know what that's like. If you have an inheritance of any size people will take quite intrusive interest in your smallest social doings, and the people you do those things with.' She gazed steadily into his eyes. 'You know I have quite an efficient network of my own. I heard rumours about Etta Beamish. Apparently, she had some mysterious illness and went abroad for a few months to convalesce at your expense.' She winced as Soames twirled her out and back again. That had been a stab in the dark but his grip tightening on her arm and fingers said it all. He pulled her close in so that his eyes were a bare hand span from her own.

'Did Jemmy tell you that? Or Clarry?' he said. 'I hear you've been interrogating them.'

'Why would you assume that?' she replied. 'I got it from one of my grandmother's WI cronies, as it happens. I've spoken to Jemmy, yes, and I also had a chat with Clarrie. And Etta. All sweet girls, I must say.'

'Sweet?' He let forth a guttural laugh. 'Good grief. Clarrie Bell is completely barking and Etta is a wolf. She's intent on getting her teeth into the biggest wallet she can find and not the least fussy how she goes about it.'

Bunch was taken aback by the venom that he did not attempt to hide for someone who, so far as Bunch knew, was very nearly the mother of his child. *No love lost there. Perhaps it's actually because of the child,* she thought. *Supposing he even knew about it.* 'Etta had designs?' she said aloud.

'I could not possibly comment. It'd be quite out of the question.' He twirled her around and dipped, as he seemed consider the thought. 'Don't get me wrong. I very much admire Etta's iron will. And her focus. She's a girl who gets things done.' He leaned forward and brushed his cheek against hers. 'She's not unlike you in that respect. Top banana.'

Bunch pulled away. His meaning was unmistakable, and the heat of his breath on her neck made her a little queasy. Soames chuckled quietly, as if her reaction pleased him, and she was confused at the game he seemed to be playing. 'I'd have said we were polar opposites,' she snapped. 'Especially in our choice of politics. Something you and Etta have in common I think.'

Soames's eyes lost all trace of their sardonic humour. 'Etta and I once shared a great many of the same political values but that is as far as it went. Her stock is good but her father comes too far down the family food chain. Three older brothers so he won't inherit much. Just his clerical stipend.'

'I read all about Archdeacon Beamish's latest address to the synod. Full throated support for appeasement, even now.' She looked up at the ceiling, to where the noises of the raid could still be heard, however hard the throng tried to ignore it.

'Goodness—' he held her away from him '—this is all a bit serious. We're here to enjoy ourselves. It's why we began this supper club in the first place. Etta's idea, back when we had a brief fling.' He drew her closer once again, far closer than she would have preferred so that his musky cologne caught at the back of her sinuses. 'The club has been sadly depleted,' he went on. 'Did you know your brother-in-law was a founder member? And his pal, Johnny Frampton? I can't recall your baby sister ever joining us very often. Not that Frampton or Tinsley did for very long. Rather more red-blooded than they could stomach, perhaps. I don't suppose you'd consider it? We heirs-apparent need to stick together, don't you think?'

'I enjoy the odd night on the town but I'm a country girl from mane to hoof.'

'You've always been obsessed with horses and hunting and what not. Shame. You're far more eligible than Etta Beamish will ever be. Or Penelope James, come to that.'

'What was wrong with Penny?'

'Where do I begin?' He laughed with very little humour in evidence. 'Far too nice and so naive. Did you know it was Penny who first met Etta? They were both at Oxford and Penny brought her on a little trip to Munich. After which Etta proved rather difficult to dislodge.'

'The grande dames' grapevine also claimed you were all but engaged to Etta.'

'God no. A thousand times no!' He gazed over Bunch's shoulder for a moment. 'Etta and I were saw each other for a very short while. That happens when a girl *flings* herself at a chap.' He grimaced. 'Your spies have that much right, and it was my "friendship" with Harriett Beamish that rather put the kibosh on Penny and me. Perhaps just as well, in the end.' Soames's face split into another of his ready grins, if a little wryly. 'Penelope disapproved of so much. A chap has to make a stand.' He raised an eyebrow and chuckled. 'You disapprove? Isn't it better we parted company than marry purely for filthy lucre? I have plenty of time to choose a wife.'

Bunch forced out a trill of laughter. 'I wonder any of you stay in this supper club of yours. It must get jolly awkward at times.'

'The past is the past,' he replied. 'People get over these things.'

Bunch glanced up at him. He seemed amused and it brought goose bumps rushing to her flesh. 'Etta said it was thriving,' she said.

'Wishful thinking. Jemmy has hardly attended for the past six months. Nor has Larry, and we hadn't seen Penny and Claude since last New Year. I suspect this evening may be our last hoorah.'

They danced for a minute more in silence. 'So what did you want to ask me?' Soames said at last.

'Pardon?'

'You and your policeman friend have been pestering me these past two weeks for a chat. What's it all about?'

'Other than two of your friends dying?'

'Come along, Rose. You can't imagine I had anything to do with that? I'm not the ringmaster of this little circus. It was all terribly sad, tragic even, but I have no notion what happened to them.'

That smile again, Bunch thought. *Ringmaster is precisely how he sees himself. All dazzling charm and complete confidence, and not an ounce of wit in him.*

The music came to an end and they applauded politely and made their way back to their seats. The band was launching into another ballad and a young woman stepped up to the microphone to croon 'When A Nightingale Sang'.

Pilkington was sitting alone at the table, watching the singer with a hungry expression on his face. He rose briefly as Bunch arrived. 'She's rather good,' he said.

'She is. Anyone I should know?'

'Calls herself Elise Balcat, though her name is Mary Roberts.

She usually sings at the Corvana Club but does a few turns here as well.'

'Pilkie here is becoming a bit of a stage door Johnny.' Soames leaned back, his arm looped over the back of the chair as he viewed his companion down the length of his nose. 'She's married, Pilkie old chap. Bruising great boxer.'

'I know, but a man can dream.' He shrugged. 'Jemmy has dragged your Inspector out onto the floor, Rose. Larry is out there somewhere with Etta. Can't think where Clarrie is. Powdering her nose, I imagine.' He tapped his nose and snorted loudly.

'And poor old Pilkie is the wallflower yet again.' Soames leaned down and whispered, 'All smoke and mirrors. It's the second trombone he really has the hots for.'

'Don't be a bloody fool, Soames.' Pilkington glowered at him and winked at Bunch. 'He likes to think he's terribly funny but then with his inheritance, women will fall at his feet like belly dancers in a harem.'

Not always. Some of them are quite the ice maidens.'

'Got the brush off for a change, Droopy? C'est la vie.' Pilkington picked up his glass and waved it in a mocking toast. 'Don't feel bad about it, old chap. Rose does that to all the chaps. Chock full of thorns.'

The two men laughed but she detected a brittle edge, an atmosphere that belied the supper club's alleged camaraderie she had heard so much about. *A private joke? Though not a terribly funny one from the look of it. Serves them right, the ratty little creeps.* 'I am sitting right here,' she snapped. 'I'm not some prize mare.'

'Sorry. That was bad of us both. Used to bantering with this crowd, don't you know.' Pilkington took out his cigarette case and offered one to Bunch.

She took one and waited as Soames produced a lighter. From outside came a boom louder than the rest. Many people looked upward, a few of the dancers paused momentarily, and then carried on, safe in the knowledge that here, sixty feet underground, they were as safe as they could be anywhere in the capital. Bunch was not so certain. The two men seated either side of her both gave her the *heebies*, though how much of that was personal dislike and how much her being in possession of evidence, however sketchy, of wrongdoing at some level.

Pilkington seemed genuinely perplexed, but Soames was eying her up and down, calculating some unnamed quantity or quality in that flint-like scrutiny. She turned away first.

'So, Aubrey. Is the war keeping you busy?' she said.

'Well, yes. Can't talk about it naturally, but this is my first night off all week.'

'You work nightshifts?'

'Not officially but even if I get away at all, by the time I get home I'm too pooped to do much but crawl into bed and sleep. Last night was another all-nighter.' He jerked a thumb toward the ceiling. 'Had a rush job, don't you know. Team didn't finish until after nine a.m. Happens a lot and our office is underground. There've been entire weeks when I've barely see daylight. Beginning to feel like a damned mole.'

'Can't just slope off, I suppose.' She breathed out and viewed him through the smoke. 'Not when your uncle is head of department.'

'*Especially* when your uncle heads a department. He tends to notice if I'm not there and he's convinced I am just the chap to set them all an example.' He offered Bunch a guilty smile.

'Yes, I can see how that could be a problem. Not that you could slope off at any time you want. Especially with a raid on.'

'No, indeed.' He sighed. 'We may be moving out soon anyway, which will make it easier. Most of the departments that can are decamping to the suburbs.'

'Sensible,' she said. 'I wish we could persuade my mother of that.'

'My mother and sister fled to the country months ago. The Manor has been infested by some wretched girl's school. They can be a nuisance but not too disruptive on the whole. They only have the East Wing. Tricky for you I suppose, what with Perringham occupied by some military squad.'

'We're not alone there. Half the county set has been ousted from their beds one way or another.' Bunch replied. 'The Howards have half the Royal Artillery tearing up the grounds at Arundel.'

'Mother has the homestead earmarked for hospital use,' said Soames. 'Thus far we've been in reserve but we have a few properties scattered here and there so we shan't be homeless.'

The band launched into a lively swing number which sent the

rest of their party scuttling back from the dance floor.

'Too much for me, I'm afraid.' Wright flopped into a vacant chair and gazed at the orchestra as they played a medley of dance tunes, Johnson conducting with his usual flamboyance. 'Sorry, Miss Harper but this is a young man's game.'

'You dance well, Inspector, but I want to swing. Come on Pilkie, let's trot.'

'Hello Jemmy.'

'Hello Rose.' Harper smiled at Bunch and seemed about to say more, but then shook her head slightly, and looked away. 'Come on Aubrey. Dance with me.' She grabbed Pilkington by the hand and hauled him into the heaving mass.

Bunch watched her go and wondered what that was about. *Jemima Harper told me about this evening and hinted she had something to say. And now she's doing everything she can to avoid me. Something, or someone, has her rattled.*

'Dammed hot in here.' Parrish mopped his brow and took a long swallow from a champagne saucer. 'Rather got used to the open seas, I'm afraid. Once this raid is over I think I shall call it a night.'

'Where are you staying?' Beamish asked. 'I'm in Town for the weekend. We could have a jolly day out tomorrow and catch up on all our news. I can drop you off on my way home.'

'Well...' Parrish smiled weakly.

'Wright here is off down to Brighton,' Bunch said. 'I'm toddling back to Wyncombe tomorrow. Daddy said he would get Sutton to drive me home, and seeing as poor Larry doesn't have a motor of his own now, I promised him a lift, so we're all scattering to the winds on the morrow.' She laid a hand on Parrish's arm to silence the argument she saw forming in his eyes. 'I promised Mummy I'd be home as close to midnight as I could if the all-clear went. Share a cab with me to the Square? We can drop by your club for your kit in the morning, wherever it is you left it.'

'I was staying at my club,' he replied, 'but a comfy bed would be nice. Your parents won't mind?'

'Absolutely not.'

'Then it's settled. Now tell us all about this secret wedding of Penny and Claude's.' Bunch sensed Beamish coming to attention and made sure she didn't look in the young woman's direction. 'It can't matter now they are both gone.'

'Nothing much to tell,' Parrish replied. We only had a few hours when we were all available to get the deed done. I had a hell of a time getting there. The other three were local.'

'I was surprised you were a witness. Why was it you were asked? Clarrie was a lot closer.'

'Bit of in in-joke.' Parrish tapped the braid on his cuff. 'Claude and I managed to get the same service and then Penny was taken in by the Wrens. We thought it was rather fun to have us all together as the Senior Service. Yes, I know Jemmy got skimmed off to the ATS, but she was Penny's best friend.' He stared across the dance floor at Harper with Pilkington, and then scrubbed his face with both hands. 'You never know what will happen tomorrow, or next week. Or the next.'

Bunch grabbed her glass and held it up, waiting for the rest to follow suit. 'To absent friends.'

'Absent friends.'

Glasses chinked against each other and she took the chance to look at each of them in turn. Only Parrish seemed to meet her gaze with any warmth and for a chilling moment she wondered if this supper club had more to it than only maintaining old friendships. *I can't imagine what that might be.*

'Have you got yourself a dog?' Beamish said, as they settled their recharged glasses.

'Dog? Oh yes, as it happens, someone has offered me a springer. Fully trained. Chap has joined up and can't keep it working as he'd like.'

'Sounds like a good match.'

'Not said I'll take it, as yet. Still giving it some thought. I mean springers are very loyal, but they're mad buggers in my experience. We shall see. What about you? Sold your pups yet?'

'No. The market for them is pretty quiet right now. Tell me now, your Inspector friend here.' Beamish tilted her head to look at her intently.

'What about him?'

'Oh come along now, don't be coy. You seem well suited.'

Bunch glanced at Wright and smiled. 'He's a friend and a colleague. Nothing more.'

'You're certain about that? He watches you rather closely.'

Wright shrugged but stayed silent. 'I had a run in with a car in the blackout and you know how men can be.'

'You might have been killed.'

'It was nothing. This blackout makes every step an adventure. Never mind the bombers.' She watched Beamish and was taken aback at how the woman gazed at her without blinking, without any apparent hint of curiosity. Bunch spread her hands. 'Bit different to Sussex. We're used to not having streetlights down there. People seem better equipped.'

'How very true.' Beamish agreed. 'Provided you have a car on the road. I'm lucky that my father's duties allow me to combine these evenings with errands for him in the Westminster Abbey precincts.'

'Your father is here in Town?'

'My father rarely leaves the diocese and his Grace, the Archbishop, doesn't get around too well with his gout, but refuses to leave the capital whilst the Royal Family remain.' She smiled. 'Total nonsense. It does mean I drive up to the Westminster Palace with papers for the Archbishop several times a week. A holy go-between.'

'That doesn't seem terribly efficient.'

'That is the Church of England. They've always done it this way. At least it gets me away from the deanery with trips up to Town – and petrol on the Church.'

'What about your dogs?'

'What about them?' Beamish scowled suddenly. 'Breeding Sussexes was my mother's wonderful idea, so she can feed them if I am not around. Small dogs for the hunting world, she called them. She wanted to give me something to do at home after— After my convalescence in the Alps. Oh, I like dogs well enough, and it started off as jolly good fun but it is becoming so very tiresome.'

If Granny's rumour mill is right, and it usually is, your mother wants to keep you out of other men's beds, Bunch thought. 'She gives a damn about what you are up to.' Bunch replied. 'That can't be so bad.'

'She gives a damn about the family reputation.'

'Don't they all? Mine is constantly trying to get me married off. Having an old maid in the family is such a trial for them.'

'Then you understand,' said Beamish. Her eyes softened to

appeal and Bunch felt a twinge of sympathy for her.

'Somewhat,' she said. 'We're all lucky to have homes these days.'

'So long as it's a roof with some life under it. I grew up in Oxford. It may be dreaming spires to some but it's on the main line into Town and a lot livelier than Chichester, I can tell you.'

'I've always rather liked Chichester. I'm surprised you're not fond of the country life. I would have thought you'd be all for it, being in the hunting dog line.'

'I like the dogs well enough but they are such a tie. Getting meat for them all now is becoming impossible.'

'Getting dog meat is hard,' Bunch agreed. The woman's dismissal of the animals' needs annoyed her but she nodded, not wanting to antagonise Harriett Beamish if there was a chance to squeeze more information from her. 'I'm sure you'll find a way,' she said. 'Like poor Larry and his car.'

'Oh yes, you're offering him a lift. I had suggested I take Larry home tomorrow. It's on my way.'

'It's all arranged now.'

'It would be no trouble. I often run him home. Know that road like my own.'

There was a brittle edge to Beamish's voice, informing Bunch without so many words that she was treading on toes, and she wondered why Etta Beamish returned to the subject. *Why does it matter to her that much?* She glanced at Wright, who seemed deep in conversation with Larry Parrish. 'Larry lives right on my doorstep,' she replied. 'Don't you Larry?'

'What's that?'

'Right on my doorstep.'

Parrish beamed at her. 'Yes, rather. Awfully good of you to offer the lift. Getting seats on trains can be tricky, even when you're in uniform.'

'Your choice.' Beamish turned to talk with Soames, shrugging as if she didn't give a hoot, but not before Bunch caught a look of sheer bile flit across her face.

Used to getting her own way, she thought. *Or maybe just plain old jealous.* She poured herself more champagne and let the matter drop.

Fatigue and a sense of tension were taking their toll. Perhaps it was the air raid, an intensity that she was not used to out in the country, or just that the tension at the table was palpably high. Bunch was more than ready to go home and was never more relieved than when the all-clear sounded a little before midnight.

As she mounted the stairs in the general exodus she was certain she spotted a familiar face. 'Henry?' she called.

Marsham touched a finger to his lips, took a single step, and vanished into the crowd. *Like an out-sized Peter Pan. What was he being so skittish over?*

'Was that someone we know?" said Wright.

'Perhaps.' She dropped back, allowing Parrish to forge ahead of them to the top of the stairs. 'Jemmy has quite obviously avoided me all evening and seemed to be making a point of it. As if she needed to prove she had no connections with me, though she danced with you. What did she have to say?'

'You are a bad influence. It seems she has been copying your sleuthing habits.' He frowned. 'She very proudly informed me that she was waiting to hear details about Miss Beamish's time in Switzerland, and also something about Penelope James's car. No idea what that might be.'

'Not a hint of a who or what?'

'She was annoyingly enigmatic. Waiting for some piece of ATS driver gossip. She promised to telephone me at the station the moment she finds anything.'

'Then we shall have to wait.'

'Did you get anything from Soames?'

'Nothing new though he was very twitchy when I talked about Etta. They may have been lovers at some point but there's no love lost where he's concerned. Trouble is, I am getting a different story from each of them, and deciding which of them is lying is proving to be quite exhausting.' Bunch yawned loudly as if to illustrate the point. 'Larry is getting impatient and I am simply bushed. Telephone me the moment you hear anything new.'

❧ Fifteen ❧

'I'm supposed to be the invalid,' Theadora observed, 'but you look quite dreadful.'

'Thank you so much, Mother.' Bunch collapsed into a chair and accepted the cup of coffee handed to her. 'I wasn't that late, as it happens, but I think Friday's accident has caught up with me.'

'There is no reason why you should get involved. There's quite enough for you to do on the estate.'

For a brief moment Bunch wondered if Theadora saw the irony in that, but her mother seemed genuinely unaware. There would have been a time when she would have been angry at that blatant challenge. She watched her mother lifting her own bone china coffee cup, noted the slight shake of he hands under even that small burden, noted the yellowing of her skin, the deep shadows beneath her eyes. *I should be grateful I don't have to battle her on every front. I'm not sure she'd be able to deal with full-scale confrontation. Though maybe she needs something to distract her.* 'I am quite capable of doing both,' she said, and smiled to take the sting. 'With Granny to fall back on, and Parsons for advice, and my super Land Girls working like Trojans. It's not so hard.'

Theadora spread her hands, and sighed theatrically. 'If you say so. We do worry, you know, and it's a little selfish of you to dive into danger when you really have no need.'

'You don't think making a drama over the spa isn't any less dangerous?' Bunch responded. 'You don't think we worry about you? Daddy is quite frantic, you know. The danger you are in is far greater.'

The two women stared at each other and Bunch wondered if she had gone too far, breaking the inviolate habit of maintaining silence over anything remotely unpleasant, even from the people, or perhaps especially from the people, closest to you. Theadora had enough American blood to make that marginally less applicable.

'Everything is fine, Mummy.' Bunch laid a reassuring forefinger on Theadora's arm. 'I shall be perfectly safe because I shall be in the company of the redoubtable Chief Inspector Wright. I promise to run away as fast as ever I can if anything looks remotely dangerous, but only if you'd agree to trundle off to Bath.'

'Is that anything like a bargain?'

'Better than the alternative. Besides, what are you staying here in London for? Anyone who can has already toddled off to the country, and who could blame them.'

'I know, darling. It's just that after Perringham House, the Dower is like being in a bloody goldfish bowl. There's no peace to be had.'

'That is so very true. I love Granny to bits but being crammed in there so tight...' Bunch chuckled. 'To carry on with the fishy theme, it's a sardine can! Even so, it's a great deal more than many people have right now.'

'I realise that and I know it's rather selfish of me. It's not just the space, you see ... not entirely. It is the feeling that my every move is being watched. By Beatrice. By Edward. And yes, my darling, by you. Even Knapp and Kimber seem to be taking turns watching the mad old lush – and hiding the booze.'

'It's all because we care about you.'

'It doesn't feel like that. It feels like a prison.'

Bunch reached out and covered her mother's hand with her own. 'I do understand. Truly I do. It felt exactly like that for me when I was invalided back from France. People hovering from the moment you wake, tutting every time you do something that wasn't on the dammed doctor's approved list of activities. All that was in Perringham House, where you could at least lose yourself when you needed to. God along knows I struggle there in the Dower House even though Granny and I get along together, for the most part.'

'Beatrice and I are not enemies. I don't know why you would think that.'

'I didn't mean to imply that you were. Though you have to admit you are not exactly bosom pals. One thing I have learned is that no house can ever have two mistresses, much less three.'

Bunch reached for a cigarette to allow Theadora to break the contact that she was clearly uncomfortable with. 'I know the spa is not your idea of heaven but at least a little stay in the West Country will give you some space.'

'Spa?' Theadora gave a hollow laugh. 'That makes it sound so acceptable. Taking the waters! We all know it's a clinic for drunks and addicts.'

'Perhaps, but please, Mummy, won't you go? If not for me and Daddy then maybe for the chance to see your grandchild growing up.'

'That was a low blow. Your grandmother has schooled you well,' Theadora said. She fell silent for a moment before finally conceding. 'Spa time it shall be, but not yet. I have a few things to do first.'

'Thank you, Mummy.' Bunch leaned in and gave her mother a light hug and drew back as the housekeeper came on.

'Ah, Gilsworth. Where is Mr Parrish? I expected to see him for breakfast.'

'He breakfasted early, Miss. He made a telephone call and asked me to tell you that he had business to attend to at his club, and he would carry on from there to Victoria to take the train.'

Oh, for heaven sake. There's some mad bugger out there wanting to kill him and he's puttering about on a train. 'I see,' she said aloud. 'Thank you, Gilsworth. I shall be going back down to the estate and won't be here for dinner.'

'No, Miss.'

'Are you going straight there now?' Theadora asked.

'I need to visit Brenda Green first, but yes I want to be home by dusk.'

'Is that the Land Girl who got herself into trouble?'

'Yes. I called the hospital and she isn't there so I called Kate for her mother's address. The Greens have no telephone, naturally.'

'I need the car this morning so you will have to get a cab, I am afraid.'

'Not a problem.' Bunch swallowed down her coffee. 'Will you take Kimber to Bath with you?'

'No staff allowed, apparently.' Theadora pulled a face. 'Rules. Don't you hate them? When I go there, if I go, and it's by no means set in stone, Kimber will be going down to the Dower. Edward feels that Beatrice could make use of her.' She checked her watch and gave her daughter a weak smile. 'I need to be off shortly. Say hello to Daphne for me and give little Georgi a kiss.'

'Safe trip, Mummy.'

'Bye-bye, my darling.' Theadora bent to drop a light kiss on her daughter's head and swept out before Bunch could get to her feet, and leaving her a little confused by her mother's uncharacteristic show of affection.

༄｡⌇༄｡⌇

After leaving a message with Wright's office about Parrish going AWOL from her tender care, Bunch called for a taxi and headed across the river into the chaos of bomb-ravaged docklands. Southwark Street was barely passable. Fire crews were damping down smouldering timber, and brick and rescue teams picked across heaps of rubble. Everywhere seemed to have a haze of smoke and river mist hovering above it. Bunch gazed at the bombed-out buildings, the tottering warehouse frontages, without rooves and minus side and rear walls, piles of rubble and timber that had been terraced homes. She passed them with a jaded curiosity, hating the fact that she was no longer surprised at what she saw, and far less shocked by it all than she felt she should be.

'Bloody criminal,' the cabbie called over his shoulder. 'Jerry's been after the railway all along 'ere. An' the docks on the other side. Amazed anythin's still upright.' He pulled off into a side street that ran close to the railway lines. ''Ere we are, Miss. Number thirty-one.'

'Thank you.' Bunch clambered out and stood on the pavement to take in her surroundings. The line of terraced houses was broken in several places along its length. At the far end she could see a clean-up team shifting rubble from the road where the newest gap still smouldered from its violent creation. The stench of smoke and burned brick mingling with damp plaster was an all-pervasive miasma she was coming to associate with London. Yet despite the carnage in the street, the door of number thirty-one was freshly painted and the step donkey-stoned into dazzling whiteness.

'Can you wait, please.' Bunch pressed a pound note into the driver's hand and went to knock. After a long minute the door was opened by a thin middle-aged, woman. Her grey hair was scraped back, her cheeks hollow and her eyes deep set. She wore a spotless wrap-over pinafore over a black dress and cardigan.

'Mrs Green?'

The woman hesitated and then nodded. 'Yes.'

'Good morning. I'm Rose Courtney.' She held out her hand. 'I came to ask after Brenda. I do apologise for calling unannounced but the number we have for Brenda seems to be out of order.'

'That would be Berry's corner shop. It got hit last week.' Mrs Green stepped back. 'You'd better come in.'

'Thank you.' Bunch stepped into a narrow hall painted in dingy cream above the dado rail and holly green beneath.

Her hostess hesitated by the only door leading off the passage, then hurried into the kitchen to the rear of the house. A large pan rattled on the range, its savoury steam misting the window over a Belfast sink. Armchairs on either side of the fire were draped with hand-knitted squares of blanket. A scrubbed table with cane chairs and a painted dresser had been crammed in to complete the furnishing.

Mrs Green opened the firebox on the small range and shoved in a few chunks of broken planking. 'Coal's a bit 'ard to get.' She wiped her hands on a cloth hanging by the range and moved the pan to the edge of the hob. 'Our Brenda's in the front parlour.'

'How is she? May I talk with her?'

The woman looked Bunch up and down, not seeming to like what was before her by the way her mouth set in a firm line. 'You 'avn't heard?' she said finally.

'The hospital had no record of her when I called. Nor the police. So I thought I should just come and see how things were.'

'I thought the Old Bill would've said something, but they don't, do they? I mean, they arrested her. Bastards – pardon my French, Miss – 'andcuffed her to the hospital bed, they did.' The woman folded inwards, wrapping her arms around herself. Her eyes were stark as she gazed at Bunch. 'The sister on the ward said they took the cuffs off cos you called their guv'nor. Thank you for that. At least she wasn't chained like a dog when she passed away. Our lovely girl's dead.'

The bald fact hit Bunch like a slap, followed by a scalding wave of guilt that she had taken a week to find time to come here. 'I am so sorry, Mrs Green. I had no idea. Please accept my condolences. When did it happen?'

'Early Tuesday.' Mrs Green rubbed at her arms. 'She's in the front parlour, like I said. If you want to see her.' There was a quiet dignity to the woman with a lurking undertone of pleading.

'Yes,' said Bunch. 'Of course.'

She followed Brenda's mother into the parlour. The blackout curtains were drawn and the room lit by a small lamp covered with a yellow cloth. It was a room like so many others Bunch had seen in cottages on the estate. A huge oak sideboard dominated one wall and a lovingly polished piano the other. Crammed between them, centre stage on the table, rested an open coffin of polished walnut, its brass handles gleaming in the lamp's glow.

Bunch approached slowly and peered inside. She realised it was something of a cliché to think that Brenda Green seemed to be sleeping, but she did look so peaceful, with the merest hint of serenity on her neatly rouged lips. *This sweet young woman is dead because some backstreet butcher doesn't know what a sterile tool is.*

'The Co-op does a lovely job,' Mrs Green murmured. 'You'd swear she was about to come out wiv one of her daft jokes.' The quiet voice at her side made Bunch jump.

'Yes. She looks perfectly lovely. What happened? If you don't mind my asking. Kate told me about the – operation.'

'She got an infection. Peree-something or other.'

Bunch shuddered. The stories of knitting needles and coat hangers she'd heard in nurse training had been the things of nightmare. 'Peritonitis? That can happen. How awful.'

'She needn't've, you know.' Mrs Green's voice cracked and she paused, gathering a suit of well-worn composure around her. 'She needn't've. It wouldn't be the first little visitor in this family. My old man weren't 'appy about it. Course he weren't, but we'd've stood by her.' She reached out to touch Brenda's cheek. 'Silly sausage. Sod the neighbours gas-baggin' about it behind your back, my pet.'

'She never breathed a word to any of the girls,' said Bunch.

'Not surprised. Brenda had a lot of pride. Just like 'er dad.' Mrs Green wiped at her face with her pinafore and forced a smile. 'Where are my manners? Can I get you a cuppa, Miss?'

'So very kind of you to offer, but I shan't impose. I have to get back to Wyncombe by tonight.' A train rattling past the back of the terrace drowned her out momentarily. She jerked a thumb in the direction of the noise. 'The trains can be so unreliable after dark though I imagine you don't notice whether they're on time or not.'

Her hostess glanced toward it, puzzled for a split second. 'Oh, we don't notice 'em any time of day. Half the trains into London come past 'ere. That's why we get such a pasting of Jerry night after night. Once it starts gettin' dark we're away down the shelters. Not this week though. Can't leave my little girl on 'er own, can I?'

The look of appeal and challenge in Mrs Green's face made Bunch swallow hard. 'No, of course not.'

'She'd be so frightened up 'ere on 'er own. So I stay.'

'With Mr Green?'

'Nah. He's bin on fire-watch down the Cathedral all week. Can't do much else wiv his back, but he does 'is bit.'

'I'm sure he does.' Bunch put her hand out, wondering if a touch to the shoulder would be strange. 'I am truly sorry. We all liked Brenda.'

Mrs Green gave Brenda's folded hands a pat. 'You sleep tight my pet. I'll just see Miss Courtney out.'

There was no mistaking her cue to leave and Bunch followed her to the front door with some relief. Coming from a world where people seldom showed emotion to each other, and never to the world at large, she found the woman's openness a little unnerving. *Which is why it's so hard to decide where people stand over two murders. And thinking about it here and now is highly inappropriate.* 'Is there anything I can do?' She said aloud.

'No, Miss, thank you for offering.' She laid one hand on Bunch's arm. 'The sergeant down the nick told me you'd left orders to contact you if our girl'd needed a solicitor. Thank you for that.'

'The least I could do. Just sorry we didn't know what was going on until Brenda went missing.' Bunch rummaged in her bag and pressed a visiting card into the older woman's hand. 'Please, Mrs Green, if there is anything we can do, no matter how small.'

'Bless you, Miss, but nothin' to be done now except bury her as proper as we can.'

Bunch climbed back into the waiting taxi and after ordering

him to drive back to Town house, sat back to examine the ideas that had come to her in Brenda's presence.

That was the rumour, as Granny had passed it on, that Harriett Beamish had a child in a Swiss clinic. That the child had been adopted, and I dutifully accepted it as the truth. But what if it had been a termination? Bunch was not sure what effect that would have ... or if there was any truth at all behind the gossip. *It's probably something I should find out.*

❧ Sixteen ❧

When Bunch set off on the cold Wednesday morning, the tracks left by the few vehicles up and out in that hour were clearly visible in the thick frost. Bare trees were uniformly coated and glinted in the low winter sun that was rising in a pale sky. The MG was still not heated and she nestled gratefully in her Irvin flying jacket, freshly delivered from the Army & Navy Stores. It fitted snugly around her neck and its length made it far less cumbersome for driving than either of the furs in her wardrobe or the duster coats in the stables. Not being cold was always a bonus.

With so little traffic she made good time, arriving in Brighton a little after eight a.m., as the message Jemima Harper had left with Knapp had requested. She could see Wright waiting for her on the steps of the small hotel that billeted the constantly changing rotation of ATS drivers.

'I hope you haven't been waiting long.' She pulled up at the kerb and eased herself out, grimacing as the biting sea-wind hit her like a battering ram.

'Just arrived. I was going to go in and wait.'

'Don't blame you. Ye gods, it's freezing out here.'

'But not snowing.'

'Small mercy,' she grumbled as she mounted the steps. 'Let's not hang around out here. Show me what you wanted me to see.'

'Harper left messages for me at the station early this morning.'

'Same here, or rather Knapp took a message at the Dower. Any hint of why she couldn't tell us things over the telephone.'

'She told Carter another driver claimed James and Naysmith left Newhaven that last day on two-days leave, and they were definitely together. Some kind of honeymoon perhaps?'

'It would make sense. Where did they go?'

'We are still trying to discover that. Not far, I would say, and almost certainly not on the coast. The other snippet of information she left concerned Harriett Beamish. It seems Beamish did go to a Swiss clinic, accompanied by Clarice Bell, and that they may have arrived there with a male companion.'

'Soames?'

'Harper said she'd have more answers by first post today.'

The foyer windows were permanently covered by blackout curtains and the only natural light came from the frosted glass panels of the main doors, making it a muted shadowy space. A low-wattage desk lamp glowered on the reception desk.

If reception is the right word, Bunch thought. She pulled off her heavy lined gloves as she approached the counter and smacked the bell with the flat of her palm.

A slightly built woman of middle years appeared after a few moments. 'Madam?' She was neat, business like in blue skirt and jacket and white blouse, and plainly not happy with her lot in life. She ran a curious glance up and down Bunch's attire before turning her attention to Wright. 'We've no vacancies, sir. I suggest you try the Hotel Alphonse down on the front.'

'Chief Inspector Wright.' He held his ID closer to her face than Bunch thought was strictly needed.

Rude but I approve, she thought. *Old battle axe plainly has the wrong idea.*

'We are not here to rent a room. We are here to see a Sub-Leader Harper. She is expecting us.'

'I am so sorry. Of course, Chief Inspector.' The concierge smiled, a hint of panic in her eyes. 'I haven't seen Miss Harper this morning. She didn't come down for breakfast, but these girls do keep odd hours. Not their fault, of course, when their duties keep them out at all hours.'

'Where will we find her?'

'Top floor. Number 307. One of our more compact rooms.' She flushed slightly. 'They were staff accommodation when we still had such a luxury. Now that our guests on the two upper floors are military, they fend for themselves.' She made a half-hearted attempt to come around the counter. 'Shall I show you the way?'

Wright held up his hand. 'We can manage. This way is it?' He indicated the staircase.'

'Up to the second floor, then turn right and the third-floor staircase is at the very end.'

'Thank you.' He tipped his hat and strode away, leaving her agog.

Bunch trotted along behind, giggling despite herself. 'She thought we were on a one-night stand,' she said. 'The nerve of the woman.'

'She'll be used to fielding that kind of thing. Brighton is still a popular spot for weekend couples even though the front is closed off. I imagine the reservations book is packed with Mr and Mrs Smiths.' Wright started up the narrow stairwell to the third floor.

'I suppose the hotel still wants return custom.'

'Most of those couples would never notice the decor. Here we are.' He rapped sharply on the white-painted door and waited. 'Miss Harper?' He hammered a little louder. 'Chief Inspector Wright and Miss Courtney here. Miss Harper?'

'Keep it down, chaps. I'm back on duty at midday and I'd like to get a few hours.' A tousled head appeared at the next door along.

'Sorry, old thing,' Bunch said. 'Can't get a reply. She is expecting us.'

'Probably still asleep. Right old racket in there when I came in from the shelters at four this morning.'

'She wasn't in the shelter?'

'Nah. Her boss wanted picking up at just gone midnight. He doesn't believe in air raids and shelters.'

'So she was out driving in the wee hours?'

'Probably.' The young woman shrugged and vanished.

'That explains why she didn't want to drag me out of bed when she called at midnight,' said Wright. He hammered on the door. 'Miss Harper?'

'Let me try. Jemima? Jemmy, it's me. Rose Courtney.' Bunch rattled the china door handle and the door swung open. She glanced at Wright uneasily.

He signalled Bunch to stay at the door, but she followed him in, nevertheless.

The tiny attic room was not merely untidy, it had been ransacked. Every movable object had been thrown around the floor and splattered with dark lines that continued up the walls and across part of the ceiling. There was a sweetish odour of recent death that Bunch recognised with a sinking finality, even without the unavoidable clue of a bloody body lying face down across the narrow single bed.

Jemima Harper's throat was a gaping sticky wound already congealing at its edges. The sheets and mattress beneath her were dark and sticky with spilled blood. Her face was turned toward them, the visible eye was wide open, and her mouth slack. The fingers of her left hand were trapped beneath her neck whilst the bloodied right hand hung limply down the side of the bed.

'Main artery severed,' Wright observed.

'I had rather drawn that conclusion,' Bunch replied. 'A sliced artery makes an awful mess.' She stared down at the body, shocked and deeply saddened. This investigation had veered into dangerous waters, yet, though her heart rate was a little high, she found herself able to take in the details with relative calm. She had not known Jemima Harper well, and once her initial shock faded she saw a crime scene as a puzzle to be solved. *Am I getting hardened to this kind of thing?* She glanced at Wright to see how it affected him. He was sombre but unhesitant. 'This is Jemima Harper,' she said. 'Without question.'

'The blood is drying so she's been dead for a few hours, I'd imagine.'

'I think we can rule out suicide.'

Wright gave her a pained look and reached inside his coat for his notebook. 'Will you run down to reception and call the station?'

ം⊱ുⴗⴖⴗⴖ

'According the girl in the next room—' Carter stood back while the ambulance drivers stretchered the body away and he consulted his notebook '—a Miss Rebecca Naylor, there was a lot of noise coming from the deceased's room at around four this morning.'

'Noise?'

'Shouting. A heated argument. At least three voices and, in her words, a lot of crashing about.'

'Do we know what these people were arguing over?'

'Miss Naylor claims she wasn't listening too closely. She does admit to hammering on the wall, and since the racket stopped immediately she didn't take any other action.'

'Did she hear anyone leave?'

'She says not. Again she claims that she wasn't really listening and was asleep again within minutes.'

'I find that hard to believe,' said Bunch.

'You say she was lying, Miss?' Carter glared at her.

'No, not at all.' She smiled at him. 'Thing is, old thing, I went to a boarding school. I was billeted with the FANY and ATS, and in my experience any argy-bargy amongst the neighbours will positively be meat and drink. Glasses against the wall would not be out of the question.' She spread her hands. 'I'm teaching my granny to suck those proverbial eggs, aren't I.'

'We shall take a proper statement later,' said Wright. 'People usually remember things once they've had time to think. Meanwhile, Carter, did you get any joy out of the staff? Was our victim at supper?'

The detective sergeant contented himself with sending Bunch a withering glance and referred back to his notes. 'The owner and a few basic staff were kept on to clean for the paying guests, and provide breakfasts. None of them live-in. The civilian guests are required to order evening meals a day in advance so most of the ATS girls eat at the barracks or in town.'

'I'm not surprised,' Bunch observed. 'If they're drivers they'll never know what time they'll be in or out. Bit rough though.'

'Cuts both ways,' Carter replied. 'The cook claims she can't cater if she doesn't know how many will be in. I hear they get fed better at the NAAFI so most days there aren't that many takers.'

'Nobody witnessed possible suspects leaving the building?' said Wright.

'No, Sir. The desk closes at nine every evening and opens at six in the morning. They rely on residents using latch keys. I gather there used to be a night porter as well as a receptionist, but he joined up just as the army requisitioned most of the rooms.'

'So we assume the killer entered the building as a guest. The doors were locked so it's the only way they would have got in.'

'Nobody recalls letting in any strangers.'

'Wonderful. A woman has her throat cut in a hotel room and no one saw or heard a thing.'

'I think it goes without saying, her murder is linked to the deaths of James and Naysmith,' said Bunch. 'It would stretch coincidence if it wasn't.'

'Probably no coincidence that she was killed after with speaking us. Why now? What has changed?'

'Plainly she had found something and was bumped off before she saw us again,' said Bunch. 'I can't see why she would divulge anything to her killer.'

'Or killers, if Miss Naylor is to be believed.'

'Perhaps they didn't know anything at all. Perhaps they were here for some other reason entirely and she let something slip. Which still points at someone she knew pretty well.'

Wright ran his hand several times over his head and replaced his hat. 'I don't think we can do much more here and now. There's nothing that tells us anything of value. We shall have to hope Letham turns something up in his post-mortem report. Can you attend, Carter?'

'Yes, Sir.'

'Wait just a moment,' Wright said when they reached the foyer. 'First post will have arrived. Let's see what she was waiting for.' He was back a minute later tearing open a long blue envelope. He took out two sheets of paper and scanned them rapidly.

'And?' Bunch demanded.

'Personal letter.' He squinted at the script. Looks like a man's writing. No address, so a close friend.'

'What does it say?'

My dearest Jemima. So good to hear from you after all this time. I have made the enquiries for you, and happy to say I have traced your friend in that year at the place you mentioned. I can say she may have been accompanied by two others as they all stayed in the guest house. It was a long time ago, so details are a little unclear. The procedures carried out are not listed but I think we can guess that. All seems to have been well. The expenses were paid in cash, and your friend left a forwarding address of a hotel in Rome. I should have that detail in the next week. Telephone me soon and we shall arrange for a dinner. Your friend, Maxime.' Wright looked at the envelope before handing it to Bunch. 'It's a London postmark. Any ideas?'

'Continental lettering.' Bunch tapped her fingernail on the crossed seven in the date. 'His syntax is a little odd, so along with the name we can assume he's not British. She said there was something in the post and here it is. Or some of it.' She flapped the paper at him. 'Address book. If this chap knows her well enough not to need to include it then she must have it somewhere.'

She paused. 'I didn't see any sign of a bag in her room and that's where most girls keep these things. Her killers must have taken it with them.'

'Our witness says it was probably a woman that Harper was arguing with.'

'Do you think people other than those on this list are at risk?' Bunch asked, staring at it.

'Someone tried to run you down,' Wright reminded her.

'True.' She looked at the list once more. 'Something fresh must have occurred after Jemmy left the supper club. Surely she would have said something to us otherwise?'

'One has to make that assumption.'

'Larry was with me, and he's the last of the crossed-out names.' She looked at him, sideways on. 'Is *he* in danger, though?'

Wright shrugged. 'There is no way of knowing. For such close friends, that circle does seem to harbour an awful lot of bad feeling.'

'You never went to a girl's school.' Bunch settled her hat and grinned at him. 'I shall call on Larry on my way home and see if he can shed any light. Call me when you get the PM results. Toodle-pip.'

∾∾∾

'Come in, Rose.' Larry Parrish waved her into the hallway of Chells and scanned the driveway briefly before closing the door. 'Chief Inspector Wright called to warn me I should keep an eye out. Do you honestly think I'm in danger?'

'Did he tell you about Jemmy Harper?'

'Not in any detail, but gosh. Poor Jemmy.'

'It was a brutal killing. She left a message saying she had information but our killer got to her before she could pass it on. Do you know anyone in London called Maxime? Possibly Swiss?'

'Not off the top of my head.'

'It plainly relates to Etta going there a few years back. It seems two people went with her.'

'We all know why she went.' Parrish arched one eyebrow. 'Etta was said to be very close to several of the chaps. If you get my drift. I would lay odds one of those people was Clarrie Bell.'

'Can you be certain?'

'It's a reasonable assumption. Let's not stand in the hallway. It's freezing.'

'Okay.' She followed him into the drawing room. 'Changing the subject, is there any reason why Penny and Claude would be trying to reach your house the night they died?'

'They were together?'

'Possibly.'

'I suspect they were…' Parrish pulled at his bottom lip as he gazed at the fire sulking in the grate. 'No,' he said, 'they knew the chances were I'd be somewhere out on the North Sea dodging U-boats. I suppose they may have thought they could throw someone off by dodging into the farm, if they were already close by. Other than that, I couldn't tell you. Perhaps it's best that I don't know. Being in the know seems to be rather dangerous. Sorry. Poor taste. Honestly, I can't think of anything that might be even remotely useful. Is this an official interrogation? Because you're awfully good at it.'

'I'm getting the hang of it, Larry. Would they have known you were not home?'

'Couldn't say. They were taking a punt, maybe? I'm sorry I'm not to be much use to you, am I?' He smiled sheepishly. 'It probably sounds completely bonkers to you, but I can't help starting to feel we're somehow cursed. First it was George, then Jonathan, and I heard Herbert Clement was killed in a raid on an airfield a few weeks ago. They were all supper-clubbers in the early days. Some of them not for very long … but still. That makes six gone now.'

'It's a war. It is a terrible thing but people die.' Bunch laid a hand on his arm. 'If it's any consolation, Larry, I was never a part of the crowd and someone had a pop at me. This is something far closer to home than a few chaps slumming around at the Café de Paris.'

'Someone tried to kill you! How? Where?'

'Up in Town, with a car.' She laughed sharply. 'Motor accidents are becoming a bit of theme in my life, it seems. I really should stick to horses.'

'I can imagine. Disturbing, having a killer in our midst. You always rather hope your pals are watching your back, not stabbing them.'

'We'll catch them. Meanwhile you need to make sure of your

own safety. Spend some time with the jolly old 'rents and then head straight back to your ship.'

'That feels rather cowardly.'

'You'll have other leaves. I know it's not far off now but hopefully before Christmas. Or over the New Year. If not, then I am sure Tilly will be most awfully glad to have you to herself just now. She misses you.' She pulled her scarf tighter for the comfort of its soft folds. The thought of young Parrish in command of a ship, albeit a coastal minesweeper, seemed mad. She could recall seeing him running across the fields in short trousers. 'Now I must go. Keep an eye out for intruders and telephone me if you can think of anything that might help.'

৯৵৯৵

'You missed Sunday service – again,' were the first words Beatrice uttered when Bunch entered the morning room. 'I've barely seen you since you missed last week's sermon.'

'Yes, Granny, I am sorry. I did try to get back earlier but you know how it can be. I've been so busy all week.'

'With this detective work, no doubt. Off to Brighton in the dark, according to Knapp.' Beatrice set down her pen and pushed the letter she had been writing into the bureau drawer.

'Well ... yes.'

'Still haring about after Penelope James's murderer? Connie Frain had been relating all kinds of rumours about the deaths of your young friends at the WI luncheon yesterday. Usual nonsense – of which German paratroopers and Bolshevik assassins are the least fanciful. I'm sure you have the real facts.'

After a moment of hesitation, wondering if it was ethical, Bunch launched into a rundown of the case, only excluding the attempts on her own life. *She doesn't need to know that; it would upset her and I'd never hear the last of it.* 'That is it so far. No need to tell you it is not to go beyond this room. Not until the case is closed, however much your pal Connie Frain tries to wheedle it out of you. As a plus, she's gossiping about the grisly deaths rather than about me. Or Mummy.'

'Indeed.' Beatrice frowned, looking into the space somewhere over Bunch's left shoulder. 'Has your mother finally trotted off to Bath?' Her voice was neutral but after years of interpreting her grandmother's coded asides, Bunch could hear a whole litany

205

lodged between invisible lines.

'If nothing else, it will give her some space to breathe,' said Bunch.

'You don't worry that she will go elsewhere once she is out of sight? You may not be aware of it but she has done something of the sort before.'

'She has?'

'September 1920. We had a stay at a convalescent home all arranged and she vanished. We eventually traced her to a small hotel up in the Lakes.'

'I didn't know. Is that why I was sent to school so suddenly? I thought—'

'That your parents had a posting to America? Your father did, it was true. He'd arranged for your Aunt Adelia to take over Theadora's consulate hostess duties until your mother was more herself. It took a great deal of effort to keep it hushed up. Could have ruined your father's career. At least we know it won't happen this time. Kimber is in charge and nobody argues with Theadora's shadow.'

'Kimber is not going to the spa.'

'No? She will be devastated about that.' Beatrice waved her hands in a resigned circle. 'You should know that Kimber lost her husband to the flu in 1919, which it is why she is so devoted to your mother. They feel the same loss.'

'I never knew that, either.'

'If you never ask, my dear, you will never know.' Beatrice rolled her eyes at Bunch's exasperated tutting. 'And you did not need to know. That is how families survives. One never discusses personal affairs unless absolutely cornered. All I am saying, is that loss can affect people in very different ways. Your mother soaked herself in alcohol. Kimber transferred her devotions to her job. As did Edward, if we are being honest. And you?' Beatrice reached up an age-spotted hand and stroked Bunch's face. 'You dealt with Jonathan's death by taking up arms. Don't think I didn't know how close you two were.'

'You knew about us?'

'That you bedded the boy? Of course I knew. You young people always assume that you invented sex and that every generation before could never have possibly indulged in anything of the kind. How you imagine you all came into this world is beyond me.' Beatrice's sad smile turned impish. 'Even we old trouts have had our moments.'

'Granny!'

'Oh Rose, for such an emancipated young woman you often display a rather prudish side. The point I am trying to make is that these crimes of yours all smack of desperation. There is no greater despair than grief. I don't wish to belittle Theadora's loss because I do know what she feels. One never recovers, nor does one forget. If you're ever blessed with children and have the pain of losing them you will come to know that.'

Beatrice busied herself with her coffee. She never spoke of her son Lucien, and the veiled reference brought Bunch up sharp. Uncle Lucien, Edward's younger brother whom she had never known though his portrait had been hanging in the gallery, had been a serving officer in India. It was easy to forget that Beatrice had lost every bit as much as Theadora. 'I do appreciate that grief explains Mother's drinking,' she said. 'I'm just not sure how it relates to this murder case, which was what we were talking about.'

'Death,' Beatrice replied, 'and how people deal with it. I should wager it being at the back of all this. It all smacks of revenge for some past loss.'

'I can't see that at all.'

'No, but then you haven't seen as much of people's darker sides as I have, despite your running around willy-nilly with that policemen chappy viewing corpses. Now there's Knapp ringing the gong for luncheon. Shall we?'

❧❀❧❀❧

Bunch had gone to settle down in the estate office with every intention of tackling the mountain of forms and reports that had accumulated in her absences. After only a few minutes she was leaning on the desk, close to the top of the small stove for warmth. She rapped a pen against the desk as she stared through the dusty window of the converted storeroom.

Though the paraffin stove took the edge off the chill, it also added a layer of fume-laden condensation between herself and the view across the Downs. She leaned forward to wipe a hole in the droplets. It didn't help a great deal. The wind had dropped and the drizzle had given way to a thickening mist coming in from the

207

coast. Even across the stable yard familiar shapes were losing definition – but her mind was not on the things her eyes were taking in.

Beatrice's incisive commentary had set her on a fresh train of thought. In normal times her cure for a restless mind or body would have been a hack across the estate and beyond. The fog was no barrier when she knew every bridleway and hill track for miles around as well as she knew her own hand, but she had promised both Wright and her father that she would not stray far from the house alone. She pushed back her chair and bent to turn off the stove. The company of horses, however, was both possible and desirable.

Bunch crossed the yard and plunged into the dusty dimly lit confines of the stable. Scents of horse and hay, and the echoless density of the familiar space, were an instant balm. This was her place and she realised how much she had missed it in the previous weeks of haring around the country in that little blue MG.

The sound of straw being trodden on, and the small snickers of greeting, preceded the heads of the stable occupants appearing at their respective stalls.

'Hello kiddies' Bunch scooped up some wisps of hay and fed some to each, patting their necks and rubbing their foreheads and muttering nonsenses as she went from Robbo to Maggie and pausing finally with the elderly Perry. She picked up a pair of body brushes, pushed her way into his stall, and twitched back his light rug. She began to groom him, settling into a mesmeric state with left-right sweeps of the brushes that were as soothing for her as for the Fell Pony. She worked methodically from his head to rump as she had so many hundreds of times before. The warmth of the pony's body and the cloistered feel of the stable allowed the things that bothered her to swirl around her mind in an almost dreamlike state. When she finished, and readjusted the rug, the equine treatment had failed to work its magic.

'Still have no idea where this is leading,' she told Perry. 'That supper club has the answer but damned if I know what it is.'

Perry nudged his forehead gently against her shoulder, snuffling greedily at her hair.

'You don't care, do you? All you want is a treat. Sorry old chap. Nothing doing. You're getting chubby, standing around indoors all day.' She laid her head against his cheek, scratching the course hair beneath the pony's chin. 'So what now?'

'Miss Rose?' Lizzie Hurst sidled around the main doors and edged nervously down the aisle, keeping her distance from Maggie's infamous jaws. 'There's a telephone message come for you.' She held out a piece of paper.

'Who from?'

'It was a young chap as I spoke to from Brighton police. He said it was from Chief Inspector Wright and how it was ever so very urgent.'

Bunch came out of the stall, her hand held out. 'Give it here.' She snatched the slip of paper and read it rapidly. *Got a lead at last. I shall be at the hut where James was discovered if you want to be in at the kill.* 'Is this it?' she said. 'There was nothing more?'

'That was all, Miss. The constable said it was very urgent.'

'Did he leave his name?'

'No, Miss, just said as he were down Brighton, and Chief Inspector Wright told him to telephone you the message.'

'Very curious.' Bunch stared at the paper. *Why didn't he speak to me? I told Carter I'd be in the office all afternoon.* 'All right, thank you, Lizzie.'

She waited for the door to close behind the maid before reading the note again. 'It sounds like Wright,' she said.

Perry snorted and she gave him a final slap to his neck before heading indoors to telephone Wright.

♮♭♮♭

'Chief is out, Miss Courtney. And Sergeant Carter.'

'But did they leave me a message?'

'Yes, Miss, there was one here at the desk when I came on duty, so I rang it straight through.'

'And you're positive it came from Chief Inspector Wright?'

'Couldn't've been left here unless it was him that left it, Miss.'

'All right. Thank you very much. Will you contact him straightaway? Tell him I shall meet him there.'

The drive along the A24, through the village of Washington and searching for the lane that Wright's note had specified, took far longer than it should. The fog was dense by now, and freezing fast, so that as she turned off the main road her tyres left twin tracks in the film of whitening ice overlaying the set already

209

recently laid.

She passed farm gates on her right and slowed a little more as the lane narrowed to a single car's width. There were bites in the tarmac to each side where rain had worn away the edges, with tufts of dried grasses poking up in the middle of the road where tyres never ran. Trees arched from the hedgerow to meet overhead, the bare branches forming a tunnel. It was a lane like many she knew in the county but she was glad when it rose up a steep incline and opened out into wider section overlooking the edge of the hill.

A black Humber Saloon was parked to one side in the lee of some scrubby gorse and brambles, its moisture-laden bonnet pointing toward the south. Bunch pulled up next to it and sat looking around her. There was no sign of Wright's Wolesley or his ATS driver, Glossop, who usually stayed with the vehicle. Nestled in a hollow a short distance down the slope was a dark smudge that she assumed had to be the shepherd's hut close to where the body of Penelope James had been discovered.

She climbed out of the MG and cupped her hands against the saloon's windows. The inside seemed oddly pristine. She walked around it and bent to look at the bumper. It was shining and clean and the matt-white dim-out paint covering the black was apparently pristine, but something in the way it caught the light made her run her fingers along its surface. She paused and retraced the move to be sure it was not her imagination. There was a distinct ripple in the steel. Well disguised but unmistakable. *So it's been repaired?* That in itself proved nothing; Bunch had dinked bumpers often enough to know that, but it was food for thought.

She stood up and peered toward the hut, shading her eyes against the light, intent on making out its shape without having to walk down across slippery grass.

The blow to the side of her head came without the merest whisper of warning.

ৡ৵ৡ৵

The numbing cold and darkness were her first coherent thoughts, closely followed by pain. Bunch tried to ease herself upright but found herself unable to move more than a few inches in any direction. The effort seemed more than she could contemplate.

She sat motionless, expecting the silence of the countryside in winter, but hearing instead the steady drone of Dornier squadrons passing overhead. Somewhere on the Downs anti-aircraft guns were pounding a staccato counterpoint.

Random thoughts flitted through her mind as she fought to retain full consciousness. She was cold, chilled deep to the bone. Blinking rapidly, she tried to focus on the view through the MG's side window, partially obscured by the beginnings of fern patterns inside the glass. She could see very little through the night-time shadows beyond flashes on the distant horizon that she told her she was somewhere overlooking the coast. Were these lights bombs blasts over one of the coastal towns? Or some naval skirmish out in the channel?

Bunch shook her head and blinked a few times. Awake now, she looked around her. It was a clear night without a hint of the earlier mist and she wondered how long she had been out there on the Downs.

The car was tilted almost on its right side, which accounted for her driver's view being of grass and chalk. The MG had rammed into something solid and unidentifiable in the deep shadows. The moon was visible through the passenger side. She noticed how it was only just past the first quarter but eerily bright, and sporting a hazy frost-halo in an otherwise cloudless starlit sky.

The cold and hard rim of the steering wheel had bent across her upper thighs, trapping her in place. Her head hurt and her joints ached, but so far as she could tell she was not seriously injured. She was just so very, very cold. Yet despite that she wanted to sleep. She snuggled her chin into the sheepskin lining of her Irvin jacket and wrapped her arms around herself.

Then Bunch realised where she was – and why, and knew that in an isolated spot the chances of anyone finding her before morning were slight. The risk of her dying from exposure if she did not get free from the wreckage was exponentially high.

Broken window glass was scattered all around her, winking in the moonlight, crunching as she tugged at the steering wheel to test its strength and structure. 'Good Midlands steel,' she muttered. 'That's not going to move in a hurry.' She tried the door handle, shoving against it as hard as she could. It gave a few inches as the latch half-freed itself and then stopped. A couple of whacks did nothing to budge it any further. It was firmly wedged against a pile of bricks and rock.

She heaved at the wheel once more and felt it move a tiny faction and then settle back against her thighs. She tried wriggling back, hearing the springs in the seat complaining at the pressure, and managed a bare inch or two of progress. She braced her hands on either side of the seat and pushed herself upwards – but her legs were held firm. *If only my knees could bend the other way, like a dog's,* she thought. She squashed herself sideways and back in the same movement, but impeded by the heavy leather jacket, which she had blessed a few moments before, she could not squeeze free.

And then something pinged around her old leg injury. Had anyone been within earshot her scream would have brought them running, but all she heard coming back to her were bleats from a few sleepy sheep and that constant drone from above and distant muffled booms. Bunch wiped sweat from her forehead and smiled grimly. *Well, it's warmed me up at very least.*

Bunch wriggled around a little more so that her feet were furthest into the right hand corner of the foot well and slid her torso to the left, wriggling her hip to squeeze a few inches around, all the while hissing away the agony that coursed up from around her knee.

She took a rest, sweating and panting, and swearing comprehensively to an empty hillside. *Because,* she thought, *a few bloody sheep and two rabbits don't count.* Her head throbbed and she could feel the stickiness of congealed blood on the side of her face and neck. Her knee hurt like the very devil. *But I'm alive.*

Grasping at the wheel, she pulled at it once more, whimpering at each fresh wave of agony – eyes screwed shut, wondering whether her teeth would stand being clenched that hard for that long without shattering. As she felt her body finally slide around she let go and laced her fingers under her damaged knee to ease it outwards. When her leg came free she lay back, panting from pain and exhaustion.

One leg was free but the other remained trapped in the foot well. Her awkward position contorted her pelvis into a painful angle. She could not rest as yet. Reaching behind her she scrabbled for the passenger door handle. It unlatched and though gravity did not allow it to swing freely she pushed against it with her head as she hauled herself backwards an inch at a time. She grabbed at the leg of her slacks and tugged her left leg free. Her head and shoulders were jutting out of the left side of the car, which in turn was suspended several feet up from the grass.

The vehicle jerked suddenly as the weight distribution changed and as it lurched toward the ground. Bunch pulled herself into a sitting position, slightly dazed and breathless. *My leg hurts like a bastard but I'm almost out.* Grabbing her bag from under the passenger seat she rolled out and onto the grass, crawling free of the wreckage.

The ground was frozen solid and the close-cropped grass was thick with frost that she could feel melting under her backside, but she sat for several minutes staring up at the sky and the last flight of bombers sliding across the stars, perhaps toward London.

It wasn't so many nights since she had been in the Café du Paris. She was certain, and felt a sinking feeling, at the potential destruction that a large flight could wreak upon it.

In her more immediate situation, she was not in much better shape than a bombsite. She attempted to stand and her head swam with the effort. Without warning her stomach reacted. She leaned to one side just in time to avoid filling her lap with vomit. As gross as that was, she did feel sufficiently better to haul herself upright and stand on one leg, balancing herself gingerly against the back of the MG. The little car's nose was buried deep into what was left of the hut with the front right wheel splayed at an impossible angle – the vehicle was not going to move anytime soon. She had driven a mile along the track, at the very least, since passing the farm.

There was no sign of the black Humber that had been parked at the top of the slope, which came as no surprise. Whoever lured her here had left her for dead. And she was very aware of how similar this was to the death of Claude Naysmith. 'It worked once, why change it?' she muttered. Her hand strayed to her neck, remembering the report of how Naysmith's spine had been neatly sliced and wondering why her would-be killers had not repeated the method.

That this was also the self-same place where Penny James's body had been dumped did not elude her. *Same killers or a very elaborate set-up.* Bunch was not inclined to wonder too much about it at that point. Her chief aim was to reach safety. The only people who had a hint of where she was were a rather dim constable at Brighton nick and Lizzie Hurst. Neither was likely to raise an alarm before dawn, at the earliest. *By which time I will have frozen to death.*

All the while she was turning the facts over in her head, Bunch was scanning around in the gloom for something she could use as a crutch. There were no walking sticks in the car, nor a blanket, which she now realised was a serious omission. *Only option is to walk, or hop, or crawl. I suppose it will keep me warm – and at least it isn't raining.*

She looked at her bag and cursed quietly. She needed both hands free and the bag was too fashionable to be practical. Its handles were too long to thread over her arm and lodge under her shoulder, yet too short to wear across her body. Bunch took out her identity card, notebook and purse, which she thrust in her pockets, and lobbing the bag on the grass she vowed to invest in a rucksack to keep in the boot, along a blanket in the event of future emergencies.

The crawl on hands and one knee to the track at the top of the slope was the hardest part. She stopped on the edge of the tarmac gasping for breath. There was not a hint of man-made light now, as she expected, and she knew that her best bet was to go back the way she had come toward the farm. But it was a long way on a wonky leg. She unwound her scarf and wrapped it around her damaged knee, pulling it as tight as she could without cutting off the circulation, and levered herself to her feet, putting most of her weight onto her good leg and using the other to balance with the tip of her boot.

The downhill portion was accomplished through a tortuous hop-step, taking frequent rests. The lower stretch of road was lined by hedgerows with hazels thrusting whippy strands toward the track. Breaking one free with her bare hands was not easy, but she managed to fashion a stave of a kind. Not strong enough to take her full weight but sufficient for her to adopt a halting dot-and-carry gait.

She had covered almost half a mile when she heard the car, the low gurgle of a high-performance engine that was struggling well below its capacity as it negotiated the narrow rutted road at walking speed.

Bunch's first thought was to step into the middle of the road and flag it down. *Why would anyone be up here in the dark in a big car?*

A tractor perhaps, or shooting brake ... but not some eight-cylinder monster?

Much as she'd been praying for help, she had no reason to believe this was bringing succour. Nor was it a coincidence, she thought. She stepped back, stumbling into the ditch, and lay shivering in six inches of semi-frozen mud and slush that lay at the bottom. She crawled around to peer through the stems of dead grasses to catch a glimpse of whoever came past, and thanked the gods that the darkness would cover any disturbance in the hoar frost where she wrestled with the hazel pole.

The car crawled through the tree-tunnel and rolled out into the moonlit stretch. An Alvis Coupe, long and sleek and darker than a bomber's moon, its engine rumbling to itself like a giant cat. As it passed she had a glimpse of the driver's profile against the moonlight and she shrank down a little further. It was unmistakable.

'Basil,' she whispered. 'Why am I not surprised?' She watched the car cruise the last of the flat ground. It was too far to see anything beyond a faint glimmer reflecting off the white-painted bumper. Soames appeared to be alone but she could not be certain.

He would reach the car in no time, and she had no doubt her car dashed against the shepherd's hut was his destination. Perhaps he had come to finish the job? If he was here to deliver the coup de grace, then who had been in the black saloon?

Bunch looked both ways along the lane. If he came back this way she would be overtaken in no time. And she was not sure she could take another leap into the ditch. The open space beyond the trees seemed her best option. She plunged into the undergrowth and fought her way through the overgrown hedge, clambering over the fence hiding at its core, to emerge on the further side at the edge of a newly ploughed field. The headland was narrow and she had no way of knowing if there was another ditch hidden in the shadows. Neither choice between long grasses full of hidden obstacle or the freshly turned earth now frozen into peaks and troughs was tempting. Her only other option was to wait for her pursuer to catch up, so she set off along the edge of the ploughed soil.

The furrows were solid enough to stand on but jarred her leg with every step, and the going was even slower than before. She had not covered more than half a mile when the Alvis growled passed her on the other side of the hedge at little more than a walking pace. He was searching the road for any sign of her, and though there was little chance of him spotting her in the darkness she flung herself face down in the solidified clay and chalk. Her heart was pounding as she listened for any sign of Soames's Alvis coming to a stop, of car doors banging, of voices, footsteps, anything at all. A breeze whispered among the branches and an owl coasted along the field edges looking for voles, but nothing more. Even the planes had vanished.

Heaving herself to her feet was an effort. Her feet and hands were numb with cold and though her knee was aching less now, she could tell that it was swollen beneath the scarf by the way it refused to bend. The farm was not far off now, she kept telling herself as she stumbled along the along the narrow headland. Another fifteen minutes and she was at the back of the farmyard, peering between the buildings for any sign of Soames's car. Satisfied that he had not stopped there, she limped toward the backdoor of the farmhouse and was halfway across the yard when a deep growl came out of the darkness. She saw a hint of movement as a pair of collies circled her. She stopped dead in her tracks. These were a sneaky breed, given to herding their prey where another dog would set up a lot of noise.

'Hello!' Bunch shouted. 'Hello in the farm.'

The dogs began to bark and the door opened in seconds. A sturdy woman appeared in the doorway, a shotgun in her arms.

ɤ∽ɤ∽ɤ

Bunch sat on the edge of kitchen table a half-hour later nursing a mug of tea whilst the farm woman knelt to bandage her knee by the light of a large Victorian oil lamp.

Bunch looked around the huge room. The only other source of light was the woodfire crackling in a vast black iron range, but she knew what would be in that room. The same things that filled every farmhouse kitchen she'd ever been in. Old ladder-back chairs at the table. A couple of saggy armchairs near the fireside along with several pairs of damp work boots stuffed with newspaper. Above them, a rack festooned with drying clothes hung from the ceiling. A large pan was simmering gently at the edge of the range filling the room with a rich meaty aroma. It was a comforting space. Ramshackle and dusty, the abode of people too busy for things like cleaning. It was a welcome refuge.

It amused Bunch that a telephone held pride of place on the dresser despite that there was no electricity in the building. She ran her hand over her hair and was a little glad that the light was poor. She knew she looked a mess, up to her eyes in mud, her slacks torn and face streaked with blood. But the woman tying off the bandage with a confident hand took it all in in her stride, as if wild-eyed women appeared in her yard every night of the week. She was a strong woman in her late forties, weather beaten from an outdoor existence. 'Your policeman from Brighton will be here any time now,' she said. 'Are you sure you don't want me to call the local constable?'

'Quite sure Mrs Tolley, thank you.' Bunch winced as the strapping pulled tight but relaxed as the pressure eased her pain. 'Thank you. Were you a nurse?'

'Auxiliary.'

'France?'

Tolley shook her head. 'No. Convalescence home up near Camberley. Jessie and I served together.'

'Jessie?'

'Jessamine Case. We own this farm. She's due back in the morning. Went to see her aunt in Cirencester.'

'Thank you, Mrs Tolley.'

'It's Vivienne. Viv.' She stood up and began repacking the first aid kit. 'We have met before, you know.'

'We have?'

'You were Land Girl officer for a short while. Settled four girls with us. It's a big house so plenty of room.'

'I thought I had been here before. Sorry. Blame the bump on the head.' Bunch nodded and slid from the table to pull her trousers back up. 'So you aren't alone here then?'

'Right now I am, yes. The girls took the bus down to Worthing. It's one of their birthdays. They should be back soon.'

'Not you?'

'Ever since that girl was murdered up there last month we haven't left the farm empty.'

'But alone? At night?'

'Our shepherd lives in the cottage across the yard. I have the dogs, and Gertie over there.' She waved at the shotgun propped against the other end of the table. 'And I keep my wits about me.'

'So you'd have seen anyone drive up here this afternoon?'

'There was a little blue sports car.'

Bunch grinned. 'That was me. But before that?'

'Yes. A black Humber. That was around two o'clock.'

'And it came back?'

Tolley thought about it. 'No, it didn't, now you say. But the track does go and lead out to Foreman's farm. Bit rough going but passable. Not too wet right now.'

'And where after that?'

'Then it leads to Storrington Road.' Tolley went to the window at the sound of a car. She pulled the curtain aside to peer out into the yard. 'Here comes your copper.'

'Don't you worry about blackout?'

'Never known a warden come anywhere near us, and if anyone thinks a pilot's going to spot the measly glow from my kitchen lamp from however many thousand feet up, they are barking mad.' She flung the door open and admitted Wright and Carter. 'Come in gents. Tea? Or maybe some homebrew? Harry makes a good drop of cider.' She held her hand out. 'Viv Tolley.'

'Mrs Tolley.' Wright stepped in with Carter hot on his heels and closed the door rapidly. 'Chief Inspector Wright, Sussex Constabulary. I believe you met Sergeant Carter when the body was discovered here last month?'

'I did. Good evening, Sergeant.'

'It's an offence to show a light,' Carter grumbled.

'So it is. And it's *Miss* Tolley.' She stared at them both, arms folded.

'My apologies.' Wright looked past her to Bunch, his expression grim. 'Rose ... are you completely mad? After everything that's happened to you these past few days – what on earth were you doing up there alone?'

'Doing my job,' she snapped. 'Someone from Brighton Police telephoned me saying you had left word telling me to meet you up there. And yes, before you say it, I did call back and check and—' She paused. 'There is no call to glower at me that way, William Wright. The PC at your station was quite positive that the message came from you.'

'We shall look into that.'

'Do. Please.' She put her hand to her head, aware that everyone was watching the exchange with far more interest than she liked. 'Without wishing to appear a little pathetic, I am not sure I can survive any more attempts on my life.'

'I am not sure anyone else would have survived as many as you have. You are the proverbial nine-lived cat.' Wright reached out to touch her shoulder. 'Do you remember anything of what happened to you up there?'

'Not really. Somebody whacked me over the head and while I was unconscious and stuffed me back into my car. They sent it careering down the hillside.'

'Same as for Naysmith...'

'The coincidence hadn't escaped me.'

'Are you badly hurt?' said Wright.

'No. I quite like being soaked in mud and blood.' Bunch snapped. 'It's quite the rage, don't you know!'

'I meant—' Wright attempted a smile. 'May we sit down Miss Tolley?'

'Of course. I'll put the kettle back on.' Tolley went to the range and moved the heavy steel kettle to the centre of the hob then turned with arms folded to lean against the wall and watch her unexpected guests. 'Carry on, chaps, don't mind me.'

'The MG is back along the road wrapped around the shepherd's hut where you found Penny James. Not a coincidence, I'm sure.' Bunch avoided Wright's glowering stare, concentrating instead on massaging her leg. 'There was a black saloon parked there when I arrived, a Humber. I thought at first it was a police Wolseley until I got close up.'

'And what time would that have been?' Carter asked, pencil poised over his notebook.

Bunch glanced at Tolley. 'Still just about light. Three o'clock perhaps? The next I knew I was jammed in the wreckage of my car and it was pitch black. Took me while to get free and walk back here to telephone you.'

'Which was around six,' Tolley added.

'And you have no idea who was waiting there for you?' Wright asked.

'I didn't see anyone there. But I did see Basil Barrington-

Soames a little later.'

'At the crash site?'

'In the lane as I was coming back down on foot. He could only have been heading there.'

'He passed you.'

'I made sure he didn't see me. I took a dive into the ditch and got soaking wet. I also have the scratches to prove it. Twenty minutes later he came back down the lane again, slowly as if he were scanning the hedges, but I'd hopped across into the field by then.'

'You're sure it was him?'

'Of course I'm damn well sure. I may have a bump on the noggin, and yes it was dark, but I know what and who I saw.'

'I saw it,' said Tolley. 'Came back down not long before Miss Courtney staggered into the yard.'

'Could you identify the driver if you saw him again, Miss Tolley?" Wright asked

'Probably not. It was dark.' Tolley glared at Carter. 'I'd know the car anywhere. Damned great Alvis Coupe. Fairly sure it was blue though one can never be certain in moonlight. It went up the lane a little after six and came back a half-hour later. I think it may have had one of those Motoring club badges on the front guard but I couldn't be sure on that.'

'You notice everything that goes along here in such detail?'

Tolley pulled a face. 'With umpteen murders on our doorstep? That is a ridiculous question, if you don't mind me saying. I have young women here under my care. Of course I take notice.'

'One murder,' Carter said.

'And one attempted,' Bunch added.

'Which should never have been possible if you had stayed at home, as I asked you to do. I am going to take you back to Wyncombe and get a doctor out to see you.'

'I am perfectly all right. Apart from the knee. There is no call to make a fuss.'

'For God sake, woman!' Wright took Bunch by the shoulders and glared into her face. 'Someone tried to kill you – again! You've been knocked unconscious! What in hell does it take for you to admit you are not indestructible?'

Bunch drew in her breath and tensed against the stinging

behind her eyes. A natural reaction to shock, she realised, but she would not give that man the satisfaction of tears. 'Don't you dare shout at me, William Wright. I will not have it.'

'No. Heaven forbid somebody tells Her Highness here that things can't all be solved by sheer bloody mindedness!'

'There are plenty of people in my own family ready and willing to do just that! You'll have to join the queue.'

Bunch was aware of Carter and Tolley exchanging looks in the silence that followed, both smothering their sniggers. *Watching the adults having a ding-dong never fails amuse*, she thought, and struggled to hold in a snicker of her own at the incongruity of it all.

'Oh, come on,' Wright said. 'I shall take you home to your grandmother. You don't argue with her.'

❧ Seventeen ❧

'Enough with your nonsense, Rose. Out with it. Was it icy? Was there another vehicle? Or were you just driving too fast in that toy car of yours?'

Bunch shook her head and fought down the urge to snap. 'No, Granny. It wasn't ice,' she said. 'Or mud, and I was *not* driving fast. But thank you for your sympathy. I do so appreciate it.'

'Don't be so ridiculous. You know very well that I worry. We all worry. And being brought home in a police car in such a terrible state last night rather proves we're right to do so.' Beatrice poured the ritual afternoon tea and handed her granddaughter a cup. 'Now stop pouting and tell me what happened.'

'It was just a little prang over on the other side of Storrington. I am perfectly fine.'

Beatrice arched one brow. 'Not what your inspector friend told me.'

'William doesn't have all of the facts.'

'But more than I do, it would seem.'

'I haven't had time to tell you.'

'No? When someone asks after a person's health it's usual to relay the pertinent facts,' Beatrice replied. 'You have a somewhat robust regard of your own importance, Rose Courtney, but you don't yet warrant royal bulletins posted on the gates.' She poured her own tea and settled back in her chair. 'I do worry. War is one thing but you have got yourself mixed up in all of this from choice.'

'Not entirely. William called me first for my advice.'

'Semantics. You are not obliged to answer his call. Oh, I understand you want a little excitement, my dear. Heaven knows, I recall being so frustrated by all the silly rules when I was your age, but you have a habit of leaving such devastation in your wake. Take your new car. Edward sent Sutton out to look at it and he

222

says it may well be beyond repair. Such a shame when you've only had it a few weeks.'

'I pranged it pretty thoroughly, I grant you. And I have no idea if it can be fixed. I know it's not his car anymore, but I dread to think what Larry will have to say about it.'

'How did you run off the road?'

'The lanes up there are so narrow and it was almost dark,' she replied.

'Bad luck.' Beatrice leaned forward in her seat. 'So much for the official version. Now tell me what really happened.'

Bunch realised there was no shaking her off. 'Well... In a nutshell, I was duped and I feel a total nincompoop. Being a little battered and bruised is my own fault. I should have known Wright wouldn't ask me to meet him there, of all places. He'd have come here first after the Saturday I'd had.'

'Just what happened on Saturday?' Beatrice demanded.

Bunch knew there was no point attempting to distract her. Edward was going to tell her at some point, and she offered an expedited version of events. 'Someone tried to bump me off, Granny.'

'Rose ... I feared it would come to something of the sort. Why on earth did you go out alone and allow this killer a second attempt?'

'I'm still here. So plainly they aren't very good at it.'

'Don't be flippant, Rose. Does your father know about all of this?'

Bunch poured tea and avoided her grandmother's eye. 'Most of it,' she replied.

'And he hasn't packed you off to a sanatorium with your mother?'

'Oh Granny— It's called a spa.'

'Call it what you will, but it won't change why she's there. And after all of this, I think you would benefit from a stay.' Beatrice silenced Bunch's protest with a glance. 'As for this accident, as you call it, would I be right in thinking it has something to do with Penelope James and Claude Naysmith?'

'More accurate to call them Mr and Mrs Claude Naysmith, Granny. And Jemmy of course.' Bunch shrugged lightly.

'Now that is a tragedy. Why would anyone want to hurt her?'

'Probably because someone knew she'd spoken to me and she was asking questions she shouldn't – and I do regret not stopping her. I probably could have. She intended to speak to me again and they silenced her.'

'Are you still in danger?'

'I don't know.' Bunch glanced toward the door as the bell rang. 'That will be William. He said he'd call.' A few moments later Knapp ushered Wright into the room. 'Good afternoon, William. How sweet of you to visit.'

Wright shot her a dark look but smiled at Beatrice. 'Ma'am, good to meet you again.'

'William. Do sit down.'

He took a seat, rubbing his hands toward the fire. 'How are you, Rose? Not too much damage?'

'I'm fine. Have you tracked down Soames?' Wright glanced at Beatrice and Bunch laughed. 'She knows. Granny is the oracle and nothing escapes her notice. Just spill the beans.'

'Oxford Constabulary and the Met have both tried Soames's various addresses. No trace of him at his London residences. But we do think we may have found the scene for Penelope James's murder. There's a cottage just outside of Thakeham owned by one of the Soames family, and Basil Soames has been known to use it on occasion. A neighbour reports activity there on the night in question. Someone has had a good try at cleaning up but there are traces of blood in the hallway.'

'Penny's blood? Do you think Soames killed her?'

'Too soon to tell. But we shall work on that assumption.'

'Any word on Beamish?'

'Chichester station sent a team to the Deanery for Beamish. According to her father, she drove up to Westminster with important papers and stayed overnight in London. She does so regularly, I gather. They expected her back yesterday.'

'So both have gone AWOL. Not by coincidence, we assume,' said Bunch.

'A very good point.' Wright took the cup that Beatrice offered him and sat back. 'It seems Harper told someone about her chat with you. She wasn't that close to either Soames or Beamish, so who else was there?'

'Clarrie Bell would be my assumption. She lives not that far from Brighton, so it's not beyond reason that she and Harper would meet up. Clarrie's not nearly as air-headed as people think, despite the drugs.'

'There are rumours she obtained those from Soames.'

'Basil?' Bunch shook her head. 'I doubt it. He's far too lazy though he may have indulged her for his own amusement.'

'I tend to agree, but here's something to think about,' said Wright. 'Soames has been expressing political aspirations and that sort of information would be less than useful to him, if it were generally known.'

'He was rather too thick with the Moseley's crowd at one point. I should have thought that would be rather dangerous now Moseley is under lock and key.'

'Seems Soames cut ties with them in '39,' Wright replied. 'He saw how the winds were blowing. Since then he's not come down in any particular camp. Hedging his bets for when the war ends.'

'What party would have him?' said Beatrice.

'I dread to think,' Bunch replied. 'Interesting background, William, but I doubt discussing Soames's career is the reason you came all this way.'

A tap on the door and Knapp appeared. 'Mr Marsham to see you Miss Rose.'

'Good God. It's like Paddington Station in here. What an absolute pleasure.' Beatrice held her hand out to Marsham as he sidled past the housekeeper. 'What brings you to our door, Henry?'

'Good afternoon, Mrs Courtney. I came to see you of course. And also to bring Rose her new dog.' He snapped his fingers at the springer by his side. 'This is Bella.' The springer bitch wagged the stump of a tail furiously at the mention of her name.

'Henry, I never said absolutely that I'd take her.' Bunch looked at the animal and held out her hand, clicking her tongue. The dog whined softly, leaning eagerly toward her.

Marsham snapped his fingers again and motioned Bella on. It scuttled across the rug to sit in front of Bunch, quivering excitedly and almost without thinking Bunch reached out to smooth the silky topknot between Bella's floppy ears. 'She is a bit eager, I'm afraid,' Marsham added. 'Needs far more training than I can give right now. And these dogs need a lot of exercise. With all your gadding about she'd be perfect.'

'She's a darling.' Bunch leaned over to envelop Bella in a bear hug. 'Surely you don't want to let her go?'

'I'd much rather not, but I am off for a longish spell and you know the requisitioning of the house is happening a little quicker than we thought. My parents are moving into the farmhouse this week and they won't have room for her as well as their own pooches. So she's all yours.'

'That must be a wrench for you. I'll take good care of her, I promise.'

'Tell your mother she has my sympathy,' said Beatrice. 'Do sit down. Can we get you a drink? We're having tea, of course, but I'm sure we can get you something stronger?'

'I would if I were able but I really can't stop. I don't want to upset Bella by hanging around too long, for one thing. I'd have sent her up by train but I wanted to see how you are after your little incident.' He peered at Rose intently. 'Not hurt too badly, I trust?'

'No, but how did you hear about all of that?'

'Oh. Bush telegraph. You know how it is.' Marsham looked to Beatrice. 'Mother sends her best wishes and asks if you're free for dinner next Saturday. Little soiree before they finally move into the cottage. Rose, you're invited of course, and your sister if she's free. Sadly I won't be there. I've things to do up in the wilds of Scotland.'

'Tell Ginny yes, I shall be delighted,' Beatrice said.

'I shall see how I am fixed,' Bunch replied. 'I shall if I'm able.'

'Wonderful,' said Marsham. 'And it's rather fortunate to see you here, Chief Inspector. May I have a private word?'

'I can take a hint.' Beatrice waved a hand at them both as they protested. 'No, it's quite all right. If William is staying for dinner I shall need to speak with Cook. If you will excuse me, gentlemen?'

Marsham and Wright stood and waited until Beatrice had made her tactical withdrawal.

'Okay, Marsham,' Wright growled. 'What is it you want to know?'

'It's more what I think you should know,' Marsham replied. 'I understand you're looking into the nefarious doings of Basil Barrington-Soames?'

'Yes we are. A murder investigation.'

'So I understand.' Marsham paused and stared down at the dog for a moment. 'Far be it from me to clog up the wheels of justice, but can I ask you to leave Soames to my department?'

'That being—?'

'Not important who we are, just that we have Soames in our purview and it could be difficult if our objectives became – entangled.' Marsham glanced at Bunch and then back to Wright. 'I am sure you will understand. I can't go into any detail, and obviously what I've already said is strictly confidential.'

'Naturally. Not that you have said a great deal,' Bunch replied. 'Is it just Soames you are watching? What about the rest of them?'

'Rest of whom?'

'Henry, I'm not an idiot. Don't pretend that was not you we saw at the Café de Paris.'

'I go there now and then. Don't want to be a dull boy like Jack.' Marsham's face was guileless, and Bunch suddenly realised she had underestimated this man for far too long. 'If we have anything to do with it, Soames is ours,' he continued.

'I thought he'd escaped service on some piddling technicality.'

'There are ways to persuade people into revising their choices.' Marsham gazed at the floor. 'Germany. 1936. I rather think there is a link between your enquiries and mine. Now I am booked on the Caledonian Sleeper so must scuttle along. No special instructions for Bella. She eats anything, including the things she shouldn't. She answers to standard commands but a word of warning, she's not overly fond of cats. I'm not sure she can differentiate between them and rats.' He stooped to ruffle the dog's neck and back and touched his forehead against the dog's. 'Behave yourself old girl. Look after Rose, d'you hear?' He got to his feet and made the door in four strides, and as Bella made to follow he raised his hand, palm out. 'Stay. Good girl. Stay. Cheerio, Rose.'

The moment the door closed Bella scampered after him, whining quietly and raising her right paw against the frame.

'Come here Bella. Heel,' Bunch called. The dog looked over her shoulder, her conker-brown eyes liquid with anxiety. 'Come.' Bunch clicked her fingers as Marsham had done and the dog scurried back to her. She reached across to grab a biscuit from the plate beside the teapot and fed it to the dog a piece at a time, muttering nothings quietly as she did so, and ruffling the dog's long satin-haired ears.

'Sugar is so bad for her,' Wright observed

'I think we can spare one biscuit for the poor thing. She'll miss Henry awfully so I think treat or two is in order, though the Marshams keep an outdoor kennel for their working dogs, so it may not be too bad.' The dog came to sit, leaning against her leg and Bunch could feel anxious tremors running through her. She stroked Bella's head, a constant smoothing until the dog began to relax. 'Well,' she said, 'bit of a day isn't it? It is fortunate Henry came when you were here.'

'I very much doubt that was anything like a co-incidence,' Wright replied.

'Oh, you are cynical. I had sort of agreed to have the dog, you know, and if he's off up north?'

'Too handy by half. I did some checking on your Mr Marsham when you said Clarrie Bell had been at the shoot. The department he works for doesn't exist.'

'He's lying?'

'No, he does work for the Admiralty, just that his department doesn't appear on any official records.'

'Doesn't stop it being sheer co-incidence that brought him here.'

'No such thing in their world. He knows exactly what we've been doing.'

'He's been spying on us? The little rat.'

'Not on us, per se.'

'On Soames.'

'Exactly. A man with Soames's connections requires careful scrutiny when he enters the political arena.'

'Another of his elliptical clues – 1936,' she said. 'I keep hearing links back to Munich. Have you uncovered anything?'

'Not as yet.'

Bunch stared into the fire for a moment, fondling the springer's ears as she mulled over the connotations. 'You think Henry knows who pushed my MG down the hill?'

'I think he knows about Soames's movements. Which is what prompted his visit, I imagine. You know him better than I do, but

I think he was telling you Soames was not there.'

'But I saw him.'

'After the event. And the Tolley woman was quite sure he hadn't been there earlier in the day.'

'If Henry was relaying information, you'd think he'd be a brick and tell us outright.'

'Henry Marsham wanted to make sure you were not injured,' said Beatrice. 'Rather sweet really, I think.' She stood in the doorway grinning at her granddaughter's discomfort.

'People don't just do that,' Bunch snapped.

'Apparently Henry just did.'

'Yes, but if William is right it's more to do with his work than me.' She sensed her grandmother looking at her and scowled. 'No, Granny, he's a nice chap but I have enough to think about without complications such as Henry Marsham.' She lit a cigarette with a spill from the fire, hoping the angry flush she felt in her face could be put down to heat. She leaned back into the cushions to gaze at Wright. 'No Carter today?' she said.

'He has some leads to follow up on in Brighton.'

'And you are here why, exactly?'

'To make sure you're in one piece. I don't need a dog as an excuse.'

'No?' Bunch began to laugh, but paused at his expression. 'Oh don't be such a sour puss, William. Whatever you might think, Henry genuinely promised me the dog. If he used Bella as a reason to visit, then so be it. I rather think his warning us off Soames was more pertinent.'

'Possibly. Even probably. I understand your car has now been recovered and towed to a garage in Storrington?'

'Yes, Daddy had his valet go—'

'Excuse me, Miss Rose, there's a telephone call for you. It's Mr Parrish.'

'Thank you, Lizzie.' Bunch threw her cigarette into the fire and got up, fighting hard to conceal the stiffness in her abused muscles. 'Saved quite literally by the bell. Will you excuse me for a moment William?'

'Hello? Larry?' She stood in the hallway, handset held to her ear, and glaring at Wright who watched from the door.

'Rose. Glad to catch you. I am probably being a worry-wart but there's a black car parked at the end of our driveway.'

'Is there anyone in it?'

'I can't see from here. And despite being a bold warrior of the sea I am not terribly inclined to go out and check.'

'Have you called Botting at the Police House?'

'Yes, but he was out. I don't doubt I'm mithering over nothing.'

'And you don't want to look ridiculous?' said Bunch.

'Do I?' Larry's breath hissing across the speaker sounded like a gale. 'I do sound rather wet, I suppose. I don't like you to think I'm a coward but…'

'Hairs on the back of your neckio?'

'Something like that.' Another susurration down the telephone and then 'Forget I called. I shall give Botting another ring. It's probably nothing and totally unfair to bother you.'

'No, don't think that, Larry. Believe me, with all the nonsense that has been going on these past few days you're right to be cautious. Look here, I have Chief Inspector Wright here with me now. I'm sure he won't mind driving over with me. Meanwhile, do call PC Botting again. It can't hurt.'

'Right-ho. I shall see you shortly.'

The line disconnected and Bunch glanced at Wright as she replaced the receiver. 'Well?' she said. 'Up for a little jaunt?'

'I will take a look. You should rest.'

'Don't talk nonsense.'

'Rose…'

'Don't say I can't go. It's almost three miles by road and under one as the crow flies. I can saddle a horse and be there ahead of you. And I would. Give me two minutes.'

She went up to her father's study and took Edward's Webley from his desk, and tried to convince herself she was not being over cautious. *No*, she told herself, *they've had two tries. I'm damned if I'll give them a third chance.* She checked that the revolver was cleaned and loaded. There was nowhere to hide it other than the pocket of her duster. Despite its shorter-than-average barrel, its weight dragged her pocket down. The alternative was walking into the Parrish's house brandishing a 12-bore. *Which does seem a little much.* After a moment's pause she slipped a moonclip loaded with six extra shells in her left-hand pocket before heading down to the front drive where Wright waited for her.

❧ Eighteen ❧

Bunch had barely climbed into the Wolseley before Bella leaped across her into the rear seat.

'Already glued to your heels, I see,' Wright said. 'I have been thinking you needed a dog though I'm not sure that idiot hound will provide much by way of protection.'

Bunch gave him a sharp look. He had a point but he didn't have to be so blunt. Bella was not ever going to be the guardian her old Lab had been. Thinking of how Roger had saved her from a poacher's bullet, she was glad she had not mentioned the Webley nestling in the duster pocket. She was not a nervous type by nature but there was logic in having some defence against another attempt on her life. Being inside the Dower was no guarantee of safety when Penny James and Jemmy Harper had both been slaughtered in their digs. *Carrying a shotgun around,* she thought, *would be rather more unnerving.*

She made sure Wright didn't see the weapon. *Because it saves and lot of questions. I don't see any reason why I shouldn't be armed. Beamish knew where to find me in London and she sure as damn knows where to find me down here. And I really would like to talk with Larry.*

All the while they drove the few miles to The Chells she could feel the gun pressing against her thigh and hoped the safety was on. Edward had taught her to handle all manner of weapon but she hadn't practised with handguns for a very long time. *Rifles I know. Shotguns yes, but revolvers – I'm not so hot on them. Dammit, I should have brought the shotgun. Who cares what it would look like?*

Bella leaned her head over the seat to get as close to Bunch she could and Bunch reached back to pat her briefly. Marsham's visit had been odd and she appreciated the gift of the dog, but had the bitch, now sitting behind her, been an excuse to call? And if she had not seen him at the Café de Paris she wondered if the excuse would have been required.

She thought about Marsham's words. He had been offering information about Soames in his own sideways fashion, but had said very little about either Harriett Beamish or Clarice Bell, and she had a notion that was partly down to both his innate reverence and simultaneous dismissal of women. *Henry can be a nice chap but a bit of a dinosaur, though that may be as much of an act as the 'Bertie Wooster' one seems to have seen? Has war brought out something that might have remained hidden?*

A black Humber was parked inside the gates of The Chells, just as Larry Parrish had reported.

Wright pulled up beside it. 'Empty,' he observed.

'Does it belong to Beamish?'

'Number plates match.' He tapped on the steering wheel, gazing about them, his brows drawn into the deep crease above his nose.

'We could have done with Carter,' said Bunch.

'Indeed.' He carried on tapping his fingers, staring toward the house just visible through the trees. 'Is there any point my telling you to stay in the car?'

'None at all.'

'Hmm. If someone is watching we can't approach by car – or on foot – without being seen, so we may as well take our chance.' He drove quietly down the drive pulling up a few yards from the front step, switching off the engine.

The sun was low in the sky but still bright enough to cast deep lanky shadows. Somewhere on the far side of the farmyard cows were calling, and a few rooks muttered from high in the trees along the farm lane. Beyond those there was little to indicate anything outside of the house.

The door opened cautiously and Parrish beckoned them, the fingers of his other hand held to his lips.

Bunch took off her scarf and slid it through Bella's leather collar and they sprinted through the door.

'Rose, Chief Inspector. Thank heavens you are here.' Parrish led them into the main drawing room.

'Not a problem I assure you,' said Bunch.

'I was looking out for the MG…'

'Ah—' Bunch glanced at Wright and blushed '—the MG had a little accident.'

'Oh my God. Are you all right?'

'Nothing a few hot baths won't cure.'

'What happened? Where?'

'Just outside the village of Washington,' Wright said.

'You were right to call,' said Bunch, 'because that Humber in your drive, it may well be the other car involved.'

'I assume it has something to do with Claude and Penny?' Parrish grunted. 'We had a prowler early this morning at the farm. The dogs frightened them off and we've padlocked the wooden gates but the iron ones on the main drive went to Scrap for Victory.'

'Did you report the prowler to PC Botting?' Wright asked.

'This morning or now?'

'Either.'

'Both. I've telephoned the Police House first thing, and there was not much to be done. Now? I've rang and left a message. I gather there's been a break in at a farm over at Stackley.'

'That is a fair way on a bike,' Bunch said to Wright. 'More than half-an-hour each way. Convenient don't you think?'

'Possibly. Have you seen anyone since you called us?'

'Yes. I was right to have the willies.' Parrish picked up a crow-gun resting against the sofa. 'After I called you I spotted intruders sneaking across the backyard. I called out and fired a warning broadside, and they ran for the barn. One of them was Etta Beamish. I shouted again and she took a bloody pot-shot at me! The bullet broke the scullery window right next to me.'

'Good God!'

'Exactly. I was going to call Botting a third time, but the lines have gone down.'

'Or cut,' said Wright. 'Is there anyone else in the house?'

'Mother and Cook. I sent them down to the cellars. They'll be safe if they keep the door bolted.'

'And you say Beamish wasn't alone?'

'There was at least one other person with her, possibly two. So far as I know they're still in the barn.'

'But she shot at you rather than as a warning?'

Parrish scratched his head and smiled a little sheepishly. 'I called out to her just as she reached the barn doors, and she just turned and raised her rifle. When I said the police were on their way – bang. Not what you'd expect.'

'I didn't think she was such a lousy shot. Nobody could miss at that range.'

'It may sound unlikely but I am sure I heard someone shouting at her not to fire.'

'Really? Dissent in the ranks?' said Bunch.

'They've been in there for twenty minutes or so, now. Quite a while. It's possible that some kind of dispute may explain why they didn't just break straight out,' said Wright. 'But they'll be getting impatient soon enough.'

'Horrible to think people we know are out there doing their best to kill us.' Parrish began to laugh. 'I've told you before, Rose. I've been playing hide and seek with U-boats all summer, so this should be small beans.'

'Yes, but you know the Kriegsmarine are out to get you. They're the enemy, after all.' Bunch said. 'A tad different when it's an old chum throwing ordnance your way.'

'That's very true, but frankly I was not sure Basil has it in him.'

'You saw Soames, too?' Wright asked.

'I'd lay odds it was him.' Parrish's lips thinned. 'We had such a jolly time in Munich, back in '36 – a merry band. These days it's mainly Basil and Etta. Or at the very least, where Basil goes she isn't far behind.'

'Jemmy seemed to think Basil was not that keen on her.'

He pulled a face. 'She's always mooned after him. She also had a brief flirtation with Claude. Even took a pass at me.' He shuddered. 'Joining up was a bit a relief. I had a good excuse to avoid the supper club altogether. Don't get me wrong, she's bright and well-bred.' Parrish shrugged. 'Perhaps they are more fond of each other than the rest of us realised. Not that he ever showed it. Rather vile to her on occasion, but never actually told her to shove off. When I spoke to Penny that last time, she asked if I thought Etta had something over him.'

'What did she say?'

'Just that. I asked her why she thought it but she said it was just a notion.'

Bunch thought about the rumours concerning the Swiss clinic. 'She hinted as much to me. And the more I hear the more likely it seems to be. And now we have the home counties answer to Alice

Diamond out there in your garage?'

'And her gang. Any thoughts on the third person?'

'I'm not sure there were three. It was just an impression.'

'But they definitely entered the barn?'

'And so far as I'm aware, they're still in there – though I'm a little surprised. She must know I'd call the police.'

'Because they have to come past here to reach their vehicle?' said Bunch. 'Did she give any indication why she's here?'

'I did try shouting at her from the house. No answers. I imagine the gun could be a clue why she's here.' Parrish pulled a face. 'Given what's happened to other people on that bloody list.'

'Agreed. What's beyond the house,' Wright asked.

'There's a lane leads to the farm one way, our gardens and orchard another, or down toward the river meadow.'

'Any weapons other than that .22?'

'I've got another two like this in a cupboard in the boot room.' Parrish cracked the weapon in his hand and checked the load and Bella took immediate notice, coming to sit close, her eyes fixed intently on him, body quivering with anticipation. 'Dog is keen,' he said.

'No shotguns or hunting rifles?' Wright asked.

'Yes, but in the gun-store down at the farm,' Parrish replied. 'I just keep these here for vermin.'

'Then it's a good job I have this.' Bunch rummaged in her coat and produced the Webley.

Wright reached out to take it from her. 'Where in hell did you find that?'

'It's Daddy's. I do know how to use it. I assume you have one of your own?'

'Yes. But I really think you should stay here.'

'Let's go and see who is out there.' Bunch peered out at the barn.

'Wouldn't it be safer to just sit tight?' said Parrish.

'Perhaps. But my job is to arrest them,' Wright replied.

'Their quickest escape route would be over the fields,' Parrish added. 'Not past the house.'

'They won't abandon the car,' Wright replied. 'They know they won't get far on foot. They need to come past us to reach the car. We need to move quickly.' Wright unlocked the door.

'You can't go on your own,' said Bunch.

'I'll go with you,' Parrish said.

'I can't allow civilians—'

'I'm not a civilian.' Parrish grinned.

'Nor me,' said Bunch. 'ATS.'

'Both of you are in danger from these people.'

'And you aren't?' said Bunch. 'I... Bella, come here.' She made a grab at the dog as it scuttled past her and went to stand a few feet beyond the door.

A gun cracked, kicking up a divot of turf close to the dog. 'Bella.' Bunch darted out, sprinting toward the end of the house calling the dog as she ran, ignoring the pain in her leg and Wright's bellowed command to come back.

Another shot rang out but she kept going until she reached the recess beside a bay window at the side of the house. 'Bloody stupid mutt,' she muttered as she unbuckled her belt to make a more substantial leash than a cashmere scarf, ignoring Wright as he pushed in next to her.

'Almost as stupid as her owner,' he said. 'What in hell did you think you were doing?'

'I lost one dog to some mad bugger with a gun,' she replied. 'Dammed if I'm going to lose a second one in a year.'

'Better the dog than you.'

'Better?' She stood up, pulling the dog to heel. In the cramped corner they were almost nose to nose. She gave him an accusing glare. 'Who left the door open, waving a rifle about? Bella's not the brightest creature. She thought we were off on a shoot.'

'Never mind that now. What's the best route into that outbuilding?'

'Where is Larry?'

'I told him to watch the main doors. Which was what I wanted you to do.'

A moment more of mutual glowering and she gestured toward the shrubbery. 'This way.' She took off, skirting along the edge of the garden. Out of sight of the old carriage house she paused to tether the dog to a fence post with a stern 'sit, stay'. Bunch led Wright along the line of trees that shielded the outbuildings from the front of the house.

'Right, now you stay here,' he hissed. 'This is police business.'

'So it is, and it's a jolly good job I'm a police consultant because that makes it mine, as well. I have the paper to prove it.' She held a finger to her lips. 'I know the place and you don't. Used to be a carriage house and stables when the Parrish's still had nags—' She suppressed a snort. 'Not the time for history lessons. Long and short of it is there's a small door at the rear of the barn directly below what was the hayloft hatch.'

'Won't it be locked?'

'Probably, but it's always the same kind of lock on these things. One swift kick and the staple will give way.'

'Hardly an element of surprise.'

'As opposed to charging the front doors across an empty yard? Neither is a brilliant strategy. As the saying goes, it's about choosing our least bad option.'

Wright shrugged. 'I'll give you that. Lead on.'

They crossed the lane and crept along the back of the building that was overgrown with brambles and the remains of nettles and grass. 'Here.' The door was as small as Bunch remembered, just five feet high and two-and-a-half wide, following the lines in the creosoted planks that made up the rear wall. The rusted stump of a Suffolk latch and a ragged keyhole were the only indications that it opened.

'One good kick?' said Bunch. She stepped aside for Wright to oblige, holding the Webley at the ready.

'I've opened a few doors in my time – just not lately.' Wright took a step back and eyed the door. 'That's what constables are for. He planted his boot against the wood, grunting with the blow and reminding Bunch that he had old wounds of his own. The ancient wood frame splintered as the metal box-hasp was ripped away. Rusted screws pulled free from rotted timber with almost no resistance. Wright staggered through the doorway on unspent momentum and pitched against a heap of boxes.

Bunch piled through on his heels and veered to one side, crouching low behind the barricade of discarded junk.

The interior beyond had the dankness of old planks and motor oil overlaid the sharp reek of cordite. An odour that was added to by both barrels of a shotgun discharge as shot rattled around them.

'Basil Soames,' Wright shouted. 'Harriet Beamish. This is the police. Drop your weapons.' The shotgun splattered another round of lead shot and Wright swore as something tore at the shoulder of his coat. 'You're under arrest,' he bellowed. 'Lay down your guns.'

Bunch expected a third blast but it didn't come. She and Wright crouched behind their barricade listening for any sign of movement. From beyond the door that was drooping on fractured hinges, the faint sound of cows drifted toward them from the direction of the farm. A lone robin, defiant in the face of gunfire, was singing from the cover of the trees. But inside the old carriage house there was nothing.

Bunch peered around the tarpaulin at the Parrish family cars standing close to the main doors. The only windows in the building were next to the main doors, and high above in the loft area, making shadows all the deeper. She plucked at Wright's sleeve and pointed upward. The light from the door picked out a trickle of dust filtering through the planking. A board creaked overhead. More dust shivered downwards.

A loud metallic click.

'Down,' Wright hissed, and shoved her into the shelter of a tarp-covered heap.

A shotgun boomed. A spray of shot and splinters peppered the space and Bunch threw her arms over her head to protect her face, but still felt a stinging on her cheek before she fell into the pile. She looked up at a surprisingly small ragged hole in the planking.

'Are you hurt?' Wright demanded.

She wiped her hand over her face and looked at the red smear on her palm. 'Okay, I think. One gets used to this sort of thing after a while.'

'Stay here.'

Wright ran for the wooden stair-ladder. Bunch hesitated. She ached all over from the punishment her body had taken over the past days and wondered if she could run fast enough to cross the space. *But what choice is there?* She ran for the ladder and limped up the steps and peered cautiously over the edge.

Soames was raising his pistol left-handed, with his right arm hanging loosely at his side, and aiming it directly at Beamish, who began to raise her own weapon in response.

'Deja vu,' said Beamish. 'You like your dramas, don't you Droopy? The gentleman fighting a duel for honour and right.'

'This is different, Etta. If I shoot you it won't be an accident.'

'Drop your weapons. Both of you,' Wright bellowed across the space. Soames turned toward Wright at the same moment as he fired. His shot went wide.

Beamish was steadier and her shot found its target. Soames fell backwards and hit the floor, sending up a cloud of ancient hay dust. Etta Beamish turned and ran, scrabbling as she attempted to reload her weapon.

'Stop! Stop right there.' Bunch emerged from the ladder cut, Webley in hand. 'Back against the wall.' She walked forward and bent to pick up the gun as Wright came sprinting across from the far side of the loft.

'Turn around,' he snapped at Beamish. 'Rose, go and see if Soames is alive.'

Bunch ran across the loft to kneel beside Soames. The red stain across his chest made it obvious where his injury was. The man's eyes were open, staring at her in disbelief. Bunch whisked his scarf from around his neck and tried to staunch the blood flow.

'I'm sorry, Rose' he whispered. 'I tried to stop her. I've been cleaning up her mess for weeks. But none of it was me.'

'Not even Claude? It wasn't your car that chased him was it?'

He shook his head. 'I...' He choked a little and closed his eyes. 'Not mine, but I ... I am sorry,' he whispered.

'Is he dead?' Wright asked?

Bunch felt Soames's pulse. 'Passed out.' She looked at Beamish, who stared down at the stricken man in silence – impassive, detached, as if she had no idea what was happening.

'Better get this one secured. Harriett Beamish, I am arresting you for the murder of Claude and Penelope Naysmith and Jemima Harper. And the attempted murder of both Rose Courtney and Basil Barrington-Soames. You do not have to say anything unless you wish to do so, but what you say may be given in evidence. And Rose,' he added. 'Thank you.'

'How sweet,' Beamish growled.

'Shut your mouth,' Bunch said. 'You've lost all right to an opinion on anything.'

'You don't want to listen to Droopy.' She sneered at the

stricken Soames laid out on the dusty floor. 'Can't take responsibility for his own—' She broke off, taking a shuddering breath.

'Child?' Bunch said. 'The child he gave you and that you had no option but to dispose of?'

'A child that was torn from me,' she snarled. 'Another death on his hands. His money. The child that was dead before it was ever a living being. I could see her. A little girl. I would have called her Emilia, but she never had a chance to live. And he didn't give a damn. Just put the money down and went back to his precious Penelope.' She straightened suddenly, the fire returning. 'Pray. Confess. Repent. I grew up having that stuff rammed down my gullet from dawn to dusk. But it didn't bring my child back to me. Damn Jemima bloody Harper. Blabbing all over the show. She had none to blame but herself. Sneaking around behind my back.'

'Jemmy suspected' Bunch replied. 'But no. She never actually told me that. Your trip to a clinic was common rumour. It was a friend at the Swiss consulate who confirmed it for me. You murdered Jemmy for no reason. We have enough evidence to lock you away for a long while. And I recognise that car. You should have hit me over the head a little harder and stayed around a little longer to make sure I was dead.'

'Oh it wasn't me who hit you.'

Bunch looked down at Soames. 'But it wasn't him,' she said. 'We know that.'

'Not him either. He doesn't have the spine. If you want someone to blame – ask Tinker.'

'Clarrie Bell?'

'You made me. You always made me.' A dishevelled figure emerged from the far corner. 'You made me.' Bell raised the rifle that she had been holding close to her leg. But the shot that deafened them all was not from her weapon. She spun under the impact of a bullet slamming into her shoulder.

Larry Parrish reloaded the single action gun and stood watching her, his wide feet apart, gun held casually over one arm, the smell of cordite and blood permeated the space like a sacrificial incense. 'Are you all right, Rose?' he said. 'Good show.'

'I'm fine. But we have a few casualties. I take it there's a phone at the farm?'

'Yes. Hopefully the line's not been cut.'

'Then call the police and ambulance as quick as you can,' Wright barked at him. He waved Beamish and Bell to the centre of the loft space. He produced a pair of cuffs from his coat pocket and started forward toward them.

'Knife,' Bunch called out. 'She carries a knife.'

Wright spun Beamish to face the wall, and with the revolver in his right hand patted her coat pockets with the left. 'Thank you.' He drew the penknife out tossed it gently toward Bunch.

It landed in the hay a foot or so from her and she scrabbled to pick it up. It was heavy in her hand, and warm from being close to Beamish's body. The same article she recalled from the Deanery kennels. This time the blade was folded into the darkly stained antler handle. 'Yes,' she muttered, 'same one.'

'How did you know she had it?' Wright said, as he secured the handcuffs and shoved Beamish down to sit next to Bell.

'Educated guess,' Bunch replied. 'Something she seemed to be fond of. Even made a point of showing it to me when I went over to see her. I imagine the pathologist will find it's the weapon used to finish off Claude. Am I right, Etta?'

Beamish returned her gaze, unblinking and intense. Steady. Silent. The only movement in her face was a slight lift to one side of her mouth.

Bunch held her stare as she pocketed the weapon. Beamish looked away first, allowing her attention to drop to Soames's pallid face, still saying nothing.

Wright made sure Beamish was secured one final time and checked Clarice Bell's injuries. 'Nasty flesh wound but you'll live. The slug went through you.' He plucked Beamish's linen scarf from her neck and handed it to Bell. 'Use this to staunch the bleeding.'

'That's my scarf,' Beamish snarled.

'You won't need it down at the station,' he replied.

❧ Nineteen ❧

'Will Etta hang?' Bunch asked.

'Perhaps.' Wright leaned back in one of the Dower house's deep sofas and stared into the depths of the whisky that she had handed him. 'Perhaps not. She's pleading insanity so she could well spend the rest of her days in a sanatorium.'

'Do you think she's mad?' Larry Parrish asked.

'Who knows. She's remarkably lucid in a chilling fashion. She never got over the man she adored forcing her to terminate her pregnancy, and then returning to his fiancé. Anger can be a form of madness.'

Bunch nodded. 'The red mist descending.'

'In the beginning, perhaps, but what came after that required planning.'

'She should have realised Soames was not going to risk all for her. A man who seduces another woman with his fiancé in the same hotel is not one to trust too far. Easy to see why Penny gave him the heave ho. Is that what Etta had over him? That he paid for her abortion?'

'Partly, but not all. It wasn't just down to their affair. You mentioned several things leading back to Munich. Soames had to flee the country after some duelling game he had been playing with a bunch of chaps. A man died. Whether Soames pulled the trigger or not, we can't say. But Beamish was using it to blackmail him.'

'So it all came down to the Munich games?' Bunch pursed her lips. 'Several people tried to hint at that, but it was almost four years ago. I couldn't see how it could be linked. But why kill Penny now?'

'Seems she had set her sights on Naysmith – and Penelope James was there yet again.'

'Claude would never have married Etta.' Parrish said.

'According to her statement she was adamant Penny James had stolen Naysmith away from her. When she heard about the wedding she turned up at the cottage – Soame's property if you recall – along with Clarice Bell and confronted the newlyweds. Whether she intended to kill is unclear but as she went armed with gun and knife, so we have to assume she thought it was a possibility.'

'Which rather destroys a *crime passionel*'

'If that ever existed in English law. It really only leaves insanity as her only escape route. Either she or Bell had fired on Naysmith – we discovered at least three extra shell holes in the walls. With Naysmith fleeing for his life and whether he was trying to reach Parrish at the Chells, we don't know,' Wright said. 'We only know how it turned out. They realised how close Parrish's home was, ran Naysmith off the road and then tried to stage it as an accident.'

'How ridiculous. Claude was stabbed in the neck. Did they think nobody would notice?'

'You would be surprised the things I've seen people do in moments of panic. Both are blaming each other but we suspect it was Beamish who stabbed him. Her actions under caution have been a little unhinged so nothing she says can be relied upon.'

'And Clarrie?' Bunch asked.

'Hopeless dope addict but not actively insane. Bell claims she can't remember half of what she's done. Between them we have an uphill struggle to build a solid case'

'I would say "poor Clarice" because she was totally in Etta's thrall.' Bunch sipped at her drink and leaned her head back against the rest to stare at the ceiling. 'But what she did was awful.'

'It will be for the courts to decide how far the coercion went. If Soames escapes relatively unscathed then she may also, though she'll remain in prison for a very long time.'

Bunch stoked the fire and poured herself another tot of single malt.

'So is Soames a murderer?' Parrish said. 'Hero or villain?'

'Less clear,' said Wright. 'He did try to stop Etta Beamish's activities, which is all to the good. It seems he did dump the body of Penny James and cleaned up the murder site. He was not involved in Jemima Harper's death, nor did he take part in any attempt on your life, you'll be pleased to hear. That was all down to Beamish and Bell.'

'He did end up shooting her, or trying to,' Parrish said. 'That will go in his favour, surely.'

'It will. And he has powerful friends in high places.' Wright replied. 'His political ambitions have gone down the pan, at least for the foreseeable future.'

'Tell me he won't get off scot-free?' Bunch demanded. 'He didn't report any of her crimes. He even spent a lot of effort covering them up.'

'He did and that is a grave offence.'

'So what's left for him?'

'Active service, I imagine,' Wright replied. 'It's not an uncommon solution. More usually reserved for working class lads on the brink of Borstal school, but in his case I suspect his family will buy him a commission with an active regiment, and we shan't see him for a rather long time.'

'Kill or cure,' Bunch muttered, and smiled sheepishly at Wright. 'Sorry. Gallows humour, if you'll excuse another bad pun.'

'You are not wrong however,' said Wright. 'He will come back a very different man.'

'If he comes back,' said Parrish.

They paused to listen to planes droning somewhere over the Downs. Having ignored the air-raid sirens sounding in Wycombe village, none of them felt inclined to pay them much attention.

'Thank you for bringing me up to speed. Tell me when you need me in court.'

'The cases will be quick,' Wright replied. 'There is no question of who killed whom. Just a case of how culpable each of them is.'

Bunch snuggled into her seat and let her left hand drop down the side to fondle Bella's ears. She revelled in the feel of the canine comfort. 'Thank heavens that is all done,' she said. 'A real test for my first official case.'

'Your father's adamant it will be your last time playing at Sherlock Holmes. His words not mine.'

'He said that?' Bunch laughed quietly. 'To paraphrase, there is nothing more stimulating, my dear Watson, than a case where everything goes against you.'

❧ Note ❦

Some historical events have been moved to fit the story. The Underground train incident at Sloane Square, for example, has been moved by a few days. I apologise for any confusion caused to railway historians.

❧ Also Available ❧

Winter Downs

by

Jan Edwards

Winner of the Arnold Bennett Book Prize!

Bunch Courtney stumbles upon the body of Jonathan Frampton in a woodland clearing. Is this a case of suicide, or is it murder? Bunch is determined to discover the truth but can she persuade the dour Chief Inspector Wright to take her seriously?

In January of 1940 a small rural community on the Sussex Downs, already preparing for invasion from across the Channel, finds itself deep in the grip of a snowy landscape, with an ice-cold killer on the loose.

Available from Penkhull Press

In Her Defence

by

Jan Edwards

Bunch Courtney's hopes for a quiet market-day lunch with her sister are shattered when a Dutch refugee dies a horribly painful death before their eyes. A few days later Bunch receives a letter from her old friend Cecile saying that her father, Professor Benoir, has been murdered in an eerily similar fashion.

Two deaths by poisoning in a single week. Co-incidence? Bunch does not believe that any more than Chief Inspector William Wright.

Set against a backdrop of escalating war and the massed internments of 1940, the pair are drawn together in a race to prevent the murderer from striking again.

Available from Penkhull Press

A Small Thing for Yolanda

by

Jan Edwards

The Paris Métro Murder is one of the most famous unsolved crimes of the 1930s.

Who was Laetitia Toureaux?

What were her links within the murky world of spies and secret political movements?

All of these things remain shrouded in mystery, despite the fact that her movements on her final day are well documented. How was she stabbed to death in an apparently empty Métro carriage?

And by whom?

Available from The Alchemy Press

Lightning Source UK Ltd.
Milton Keynes UK
UKHW010033220520
363596UK00001B/111

9 781916 437371